SOUL STORM

OVERWORLD CHRONICLES BOOK EIGHTEEN

JOHN CORWIN

BOOKS BY JOHN CORWIN

THE OVERWORLD CHRONICLES

Sweet Blood of Mine

Dark Light of Mine

Fallen Angel of Mine

Dread Nemesis of Mine

Twisted Sister of Mine

Dearest Mother of Mine

Infernal Father of Mine

Sinister Seraphim of Mine

Wicked War of Mine

Dire Destiny of Ours

Aetherial Annihilation

Baleful Betrayal

Ominous Odyssey

Insidious Insurrection

Utopia Undone

Overworld Apocalypse

Apocryphan Rising

Soul Storm

Assignment Zero (An Elyssa Short Story)

OVERWORLD UNDERGROUND

Soul Seer

Demonicus

Infernal Blade

OVERWORLD ARCANUM

Conrad Edison and the Living Curse

Conrad Edison and the Anchored World

Conrad Edison and the Broken Relic

Conrad Edison and the Infernal Design

Conrad Edison and the First Power

STAND ALONE NOVELS

Mars Rising

No Darker Fate

The Next Thing I Knew

Outsourced

For the latest on new releases, free ebooks, and more, join John Corwin's Newsletter at www.johncorwin.net!

JUSTIN SLADE IS DEAD

When Baal launches a surprise attack against Justin and gang on Emily's wedding day, Justin overuses his Apocryphan powers and nearly kills himself.

With his body hanging on in a preservation spell, Justin is trapped in the afterlife. While there, he discovers that Baal's plan to collapse the realms back into one world might not only kill billions, but also wipe out the souls of the dead.

Turning to old friends and enemies, Justin pools any resources he can in attempts to fight his way back to the land of the living. Can he make it in time to prevent Baal from locating the final Relics of Jura? Or will he be powerless to do anything but watch as the body count rises?

CHAPTER 1

My head didn't hurt anymore.

Come to think of it, neither did the rest of my body. The world seemed to sway back and forth even though I was flat on my back. Everything looked fuzzy around the edges one moment and sharply in focus the next. That was when something alarming occurred to me.

"Where in the hell am I?" I lay on a large bed, staring up at a massive painting that spanned a domed roof. In the painting, pudgy babies surrounded a young man with a thick brown beard. The bearded man reached his hand across an expanse of sky, just shy of touching the outstretched hand of a naked man who reposed on a strip of grass. It looked vaguely familiar, but I couldn't place where I'd seen it.

I sat up and shook my head woozily.

"I feel strange," a familiar voice said.

I yelped and jumped off the bed, twisting and turning to see who spoke.

Another me stood on the other side of the bed, eyes wide. Except this me had blue skin and pointy black horns about three inches long protruding from his forehead.

"Cain!" I drew upon my Seraphim powers, ready to blast him. Nothing happened. I should have felt aether flowing into me, but I couldn't even sense a hint of magical power in the air around me.

So I switched to my infernal skillset and tried to spawn into demon form. A wisp of soul essence drifted from me and connected to my blue clone.

He frowned. "Justin?"

I frowned back. "Holy shit—Kalesh?"

He nodded. "We are not in Kansas anymore."

"Understatement of the year." I held out my hands and rubbed my fingers together. I pinched my arm and felt pain. Then I walked over and put a hand on Kalesh. He felt as warm and alive as I did. "Am I unconscious?"

"We are not in your subconscious," he said. "We are somewhere else." He walked to one of the windows and looked out. His eyes grew wide. "Oh no. We're in terrible danger!"

The city outside the arched windows looked as if someone had copied ancient Greek architecture and then super-sized it. White marble buildings with columns, domes, and even pyramids dominated the cityscape. Buildings of opaque crystal broke the monotony, casting rainbows where the sun struck them.

A wide avenue ran from one of the crystal buildings to a plaza ringed by towering marble statues. The statue of a bearded man stood in the center, fist upraised to the heavens. It was the only figure I didn't recognize. The others I knew all too well. Posthanied wore a helmet over his oval head, a cape draped about his square shoulders and blocky body. He stared at the center statue, arms crossed, face brooding.

Zon stood to his right, hands clasped behind his back, shoulders straight, as if standing at attention. The arachnid demigod, Araxos, was next, crouched on eight legs as if either bowing or readying to pounce. Tall and curvy, Couriondral stood to her right, hair lifted from her shoulders as if flowing in a breeze. And outside the circle was the outcast. Unlike the others, Xanos knelt, head bowed, hair hiding her face.

That meant the statue in the middle was Kathazal, father of the Apocryphan. After their banishment to the Abyss, Xanos had tricked the others into killing Kathazal. She'd been exiled to the fringe, a ring of mountains and intense gravitational forces around the edge of the prison. From there, she'd launched a plot that would eventually free her, thanks to little old me.

Now all the Apocryphan but Xanos were dead. Couriondral, Posthanied, and Araxos had been murdered by their own mother, Eve. I'd killed Zon, with stolen Apocryphan powers, and then banished Xanos to the small realm where Eve lived.

But there was no place in the Overworld that had statues of the Apocryphan—at least not that I knew of. "Where in the hell are we, Kalesh?"

He growled. "The capital."

I blinked. "The capital of what?"

Kalesh gave me the side-eye. "Haedaemos."

I shook my head like a wet dog. "Say what?"

Someone slow clapped behind us. "I wasn't sure you'd recognize the location." His voice was deep, rich, and smothered in smugness.

I'd heard echoes of that voice in the infernus hosts he used as puppets in the physical world. Hearing it in person was something else entirely. "Baal." I turned slowly, giving myself time to hide shock and dismay behind a stony mask. On the inside, I was about to lose my shit. *I'm in Haedaemos? That's impossible! If I'm really here, Baal can eat my soul for breakfast!*

He continued to slow clap. "Yes, grandson." Baal stroked a long black beard. His irises glinted red and orange, as if speckled with rust. In fact, he looked remarkably like the flying man painted on the ceiling.

I couldn't help but glance back at it and then to him.

Baal smiled. "Michelangelo did a wonderful job copying it, don't you think?"

"Huh?"

He sighed. "It's the original version of *The Creation of Adam*. Michelangelo used it for inspiration."

"Uh, how did he even know about it if it's here?" I said.

Baal snorted. "Demonic possession, of course."

"Why are we here?" Kalesh said.

I grunted. "Better yet, how?"

"First of all, welcome to the capital of Haedaemos." Baal spread his hands out toward the city. "I give you Juranthemon."

My jaw nearly hit the floor. "Juranthemon? Impossible! It was destroyed in the Sundering."

Baal nodded. "Yes, and the incredible explosion killed so many beings so fast, that it left behind an echo—a spirit realm, complete with the ghost of a destroyed city." He walked to the window and leaned on the balustrade. "Many beings had no idea anything had happened. One moment there was a bright flash of light, and the next, everything looked perfectly normal." He clasped his hands in front of him. "A spirit is a faded copy of flesh and blood. We don't feel things quite the same. Nothing is as sharp or as focused as being truly alive."

"This is nothing like what I expected." I backed away from him, casting about for a gateway out of this world. "How did you bring us here?"

Baal smirked. "I couldn't have done it without your help." He sat down on a red leather couch that hadn't been there a moment ago. "As we speak, your physical body is battling to stay alive."

"My body?" I clenched my fists. "What did you do to me?"

He held up his hands defensively. "You have only yourself to blame for that part. When I planted the demon seed in you that eventually became Cain, I also captured a fragment of your essence in a soul vessel."

I blinked "A what?"

"It's similar to a soulstone, but it does not absorb an entire soul on death." Baal conjured a black crystal in his hand. "When the bond between flesh and soul grows weak, it is able to redirect the soul else-where for a brief time."

"So instead of going where I'm supposed to be, I end up somewhere else?" I said.

Baal nodded. "In a sense."

Kalesh's forehead pinched with worry. "How did we die?"

"Why spoil the surprise?" Baal tilted his head to the side and looked me up and down. "You're not quite dead yet, anyway."

"Fine, I get it." I threw up my hands. "I'm at your mercy. Are you going to eat my soul?"

Another grin. "As much as I'm enjoying this moment, I suppose I'll let you in on a little secret." Baal leaned forward, elbows on knees. "You're not really here. You and your spirit are being held by the soul vessel in the living world. It's projecting your consciousness here."

"You're confusing the hell out of me," I said.

He grinned. "Easily done."

Kalesh gave him an uneasy look. "So we're safe?"

"From me, at least." Baal pursed his lips and watched us for a moment. "Now, as to why I brought you here."

I put my back against the wall because I didn't trust a thing Baal told me. Plus, I figured I could jump from a window if he tried anything. "I'm listening."

"Are you familiar with the afterlife?" he said.

I blinked a few times. "No, but maybe in the next few minutes I will be." For some reason, I wasn't as worried as I should have been. Then again, the situation seemed so surreal, I could hardly believe it was happening.

Baal nodded. "I think that's likely." He stood up and took a step closer. "Haedaemos was an accident—a purgatory that was never meant to be." He turned back toward the windows. "Nearly everyone who died in the instant of the Sundering had their souls trapped here instead of moving on to the afterlife. The higher forms that you call ruby spirits are the remnants of beings like Seraphim and Sirens. Many of the caustics are human in origin. The jades and sapphires are a mixture of more powerful beings, including a few humans. Over the millennia, most of the originals are gone—devoured or faded to nothing."

It sounded reasonable, so I played along. "So what we call demons are actually the spirits of the dead?"

"We're not demons in the classical sense," Baal said. "Demons in those days lived in Hell. Some of them also died in the Sundering and became the shadow creatures you know as crawlers and scorps. We are simply spirits and souls trapped for eternity in the copy of a world long gone."

"You want to remake it," Kalesh said. "You think it will give you life again."

Baal shook his head. "My goal is to free our spirits so we can finally escape this prison and join the others in the afterlife." He gave me an imploring look. "Justin, combining the relics into Saila will not recombine the realms. It will only recreate Juranthemon for an instant. And in that instant, Haedaemos will cease to exist and our spirits will finally fly free."

I ran a hand down my face. "Hang on—you brought me here because you thought I'd help you find the remaining relics? You really think after everything we've been through, that I'd trust you?"

"I'm asking you to do the right thing, Justin." Baal lifted a hand toward me though I stood well out of reach. "Help me, and I'll return your father whole and unharmed to you."

"Using Dad as a hostage isn't going to earn my trust," I said. "Evict Cain from his body right now and show me proof that your plan won't destroy the world. Then I'll help you."

"I need the dagger." Baal stared at me as if I might answer, then said, "I need the heart." Again, he watched intently.

"Why don't you make me a list, and I'll run down to the grocery store and grab them?" I said. "Need some bread and milk while I'm there?"

Baal continued speaking as if I hadn't said a word. "I need the sword."

Kalesh grabbed my arm. "Justin, how did Vallaena die?"

The question caught me so off guard I couldn't speak for a moment. Images of her body, crushed in the Battle of the Grand Nexus, replayed through my head. Everything else fled from my thoughts and all I could think of was her, as if some outside force projected it into my mind.

Baal chuckled. "I'm afraid you caught on too late." He stood. "Your spirit has grown smarter, boy. I can't say the same for you."

I looked back and forth between Kalesh and Baal. "What are you talking about?"

"It was a lie," Kalesh said. "He led your mind down a path. He made you think about what he wanted you to think so he could steal your thoughts."

"Yes, another useful side-effect of the relic," Baal said. "All your active thoughts were recorded."

"You read my mind?" I laughed. "You didn't even ask me anything useful."

"As you know, I'm missing a few relics and I suspect you know where they are."

"Not anymore!" I rushed forward, grabbed the crystal, and smashed it on the floor.

The pieces turned to black smoke and dissipated.

Baal chuckled. "The crystal is in the physical world, you idiot. That was just a representation."

A woman in a red dress appeared in the doorway, a scroll in her hand. "The information has been fetched from the crystal." She knelt and held it up, eyes fixed firmly on the floor.

He took it from her without even acknowledging her existence and read it. "Goodness. It seems the Apocryphan statues outside triggered a few things I didn't know." Baal looked at me. "God damn, you amaze me, boy. You might be a fool, but blind luck follows you everywhere." He shook his head. "All the Apocryphan are dead except for Xanos? And you banished her to live with Eve." He rocked back on his heels, roaring with laughter until his face turned red. "My God, that's hilarious." He stopped. "Oh, wait, that's me!"

I didn't get the joke at first, but then I realized what he meant. "Then you know that I know your true identity, Elohim."

"You've discovered my secret." A pair of glasses appeared on Baal's face. He removed them with a flourish. "Yes, I'm God."

Fuck my life. How much info had I given him? I couldn't remember everything I'd thought of since waking up here. Now I knew why Kalesh asked me about Vallaena—he wanted me to think of something that didn't matter to Baal. The longer I stayed here, the more I risked giving away.

"Let me go, Baal." I tried to focus on something inconsequential. High school home room class came to mind. I imagined skipping down the hallway, a juice box in hand. "Let me go."

8

"I'm afraid I wasn't entirely honest about your condition in the real world either." Baal sighed. "You're definitely going to die, Justin." He stepped onto the balcony and basked in the sun. "But I wasn't lying about one thing. Haedaemos really will stop existing when Saila is rebuilt. All the trapped spirits here will be freed."

"And you'll get your body back," I said.

"Yes."

"How? Wasn't it annihilated?"

Baal shook his head. "You see, I was there that day, only a few feet away from Saila. I thought it would be entertaining to see the mighty Apocryphan destroy each other. But on that day, I shared one thing in common with them—I didn't realize we had all been lured there by Xanos. I didn't realize I would be used as the tool to destroy her siblings." He chuckled. "Things didn't go quite as planned for any of us."

"So you were at ground zero?" I said.

He scoffed. "I was the catalyst, boy. Xanos revealed my identity, the Apocryphan tried to annihilate me, and when I struck back, it destroyed everything." He shook his head. "To this day, I don't understand how the Apocryphan survived, while I was sentenced to eternity in purgatory."

I tried to speak, but my mouth went slack and I felt lightheaded. "Ungh."

"I'm afraid we've reached the end, grandson." Baal feigned a sad look. "Thank you for your help."

I tried to speak again, but stumbled back and fell to the floor, too weak to even move. *So this is death.* I wished I could remember what in the hell I'd done to end up dead.

Maybe I'd find out in the afterlife.

CHAPTER 2

Baal rubbed his hands together and laughed as Justin and Kalesh faded to nothing. "Damn, that felt good." It was rare to have such delicious moments, and he wanted to savor them. Justin had done everything Baal wanted and then died, leaving nothing between him and victory.

Well, nothing except Emily Glass.

Xanos was powerless, and the other Apocryphan were dead. All that was left was to sweep in and take the remaining relics. According to Justin's thoughts, the dagger was in the Glimmer, hidden in the roots of the Soul Tree. Underborn had the heart, and Eve possessed the sword in her cottage.

The nose was also important, but it would come of its own accord, Baal hoped, once he had at least three of the remaining artifacts recovered.

He remembered the day of the Sundering as if it were yesterday. Word of massive armies converging on Juranthemon had caused mass hysteria. The population fled even though the city was considered neutral by the Apocryphan. While the looming conflict drove away the masses, it had drawn Baal in. Eve and her loathsome children had wreaked havoc on the world. They'd marred what should have been perfection.

He wanted to see them destroy each other.

It was not the Apocryphan Baal most despised, but the humans. The Sirens, Seraphim, and Fae were beautiful and noble creatures, worthy of keeping company with the gods. Then Eve, the insipid little fool, decided to create humans in her image, but make them powerless. They were inferior creatures, breeding and swarming across the world like rodents.

When Baal arrived in Juranthemon on that fateful day, he watched the brave Saila confront her father, Kathazal, and his other children. Only Araxos had not been present, for she had no desire to rule a kingdom. Xanos had likely watched from somewhere nearby as well, another hidden observer waiting for the mighty god, Elohim, to appear.

"Why do you bring your armies to Juranthemon?" Saila had asked. "We are neutral, Father. We will not break the accords."

"Because we learned of treachery, daughter." Kathazal looked down on her from his place in the sky. "An old god intends to name Juranthemon his capitol and launch a war against us so he might rule."

"An old god?" Saila looked confused. "They have all left. Only Eve remains and she cares nothing of our affairs."

"No, we have definitive word. Today, our armies gathered not to battle each other, but to kill the old god once and for all."

Baal growled at the memory. At his stupidity. Not once had it occurred to him that they meant him. He'd assumed another of the old gods had returned. And then an eclipse had darkened the sky, leaving only a spot of light where Baal stood. A great booming voice announced, "You will never defeat me!"

It was in that moment, Baal realized what had happened. The resulting fight had broken the world.

That had been one of the worst days in his life. A close second would have been when Eve birthed humans and dumped them onto the precious world he'd sculpted. But the moment of his undoing would soon be undone. Even though he'd long fantasized about destroying the Apocryphan for that day, he was more than satisfied that they'd died by Eve's hand.

Even more enjoyable would be killing Eve. But that could wait. First, he would burn the scourge of humanity from the world and leave only those worthy to carry on its perfection. The long journey was almost at an end. But even with Justin dead, there were others who would stand in the way. And he was most disappointed in his servants.

Baal reached out with his consciousness and peered through the eyes of his hundreds of infernus in the real world all at once. One spoke to the U.S. Congress, demanding retribution for a terrorist attack.

"We must attack them and show their population that America will not be cowed!" He raised an arm and the members of his party cheered in support.

Another infernus sat in a café halfway around the world. He smoked a hookah with two other men as they spoke about the success of the bombing that so enraged the Americans. Yet another infernus incited a mob in India, demanding the death of a local politician whose only crime was to negotiate peace.

Victus's crowning achievement had been the infernus. With them, Baal could have achieved his goals centuries before. For now, they were promoting chaos around the globe, keeping the mortals distracted so they wouldn't realize the end was nigh.

None of the infernus laid eyes on the people Baal sought, but he had a good idea where they were. His special infernus were the only ones capable of hosting a fragment of his power. As a result, he felt partially numb and disembodied whenever he possessed one. It was a cruel feeling, to be so close to flesh and blood, but not fully feel pain or pleasure. But it was enough for now.

Baal shoved aside the consciousness in the infernus. He flexed his hands and rubbed his face, as if this time would be different. As if this time, he would feel everything. But the sensation, as usual, was muted and unsatisfying. So he straightened his shoulders and stood from the chair the body had occupied.

He was in a mansion in the middle of nowhere—specifically, deep in the Australian outback. The house stood on the shores of Lake MacKay and was significant because it was located almost directly above where the infernal fount flowed in this physical plane. Several miles below the surface, the lake of fire bubbled and burned in the mythical underworld, the place many called Hell.

Baal never could have imagined he would be the perceived ruler of that place. That God himself had fallen was the ultimate irony.

He marched out of the foyer and walked through the house. The place swarmed with other infernus, all dedicated to coordinating Baal's plans around the world. Not a one of them spoke to his infernus or met its eyes as he walked past. They were beings of a sort, but still less than nothing to him. They were cogs in a plan, tools of flesh and bone.

Olivia was not in the bar getting drunk, nor was she outside at the pool, demanding margaritas from the cabana boy. But Baal sensed Cain nearby and knew Olivia would also be in the vicinity. He walked up a winding staircase and down a hallway. From the sounds emanating ahead, he knew he'd found Cain.

Baal opened the door and strode into the master suite, a sprawling bedroom with its own swimming pool and spa. Cain and Olivia were on the bed, naked and enjoying other recreational activity.

Olivia's eyes widened when she saw Baal. "Shit!" She shoved Cain off her.

"What the fuck?" Cain rolled over and saw Baal. He laughed. "Damn, Dad. You scared her!"

Baal gripped Olivia by the neck and raised her struggling, naked form off the bed. She choked and gagged.

Cain laughed harder. "I didn't know you wanted to join in."

Baal slammed Olivia against the wall. She could easily defeat this infernus if she desired, but she knew better. "You failed again."

"Failed what?" she gasped.

"You still haven't brought me Emily Glass."

Legs flailing, she tried to answer but couldn't draw enough air. Baal dropped her to the floor.

Olivia sucked in a ragged breath. "I tried!"

Baal continued to stare. "On the other hand, you did kill Justin Slade."

Cain hopped off the bed. "Whoa, he died?"

"We actually killed him?" Olivia looked just as surprised. "But we had to retreat after the fight. How do you know he died?"

Baal tapped his temple. "I have my resources."

"Emily's too damned powerful." Cain threw up his hands. "And then Justin was a lot stronger than before. He shot these huge green rays at us. He blasted a hellfire demon to dust!"

"Emily stole the power of an Apocryphan and gave it to him." Baal continued to watch Olivia's face. "Even he can't handle that kind of power. He probably overused it and killed himself in the process."

"Is that a good thing?" Cain said.

"The good thing is that all the Apocryphan are either dead or powerless to stop me now." Baal smiled reassuringly. "I also know where the remaining relics are. But I need Emily Glass to complete my plans."

"Why her?" Olivia said. "I'm better."

Baal slapped her hard enough to leave a mark on her cheek. "Because you're not better, as you've proven time and time again."

Tears pooled in her eyes, but she said nothing.

Cain laughed.

"You're as culpable as she is, boy." Baal turned his glare on him. "Don't make me devour your soul."

Cain's face paled. He gulped and backed up a step. "I won't fail you, Father."

"With Justin Slade dead, perhaps you won't." Baal sighed. "I need you to search the Glimmer. To do that, we'll need a fragment of anchor stone and the Bird of Jura. That will allow you to remain hidden from the Glimmer Queen."

"Why us and not an agent?" Cain asked.

"Because the dagger is a challenge to handle." He smirked at Olivia. "It causes the most intense pain you can imagine. The sort you can handle, I think."

Hate flashed into her eyes, but she nodded demurely. "Can't we just put it in a satchel, my lord?"

"You can, but I prefer you carry it, dear." Baal caressed her cheek. "It will turn you invisible."

Cain wrinkled his nose. "Why do you want to put her through so much pain, Dad? I mean, we're trying really hard."

Baal didn't have an answer. Maybe it was because Olivia looked so much like Eve, that he intrinsically hated her. Perhaps it was because she continually failed when it came to Emily Glass. He decided to relent this time. "Fine. Put it in a satchel. Fail to bring it to me, and the consequences will not be pleasant."

Cain nodded. "We'll get it, Dad."

Baal held their gazes another moment, then turned and left.

Retrieving the dagger would be child's play compared to stealing the heart from Underborn and the sword from Eve. As important as those relics were, there was yet another mystery to solve. The Apocryphan had also guarded relics--or claimed to. Baal didn't think they knew which relics or where they were hidden in the Abyss.

He'd sent agents to search from time to time, but the Apocryphan would destroy their bodies or consume their spirits. "If only I had the Nose of Jura." It could sniff out other relics and would make searching the Abyss less of a chore. But since the Apocryphan were dead, Baal could send more agents to conduct a search. He could even take his own infernus inside now that there was no danger of losing part of his spirit to an Apocryphan.

Baal stopped a nearby infernus. "Gather five hundred and meet me in Hell."

The infernus bowed deeply and raced away to complete her task. Baal walked up the center stairwell to the top floor and entered his private quarters. Dozens of half-naked concubines put away smartphones or roused from slumber and stood at attention when he entered. They were all real humans, males and females of all body types. Though physical sensations were muted, he still liked to indulge from time to time.

Now was not one of those times.

Baal clapped his hands. "Go dress yourselves for adventure. We're going on a field trip."

Concerned looks flashed through the room, especially among the more corpulent males and females. Then they scrambled to comply. It was likely some of them would not survive the rigors of the Abyss. The prison held dangerous spirits and physical creatures alike. So many humans would likely attract their attention and lure them to easy prey.

Just as Baal intended.

With the Apocryphan gone, some of those spirits would be more likely to talk. He would offer them freedom provided they told him where the relics were hidden.

Within five minutes, the concubines were dressed. They wore matching camouflage cargo pants and tank tops imprinted with name tags. Across the middle, each one had the words, *Baal's Little Bitch.*

Baal chuckled. "Damn, I crack myself up." He snapped his fingers and they stood at attention. A curvy brunette in the front row cast sultry gazes at him, but he wasn't in the mood for play right now. "Gather before the main elevator downstairs. An infernus will take you where you need to go."

Belinda, a plump redhead raised her hand. "Daddy, will we have to eat spiders again?"

"Not this time, dear." He approached and caressed her cheek. "We're going somewhere really fun today." Judging from the fear flashing in their eyes, he realized they knew him all too well. *It's time to refresh my stock, I believe.*

They left the room, and Baal went into his bedroom. Golden doors surrounded by ivory trim slid open when he approached. He stepped into the personal levitator. There were only three buttons. He pressed the one labeled *H.* The doors slid shut and the floor dropped out from beneath him.

He fell through the darkness, hurtling at terminal velocity miles beneath the surface. Moments later, his descent slowed gradually until he gently alighted on polished black stone inscribed with demonic symbols. Golden doors slid open. and Baal stepped into a great cavern. The ceiling sparkled like diamonds, primarily because it was covered in diamonds, many of them as large as boulders.

Glowing crystals on the floor and walls cast some of the light, but most of it was provided by the lake of fire in the middle of the vast cavern. The fire was, of course, the infernal fount.

Demons gathered around the fount, warming themselves like cats in the sun. They saw him approaching and scattered like roaches. Black-winged phegors took to the air. Lumbering stone giants fled down adjoining corridors. Red-skinned manikins fluttered their useless wings, hoofs clacking on stone as they pushed their stubby legs to the limit. Even the octopods rolled away, tentacles slapping wetly against stone.

Baal snapped a finger and the remaining demons stopped and bent knees in the presence of their lord. "We will soon have human guests. You will leave them unmolested."

They replied in the guttural demon tongue. Baal considered using the phegors to aid in the Abyssal search, but they were not bright creatures, easily distracted. So he waved them away and they vanished down tunnels and corridors.

Baal walked over to wide levitator doors and waited.

Distant screams grew louder and, a moment later, the doors slid open. Terrified concubines stared out at him. Judging from the odors, some had completely lost their composure. He grinned. "Welcome, little humans. Consider yourselves fortunate, for few ever see this domain while they live." He flourished his hand toward the fount in the distance. "I give you Hell."

The resulting cries and fainting warmed his heart.

Stone-faced infernus herded the concubines out of the elevator, dragging the unconscious ones unceremoniously by their ankles. Four more loads of infernus arrived over the next few minutes and the search party was complete.

Concubines huddled in fear among the small army of infernus, faces glowing in the light of the infernal fount. Baal traced a pattern over the surface. Tendrils of lava snaked out, weaving a vertical disc of fire at the edge. The flames cooled and faded, leaving behind a gateway to a barren landscape.

Baal gave the order, and the infernus marched through twenty abreast, the concubines sandwiched in the middle. He paused a moment once they were all through just to make sure there were no surprises, and then stepped through after them.

The gateway was a distance from the underside of the infernal fount at the center of the Abyss. He usually closed it right away to prevent escapes, but this time he left it open since there was no one on the other side who could open a new one.

Baal turned to an infernus. "Take the concubines to the middle. Spread out and inform me of any sentient predators who come close. Drive away all others."

"Yes, lord." The infernus relayed the orders and the army marched for the Abyssal fount.

The relic hunt had begun.

CHAPTER 3

O NE DAY AGO

The Mansion was a slagheap.

Zon's explosive charge had destroyed most of the first floor supports in the west wing, leaving the rest of the structure unstable. Luckily, the only deaths had been those of the traitors who conspired with the Apocryphan.

"How many damned houses are we gonna go through?" Harry Shelton booted a pile of rubble. "Do you know how much bacon we lost when the kitchen collapsed?"

"The loss of even one slice of bacon is horrendous," Adam Nosti said. "I suggest we hold a funeral for those poor, uneaten swine."

Shelton grimaced. "Don't mock my pain."

I saw the opportunity and jumped right in. "Life is pain, Highness."

Elyssa high-fived me. "Nice one."

I grinned. "Seems like opportunities for *Princess Bride* quotes are rare these days."

Maxwell Tiberius regarded the blood-stained earth where the traitors, his father, Xander, and brother, Rhys, had died in the explosion. "I think bacon deserves a funeral more than my father."

Ambria Rax patted him on the back. "Max, I don't know whether to be sad for you or not."

He shrugged. "I'm not happy, but I'm not sad. I think what bothers me the most is that my father actually called me over to him before the blast. I think he wanted to save me, but I don't understand why."

"Family is strange like that." Conrad Edison sat on a slab of broken stone, his gaze lost in the distance. "Xander didn't really care about anything except himself and his legacy. I hate to say it, but I think he tried to save you because he thought killing his own son would look bad."

Shelton growled and clapped Max on the back. "You're the best of all of them. Sometimes, even a piece of shit like Xander can make gold."

A wan smile touched Max's lips. "I'm just in a weird place right now. I don't know what to feel."

"Well, with Xander dead, the treaty with him is dissolved," Elyssa said. "The Arcanes are already voting for a new Arcanus Primus as we speak."

"What about the rest of Max's family?" Adam said.

"Devon's in a detention cell beneath the Ranch. Max's mother and sisters are in Milan." Elyssa shrugged. "We don't think they even know what happened yet."

"Does this mean we can freeze the family assets now?" Max said.

Elyssa raised an eyebrow. "Is that what you want, Max?"

Ambria rubbed Max's arm. "That will put them out of house and home, Max."

A grin spread his lips. "Would it really?"

Ambria nodded. "Yes. They'll be poor as dirt."

The grin broadened. "Oh, please, Elyssa, can you please freeze their assets? I'd love nothing more than for those useless humans to have to find honest work."

Elyssa nodded. "I believe we can. I'll speak with my father."

Max clapped his hands. "I can't wait!"

Shelton chuckled. "Well, now we know what makes you happy."

"Max's brothers tormented him constantly," Ambria said. "His parents did nothing to stop them."

"My sisters weren't much better," Max said. "I think horrible people should suffer."

"Agreed." Conrad squeezed his friend's shoulder. "Let them reap what they've sown."

A group of Templars sauntered into the cavern. Their gray uniforms identified them as members of the Eden Templars, those who'd joined the organization or been left behind when our army was stranded in Seraphina. They were so bad at their jobs, they weren't even pale imitations of real Templars.

Elyssa shook her head. "Why do they even bother patrolling?" She grunted. "Look at them. They're not in formation, and they're so busy talking to each other that a rampaging bull would catch them off guard."

The lone female of the group pointed excitedly at us and ran over. "My god, it's the heroes of Eden!" She took out a phone. "Can I please get a selfie with you guys?"

"Um." I looked around at the others. They shrugged, nodded, and gathered around me. "Sure."

She waved over her comrades and made one of them hold the camera.

"You realize it's not a selfie anymore, right?" Adam said.

The Templar took several pictures then handed the phone back to the woman. She giggled. "Thank you so much!"

"No problem." I sat back down on a stone slab.

She began showing the pictures to her companions as they walked away.

Elyssa grimaced. "They shouldn't even call themselves Templars."

"Amen to that," Shelton said.

"I still don't know what to do with all the noms Xander recruited." I picked up a rock and tossed it at one of the few unbroken windows. It bounced off. "A few hundred took that super potion of his, and we can't very well just put them back on the streets again."

"Before Xanos attacked Queens Gate, we evacuated most of them to the Ranch," Elyssa said. "The bad news is dozens just left of their own accord and we still haven't found a roster of everyone who signed up. Not all of them were average Joes and Jills. We found evidence Xander had recruited a number of them from jails and penitentiaries."

I face-palmed. "So we've got super criminals roaming the streets now?"

"It's only been a few weeks since the battle, and we've already heard reports of robberies carried out by people with unbelievable strength." Elyssa shook her head. "The Templars are stretched too thin to deal with them."

"Ah, yes. I hoped I might find you all down here." A tall bearded man with a pointy wizard's hat approached. Galfandor had fought Xander's forces before our return from exile, but things hadn't gone his way, and the old headmaster had been thrown in jail for treason. With Xander dead, Captain Takei had appointed him headmaster again.

Ambria raised an eyebrow. "Galfandor, what are you doing here?"

"It's not a matter of supreme urgency, but it should be addressed." He nodded at Elyssa. "Commander, the blast which decimated this house shot up through the cavern ceiling, emerged aboveground, and nearly destroyed my house directly above. Thankfully, it was unoccupied at the time."

"I'm not the person to talk to about repairs," Elyssa said.

"I didn't know it blew up your house too." I looked at the gaping hole in the cave ceiling. I'd funneled the explosion up and out of the Mansion using a cone of Murk. I hadn't even considered it might blast all the way to the surface.

"Now that I'm headmaster again," Galfandor said, "I would like to take back my old quarters in the university." He smiled. "Knowing the history of the land above, I'd be honored if you would consider rebuilding your home in place of the wreckage now there."

Shelton's mouth dropped open. "Really?"

Galfandor nodded. "Yes."

Shelton's eyes watered up. "That's a beautiful gesture, man." He walked over and hugged the headmaster, clapping him on the back. "I don't know what to say."

"Jesus, Shelton." Adam shook his head. "I had no idea you were so emotionally attached to the place."

Shelton backed away and looked at Adam, aghast. "Dude, that was the O.G. Mansion! Justin and I cleaned up that place and made it our own." He chucked a rock toward a stone pillar. "This place was cool, but it never felt quite like home."

Elyssa nodded. "I know exactly what you mean."

I hadn't wanted to admit it, but Galfandor's offer hit me right in the feels too. I sniffed and wiped my eyes to avoid any tears. "This means a lot to us, Galfandor. Thank you." I still had nightmares of the day Daelissa annihilated the original mansion and burned Jeremiah Conroy to ashes. It'd be nice to finally reclaim it.

The headmaster smiled. "My pleasure. I have already submitted the original plans for the previous mansion to some local builders. They said they would gladly do the work at cost."

"Then it's settled." Elyssa smiled at me. "Let's rebuild our home."

"Yes!" Shelton tossed his hat into the air. "I can't wait!"

For the first time in a while, I felt happy. Elated, even. We had a long row to hoe, but with my nifty new Apocryphan powers, fighting Baal and his dragon army wouldn't be as hard as before. And it would be super cool to have the old Mansion back.

A portal slashed open to our left. Emily Glass and her boyfriend, Tyler Rock, stepped through. Crystal blue water lapped a white sand beach on the other side of the gateway. Tyler looked tanned and happy. Emily looked a little sunburned, but the smile gracing her face told me her vacation had gone well.

"I was told I could find you here," Emily said.

Tyler cleared his throat as if to speak, but Emily put a finger over his lips. She turned to us. "I've only known you all for a short time, but Tyler and I have decided to make today something of a big deal."

Tyler rocked on his heels like a happy little boy. His eyes shone with such happiness that I knew where this was going.

Emily continued. "Would you all do us the honor of attending our wedding?"

"Of course!" Elyssa clapped her hands and hugged Emily. "Congratulations!"

"How romantic!" Ambria hugged Emily too. "When did he propose?"

"Oh, about ten years ago," Tyler said. "I resigned myself to thinking it was never going to happen."

Ambria's eyes flared. "Ten bloody years?"

"What date should we mark on our calendars?" I asked.

"Today." Emily motioned toward the portal. "Right now."

"Damn." Shelton clapped his hat back on his head. "Bella's gonna be real upset to miss a wedding."

"Where is she?" Emily said.

"In the Glimmer," Shelton said. "You mind letting me get her?" He took out his arcphone and found a picture of a room in the Glimmer Queen's castle.

"It would be a delight to meet her." Emily concentrated and a new gateway slashed open right next to the one leading to the beach.

"Be right back," Shelton said. He ran through and into the room on the other side.

"Anyone else?" Emily said.

"My parents would probably like to come," Elyssa said. "Since you're sort of a Custodian, and all."

"I'd be honored if they attended." Emily opened yet another portal to the Ranch, the Templar headquarters. Elyssa dashed through.

"I wish I knew where Felicia is," Adam said wistfully. "I haven't heard from my sister since we got back, and I don't even know where to begin tracking her down."

"She'll eventually hear that we're back," I said. "I wouldn't be surprised if she stayed near Atlanta just in case."

Adam sighed. "I'll bet she married Larry."

"Wouldn't doubt it." I tapped a finger on my chin. "Maybe Stacey would like to come to the wedding."

"Do you have a location?" Emily said.

I retrieved a picture Stacey sent me not long ago with a quaint cottage in the background. After I'd rescued her from a Razor facility, she'd returned home to Ryland and her kids and we hadn't had a chance to catch up.

Emily opened a portal to the cottage.

"How many rifts can you keep open at once?" I said.

She smiled. "A few."

Tyler looked impatient. "I thought we were just coming to grab a few witnesses really quick. By the time everyone's ready, Emily's going to change her mind."

Emily laughed.

I dashed through the portal and knocked on the cottage door. Stacey answered a moment later, completely naked, of course.

"My little lamb!" She hugged me, pressing her soft bits against me. "Oh, you've finally come for a little romp, haven't you?"

"You're impossible, you know that?" I gingerly separated myself from the sexy felycan. "I don't know how Ryland is, but I'm a one-woman kind of guy."

She smiled. "Let us say that we're rather adventurous."

A tall man with mutton chops and a thick head of hair appeared behind Stacey. "Justin!" Ryland reached out and shook my hand with an iron grip. He glanced at the portal behind me. "Social visit or something else?" He didn't seem the least bit concerned that his wife was stark-naked in front of me. Then again, he wore only a pair of gray boxer-briefs.

"A wedding, actually." I cleared my throat and kept my eyes averted from Stacey's generous features.

"Oh my!" Stacey clapped her hands together, tears pooling in her eyes. "You and Elyssa are finally getting married?"

My heart just about stopped. "Say what?"

Ryland chuckled. "Apparently not."

"I mean—no, not yet." It was one of those things I hadn't given much thought. Marriage seemed nice and all, but it felt like more of a nom thing. Plus, Elyssa and I were still so young. "Some friends are getting married. They just recently helped us save the world, and I thought it might be nice to have a little reunion while we're at it."

"Then count us in." Ryland pulled Stacey inside. "Go throw on something sexy, hun."

She pinched his butt. "You too, dear."

Ryland motioned me in after him. "Want anything to drink while we get dressed?"

"No, thanks." I looked around. "Where are the kids?"

"Out camping with friends." He flashed a grin. "They grow up so fast."

"Yeah, I guess they do." I leaned against the door frame. "I'll be here."

"Ready!" Stacey leapt around the corner, wearing a tight red dress. She wore no makeup, but looked pretty damned fabulous.

"Damn, and I thought Elyssa got dressed fast."

Ryland stepped past her. "Hun, where's my belt?"

Stacey didn't even look. "Right in front of you, dear."

"Ah, here it is."

Stacey stepped over to me and laced her arms around my neck. "Darling, why haven't you married your sweetheart? Are you still holding out hope for us?"

I laughed uneasily. "You realize your husband has super hearing, right?"

"You're the one conquest she regrets never having," Ryland called from the other room. "Life's too short for regrets, even if you live as long as we do."

Stacey licked her lips.

"Not going to happen!" I said. "Elyssa is the only one for me."

She winked. "Perhaps in a few years, you'll realize that physical enjoyment need not be limited to one person."

"Babe, where's my good plaid shirt?" Ryland called.

"In the closet next to your white shirt," Stacey said. "Right in front of you."

"Oh, yeah, found it." He emerged a moment later in jeans, boots, and a plaid shirt. I wasn't sure if he thought we were going to a rodeo or a wedding. "Let's go!"

We stepped back through the portal and found a considerably larger crowd waiting on the other side.

This wedding looked like it would be an adventure in and of itself.

CHAPTER 4

"Justin!" Mom squeezed between Shelton and Adam and hugged me a little too hard. "I'm sorry I haven't come back sooner. Cora has kept us so busy trying to wake up Glimmer folk."

I kissed her cheek. "It's okay. The past few weeks have been slow, thank god. Gave us a chance to rest up."

"Big bro!" Ivy nearly knocked me over with an enthusiastic hug. She backed away, face clouded with anger. "I'm so mad I missed the big fight against Xanos!"

I sighed. "Believe me, there wasn't much you could have done."

"Yeah, but I didn't get to see your new power!" Ivy inspected my hands as if they might look different. "I saw the ASE footage. You blew a hole in Zon's head! Maybe you can do the same thing to Baal."

Mom's jaw tightened. "I'll settle for getting David back in one piece."

"Me too." I put an arm on her shoulders. "We came really close the last time. With my new powers, Cain won't escape next time."

Stacey had cornered Emily and was eyeing Tyler hungrily. "You are a delicious couple, I must say."

"Your accent is so quaint." Emily tilted her head slightly. "It sounds almost Victorian."

"And your hearing is spot-on." Stacey took Emily's hand. "Thank you for inviting me to this lovely soiree."

"This isn't the party." Tyler jabbed a finger toward the beach through the portal. "It's supposed to be over there."

"Emily and Tyler, this is Alysea, my mother, and my sister, Ivy." I squeezed us in between Tyler and Stacey to ward off the insatiable felycan.

"A pleasure." Emily shook their hands. "I've heard so much about you from Justin." She turned her gaze on Ivy. "And the story of how you overthrew Victus Edison is inspirational."

"Gee, thanks." Ivy's face flushed pink. "I still don't remember how I did it. Cumberbatch really messed up my memory when he kidnapped me."

Shelton led Bella to the other side of the group. "Emily, this is my wife, Bella."

"It is so nice to meet you." Bella took Emily's outstretched hand in both of hers and squeezed it. "Harry says you're practically a goddess."

Emily laughed. "Not even close."

Shelton snorted. "Close enough."

Even though I knew Tyler really wanted to herd us back to the beach, he wore an amused smirk and managed to look completely calm in the chaos. Judging from the look of pain in Mom's eyes, I could tell Tyler reminded her of Dad. They might not look alike, but the attitude was nearly identical.

"Wow, a wedding!" A girl with long green hair and silvery skin flitted among the crowd, a mad look in her inhumanly large eyes.

"Evadora!" Ambria managed to catch the girl and hugged her.

"Ambria!" Evadora kissed the other girl's cheeks. "I missed you all so much." She snagged Conrad and Max and gave them the same treatment.

Cora, the orange-haired Glimmer Queen, stepped up behind Evadora and patted her shoulder. "Darling, perhaps you should calm down before the wedding."

"Oh, but I'm so excited!" Evadora danced in place. "I've heard of weddings, but never saw one before."

A genuine smile spread across Conrad's face. "Hello, Mum."

"Conrad." Cora hugged him and kissed the top of his head. "I'm sorry I wasn't here to help against Xanos."

"Well, Justin and Emily handled her quite nicely," he said.

"Conrad was invaluable," Emily said. She curtseyed. "I'm honored to meet you, Queen Cora."

Cora laughed. "I'm the queen of no one. All the Glimmer folk sleep."

"Yes, so I've heard." Emily's forehead pinched. "Perhaps I could take a look and see if I can sense what binds them."

"Any help is appreciated," Cora said.

A miniature woman fluttered over to us on amber wings. She landed and stood tall, all four feet of her. "Justin, I am pleased to see you again." Thal was a dark fairy, but they preferred the term Unfae.

I nodded at her. "How have you been, Thal?"

"Good." She cocked her head slightly. "Now that the human need for greetings is over, may I ask what a wedding is?"

Tyler chuckled. "It's supposed to be a blessed union of two people in love. But I'm beginning to wonder if it'll ever happen."

Emily raised an eyebrow. "Point made, Mr. Rock."

He grinned. "I love making points with you, Miss Glass."

Shelton snorted. "Jesus, it's like fifty shades of sexual innuendo with you people."

Tyler's grin broadened. "Believe me, there's far more than innuendo."

"Oh, Mr. Rock." Stacey fanned her face with a hand. "I believe you and Emily are our new favorite couple."

"They're not even married yet!" I said.

Stacey giggled.

Elyssa and her family stepped through the portal from the Ranch. "Sorry it took so long," Elyssa said. "There's a lot going on."

Thomas Borathen extended a hand to Emily and shook it. "Congratulations, Templar."

Her face flushed. "Thank you, Commander Borathen."

Elyssa's mom, Leia congratulated them next, followed by Phoebe and Michael. Now that Elyssa was a little older, she and Phoebe looked more alike than ever. It was hard to believe Elyssa's sister had been one of Daelissa's henchmen back in the day. Now she was training to eventually be a legion commander—provided the Templars could bulk up their numbers anytime soon.

Nightliss came through after them, looking a bit confused. "Where did you say we're going?"

"To a wedding!" Ivy shouted. She bounded over to Nightliss and wrapped her arms around the angel.

"Nightliss!" Evadora flitted through the crowd and nearly bowled her over. "I love you so much!"

Nightliss met my amused gaze with a smile of her own. "There is nothing better than being loved."

I blew her a kiss.

"Well, it seems everyone's here." Emily cast an award-winning smile at the crowd. "Let's move on to the beach, shall we?"

"Actually, we have two more people coming," Thomas said. "They should arrive any minute."

"Oh, okay." Emily looked a bit uncertain. "Are they third cousins or something?"

Tyler laughed. "Hey, maybe I can invite my human family too."

"Human family?" Shelton said.

"Yeah, the relatives of the original owner of this body." Tyler scoffed. "Talk about real demons."

"Indeed," Emily said.

Two men in black suits and ties emerged from the portal. With brown hair combed to the side, a round jaw, and glasses, the man to the left looked rather ordinary. The tall, thin man with him bore a scowl that marked him as anything but. Two more people emerged from the portal, a beautiful woman with almond shaped eyes and long silky hair. A tall muscular man held her hand, grinning as if he was the luckiest man alive.

The woman squealed with glee. "Em!"

Emily's eyes flared and she spun around. "Izzy!" She clapped her hands and danced in place like a little girl. The pair dashed toward each other and embraced, hopping up and down. "Oh. My. God! It's been so long!"

"I thought you died!" Izzy hugged her tight, tears streaming from her eyes.

Her escort wiped his eyes and smiled even wider.

"They must know each other," Adam whispered to Shelton.

Shelton scoffed. "Damn, Nosti, you're a world-class mind-reader!"

Emily finally released Izzy and hugged the man next to her. "Oh, Jack, I'm sorry Tyler and I disappeared on you two." Her eyes lit on the men in black behind them and flared again. "George? Mr. Sticks?" Despite their obvious discomfort, Emily gave them brief but firm hugs.

"A pleasure as always, Miss Glass." George put a fist to his chest in a Templar salute. "From what I've heard, you've come a long way since the last time we spoke."

Mr. Sticks didn't say a word, but stared at Emily. She gasped. "Thank you." Fresh tears gathered in her eyes. "For finally speaking to me after all this time."

A faint smile tugged on the man's lips.

"Uh, am I deaf, or did he not say anything?" Adam said.

"You're deaf," Shelton said. "He said, congratulations, Emily. Nice dress."

I repressed a snort. "Yep, that's what I heard too."

"Really?" Adam pushed a finger up the bridge of his nose even though he no longer wore glasses. "I didn't even see his lips move."

Elyssa rolled her eyes. "Will you two stop picking on Adam?"

Shelton laughed. "He loves it."

"Not really," Adam said. "I seriously thought I lost my hearing."

Emily wiped her eyes and turned to Thomas. "How did you find everyone?"

"We finally located Agents Walker and Sticks last week," he said.

"We left the Templar organization once it began its downward slide," George said. "It seemed more effective to freelance. Once we heard Commander Borathen was back, we decided to return and reenlist."

"I knew about Isabel and Jack from your records," Elyssa said. "It took a little bit of work, but I tracked them down and used an omniarch portal to bring them through."

Isabel looked down at her sapphire blue dress. "I didn't even have time to dress properly."

"Oh, Izzy, you could wear a paper sack and look like a runway model." Emily sighed happily. "This day has already turned our wonderfully, and I'm not even married yet."

Tyler rubbed his hands together. "Then let's do it, so I can finally stop living in sin!"

Emily sighed. "What about my father?"

Elyssa shook her head sadly. "He's still off the map, I'm afraid. He left the Templars not long after Agents Walker and Sticks."

"Wow, what's going on?" The Templar woman and her pals had returned.

Thomas glanced at her, but since he didn't officially have authority over the Eden Templars, he ignored her and stepped through the portal to the beach.

"It's a wedding!" Ivy said to the woman. "You should totally come."

"Oh, may I?" the woman said.

Tyler snorted. "At this point, we might as well have invited everyone in Queens Gate." He waved her through. "Come on."

Everyone made their way through the gateway. The portal offered only a glimpse of what waited on the other side. Bright sunshine warmed my skin and a pleasant ocean breeze carried the sweet scent of flowers. The portal stood between tall boulders, hiding it from view and I soon found out why.

About fifty yards down the beach, workers had set up chairs and erected a small platform where I assumed the ceremony would take place. Not far away, a straw-roofed hut held a well-stocked bar. Wooden stairs led up a hill and to a quaint cottage at the top.

The workers looked surprised at the group coming down the beach.

Since we seemed far from civilization, they probably couldn't figure out where all of us had come from.

"Where are we?" I asked.

"Fiji," Tyler said. "Found a nice private beach house and rented it."

"I could use a vacation," Elyssa said.

Phoebe laughed. "I think all of us could at this point."

Bella raised her hands in praise. "Amen!"

Thal, thankfully, had hidden her wings and assumed a normal human height. "It reminds me of home."

"I love the beach!" Evadora dashed into the water and began splashing around like a wild dolphin.

"Yes!" Ivy dove into the blue waters, laughing and thrashing without a care in the world.

Mom and Cora sighed in contentment, then grinned at each other as if sharing a moment.

"By the way, I'm Vicky." The Eden Templar woman held out her hand to me.

I shook it, nodded. "Um, nice to meet you."

I expected her to introduce the three men with her, but she looked at the bar and licked her lips. "I hope they have margaritas."

"They have everything," Tyler said. "Open bar."

The men with Vicky cheered and made a beeline for alcohol.

Michael shook his head. "They're a disgrace to the uniform."

"The very reason we left," George said. "After the purges during Victus's rule, only his puppets remained."

"Oh, bother." Emily put her hands on her hips. "Where's the priest?"

Tyler groaned. "I don't see him."

Thomas raised an eyebrow. "As the Templar commander, I can perform wedding ceremonies."

"Oh, I wouldn't want to impose," Emily said.

Tyler waved away her objection. "I will totally impose on you. Having you perform our ceremony would be more official than anything in the entire world."

Adam cleared his throat. "Hey, should we invite Eve?"

Shelton burst into laughter. "Nosti, you're insane and I love it!"

Adam persisted. "I mean, she's your grandmother and all."

Emily gave him a sad smile. "The sentiment is nice, but I'd rather not deal with Eve. I'm still furious with her."

Tyler still spoke to Thomas. "So you'll do it?"

"Yes." Thomas started toward the raised platform. "Shall we?"

"Yes, we shall!" Tyler put fingers to his lips and whistled. "To your seats, everyone!"

Emily took Isabel aside. "Be my maid of honor?"

"Absolutely!" her best friend squealed.

Tyler tapped Jack for his best man, and just like that, they were good to go.

Shelton grunted. "Damn, they know how to throw a fast wedding."

"I just wish Dad could be here." Emily sighed.

Tyler kind of gave her a *what can you do?* shrug but didn't respond.

"Tyler dodged that bullet," Shelton whispered. "One wrong word, and a woman will just call everything off."

Bella slapped his shoulder. "Harry, hush, and get into a seat."

"I'm just saying." He hustled to the chairs and we followed him.

There was no walk down the aisle, or stand-in father giving away the bride. Emily started up front next to Tyler and Thomas got right into the ceremony. It was a little different than what I was used to, but I assumed it would have a Templar twist to it.

Thomas clasped his hands in front of him. "Today we gather to honor the union of Tyler Rock and Emily Glass. Today, they formalize their bond with an oath to declare their undying loyalty before these witnesses here today." He looked at the couple. "A ring has neither a beginning nor end. By placing a ring on the finger of your loved one, it symbolizes your unending oath."

He turned to Tyler. "Do you, Tyler Rock, declare unending loyalty to Emily Glass, until death does end all obligation?"

"I do."

Thomas turned to Emily. "Do you, Emily Glass, declare unending loyalty to Tyler Rock, until death does end all obligation?"

She smiled. "I do."

"Do you have any further vows to declare?"

Emily and Tyler shook their heads.

Thomas continued. "Tyler, place the ring on Emily's finger."

He grinned and slid a silver ring onto her finger.

"Emily, place the ring on Tyler's finger."

Eyes brimming with happy tears, Emily pushed a black ring onto Tyler's finger.

"I declare the oath complete." Thomas motioned toward the crowd and the couple turned to face us. "I present to you—"

Emily leaned back and whispered something to Thomas. He nodded.

Thomas spread his hands apart. "I present to you Emily Glass and Tyler Rock, now and forevermore until death, husband and wife."

Tyler swept Emily into his arms and kissed her. We rose to our feet and cheered.

"Man, that was short." Shelton sounded disappointed.

"But to the point." Adam shrugged. "I can't picture Thomas getting all flowery even for a wedding."

I snorted. "Yeah, he's definitely not the one for sentiment."

Our applause died down, all but for one person slowly clapping. I looked down the beach to our left and saw a lone figure with bright orange hair walking slowly toward us, a malicious grin on her face. The orange hair made me think it was Cora at first, but I knew that face all too well.

The woman rose into the air, hair blazing like an inferno, a halo of orange flames around her. Olivia shook her head. "Wow, Emily, you didn't even invite your own sister to your wedding?" She thrust a hand in the air. "Big mistake."

A portal sliced open and an army of demons on the other side rushed through.

CHAPTER 5

The first wave of demons looked like baby devils, complete with red skin, tiny horns, forked tails, and bat wings. They even had little mustaches. I hated to admit it, but they looked kind of cute in a creepy sort of way. Then they swarmed into the sky, shrieking like banshees and all I wanted to do was shut them up.

Giant hellfire demons tromped through next, lava feet melting the sand to glass. Behind them came dozens of squirming masses that seemed to be nothing more than groping tentacles. Despite having no visible heads or eyes, they bounced and rolled with precise coordination.

In the far back stood a naked humanoid form, but it had no face, hair, nipples, or genitals. Its only discerning features were two long antennae with flat discs atop them. It stood a little less than half as tall as the hellfire demons, maybe ten feet tall.

Cain jetted into the air on orange flames and hovered next to Olivia. He looked at me and smirked. I wanted to punch him in the throat.

The locals screamed and fled for their lives. Whether by instinct or some command, the rest of us gathered around Thomas and Elyssa who started barking commands and assignments almost immediately.

Emily gripped my shoulder. "Justin, remember what I told you. Don't overuse your powers."

I nodded. "I'll go easy." It wouldn't help anyone if I burned myself out.

"I count four hellfire demons," Shelton said. "How in the blazes do we deal with that many?"

I found Ivy and Mom nearby. "Come with me." I took them to Nightliss. "If we focus on one demon at a time, we can take them down faster."

"By blasting them?" Ivy said.

I shook my head. "Stasis is the only thing that works." I was reluctant to use my Apocryphan powers on them unless absolutely necessary. "We need to coat them from head to toe in Stasis and that will kill them."

Mom looked at the lumbering hellions. "They're nearly thirty feet tall, and we don't have flying brooms."

"Ivy and I will take care of the head and torso. You and Nightliss do the feet up."

Ivy frowned. "I can levitate, but I can't fly fast."

"Don't worry, I got you." I reached over a shoulder and patted my back. "Piggy-back ride."

She laughed. "Are you serious?"

I nodded. "As a heart attack."

Ivy clambered onto my back, arms wrapped loosely around my neck. "I don't know how this is going to work, bro."

"You'll figure it out real fast." I jogged across the sand to Elyssa. "We're hitting the hellfire demons first. We'll need cover from those baby devils."

"We've got you." She drew her light bow and flicked it out to full length. Shelton and Adam held their staffs at the ready. Stacey had shifted into hybrid form, a black-furred human body with the head, tail, and claws of a panther. Ryland assumed his hybrid wolf form.

Emily hovered above, gold and blue flames flickering around her body. Max, Ambria, and Conrad joined Shelton and Adam.

We didn't quite have an army, but this would be good enough.

"We could just escape through a portal," Shelton said.

Emily nodded. "We could, but we have a secret weapon they don't know about." She glanced at me. "Perhaps this is the day we take Olivia and Cain out of the fight."

I grinned. "Sounds good to me." I looked over my shoulder at Ivy. "Ready?"

She nodded eagerly. "Let's go, bro!"

Magical flames erupted from my feet and I jetted into the sky. Cain's eyes bugged and Olivia's mouth dropped open. *They have no idea what I can do now.*

Ivy whooped with joy. "How did you learn to fly?"

"Ancient Chinese secret." I leveled out into horizontal flight. "Can you sit upright?"

She pushed herself up. "Yep. This'll be easy as pie."

"Good." I looked down and paced Mom and Nightliss as they ran toward the nearest hellfire demon. "These things spit fire, so watch out."

Mom looked up and nodded.

Emily flew ahead of us and met the flying baby devils as they swarmed to intercept us. Beams of golden light speared from her fists. Smoking devils screamed piteously as they spiraled to the ground. Elyssa unleashed a volley of light arrows, spearing the little demons left and right. Shelton and the others opened fire with staffs and wands, clearing a path for us.

Ivy and I fired twin beams of Stasis at the head of the nearest hellfire demon. Mom and Nightliss blasted its feet. It roared and threw up clawed hands but couldn't defend itself against the onslaught. The first hellfire demon froze into dead rock and crumbled to ash in seconds.

Then we went for the next one. Before we could reach it, the balls of squirming tentacles bounced and rolled in Mom's and Nightliss's path. I wove Stasis and hit one. It froze into a solid lump and went motionless. But the next one dodged my attacks and bounced into the air. A maw of shark teeth opened in the middle of the ball. Tentacles reached for me.

I rolled to the side and it narrowly missed. Ivy shouted in alarm and her legs tightened around my waist. "A tentacle got me!"

I craned my neck and saw a glistening black coil around her shoulders. It stretched like a rubber band, growing so thin, I thought it would snap. Instead, the tentacle retracted, and the monster at the other end flew toward us, sharp teeth ready to chomp on my sister.

"Can you free your arms?" I said.

"No, it's too strong!"

I channeled Brilliance from a finger and slashed the tentacle. The destructive energy splashed off without even leaving a mark. The mini devils weren't magic resistant, but these things certainly were.

"Let go of my waist!" I said.

Ivy unclenched her legs. I spun around, grabbed the tentacle, and yanked it upward, but it didn't budge. Ivy screamed. I slid a hand beneath the tentacle. Something sharp burrowed into my skin. I shouted and yanked out my hand. "Jesus, it has teeth!"

Ivy's eyes welled with tears. "It hurts, Justin!"

The monster was nearly upon us, so I did the only thing I could. Holding her aloft with one arm, I channeled Brilliance and Murk from my eyes, weaving it into Stasis and hit the monster with everything I had. It froze into a solid lump and dropped like a rock. The tentacle went slack and the monster thudded in the sand.

I tossed Ivy into the air, spun around, and she landed on my back.

"So tired," she moaned. Blood and green liquid oozed from wounds in her skin.

"It poisoned you," I said. "We've got to get you away from them." I checked the bite mark on my hand, but luckily the fang hadn't penetrated the skin.

The tentacle demon began to move again, slowly returning to life. Stasis might kill the hellfire demons, but it only put this kind to sleep.

Mom and Nightliss fought off two of the tentacle monsters with shields of Murk. I flew back to Thomas and set Ivy on the ground. "She's poisoned. We may need to retreat."

Thomas checked her wounds and nodded grimly. "You'll need to go tell Emily. She's not wearing a com badge so I can't contact her."

"Yes, sir." I soared back into the air and made a beeline for her. Scores of smoking mini devils lay on the beach. Two of the tentacle demons rolled around helplessly, their arms cleaved off. It seemed Emily was strong enough to punch through their magic resistance.

"We've got to retreat!" I said. "Ivy's been poisoned."

Emily clenched her teeth. "How badly?"

"Really bad," I said.

Olivia, still hovering behind the safety of her minions gave us a gloating smile. "Come with me, Emily, and I promise not to kill your friends."

Emily glared back. "How did you find me?"

"The old-fashioned way." Olivia folded her arms. "Now come here, sister dearest. Baal would love to say hello."

"Another time, perhaps." Emily looked into the distance where Thomas stood next to Ivy. She slashed her hand and a portal opened. "Until the next time."

Olivia laughed. "Where do you think you're going?" She snapped her fingers, and the tentacles on the blue demon emitted a pulse wave that raced across the beach. It struck Emily's portal and collapsed it instantly.

"What the bloody hell?" Emily opened another portal, but the blue demon closed it with another pulse. Emily bared her teeth and fired a blast at the blue man, but Olivia shielded him easily.

"Come with us or watch your friends die," Olivia said.

Scores of tentacle demons—squirmers—rolled toward us, the hellfire demons stomping close behind. Conrad, Ambria, and Max lined up with Shelton and the others. Max grabbed a handful of yellow marbles from inside his side pack and handed them out. "I don't know how well these will work in the sand, but we might as well try."

Stacey held one up between thumb and forefinger. "What the bloody hell is this?"

"Banana peel," Max said. "Now throw them!"

We launched a volley of the marbles. Most landed about fifty feet from our position, but Stacey and Ryland's landed right in front of the squirmers. Yellow liquid spread across the sand, each marble coating it about twenty yards in diameter. The squirmers slid across it, unable to gain traction. One of the hellfire demons stepped on it. Its foot flew up and the monster landed on its ass, throwing molten sand in all directions and crushing several squirmers.

Tentacles writhed and went still. Horrifying shrieks went silent. But there were still dozens of the monsters and not enough of us to deal with them.

Elyssa, Shelton, and Adam continued picking off baby devils to deprive them of their aerial advantage. Max and the others threw more banana peel bombs to create a line in the sand. It might cause the squirmers to lose their grip, but it wouldn't slow them down. They'd just slide across it like the last one.

Thomas seemed to have already considered that, because the moment they were done, he pointed a finger down the beach toward a rocky cove. "Everyone retreat. We'll take cover so Emily can open a portal they can't close."

Before we could make a run for it, a portal ripped open thirty yards from our flank. Olivia had opened a gateway from one part of the beach to the other. All the squirmers in front of us were suddenly just on the other side of a gateway behind us. The huge pool of banana peel meant to protect us, was suddenly a barrier pinning us in.

Thomas shook his head. "Clever girl." But he wasn't done yet. "Into the jungle." He pointed up the rocky path leading away from the beach.

"I hate that bitch!" Shelton shouted. He started running, but his boots were made for walking, not running.

"I've got you, my love." Bella slung him over her shoulder like a sack of potatoes and raced toward the cliff.

But there were others among us that didn't have supernatural speed, and the squirmers were too fast for them to outrun. I snagged Max and tossed him over my shoulder. "Stacey and Ryland, grab someone!"

Mom picked up Ivy and Nightliss ran alongside her. Ivy's skin had a greenish cast. She threw up all down Mom's back before they'd gone two strides.

"I'll get the boy." Stacy grabbed Conrad, and Ryland hefted Ambria.

"Apologies, Mr. Nosti." George Walker threw him on his shoulder.

"Fine...with...me!" he gasped as his shoulder drove the air out of him with every stride.

"Where are those damned Templars?" I said. I didn't see them at the bar

47

or anywhere else. They'd probably run for the hills the moment Olivia and pals showed up.

Mr. Sticks bared his teeth but said nothing.

Michael and the other Borathens formed a perimeter along our flank as we made our retreat. The squirmers were fast, but we were easily outpacing them.

Olivia and Cain rained down destruction on the path ahead of us, filling the path with burning trees and rubble. A huge boulder rolled down the cliff straight at us. Nightliss formed a shield of Murk and diverted it to the left. But the stairs leading up the steep cliff were gone. Scaling it wouldn't be a problem for most of us, but it wouldn't be easy for those of us carrying someone, especially not with Olivia and Cain firing on us.

"I'll take care of them." Emily zipped out on her own, trading shots with the pair.

"I've had enough of this." Cora reached into a pack on her side and sprinkled seeds on the ground.

Squirmers closed in to within a few feet. The Borathens, George, and Mr. Sticks drew swords and prepared to engage.

Black vines shot up from the ground, impaling squirmers with glistening thorns. The monsters screeched, tentacles flailing violently. But more vines exploded from the sand, constricting the creatures, cutting and slicing them open, flooding the sand with green ichor. Those few who made it through met Templar blades. The squirmers might be magic resistant, but the enchanted blades cut into them easily enough.

"Get everyone up the cliff," Thomas shouted.

I flew Max to the top, then returned for Conrad and Ambria. I hefted them under my arms and flew them to the top.

Ambria rubbed her ribs when I set her down. "That wasn't pleasant at all."

"Sorry!" I dipped back down and got Ivy to the top. Without cargo, the others were able to quickly scale the cliff.

Olivia disengaged from Emily, leaving Cain to fight her. A malicious grin clear on her face, I knew she was up to something terrible. We had to get everyone up the cliff so Emily could portal us to safety.

Then the trees began to shake. Ambria shouted in alarm, and Conrad began firing at something in the jungle. Within seconds, the problem became clear. Olivia had opened a portal on the cliff and the squirmers were about to kill everyone up there.

CHAPTER 6

The smirk on Olivia's face superheated my anger. "I've had enough!" I roared.

"Aw, is baby mad?" Olivia shouted. "Maybe your mommy can kiss it better."

That was all it took to push me over the edge. I flew toward the cliff and unleashed holy hell on the squirmers. They might have resisted Brilliance, but they had no protection against Apocryphan magic. Jade energy cleaved through a group of them, giving Conrad and the others enough time to group with Mom and Nightliss who'd just reached the top of the cliff.

Nightliss channeled a shield, and I mowed down the monsters around it until the forest was drenched in sizzling green blood and body parts. The flesh around my fingernails cracked and blood seeped out. The amount of energy expended was already taking a toll on my body.

But I wasn't done yet.

The hellfire demons were ripping through Cora's vines. Tough as the plants were, they burst into flames when they touched the lava skin of the demons. Michael, Thomas, and the others had nothing but swords to defend themselves. A giant claw slashed toward Elyssa's family, threatening to orphan her in one swipe.

I dove down and shielded them. The claw glanced off. Shielding my fists, I summoned all my Apocryphan strength and slammed the nearest demon in the face. Its monstrous face cracked. It stumbled backward, roaring in pain. The other two hellfire demons stomped through the remaining vines and spat fire at Cora and the others.

"No!" I barely shielded them in time.

Emily threw up a shield of her own. "Justin, you're past your limit. You've got to stop!"

"I can't!" If I did, the hellfire demons would kill Elyssa's family. I flew forward and slammed the other two in the face. I couldn't kill the bastards with Stasis—not without help. And for all I knew, Ivy was dying of poison from those damned tentacles.

The relentless demons slammed their fists against mine and Emily's shields. Thomas, Phoebe, Michael, and Leia had nowhere to go. Cora could probably escape, but the demons would kill everyone else.

Elyssa scrambled down the cliff face. There was nothing she could do but die if she came down here. I had to stop the demons at any cost.

I took one last look at Elyssa then summoned everything I had. "Whatever it takes."

I unleashed a torrent of jade energy into the nearest hellfire demon's chest. It roared defiance, struggling forward. I widened the beam and engulfed the top half of the demon. When I relented, only ashes remained. The bottom half staggered back, but it was already growing, trying to regenerate. So I unleashed another broad swath of jade destruction until there was nothing left but black ash.

Then I turned on the next one.

My fingers and hands blackened and burned. The skin along my arms turned crimson, cracked and bleeding. My insides were on fire. But there was one more demon left.

I destroyed its legs first. It crawled forward on its hands, still trying to kill Elyssa's family. "Go to hell!" I roared and blasted it to dust.

"Justin!" Emily grabbed my arm. "What have you done?"

My lips were cracked. My mouth felt dry as cotton. Somehow, I managed to speak. "Whatever it took."

The hellfire demons were dead, but one last threat remained.

The tall blue demon came closer, its antennae twitching wildly. A low hum grew louder, and energy crackled along its body. A pulse wave fired from its antennae with a razor edge. Emily cried out in effort and blocked it with a shield. But the demon was already charging up a second wave.

I didn't have much left in me, but that didn't matter.

I saw Olivia in the distance. Her smirk was gone. Cain hovered beside her, a frightened look on his face.

I streaked toward the blue demon and landed in front of it. "Fucking die!" I channeled a jade blade and lopped off its antennae. The pulsating energy sparked and vanished. I slashed again and separated its head from its shoulders. The demon dropped to its knees as blue blood soaked the sand.

Something smelled awful, and I soon realized my hair was on fire. I rubbed it out with a hand. I bared my teeth at Olivia and Cain. Raised a hand and gave them a come-hither motion.

It took everything I had to speak. "Let's finish this, you frightened little bitches." I couldn't have channeled another ounce of power if I'd tried.

My skin felt so dry and burned, I felt it crack when I tried to move. The pain was unbearable.

I gasped and felt myself falling.

EMILY

"Justin!" Emily dropped down beside Justin's still form. The odor of smoke and burning flesh stung her nose.

Olivia cackled with mad laughter. "He killed himself!"

Cain's forehead pinched. "Where the fuck did he get that power?"

"Justin, you bloody fool!" Emily gathered more power and rose into the air. "Well, sister, your demon army is gone. Shall we finish this?" She opened a portal, bridging the gap between Justin and the rest of their people.

Olivia bared her teeth. "I think next time it will be easier." She backed through her portal, and Cain flew alongside her. "Until next time." The portal winked shut.

Emily sagged with relief. She was beyond exhausted and couldn't have lasted long against Cain and Olivia. She dropped back to the ground. Elyssa and the others had already rushed to Justin's side. Even the cowardly Templars who'd come with them finally showed their faces.

"He's still alive!" Tears streaked down Elyssa's face. "He needs a healer right now."

"What's wrong with him?" Shelton dropped to his knees. "Jesus, he's burning up!"

"We've got to do something!" Shelton, who rarely seemed to care about anything practically screamed with emotion now.

"Oh god." Adam Nosti blanched. "Oh, Jesus, he looks bad."

"Justin!" Alysea cried out in anguish, her deathly sick daughter cradled in her arms.

Thomas inspected Justin's blackened skin. "I don't know if even healers can help him now."

"I know who can." Nightliss gripped Elyssa's arm. "We need to go to Utopia."

Elyssa stared blankly at Justin.

Nightliss shook her. "Elyssa, do you have a picture of Utopia?"

The other woman shook out of her shock. "Yes, but what's on Utopia?"

"Flava."

Elyssa fumbled with her phone and found a picture of twin chrome buildings standing side by side. "Emily, can you get us there?"

Emily's hands trembled with exhaustion, but she nodded. "Yes." She took out her own arcphone and retrieved the list of realms Vitania had given them. She found the symbols for Utopia and burned them into her mind. Then she filled them with power and slashed open a gateway. The twin buildings appeared on the other side.

Elyssa hefted Justin and carried him through. The others followed close behind.

Cars screeched to a halt and pedestrians stared in shock as people appeared out of nowhere.

"This is fucking awful." Shelton paced alongside Elyssa. "He looks like someone nuked him!"

Adam wiped his face. "Do you think he'll be okay?"

Elyssa looked back at Nightliss. "Where's Flava?"

"She came here with the other refugees from Seraphina," Nightliss said. "She's their ambassador, so she lives here full time."

Alysea carried Ivy like a baby. Vomit stained the girl's lips and her face looked white as death.

Elyssa sprinted to the door of the chrome skyscraper on the left. She ran back outside a moment later. "Flava is in session with the Utopian council." She pointed to the building on the right.

The group hurried inside. A surprised woman watched them walk across the lobby. "Can I help you?"

"Medical emergency," Nightliss said. "We must speak to Flava."

"But she's in session," the woman said. Then she saw Justin and her eyes flared wide. "It's the Savior!" Without another word, she ran over and slammed a hand against the elevator button. She picked up a nearby phone and dialed a number. "Medical emergency for the Savior! Please alert Ambassador Flava that he is incoming!"

Shelton paced back and forth in front of the elevator. "How slow is this damned thing?" Red rimmed his eyes and he looked like a man on the verge of breaking down.

Justin's eyelids fluttered.

He's still alive, Emily thought. *But for how much longer?*

The doors finally slid open. Only a few could fit inside with Justin, so Emily, Alysea, and Elyssa went. Michael gravely handed Ivy over to Emily.

"Save him," Shelton said, and then the doors closed.

The elevator rose quickly and opened into a large chamber a moment later. There were ten people just outside the elevator, murmuring in concern.

"Elyssa, my dear, how is he?" An older man asked.

"Not good."

A petite woman with dark brown skin motioned to the floor. "Set him down there." Her brown hair was long, braided along her right temple and completely shaven on the left. "What happened to him?"

Emily explained the Apocryphan powers and how Justin had channeled too much power through his body. "He nearly cooked himself from the inside out."

Nightliss knelt next to Justin. "Can you help him, Flava?"

The other woman bit her lower lip. "I will do everything in my power." Ultraviolet mist spread from her fingers, covering Justin entirely. Then she closed her eyes and put hands to his head. She remained silent, wincing from time to time as she probed from his head down past his chest.

Emily laid Ivy next to him, then took a moment to sit against a wall and rest.

The rest of the group came up in the elevator. Tyler sat down next to Emily and put his arm around her. She leaned against him and closed her eyes.

WHEN SHE OPENED her eyes again, everything had changed. They were no longer in the chamber, but in a dark room. Dim light filtered in through orange curtains, lighting pea-green wallpaper. She summoned a ball of light and sent it upward, lighting the rest of the room. From the shag carpet to the orange laminate furniture, everything had a distinct seventies vibe to it.

Tyler blinked open his sleepy eyes and smiled. "How you feeling, baby?"

"Like shit." She pinched the bridge of her nose to ward off the growing headache. "How long have I been out?"

"All night." He sat up and rubbed her shoulders.

Emily sighed and let him work his magic. The aches in her muscles melted and the headache faded away. But it didn't remove the nauseating feeling in the pit of her stomach. She'd stretched herself past her limits yesterday, and the resulting aether sickness would be an unpleasant reminder for a few days.

She thought of Justin and felt even sicker. The dreaded question lingered on the tip of her tongue for a moment until she summoned the courage to ask it. "How is Justin?"

Tyler's forehead pinched. "He didn't make it."

Emily's lips trembled and her face contorted with anger. "Why didn't he fucking listen to me?" She flung her pillow across the room. Polyester stuffing exploded. "I fucking told him to stop! But he kept killing them!"

Tyler gently took her hands in his. "Baby, he saved our lives. If he hadn't killed the squirmers and the hellfire demons, we would have lost a lot of people."

Emily wiped the tears from her cheeks. "I'm certain he crossed the point of no return when he killed the third hellfire demon." She shook her head. "I couldn't even help him stop it."

"Because you were shielding Thomas and the others." He rubbed her arm. "It was a no-win situation."

"He sacrificed himself." Emily hadn't known Justin long, but he'd never hesitated to throw himself in harm's way if it meant saving his friends— his family. Justin did whatever it took to save people.

And now he was gone.

Tears burned her eyes. Emily didn't even know if she was angry, sad, or just so stressed out that she couldn't understand what she felt. One thing was certain—she couldn't stand to be in this room a moment longer.

She took a quick shower and changed into clothes provided by their hosts. The green polyester skirt didn't quite reach her knees, and the black sandals looked like something pilfered from the dumpster behind a Goodwill store, only because the style was decades behind.

"What is wrong with this place?" She said.

Tyler examined his wide-collared shirt and brown polyester slacks. "Nothing is wrong. It's about time the seventies came back."

"I don't think it ever left this place." She looked in the mirror and wiped at her red eyes. She couldn't imagine how the others felt if she felt so awful. She and Tyler left the room. A helpful woman in an awful orange dress pointed them to the elevator and told them where to find their friends.

They went up several floors and found the others gathered inside a large room. Justin's still form lay beneath a shroud of ultraviolet crystal. Elyssa leaned over him, unable to touch him because of the shroud. Her shoulders shook with sobs. Shelton sat against the wall, face miserable and wet. Adam didn't look much better. Thomas, Michael, George, and Mr. Sticks remained stoic in the face of tragedy, but even their faces betrayed anger and sadness.

Flava sat in a nearby chair, wiping away her own tears. Ivy clung to Alysea, the pair of them sobbing. It seemed Ivy had been healed of the squirmer poison and had woken up to this tragedy.

"There's no justice in this fucking world." Emily wiped her eyes again. "How are we supposed to stop Baal without Justin?"

The old man from yesterday stepped inside the room and walked over to Elyssa. "I'm terribly sorry, dear, but none of our healers can help."

"What do you mean help?" Emily walked over and looked down at Justin. "How do you help a dead man?"

Flava walked over to her and spoke softly. "He clings to life by the barest of threads. Only the preservation magic keeps him alive."

"Can't he heal, given enough time?"

"Not with the preservation field." Flava sighed. "He suffered extensive damage. I cannot heal the body in time to prevent his soul from slipping away."

"That bloody fool had to go and be a hero," Emily hissed.

"Yes, all the time." Flava smiled sadly. "When Elyssa was near death, he sought a healer in Seraphina and found me. I was able to bring her back from the brink. I regret that I cannot do the same for him."

Two women exited the elevator. One of them was short with dark skin, the other tall and muscular with long blonde hair. The tall one walked over to Justin and scowled down at him. "It pains me to see a great warrior reduced to such a hollow shell."

"I cannot believe it has come to pass," the shorter woman said.

"Ah, Ki and Gemma, it is pleasurable to see you this day." The old man from earlier offered them a curt bow. "I am sorry the circumstances are so dire."

"It is tragic, Magus Agula." Ki's eyes wandered until they found Elyssa. "There is great pain in this room."

Emily didn't know much about Utopia—only the little Justin had told her—but the people here seemed unfailingly polite.

Shelton pounded a fist on the wall. "If nobody else is gonna say it, then I will."

"Dude, it's a terrible idea!" Adam gripped the other man's arm. "It might not even work."

"Hell, it worked on most of the population here." Shelton jerked his arm free and walked over to Agula. "Vokan can save Justin."

Agula's eyes widened. "Vokan?"

"Yep." Shelton waved an arm at Justin's still form. "But we need to get him up here right now."

Elyssa dragged herself up out of her chair. "How is Vokan supposed to help, Shelton?"

"Easy." Shelton explained his theory.

It sounded positively awful. But faint hope lit Elyssa's eyes.

"I'm willing to try anything," Alysea said.

"Please!" Ivy clasped her hands in prayer.

Magus Agula nodded somberly. "Then let us try." He turned to Ki. "Would you bring up the prisoner?"

CHAPTER 7

A middle-aged man looked me up and down. He looked somewhere over thirty with a healthy complexion, but his hair and eyebrows were stark white. He wore a white suit and held a black cane. A pipe jutted from his mouth. He looked like a young Colonel Sanders.

We stood in a field teeming with other people. Some screamed in terror. Some collapsed to the ground. Some cried with joy and kissed the ground. But most of them looked just as confused as I was.

Other people in white mingled among the crowd, handing them brochures and directing people to follow a white line painted on the grass.

"I must admit this is quite a shock." The young man's genteel accent sounded strangely familiar. "I hadn't expected to see you for quite some time."

I quirked an eyebrow. "Um, who are you and how do you know me?" I tried to make sense of all the activity around me. "Where in the hell am I?" The crowded field seemed to be growing even more so with every passing second. People of every race, shape, and size seemed to step out of thin air at the end of the field. They'd walk forward, eyes unfocused like zombies and then seem to blink awake.

Eventually, the people in white spoke with the newcomers and prodded them on their way along the white line.

"Come with me and I'll tell you." He followed the white line.

I figured he knew what he was doing. "Okay." We followed the white line and entered a warehouse-sized space that reminded me of a place I couldn't quite name. It was packed to the gills with people. Signs in hundreds of languages hung from rafters. Dozens of colored lines split from the white line and led people to distant doors of the same color.

The sign in English said, *Follow the red line.* But my guide ignored them and walked to a door that had no lines. He opened the door and ushered me through. I stepped into darkness.

"What the hell?" I tried to go back through, but he closed the door. I balled my fists. "Let me out of here!"

"No need to worry, Mr. Slade." A light came on, illuminating a small room that seemed to materialize around us. "Nothing can harm you at the moment."

"Yeah?" I backed away a step from him. "How would you know?"

He pursed his lips. "Because you're dead."

"Say what?" I nearly fell over backward trying to get away from him. The room vanished, replaced with concrete walls and lockers. I instantly recognized my high school. "How did you do that?"

He sighed. "Most people don't realize they're dead so their subconscious constructs something familiar."

My skin itched. I looked down and gasped at the sight of dry, cracked skin. Blisters formed on my fingers, and the skin began to blacken. Violent images flashed through my head—giant flaming demons, squirming balls of tentacles, little flying devils. Memories flooded back, hitting me like a punch to the gut. My skin returned to normal and I realized the man was right.

I also knew who he was. "Jeremiah?"

Jeremiah Conroy, also known as Ezzek Moore, Moses, and the first Arcane, nodded. "Very good, Mr. Slade."

Jeremiah pursed his lips. "I'm surprised, but considering how often you threw yourself into harm's way, perhaps I shouldn't be."

"You knew I was dead?"

"I knew that Baal and Xanos threatened Eden," he said. "Several Templars have been through here lately. I try to get as much news from them as possible."

"So you weren't waiting on me?" I said.

"No. Others like me volunteer for death duty. We guide the newly deceased into the afterlife." He pointed a thumb over his shoulder. "Everyone enters the prairie from the death chamber. I figured it was the best way for me to monitor what's happening in the living world."

"Holy shit." I felt another punch in my gut. "I'm really dead." I wanted to fall on my knees and burst into tears, but I didn't want to look stupid in front of Jeremiah. "Why does this place look like my school but the first place was a field and the next was a warehouse?"

"The prairie has always existed," he said. "The warehouse formed when a group of humans decided it was better to organize newcomers instead of letting them wander aimlessly, only to end up in the wrong collective by accident."

"Collective?" I said. "Like the Borg?"

That earned me a blank stare.

"Sort of like nations in the afterlife." Jeremiah's nose wrinkled. "People cling to the familiar, even when dead. Neutral representatives give newcomers a brief orientation and tell them about the various collectives so they can choose one that best fits their afterlives." He scoffed. "Most don't even want to believe they're dead."

"Sounds a lot like normal life," I said.

"Almost depressingly so," Jeremiah said. "But there are plenty who go their own route."

My knees felt weak. I imagined a chair so I could sit down, but nothing happened. I focused harder, but still, no chair.

"Son, you look like you're having a stroke." Jeremiah folded his arms across his chest. "What are you trying to do?"

"Make a damned chair!"

"You'll need to be more specific." A wooden rocking chair slowly faded into being next to him. He sat down, took out a pipe, and began packing tobacco into it.

"They allow smoking here?"

He snorted. "Here in the darkness you can do what you want." He finished packing the pipe and put it into his mouth without lighting it. "Now, before you get too comfortable, I suggest you tell me how you got here." He motioned behind me and another rocking chair appeared.

"Got anything softer?" I asked.

He frowned, but a seat cushion appeared.

I sat down and wiggled my butt to get comfortable. "Oh, it's memory foam."

Jeremiah lit his pipe. "Do you mind the smell?"

I shook my head. "No, pipe tobacco is kind of pleasant."

"I agree, though Mrs. Conroy put up quite a fuss whenever I smoked." He sighed. "From what I've learned from dead Templars, you've prevented several world-wide catastrophes. You beat Daelissa, handled Cephus and the crystoids, and now Xanos and Baal are up to no good."

"Is Daelissa here somewhere?" I asked.

"She is." Jeremiah puffed a smoke ring. "I saw her when she appeared on the prairie. But she's nearly as unstable as before. Hitting her with Clarity purged her of insanity but unleashed a flood of repressed guilt. She was barely functional when I sent her on her way."

"She deserves her fate," I said. She'd overseen a reign of destruction back in biblical times before making another play for Eden thousands of years later. Daelissa had been sane enough when she'd made those decisions. Clarity had just revealed the utter and inescapable truth about who she really was. Even the most obstinate of people couldn't escape the revelations of Clarity.

"Were you furious with her for killing you?" I said.

Jeremiah shrugged. "I was not magnanimous when I saw her."

I waited for further explanation. When he didn't continue, I prodded him. "What did you do?"

"I sent her to a collective that would not be kind." He sighed. "She didn't even recognize me."

"Wow." I blew out a breath. "I mean, you look a lot younger."

"This is my true appearance," he said. "The old age was a disguise. People gave me more respect than I was due, all thanks to gray hair."

I squeezed my eyes shut, still trying to shake the surreal disconnection I felt. Sitting in rocking chairs in the hall of my high school with a dead man wasn't exactly helping. I felt disconnected from emotions one moment, then on the verge of tears the next. A sense of immense loss crushed my insides whenever I thought of Elyssa, Shelton, or my other friends. I might not see anyone I loved until they died. I'd never save my father and couldn't help the others fight Baal.

If Baal won, billions of souls would soon pack the prairie—or maybe they'd go on to form another Haedaemos. I felt trapped. Helpless. I was furious with myself for dying, for not listening to Emily when I should have. At the time, it seemed like I hadn't had a choice. Those demons would've killed Elyssa's family. But without Apocryphan powers on their side, my friends might not even have a chance against Baal.

I wanted to be numb to it all.

Jeremiah seemed to know what I was thinking. "It's common to feel horrible once you start thinking of what you left behind. Of the mistakes you made." He puffed on his pipe again. "All that is left of you is this ghost—this soul."

"Wonderful."

Depression sagged like a lead weight in my guts.

"Araxos, Couriondral, and Posthanied caused quite a fright when they arrived on the prairie," Jeremiah said.

"I imagine they did." The Apocryphan were big and purple, and Araxos looked like a giant spider.

"Araxos alone was enough to send the dead screaming in all directions." Jeremiah chuckled. "Unfortunately, the Apocryphan weren't eager to talk. They left the same way we did and are probably wandering the outlands."

"Well, they wouldn't fit in with the human souls very well."

"True." He gave me a direct look. "It's important we discuss how you got here."

I drew in a deep breath. "Well, since you know about the Crystoid Incident, I guess I'll start from there and work my way forward." I caught him up on my adventures and told him about Conrad and Emily as well. I probably left out a lot of important events and facts but talking without crying was a major struggle.

Jeremiah listened without comment until the end. Then he whistled. "I'm not even a little surprised Eve snapped and killed the Apocryphan.

She could be out exploring the universe but chooses instead to live in boredom and misery." He stood. "Wait here. I'll be right back."

I gripped the arms of the rocking chair as if they somehow anchored me here. "You're leaving me alone?"

"Only for a minute." He opened an invisible door and stepped back through into the warehouse on the other side. He kept his promise and returned about a minute later, taking his seat again as if he'd never left. "We'll have company in a moment." He began cleaning out his pipe.

"Company?" I looked around, but the school halls were empty. "I hope it's not Nathan." That asshole had bullied me relentlessly in school.

Jeremiah didn't comment.

"Did the Apocryphan keep their powers?" I said. "Did you keep yours?"

Jeremiah shook his head. "Abilities don't work here."

I reached inside for Kalesh and found nothing, not even a void. Anxiety beat my heart like a timpani drum. "He's gone!" I tried to channel magic, but there was no aether to draw on. Tears stung my eyes. "I—I'm normal."

"You're dead," Jeremiah reminded me.

I gulped. "Can dead people die?"

"That is a good question." Jeremiah tucked away his pipe. "There will be plenty of time to discuss such things later. We need to focus on the living for now."

I tried not to panic. "But I'm dead and powerless."

Jeremiah waggled a hand. "Technically, we are alive, but not in the same way as before."

The school hall flickered and vanished. Suddenly, our chairs sat on a wide balcony overlooking a gravel road and forest. I blinked and shot up from my seat. "Hey, it's the old Mansion before Daelissa destroyed it."

Jeremiah looked around. Nodded. "Indeed."

I looked down at the place where Jeremiah met his fate, incinerated by Daelissa. He and I had only been allies for a short while. Before then, he'd tried to kill me at least twice. I'd forgiven him and we'd come to respect each other. It brought up another question. "Did you find your wife, Thesha?" Daelissa had killed Jeremiah's wife way back when he was Moses, and he'd nursed that grudge all his life.

Jeremiah rocked back in his chair and laughed and laughed and laughed until I wondered if he'd gone insane. He finally recovered and sighed. "Yes, I found her living in Kalifa—a superstitious collective not far from here. I held onto her memory my entire earthly life, planned and plotted to avenge her death. But Thesha had long since moved on. It has been thousands of years since she died. She also didn't like the person I'd become."

"Wow, what a bummer." It had to suck something awful to devote your entire life to revenge, only to find the person you did it for couldn't care less.

A beautiful blonde woman stepped onto the balcony. She looked as young and vibrant as the last time I'd seen her even though she was as old as dirt. I remembered holding her crushed body in her final moments at the Battle of the Grand Nexus.

The world shifted again, and we sat in a massive cavern next to a mountain of rubble. We were back in the place where she'd died.

Jeremiah looked around and grunted.

"Aunt Vallaena!" I jumped up and hugged her.

She kissed my cheek and backed away with a broad smile. "My mighty nephew. I am happy and sad to see you."

A red leather sofa appeared, and she sat down on it. "I'm sorry you ended up here so young, nephew."

Jeremiah tapped a finger on his chin. "Now, where is she?"

"I'm here." A lovely older woman stepped onto the balcony and looked around at the scenery. She looked familiar, but I couldn't place it.

I turned to face her. "And you are?"

"Victoria." She sat down next to Vallaena. "Emily's mother."

"Oh, wow." I frowned. "Where did you come from?"

"We also work with the greeters," Vallaena said. "It's the only way to keep tabs on the living world."

"Unless my daughter summons me to Nowhere," Victoria said. "But it's interesting to interview the newly dead and find out what happened."

"What if they don't speak English?" I said.

"Someone translates," Victoria said.

"Is there any way to communicate across distances?" I said.

"Oh, some collectives have working phone systems." Jeremiah shrugged. "But nothing that allows communication across collectives."

"I'm confused." I thought of Nookli, and my arcphone materialized in my hand. The screen turned on and the apps seemed to work, but the map just showed a big blank space. "If I can create an arcphone out of thin air, why can't I call someone with it?"

"Think of the void as a big blank slate." Jeremiah waved his hand, and everything vanished except our seats. "Anything you imagine can be made here. But unless a construct is held together by many minds, it's just as easy to wipe it away." He looked at my hand and my phone vanished.

"The collectives get their name because the subconscious perceptions and beliefs of those living there create a semi-permanent environment." Vallaena pointed into the void. "The further in you go, the longer the constructs last."

"We don't know why," Victoria said. "None of us have ventured much further than Heavenly and Kalifa."

"Heavenly?" I snorted. "That's a collective?"

Jeremiah scoffed. "One you don't want to visit." He fiddled with his pipe. "I should have waited for the others, but they were busy with newcomers at the time."

"He already told you how he got here?" Vallaena tutted. "Jeremiah, you should have waited."

"I don't mind repeating it." I did, considering how much there was to go over, but I put on a smile and gave them a thirty-minute tour of my chaotic life.

"My daughter finally married." Victoria sighed. "If only it weren't meaningless."

"Meaningless?" I blinked in confusion. "Why do you say that?"

"Baal wants to undo the sundering." Victoria's eyes lost focus. "Billions will die."

"And flood the afterlife," Vallaena said.

Jeremiah pursed his lips and stared into the darkness. "It might be even more disastrous than that." His pipe vanished. "If Haedaemos was created during the Sundering, it's possible the vast energy from a collapse would kill billions in an instant and create another spirit realm."

"What would that kind of energy do to those of us already in the afterlife?" Vallaena said. "Souls cannot die, but they can be drained, as they were when the Grand Nexus exploded."

"Good heavens." Jeremiah's eyes widened in horror. "It could consume living essence from our souls and turn us all into consumed."

The consumed were mindless black souls, drained of their light or living essence, doomed to circle the infernal fount for eternity. Daelissa had done that to thousands of humans during her lifespan. Rogue Daemos and Seraphim were likely responsible for countless others.

"The entire afterlife, consumed." Victoria shuddered. "From what Justin's told us, Baal's practically won already."

I wanted to respond, but my vision went hazy and I heard more voices around me.

"I cannot help him," said an imperious voice. "Had you not destroyed my cantrap, perhaps I would have had the power."

"Liar!" A female shouted. "Fix my brother!"

"Ivy?" I called out. "Is that you?"

But the voices faded.

Jeremiah and the others fixed me with confused looks.

Victoria broke the silence. "Is something wrong?"

"I heard voices." I looked around as if I might find someone hiding in the void around us. "One sounded like Ivy." But who was the other one? Whoever it was sounded like such an asshole I just wanted to punch their invisible ass. I snapped my fingers. "The other was Vokan."

"The man from Utopia." Victoria frowned. "What did they say?"

I told them.

"Afterimages?" Vallaena said.

"I don't think so." Jeremiah's pipe appeared again. "Afterimages from life usually occur within minutes of death. This sounds similar to the other stories we've heard."

Vallaena pursed her lips. "You think his body is still alive."

"Probably under a preservation spell," Jeremiah said.

"Hovering on the verge of death, but unable to pass either way." Victoria grunted. "It means a part of him remained tethered to the living."

"Justin is their only hope for defeating Baal." Vallaena sprang up from the couch. "We must return him to life. It's our only hope for preventing an afterlife apocalypse!"

Jeremiah didn't look convinced. "How in tarnation are we supposed to return him to life?"

"You're so bloody daft sometimes," Victoria said. "We take him to the birthing chamber—the place where you met your grandson."

He stiffened. "I told you I don't remember how I got there." Jeremiah's pipe vanished from his mouth as if whatever thoughts holding it there were shattered. "I remember a bright light and waking up there. Somehow, I just knew what I had to say, as if some outside force controlled me. And then I was back here."

"My point is, the birthing chamber exists," Victoria said. "We know from rumor that it lies in the core right next to the primal fount."

"And the core is where, exactly, hmm?" Jeremiah's pipe flickered into existence again. "I've heard a hundred different stories from a hundred different people."

Victoria sighed. "But how many of them were guides, Jeremiah? Those are the people that actually make sure newcomers reach their collectives."

He grunted and looked away from her. "I didn't count."

"Stubborn old man." Vallaena smiled. "You just don't care anymore, do you?"

"What's there to care about?" Jeremiah waved a hand around. "The afterlife is simply another version of hell. Hundreds of clueless newcomers arrive every day and all we do is make sure they're ferried to a place that's nearly identical to the one they came from."

"It makes them comfortable," Victoria said.

"Comfortable? Bah!" Jeremiah threw his pipe into the darkness. "What's the damned point of the afterlife if it's just a continuation of the same old shit you left behind?" He pounded a fist on his chair. "Victoria, you died to save your daughter and prevented Domathus's demonic war on Eden." He thrust a hand at Vallaena. "You died to stop Daelissa from world domination."

Jeremiah seemed to deflate as he looked at me. "And after all the good you've done, you end up here just like the rest of us." He shook his head. "It's a god damned joke."

Vallaena's smile faltered. "Yes, I suppose it is. Dedication to duty and honor earned me no rewards. There is no Valhalla except for the collective. And even it is filled with eternally drunk and fighting Vikings."

"Wow." I dropped into my seat and ass-planted on the ground because the rocking chair was no longer there. I crossed my legs and stayed on the disorienting blackness that was the floor. "You sound so defeated."

"There is no defeat or victory, son." Jeremiah sagged. "There's just a never-ending rehash of life waiting in the collectives. And since we're stripped of our powers, we're just as weak as the noms."

"And some collectives are too dangerous to visit," Victoria said. "Some who venture there are enslaved and may never escape."

"That's why we're here." Vallaena offered me a sheepish smile—one that I had never seen on her bold face in life. "It's safer to remain here. It's easier to advise newcomers on the dangers of the afterlife and point them to places that are boring, but safe."

I looked up at the endless black sky. There was no sun, but somehow there was light. It was disorienting to say the least, but not focusing on it helped. It seemed terribly easy to go insane in this endless black void. I felt the invisible weight on my psyche, sensed it trying to drag me down and depress my spirits.

"We're moving him back to the Ranch." Thomas's voice was a distant echo in my head.

Someone sobbed nearby. I bolted to my feet and looked around.

"Thomas?" I shouted.

"His eyes are moving under his eyelids," Elyssa said. "Does that mean he's dreaming?"

Someone else spoke but the voices faded to silence.

"Elyssa?" *My eyes are moving?* Jeremiah spoke, but I was too lost in my thoughts to hear him. "What if I'm unconscious and dreaming?"

"You heard the living again?" Victoria said.

"Is this a dream?" I pinched myself and it hurt.

"I'm afraid not." Vallaena walked over and slapped my cheek hard. "Life is pain. Death is also pain."

"Son of a bitch!" I held my stung cheek. "I believe you, okay?"

"I am sorry." Vallaena sighed. "You are truly dead."

"Not quite." Victoria fixed me with her gaze. "He's only mostly dead."

CHAPTER 8

I just couldn't keep it together anymore. I burst into maniacal laughter and cried my eyes out. I didn't know if I was happy or sad and could barely think straight. I gasped for breath. "I'm only mostly dead!" And then I started laughing and crying again.

The others watched me patiently, as if a complete emotional breakdown was normal. I kept sobbing, laughing, and wrestling with the desire to hurl myself off a cliff. The environs flickered, changing to places I'd been, Thunder Rock, the Ranch, the original mansion, and even the gym in my high school.

I pounded the invisible ever-changing ground with my fists, howling like an infant throwing a tantrum. There was too much pain, too much loss. I felt as if I'd completely lost my mind.

At long last, I was physically and emotionally exhausted. The surroundings stabilized, forming the war room in the original mansion. Oddly enough, this room brought me peace. It was where we usually came up with plans that would defeat evildoers and save the day.

So many times we'd been on the verge of giving up, but gathering together and reminding ourselves why we fought had always helped us pull one more miracle out of our collective hat.

I will not go quietly into that good night.

I refuse to give in. I would be strong and determined to find a way out of this mess. And then I wiped my eyes and sagged with embarrassment. "Jesus, that was an epic meltdown. I don't know what came over me."

Jeremiah shrugged. "It happened to all of us. When I first arrived, I thought I would be okay. But then depression hit me, and I stayed all alone in the void for days, unable to cope with this strange new eternity."

Victoria looked down. "I thought I was strong, but this place will eventually break your spirit."

"Even I couldn't avoid despair," Vallaena said. "I thought I would return to Haedaemos upon death, so imagine my surprise when I found myself cut off forever from everything I'd known for thousands of years."

It made me feel better to know that I wasn't alone. "Mostly dead." I sighed. "Where's Miracle Max when you need him?"

No one got the reference.

Despite the hope that I might not be completely done with life just yet, I still couldn't shake the soul-crushing sadness of knowing I might not see my true love until the day she died. Nothing could replace the Elyssa-shaped hole in my heart. At the same time, I didn't want her to die anytime soon. If I couldn't make it back to her, I hoped she found happiness.

Of course, a whole lot of people would be dead if Baal had his way. And if Jeremiah was right, most of us in the afterlife wouldn't be here to greet them. "So everyone in the afterlife might be drained of their essence and the billions who die might create another Haedaemos. We can't let that happen."

"For all we know, the current Haedaemos might return to the land of the living." Vallaena traced a finger in the air and an image appeared as if viewing it on a television. A great forest stretched for miles across a pristine landscape, interrupted only by a massive wall that seemed tall enough to reach the sky.

"Whoa." I got up and walked over to the image. "Where is that?"

"That is the wall protecting the forbidden zone in Haedaemos," Vallaena said. "Only Baal and a few of his trusted inner circle are allowed there."

"Can't spirits just walk through walls?" I said.

"In Haedaemos, everything is solid to those who live there." She conjured another image, this one lower and inside the forest. Though the green canopy above basked in golden sunlight, the underside was another story.

Glowing eyes peered out from foggy gloom. Familiar shapes hung from trees, shapes with more legs than I wanted to count. "Are those crawlers?"

She nodded. "The forbidden zone is infested with lesser spawn. Any Daemos strong enough to draw their summons from there will find the most powerful spirits."

"Like powerful enough to take on hellfire demons?" I said.

She shrugged. "Having never dealt with such creatures, I cannot say."

My eyebrows rose. "In all your long life, you never dealt with hellfire demons?"

"Demons from Hell were long considered a myth." Vallaena shook her head. "I suspect they were another of Baal's closely held secrets. But what I have long suspected is that beyond the wall is the dead city of Juranthemon."

Neither Moses nor Victoria looked surprised to hear this, meaning they'd probably heard it before.

I took a moment to think about what she'd said. If Haedaemos was created at the moment of the Sundering, and if it was a spirit world, then that meant—"Haedaemos is an afterimage of the world the day of the Sundering, isn't it? Most of the people who died that day ended up there."

Jeremiah nodded. "The spirits in Haedaemos are not like the souls in the afterlife. They are, in a sense, closer to life than we are. That is why they can possess bodies and be summoned to the mortal plane."

"Will they return to life if Baal recombines the realms?" I asked.

"We don't know," Victoria said. "Perhaps they'll be erased or perhaps they'll remain spirits."

"Or a new Haedaemos will spawn," Vallaena said. "Except this one will look more like modern Eden or a combination of the realms."

"What I don't understand is how Baal plans to avoid the same fate as other spirits," Jeremiah said. "He is too clever to risk oblivion."

In the rush to catch them up on current events, I hadn't mentioned something pretty important. "The reason Baal is so convinced he'll survive, is because undoing the Sundering will give him back his physical body."

That drew a round of uncertain frowns and pinched foreheads.

"It stands to reason Baal was a physical being before the Sundering," Jeremiah said. "But what makes him think he'll return to flesh?"

"Because Baal was an ancient god." I pointed up even though technically we were in the afterlife already. "He was known as Elohim to some, but most humans simply call him God."

Their eyebrows shot up in surprise.

"This just keeps getting worse," Jeremiah said. "Elohim was not known for his benevolence."

Victoria looked the most distraught. "It's no wonder any holy books related to him have brought nothing but ignorance and terror to the world."

I turned to Vallaena. "You don't know what it looks like on the other side of the wall?"

"Only rumors and third-hand accounts," she replied. "What puzzles me the most is why Baal would want to keep it secret. He didn't bother hiding Babyl, Mereania, or Nimbus, all of which existed before the Sundering."

"I've never heard of those places," I said.

"Babyl was the earliest human city," Vallaena said. "Mereania was the underwater city of the Sirens, and Nimbus was the cloud city of the Seraphim."

"Whoa." I whistled. "Yeah, I guess they all lived on the same planet back then." I frowned. "You seem to know an awful lot about the Sundering, but you never mentioned it to me during my training."

Vallaena shrugged. "I did not know about it until after I died. Only in retrospect did I learn about those cities and why they exist."

Jeremiah chewed on the stem of his pipe thoughtfully. "Then it stands to reason Baal has something to protect in Juranthemon. As the focus of the blast that sundered the world, there's likely something important about the place."

"Maybe he's hiding something vital," I said. "Maybe the real secret to stopping Baal is in Haedaemos." I frowned. "Is there any way we can go there?"

"Not that we know of," Jeremiah replied. "But perhaps there are those in the core who would know."

"And that's the area near the birthing chamber?" I said.

"Yes, the rumored center of the afterlife." He waved toward the darkness. "Somewhere next to the primal fount."

"It's said that there are ancient beings in the core," Vallaena said. "It is even rumored some dead gods live there. If anyone knows how to bridge the gap between us and Haedaemos, or return you to life, it would be them."

"Well, like everything in my life, it's a long shot." I shrugged. "But if reaching the birthing chamber means I can return to life and fight Baal, then I'm in."

Jeremiah cleared his throat. "Perhaps."

Victoria and Vallaena exchanged uncertain looks.

Something wasn't right. "What aren't you telling me?"

Jeremiah cleared his throat again. "Even if you return to your body, it's a long shot that you'll survive without the preservation spell."

"So I'd just die all over again," I said.

"The safer collectives are all around the fringe." Vallaena bit her lower lip. "Travelling toward the core means risking our freedom."

Victoria nodded. "We could be enslaved forever."

"Oh." I was a little disappointed. "I thought for sure you'd all be ready for a quest just to liven things up a bit."

Victoria sighed. "But what if your body dies before we reach the birthing chamber? Or what if you simply die again?"

Jeremiah stood and kicked his chair. "We're hemming and hawing like a bunch of lily-livered cowards when what we should be doing is helping the boy."

Vallaena looked away. "I'm sorry. I'm not the person I once was. Now I am but a hollow shell."

I took her hands. "Aunt Vallaena, your training made me the man I am today. Without you, I wouldn't have survived as long as I did." I blew out a breath. "If you spend eternity sitting in one place and not taking risks, one day you'll look at yourself and realize the person you used to be is completely dead, replaced by someone you hate."

Tears welled in her eyes.

I turned to Victoria. "Emily always told me how strong you were. How you never let anything get in your way. Has the afterlife really broken your spirit?"

Her face hardened. "I'm not a weak-willed ninny. I'm just being realistic."

"I will go," Vallaena said. "I'm ashamed for not agreeing right away."

"I've already allowed myself to become a prisoner of this place," Jeremiah said. "I think it's time to move on."

"Pack your bags, everyone." Victoria didn't quite smile, but she tried. "We're bound for adventure."

"Let's get the boy to the birthing chamber and pray for the best." Jeremiah shook his head. "Heaven knows I've done more for far less."

Despite their words, they really didn't look enthused at all. It was tragic seeing how the afterlife had whittled their spirits down to almost nothing. Then again, they'd been stuck here doing the same thing for years, witnessing an endless parade of the dead—sending them to a new existence that was just a pale imitation of what they'd known.

"This place is cancer," I said. "It eats away at you until you're just a hollow shell."

"Absolutely." Victoria looked at her hands as if she could hardly believe they were hers. "Perhaps this is what we need to recover even a little bit of what we used to be."

"It's hard," Vallaena said, "so hard to leave the familiar."

I clapped my hands together. "Well, no time like the present."

"We can't just set out willy-nilly," Jeremiah said. "The greeters don't wander in further than the outer collectives for a reason."

I raised an eyebrow. "I'm having a hard time envisioning what you mean."

Vallaena conjured a two-dimensional circle. The outer edge was labeled *void*. A small square area was labeled *prairie* and next to it, *greeting room*. The next ring was comprised of irregularly shaped blocks.

"Where's the death chamber?" I said.

Jeremiah shrugged. "It doesn't seem to be reachable from the prairie, but we suspect it's somewhere there."

A blue dot appeared next to the prairie—our current location if I had to guess.

Vallaena tapped the outer ring of the circle and shaded it green. "These are the safe collectives."

The closest green territory, Britannia, sat due north. To the left was Little America, Little Germany, and a string of other European countries similarly named. Big China dominated a wide space to the right of Britannia. Collectives named after other Asian countries were barely a quarter the size.

"Are these borders accurate?" I asked.

"Mapped precisely by adventurous people," Jeremiah said. "You'll notice there's a blank space between the collectives."

"What's there?" I asked.

"A small seam of void," he said.

Victoria traced a finger along the map, north through the middle of Britannia, continuing north through the seam between Heavenly and Kalifa. Still following the seam, we went left and then north again to avoid Freedom. She stopped at the blank space beyond. "We'll simply have to wait and see what comes after that."

"Freedom is a bad collective?" I said.

"Let's just say it has mixed reviews," Victoria said. "Freedom isn't free for everyone."

"What's wrong with Heavenly and Kalifa?" I asked.

Victoria answered. "Religious zealots rule one, and the other is full of genies and dangerous spirits."

"Cool!" I rubbed my hands together. "I want to see genies."

"The place is full of superstitious desert tribes," Jeremiah said. "Their beliefs make Kalifa a land of countless dangers."

"Giant sandworms, scorpions, and even sand spiders." Victoria shuddered. "I've never been, but the tales are enough to convince me."

"I'll take your word for it." I leaned in and examined the route. "Looks easy enough. Let's go."

"Yes, I suppose there's nothing else holding us back." Jeremiah looked at the others uneasily. "Is there?"

I scoffed. "You sound as if you wished something held us back."

Victoria took a breath. "Just keep to the void after Britannia and Bob's your uncle."

"Cool beans." I walked toward the place where they'd opened the invisible door and encountered an invisible wall. "How do we get out of this place?"

Jeremiah cleared his throat. As if prodded by some unseen force, he finally walked over and pulled at the air. The door back to the warehouse appeared and we all stepped inside. My companions looked around as if this might be the last chance they had to see this place, took a collective breath to gather themselves, and then started walking.

Jeremiah and Vallaena were nothing like I remembered them. They were just pale imitations of the people I'd known. I just hoped if things got tough I could count on them. Otherwise I had no hope of making it back to the land of the living.

CHAPTER 9

The warehouse was packed wall to wall with people shuffling along the lines. Despite the guides in white trying to keep order and calm, the newcomers were freaking out. Screaming, wailing, many of them sitting on the floor, refusing to budge. Some looked bloodied and bruised, as if somehow injured here in the afterlife.

"What in the bloody hell?" Victoria looked stunned. "I've never seen so many people here all at once."

Jeremiah touched the elbow of one of the women in line. "How did you get here?"

The woman frowned and spoke in a foreign language. Jeremiah replied in the same language and they conversed for a moment. Then he came back over to me. "Apparently, wars have erupted in several Eastern European countries, and some of the larger nations are rattling their sabers. I suspect the timing of these conflicts points to Baal."

"How?" I said.

"He probably has agents in dozens of governments," Jeremiah said.

"Sowing chaos before the storm is the best way to keep your opponents occupied."

Vallaena grimaced. "He could control entire governments with the infernus you spoke of, Justin."

"Wouldn't be the first time." I pressed my back to the wall to make room for more people. "Can we get out of here?"

Jeremiah grunted and walked back through the door to the void. "Let's take a different route. We'll never get through the crowd in there." He pointed to his left. "Britannia should be that way."

"How do you know which way is which around here?" It all looked pitch black to me.

He shrugged. "Because Britannia is at the end of the warehouse."

I imagined a yellow brick road, so it stretched in the direction he indicated. "We're off to see the wizard."

Victoria raised an eyebrow. "Amusing."

The others exchanged a confused glance and started walking.

I turned around and walked backward so I could talk to them. "Is it possible to reach Nowhere from here?"

"I've only been able to reach it when Emily calls me there," Victoria said. "Why do you ask?"

"I want to tell my friends not to give up hope." I faced forward. "I want to make sure they don't pull the plug on me before we reach the birthing chamber."

"I didn't know about Nowhere when I died," Victoria said. "I sat in the outlands for weeks, concentrating on finding Emily. Somehow, I reached her through her dreams. Perhaps you can do that with Elyssa."

"We don't have weeks," Jeremiah said. "Justin's body might only survive a few days without a soul, even if it's in a preservation spell."

He was right. Reaching the core as fast as possible was the best course of action. But I also yearned to see Elyssa, to feel her body against mine. A ghostly image of her appeared before me. I reached out and tried to caress her cheek, but my hand went through it.

Victoria's eyebrow rose. "How did you do that?"

I snapped out of fantasy land and let the Elyssa ghost fade away. "I just wanted to see her, so I did."

"Interesting." A ghostly woman in Middle Eastern garb appeared in front of Jeremiah. "I never attempted to replicate a person."

Vallaena's chin rose. "The student becomes the teacher."

Victoria scoffed. "Give it a bloody rest, woman."

I sighed. "Well, we should get going." I hooked my arm around Vallaena's and sang, "We're off the see the wizard, the wonderful Wizard of Oz!"

Her prideful chin dropped a couple of inches. "Some things haven't changed."

Victoria smirked.

I doubled down and dreamcasted Scarecrow, Tin Man, and Cowardly Lion arm-in-arm with each other on my other side. Jeremiah gave me a blank stare, then turned and began walking. I marched behind him with my imaginary friends, chanting, "Follow the yellow brick road. Follow the yellow brick road."

Vallaena was not amused.

We hadn't gone far when my next step carried me onto a cobblestone road. I blinked in confusion and looked around. Scarecrow, Tin Man, and Cowardly Lion began to melt like wicked witches, turning to puddles of gray goop in seconds.

Dark clouds covered the sky, and a light mist drifted across rolling hills of green. Sheep grazed in nearby fields. There was a quaint cottage with a thatched roof not far from the road, and in the distance, a stone castle.

JOHN CORWIN

It would have had a medieval feel to it if not for a small town with modern buildings not far from the castle.

"I'm guessing we just entered Britannia." I looked at the evaporating puddles of gray goop. "That's gross."

Jeremiah frowned at the puddle. "Almost like demon flesh."

"Yeah, it does resemble it." I wanted to experiment, but the others continued walking briskly down the street, so I hurried to catch up. The air smelled as fresh and clean as a spring morning. "What's with the sheep? People don't have to eat, do they?"

"Collectives offer a sense of the familiar," Vallaena said. "Some people can't handle being dead, so they continue on as if nothing happened. Their subconscious thoughts molded by life experience create the world and its rules."

Jeremiah grunted. "It's the purest form of mob rule and most of them don't even realize it."

"I don't think it's all bad." This was the first time since arriving in the afterlife that I felt grounded. I tried to dreamcast Scarecrow again, but something pushed back against me. It was like trying to exert my will over a demon. I concentrated harder, trying to force the brainless character into existence. It was like pushing through a crowd of tightly packed bodies, but in this case, it was hundreds of minds subconsciously pushing back against mine.

I tried harder, but there was no smashing through that wall.

"You can't overpower thousands of minds," Jeremiah said.

I nodded. "It's like trying to control a hundred demons at once."

"One mind against many," Victoria said. "It would take a small army of strong wills to overwhelm them."

Jeremiah nodded. "And this is why we must be very cautious. Because the rules of the collectives make us as helpless as noms."

CHAPTER 10

helton

Thomas Borathen displayed a holographic map of Eden and declared, "Eastern Europe is at war." Ukraine, parts of Russia, Georgia, and other nearby countries turned red.

Colin McCloud of the lycans frowned and looked at Komad Rashad, but the vampire leader didn't seem overly concerned.

Kassallandra raised a fiery red eyebrow but said nothing.

"Oh, my." Arcanus Primus Takei shook his head. "This isn't good."

Who gives a flying rat's ass? Shelton lifted his cowboy hat and scratched his head. "You called a meeting to talk about nom wars? Those idiots are always fighting about something."

"These countries have been at relative peace for years." Thomas rotated the holographic globe to the United States. "To make matters worse, officials in the U.S. are calling to enter the war on the side of Ukraine."

Adam Nosti wrinkled his nose. "Why in the hell would the U.S. stick its nose into a war in Eastern Europe? It'd throw the world into chaos."

Elyssa, standing next to her father, nodded. "Exactly. Baal's fingerprints are all over this."

"We've known for some time that he's been planting infernus agents in various governments," Thomas said. "Now we know to what end."

Shelton didn't see a connection. "How does this help Baal?"

"It weakens nom militaries, culls the herd." Thomas looked around the table in the conference room. "But I suspect the main reason is that Baal wants to force the Templars to intervene. He knows we're stretched thin as it is, and that making us expend manpower to enforce Overworld law means we can't interfere with his plans."

Shelton waited for Justin to chime in and choked up when reality punched him in the guts. *Justin's dead.* He slumped in his seat and tried not to think about the day before, but it was impossible not to. Bella gripped his hand under the table and wiped away tears of her own. Shelton managed to give her a weak smile.

"What are Baal's plans?" Emily Glass asked.

"We think he's making the final push to recover the other relics," Thomas replied. "Eve has the Sword of Unmaking, Underborn has the Heart of Jura, and the dagger is in the Glimmer. An unknown relic is somewhere in the Abyss."

"I don't see how Baal could get into the Glimmer, much less steal anything from there," Emily said. "And Eve won't give up the sword."

"We're sending a team to secure the relic from the Abyss and find out if Underborn still has the heart," Elyssa said.

"I can assure you that Baal's agents will not get into the Glimmer undetected," Cora said.

Elyssa frowned. "There's no way they can sneak in?"

Cora shook her head. "Not while I'm there."

Shelton grunted. "So, they could sneak in right now?"

"No," Evadora said. "The guardians would kill them."

Conrad frowned. "What if Baal send infernus through the reflected world?"

"They'd still have to navigate the dangers of my realm," Cora said. "The creatures are on guard."

"I'd feel better if you could keep vigilant," Thomas said. "Baal always seems to have a way around our defenses."

Cora nodded. "I'll return at once." She looked at Emily. "You once told me that Vitania, the former queen of the Sirens, might help awaken my people. Have you heard from her?"

Emily shook her head. "Vitania traveled to Aquilis to petition Queen Dactia for help, but that was some time ago. Dactia doesn't like her, so there's no telling how things are there."

"We haven't heard anything from Lumia either," Elyssa said. "But I don't know what we can do about it."

Shelton sighed. "Well, we sure as hell can't sit around doing nothing." He stood up. "If Justin was here, he'd say we should go to Aquilis and find Vitania."

Elyssa seemed to swallow a lump in her throat. "Why do you think that, Shelton?"

"Because if she can wake up the Glimmer folk, then we'll have a lot more people guarding the relics in the Glimmer." He shrugged. "And we might get the Sirens to help us too."

"Aye." Colin McCloud slapped his hand on the table. "I think the lad's plan makes sense."

"There's no reason we should put all our resources toward guarding a few remaining relics," Kassallandra said. "We need to find where Baal keeps the relics he's already acquired and take them by force."

Komad nodded. "I agree."

"But we don't have a bloody army anymore," McCloud shot back. "We were already running thin when Xanos and Zon attacked, and they wiped out hundreds of our people in seconds."

Shelton huffed. "Look, we don't have any idea where Baal keeps the relics. Until we do, it's better if we do something productive. I say we check in on Vitania."

Emily nodded. "I agree. I can get us there, but without a Siren to help us, we can't easily reach the underwater cities."

"Then let's ask Dolpha or one of her sisters to help," Shelton said.

Elyssa swallowed hard again and nodded. "I agree with Shelton."

Thomas dismissed the holographic map. "I concur. We have no intel on the relics in Baal's possession. While Elyssa plans this mission, I will make contact with Underborn and ask if he still has the Heart of Jura."

"Evadora and I will return to the Glimmer to guard against Baal's agents," Cora said.

Ivy wiped tears from her face. "I want to do whatever Justin would have done."

Alysea kissed her forehead. "I think he'd want us to help guard the Glimmer."

"Okay, Mom." Ivy's lips trembled. "But when we find Baal's secret lair, I want to be the one to blow it to bits!" Her declaration ended in a scream.

McCloud cleared his throat uneasily. "We still haven't talked about the elephant in the room. When are we honoring Justin properly?"

Elyssa tried to speak, but her voice broke.

Shelton fought back another lump and tried not to think about his best friend's body lying on a slab.

"Justin will remain under the preservation spell for now." Tears trickled down Alysea's cheeks, but she made no move to wipe them. "When this is over, we'll lay his body to rest."

Thomas nodded somberly. "Justin wouldn't want us taking time to mourn him when there's an imminent threat to Eden."

Shelton couldn't hold back tears of his own no matter how many deep breaths he took. *Damn it, not again.* "Yeah," he said in a hoarse voice. "Justin would want us to kick ass first, so that's what I'm gonna do."

"Let's break for thirty minutes," Thomas said. "We'll have assignments ready by then."

Normally, Shelton would have grabbed himself a snack. A bacon sandwich, a bacon-wrapped burger, or even pizza topped with bacon usually hit the spot. But his appetite had gone on vacation. Still holding Bella's hand, he left the conference room and walked down the underground corridor to the room he dreaded to enter.

Bella squeezed his hand. "Shelton." Her voice broke and she pressed her face against his shoulder.

Shelton opened the door. The room was cold as death, bathed in the ultraviolet light of a preservation spell. They stepped up to the stone slab where Justin's body rested beneath a transparent barrier. Most of the burn marks were gone from his skin, but Flava had explained that the damage was mostly internal. Not even Justin's demonic regeneration could overcome the damage to his heart and other organs.

Justin looked strange without any hair. Shelton wished he could give him a hard time about it. Wished he could just talk to him one more time and say goodbye. "God damn it, man. I'm gonna miss you."

Bella released a shuddering breath. "It seems like just yesterday when he wandered into my small town and turned everything upside down within a day." She laughed through her tears. "He had a way of stirring things up."

"Yeah." Shelton wiped his cheeks. "I didn't know what I was getting into when I tried to arrest him and his dad for a bounty. Got more than I bargained for."

Elyssa stepped up beside Bella. "I think we all did."

"Oh, hey." Shelton tried to dry his face, but his damned tear ducts wouldn't cooperate. "Shouldn't you be coming up with a plan?"

"We've got most of it figured out." Elyssa tore her eyes off Justin's body and turned to Shelton. "Emily and Nightliss are going to Aquilis. Cora, Evadora, Alysea, and Ivy are going to the Glimmer. Conrad, Max, Ambria, and a few hundred Templars are going to the Abyss to start the search for the relic there."

"Without Emily to get them out again?" Shelton said.

"She'll get them there. We hope Emily won't take too long in Aquilis, but we also have Cinder's portal device as a backup."

Shelton frowned. "He finally got it working?" After defeating Xanos, they'd found loads of Razor tech at her base in Thunder Rock, but the portal device she'd used to reach the Abyss had been destroyed.

Elyssa shrugged. "He's close."

"Hang on a damned minute." Shelton scowled. "You didn't mention my name. Where am I going?"

"Hopefully, to stop a war." Elyssa seemed to force herself to turn away from Justin's body. She stepped into the corridor and waited for them to join her.

Shelton closed the door behind him. "I'm listening."

"We can't afford for the U.S. to jump into a war," Elyssa said. "It won't do much good to save the world if the noms nuke each other."

Shelton grunted. "You want me to run for president?"

"We want you and Adam to get rid of the infernus infesting the government." Elyssa folded her arms over her chest. "Baal has improved the infernus. The Mzodi gems we used to detect them aren't working on the new models."

"Let me get this straight," Shelton said. "You want me and Nosti to infiltrate the nom government and assassinate government officials that are infernus?"

"Exactly."

Shelton scoffed. "Why not send Custodians?"

"Because every single one of them is headed to Eastern Europe," Elyssa said. She turned to Bella. "I'd like you to go with Shelton and Adam. They'll probably need someone to watch their backs."

Bella managed a wan smile. "I have no doubt they will."

Elyssa's eyes locked on the door to Justin's room. It took visible effort for her to look away and back to Shelton. "What do you say?"

"We'll do it," Shelton said.

Bella nodded. "We will rip them out, stem and root."

"One other thing," Elyssa said. "If you have to eliminate a large number of infernus posing as top government officials, it might look like a foreign country is assassinating them. You'll have to figure out how to fix the problem without creating an even bigger one."

"My specialty is creating big problems out of smaller ones," Shelton said.

Elyssa smiled. "Just like Justin." The smile faded. "Meet with George Walker before you go. He can probably give you some tips before he heads to Russia."

Shelton nodded. "You got it."

Elyssa nodded and left.

Shelton turned back to the door and considered going back in. Then he turned away, took Bella's hand and walked away from the room.

George Walker and his weirdo sidekick, Mr. Sticks waited near the conference room when they returned moments later. George smiled affably but didn't move to meet them. Sticks watched with a stony face.

Shelton glanced around but didn't see Adam anywhere. So he walked up to George and got to business. "Elyssa said you might have some tips for our mission."

George held out his hands in a shrug. "You were a registered bounty hunter for a time, Mr. Shelton, so I suspect you know how to deal with noms."

"Been a while, but yeah," Shelton said. "Dealing with the government types in Washington is something else, though."

"I'm afraid you'll have to dress differently," George said.

Shelton groaned. "I'm gonna have to wear a suit, ain't I?"

"I'd suggest a different route," George said. "We've found it much easier to infiltrate by dressing down for the occasion."

"People never look twice at the help," Bella said.

Mr. Sticks stared at Bella and his forehead pinched into a V.

"My associate senses that you might have some experience in infiltration," George said.

Shelton narrowed his eyes. "Is Sticks a mind reader or something?"

"No, just very observant," George replied.

Shelton didn't buy it, but he also didn't really care. "Yeah, Bella's got a history. She'll be way better at this than me and Nosti, that's for sure."

"Then you're already in good hands." George nodded at Bella. "My only other suggestion is that you positively identify as many infernus as you can and then decide how best to deal with them. Even a handful of dead officials might be enough to spark war."

"Already heard that speech," Shelton said. "Don't worry. We'll figure out something."

"I've assigned you one of our cars," George said. "You're familiar with them, I trust?"

Shelton brightened a little. Custodian cars had even more gadgets than the Templar versions. "Mostly. I can figure out the rest."

George handed Shelton a black key fob imprinted with *TESLA* across the top. "It's modeled after the nom division of Tesla Labs, but it was equipped by Science Academy."

"So this ain't no ordinary Custodian car," Shelton said.

"It's a new model, so please take care of it."

Shelton chortled. "I'll love it like the last living pig in a bacon apocalypse."

George blinked a couple times, then nodded. "Then I wish you luck." He and Sticks went into the conference room.

Shelton took out his arcphone and punched in a text. *Nosti, where are you?*

Adam's reply came a moment later. *Cinder's lab.*

On the way. "Back to Arcane University," he told Bella.

Bella nodded as if she'd expected it. "What about the car?"

"We'll pick it up when we get back." Shelton pocketed the key fob and headed down the corridor to the levitator. He hoped Bella and Adam had some ideas, because Shelton had no idea how they were gonna pull this off.

CHAPTER 11

J ustin

It felt like we'd been walking for hours even though we'd barely gone a few miles. And my head hurt from trying to dreamcast random objects in Britannia.

"Perhaps you should give it a rest," Jeremiah said. "Despite my centuries of practice, I have been unable to break the rules of a collective."

I pinched the bridge of my nose. "Not even once?"

"Unfortunately, no." He shrugged. "Except perhaps when I instantly traveled to the primal fount, but that was not my doing."

That reminded me of something. "So Conrad's ghost showed up there and you talked to it?"

"Yes." Jeremiah spread his arms helplessly. "I believe the fount used me so Conrad could access its power."

"Why can't I use the primal fount?" I said.

"It simply hasn't chosen you," Jeremiah replied.

I'd heard the reasoning before, but it kind of chafed that I wasn't special enough to be chosen.

We reached the outskirts of another town. Red-brick row houses took over where thatched cottages left off. A few locals walked the streets, many of them going about their day as if in the real world. Some wore suits and bowler hats. Others were garbed in sackcloth or ragged wool and carried bundles of hay on their back. There were those in seventies gear, those in modern apparel, and then the few sporting goth and punk clothing.

Most of them seemed oblivious to each other, as if they didn't want to acknowledge that people from centuries past now coexisted with those from modern eras. A group of men in old military uniforms gathered at a pub, drinking beers and laughing. Some even wore helmets and looked slightly dirty or bloody, as if they'd just come from the war front even though none of them had any weapons I could see.

"Man, this place is weird." Though at first I'd liked the familiar environs, now I was starting to feel out of place. On the upside, hardly anyone gave our group a second glance. I cracked a yawn and stretched. My feet hurt and a headache pounded my temples.

Something occurred to me during my third yawn. "Why am I yawning? Why do my feet and head hurt? Dead people shouldn't feel anything."

"The rules of the collective," Jeremiah said. "These people could create a paradise if they put their minds to it, but their subconscious thoughts are too entrenched in the ways of the living."

"So my feet don't really ache, but this place makes me think they do." I watched a group of gossiping women in drab clothing lower a bucket into a well. They spoke English, but their strong accents made it hard for me to comprehend anything they said.

"It's depressing, really." Victoria watched them disapprovingly. "They've probably been living the same afterlife for centuries now, and in all this time haven't even sought to enlighten themselves."

99

"Most people aren't taught to think for themselves," Vallaena said. "And there certainly isn't anyone here who will show them otherwise."

I shrugged. "What's the point? Maybe this is happiness for them."

Victoria wrinkled her nose. "Only because they refuse to see the possibilities."

It was obvious that the subconscious minds of the many didn't quite mesh into one coherent whole. For example, the road leading through town was paved with cobblestones one mile and asphalt the next. Contemporary houses and thatched huts vied for space with Victorian estates and brick cottages. There were very few cars on the road or in driveways. Horse-drawn carriages and carts were far more prevalent.

It was a wonder all these vastly different people coexisted.

We managed to get a lift from a peasant hauling hay in a cart. He and his donkey gave us dubious looks but allowed us to sit in a bare spot near the back. Before long, the paved road turned to gravel. After a short distance, the road transitioned to dirt surface, which became mud as rain started. The man driving the cart didn't seem to mind. If anything, he seemed happier than a fly in shit and even began singing an ancient tune I had trouble understanding with his archaic accent.

Vallaena and Victoria tied their wet hair into ponytails, somehow managing to look dignified. Jeremiah stared out at the countryside, seemingly oblivious to the miserable weather. I desperately wanted to ask how much farther it was until we were out of this place, but a better question came to mind.

"Why are there hardly any cars?"

Jeremiah blinked from his thoughts. "I don't know."

"Probably because of the tug of war between the old people and the new," Victoria said. "Most people here accept carriages and cars, but those who never saw cars probably have a hard time accepting their existence."

"And yet a few cars exist." I bit my lower lips and tried to nail down the significance of that fact. "It might mean there are sub-collectives with slightly altered rules within a collective."

Jeremiah nodded. "That would be a logical assumption."

I sighed. "Sure wish we'd stolen a car."

The farmer eventually stopped when he reached a fork in the road. We thanked him for the lift, and he continued on his merry way. Then we trudged down the muddy road in the rain.

"This place sucks!" I stared ahead and wondered if it ever ended. "How long does it take to reach the end?"

"Too bloody long," Victoria said.

She wasn't wrong. We reached a modern village at dusk and stopped at the tavern. An old man with a guitar sang drinking songs to a raucous crowd inside. Jeremiah squeezed through the crowd and went to the bar. He returned a moment later with a brass key.

"There's no barkeep, so I helped myself," he said.

"There's no wait staff either," Vallaena said.

I frowned. "How does a place operate without workers?"

"I suppose it operates like everyone expects it to," Jeremiah said.

By the strange logic of the afterlife, it made sense. Everyone wanted to drink and have fun, not work. As long as everyone expected there to be alcohol, it would probably be there for them. They were the same kind of subconscious expectations that made my feet feel as if I'd walked for two days straight.

Though the tavern looked old on the outside, my room had a modern shower and claw foot tub. I happily shed my clothes and soaked in a hot bath until I dozed off. When I woke up, I was underwater. I almost gasped but realized that would be a terrible mistake. How had I not drowned?

Because you're already dead, stupid!

I sat up and wiped the water from my eyes. Sunlight filtered through the curtains and a bird chirped outside the window. "It's morning already?" I climbed out of the tub and wrapped a towel around myself. It was definitely morning and I'd definitely slept some part of the night submerged in water.

"Dude, the afterlife is really fucked up," I said to myself. I kept hoping to feel a hint of Kalesh somewhere in my subconscious, but he was nowhere to be found. It felt terribly lonely not to have his voice inside my head.

As I dried off, I noticed my fingers weren't even wrinkled from soaking so long. When I reached into the water to release the drain, the water was still hot. Apparently, not everything worked as it did in the living world.

When I stepped into the bedroom, I found clean clothes neatly folded on top of the blankets. I didn't know how they ended up like that, but I wasn't about to complain. I also found an umbrella and long raincoat in the closet. I decided they were meant for me.

There were probably more important things to worry about, but the empty space where Kalesh used to be was driving me crazy.

The afterlife reminded me of the Gloom in all the wrong ways. In that shadow realm, I'd been separated from my demon side, but it had felt different. When I tried to contact my demon in the Gloom, a mental barrier separated us. He was there, but just out of reach. In this place I couldn't sense him at all.

During my time in the Gloom, Dad had taught me how to meditate into a lucid dream state so I could dreamcast people and objects. The trick in the Gloom was allowing the subconscious mind to control the dream-casting while your conscious side only nudged it instead of allowing it free reign as in most dreams.

Since I couldn't contact Kalesh by the normal methods, it meant I had to probe deeper into my subconscious. I had to meet him more than halfway instead of trying to bring him to the surface.

It had been a while since I'd tried this, but hopefully it was just like riding a bike.

I SAT down on the bed, relaxed my mind, and shifted into a lucid dream state. Kalesh usually prowled the darkness of my subconscious, but this time I was surprised to find a small room with a twin bed, a computer on a desk, and an old-school television with an Atari 2600 hooked up to it. It seemed Kalesh had created his own little nook.

He was like a passenger, able to sense and see everything I did, but unable to take the steering wheel unless I allowed him. That was probably frustrating as hell, so it made sense that he'd come up with ways to amuse himself. I'd never given it a lot of thought, but was he literally a prisoner in my body?

I grimaced at the thought.

The studio loft had no bathroom, but it had a kitchen with a tea kettle on a gas stove. The walls were red brick, and the floor, polished concrete. There were no doors, just a single window on the wall. That seemed like the most significant feature, so I looked through the glass.

A red-brick apartment building stood alone in the void outside, its countless stories vanishing into the pitch black below. There was no street, no trees, no sky—just the other apartment building. It had hundreds of windows, but only one glowed with light.

The glass of the other window was foggy, but I saw a faint silhouette moving back and forth on the other side. I tried to open my window, but it wouldn't budge. I tried to break it with my elbow, but it didn't even crack no matter how many times I hit it.

"Kalesh!" I shouted.

The silhouette stopped pacing and came closer to the window. Hands pressed to the glass but seemed to be unable to break though.

"Son of a bitch!" I grabbed the television and threw it at the window. It bounced off and the screen shattered on the concrete.

Lightning flashed, outlining something even darker than the void. Lightning flashed again, and wind howled. But as the sound grew louder, I realized it wasn't the wind making the noise. It was something else. Something awful. Black shadows slapped against the window.

A cacophony of screams shattered my concentration.

I jerked back to consciousness with a shout, heart pounding in my chest. "What in the hell was that thing?" And why was my heart pounding when I no longer had one? I was probably so used to being in a physical body that my mind simulated the effects. Or maybe it had something to do with the will of the collective.

Had that been Kalesh behind the window? Or was it just a manifestation of my dream state? Everything here was so confusing and new.

My stomach—another non-existent organ—rumbled. It was time to eat. My mind was too flustered to attempt another lucid dream anyway.

I knocked on the other's doors, but they didn't answer. I found them downstairs feasting on eggs, sausage, and bread. Apparently, an invisible chef had prepared a buffet. I heaped a plateful and joined the others at the table.

"Where does the food come from?" I asked.

Jeremiah shrugged. "I suppose it's simply willed into existence."

"Wish they'd will a car into existence," I grumbled. Despite its dubious origins, the food was excellent and filled me up quite nicely. I tried not to think about how I shouldn't have to eat and couldn't really be full since I was dead but couldn't stop thinking about it the moment the thought crossed my mind.

I told them how I'd tried to contact Kalesh and what I'd seen.

Vallaena gave me a doubtful frown. "I think you imagined it."

Considering the trauma I'd been through in such a short period of time, she was probably right. So I shrugged it off for the time being.

The clear morning skies turned gray by the time we finished breakfast. I tugged on my new raincoat. "Great. Another day in the rain."

"One of the few constants of Britannia," Victoria said. "Just like the real thing."

I offered up a prayer for a car before stepping outside and wasn't surprised when I found none waiting in the parking lot. But right near the end of the village, I noticed an old pickup truck sitting next to a stone house.

"Please tell me we can hotwire that thing," I said.

Vallaena tugged on the handle and the truck door squeaked open. She slid onto the bench seat and reached around the steering wheel. The truck rumbled to life. "The key is in the ignition."

"Well, it would appear we have a ride." Jeremiah walked around and climbed in on the other side.

I didn't feel like squeezing in next to him, so I sat in the back. Victoria joined me.

"Who's in me bloody lorry?" someone shouted from the other side of the wall.

Vallaena made a U-turn onto the road and took off, just as an old man with a pitchfork rounded the corner.

"Thieves!" he screamed. "Help! I'm being oppressed!" He gave chase for a few seconds before slipping and falling in the mud.

I winced. "Man, I feel bad now."

Victoria shrugged. "It's not like he really needs the truck."

105

"It's not like any of these people need anything," I said. "They just think they do." I couldn't help but think that everything in this place was just a reenactment of old lives, and we were trapped in the asylum with the inmates. Then again, judging from the glum looks on my companions' faces, they'd already become inmates themselves.

I thought of Kalesh and being powerless again. Another surge of anxiety and hopelessness threatened to drown me. If I didn't reach the primal fount soon, I'd probably succumb just like everyone else.

The truck didn't go fast, but that was just as well considering the road was muddy and heavily rutted. We made good progress, but the constant bumps and sliding really chafed my ass. We passed through several small villages and across open countryside. We passed legions of redcoats battling an army in blue uniforms.

Cannons boomed and muskets popped. Soldiers fell in droves, leaving ragged holes in neat formations. The battle was only a hundred yards away, but the combatants completely ignored us.

Victoria grunted. "Some people haven't accepted that the American Revolutionary War is over."

"There are Americans here?" I asked.

"Of course." She watched the battle with mild interest. "There were many first-generation immigrants who fought and died in the war."

As the battle faded into the distance, I wondered how awful it must be to fight an eternal war that was nothing but a distant memory to those alive now. Before I had a chance to brood on it very long, a new spectacle ahead caught my gaze.

A huge clock tower stood hundreds of feet high, towering over even the tallest trees. For a time, it was the only landmark we could see. Then the road left the forest, straightening out across an urban landscape. The houses were small, mostly white and red brick. At least ten bridges spanned a wide river. Some resembled the tower bridge in London.

Others looked more modern. Some looked as if the architect merged Big Ben into the towers on the four corners.

It was as if someone took the most touristy parts of London and crossbred them into the most London town in all of existence. I stood in the back of the pickup and leaned on the roof of the cab. "Someone messed up London."

"This isn't even the only London in Britannia," Victoria said. "There are four more cities by the same name. But this one does have the most bridges and the tallest version of Big Ben."

On the upside, the road was paved and smooth. The sidewalks teemed with people from all walks of life, just as I'd seen in the other towns. Traffic was actually a thing here, clogging the roads and generally making our life miserable.

The worst part was that many didn't even have drivers. At first it didn't make sense to me, but then I gave it a little thought and realized the awful truth. "These people have literally willed bad traffic into existence just because that's what it was like."

"The dead make their own chaotic hell." Victoria stared blankly at a group of thugs harassing a man in a suit and bowler. "At least they're free."

"This isn't freedom." I almost jumped out of the pickup to help the man in the bowler but reminded myself that the thugs couldn't really kill or hurt him. "It's a prison of their own making."

"Better a prison of your own making than that of another's." Victoria blinked as if waking from a stupor. "I'm sorry. I shouldn't be so bloody negative."

I shrugged. "I've only been here a few hours and this place is already getting to me."

We finally broke through traffic, crossed a bridge across another river, and emerged into open countryside. The road abruptly ended about a mile out of town even though the grassy plain seemed to stretch on forever. Vallaena stopped the truck, got out, and stretched.

"We're here," Jeremiah said. "The end of Britannia."

"Yay," I said with very little enthusiasm. "What now?"

Vallaena walked to the end of the road. "Now we travel the void between Heavenly and Kalifa."

"Why not take the truck?" I said. "Won't it continue to exist in the void?"

"It's part of this collective," Jeremiah said. "It'll vanish. We could probably make our own, though."

I didn't understand why the truck would vanish just because it was part of this collective, but figured he knew better than I did.

Vallaena stepped forward. The air rippled like water and she vanished.

"Whoa, that's weird." I followed her. There was no sensation, but Britannia vanished in an instant, and once again I stood in the void.

It took a moment to register that not only was Vallaena there, but a dozen or more men wearing white business suits. For a moment, I thought they were the same folks who greeted the newly deceased on the prairie. But a pair of them grabbed Vallaena and dragged her away. Before I could react, another pair took me and hauled me forward.

The void vanished and I stumbled into a grassy meadow. Bells rang in the tower of a small white church not far from us. Dozens more of the men in white business suits applauded when they saw me and Vallaena. I heard cursing and looked back to see Victoria and Jeremiah also being forced along the path to the church.

I wrenched free of the two men and tried to ram the ones holding Vallaena. But the other men mobbed me, pinning my arms to my sides. Without Kalesh, I was helpless as a baby.

I struggled helplessly. "What the hell do you want with me?"

"We're saving you," one of the men answered.

"From what?" I shouted.

"Your sins." One of the men cuffed my head. "Be quiet!"

Victoria wriggled helplessly. "Bloody Heavenly!"

The bells stopped ringing when we reached the outside of the church. A fat, balding man with a fringe of white hair on the temples stopped at the bottom of the steps. "Hark, the ushers have brought new souls for cleansing."

The French doors opened and a woman in a white dress stepped outside, followed closely by a man in a dark red suit.

The woman spoke. "The church gladly accepts the duty of cleansing. Ushers, please bring the sullied inside."

"Oh, shit," I hissed. This didn't sound good at all.

The man in the red suit blurred forward at inhuman speed and back-handed me so hard, I saw stars. "Quiet, sinner! We will have no vulgarities here."

I was about to reply with a nice stream of vulgarities, but when I tried to talk, only a faint squeak emerged. *What in the hell?* The ushers dragged us into the church. The woman in white led us down a flight of stairs and into a dank-smelling basement lined with prison cells.

Screams echoed from another stairwell leading deeper underground. Thankfully we didn't get to discover what lay below and our captors shoved us into individual cells. Three brick walls, a cot, and a bedpan greeted me in the cramped space.

I spun around and gripped the barred door. I tried to speak and discovered my voice was back. "Look, we're on an important mission for God. If you'll just let us go on our merry way, you'll be doing God's work."

The man in the red suit stepped forward. This time, I got a better look at the bastard. He was my height, barrel-chested, and broad-shouldered.

His eyes were washed-out blue, and he wore his gray hair combed over to the side. He had old-man skin, flushed and pink but not too wrinkly. I placed him in his late fifties or early sixties.

He brandished what looked like a riding crop except it was white instead of black. "Keep quiet, sinner, or feel holy wrath upon thee."

I whistled. "You are so kinky."

He bared his teeth and raised the crop.

The woman put a hand on his arm. "Peace upon thee, Gerald. We must be patient with the newcomers and their ignorance."

Gerald lowered the crop but flogged me with his fierce glare.

"Madam, if I might have a word," Jeremiah said. "We did not willingly enter Heavenly. The collective bylaws clearly state that travelers are not to be interfered with so long as they remain in the neutral zone between collectives."

"God's word does not recognize mortal boundaries, young man." The woman gave him a sweet smile heaped with condescension. "It is the duty of Heavenly to prepare all souls trapped in this purgatory for our ascension to paradise. You will be cleansed."

The balding usher spoke. "Mother, we leave these sinners in your holy care."

"Thank you, brothers." Mother bowed and the ushers headed up the stairs.

Gerald snarled at me a moment longer, smacking the crop against his hand. "You will soon feel the holy cane upon thine flesh, child. It is best that you repent, or your trials will be unpleasant." Then he spun on his heel and followed the others upstairs.

I couldn't see my companions, but I heard them moving around in the neighboring cells. "We are well and truly fucked, aren't we?"

Jeremiah sighed. "Son, that is an understatement."

CHAPTER 12

I didn't even want to think about what lay in store for us at the hands of Mother and Gerald, but they forced the issue before I even had time to get comfortable on my cot. A PA speaker squawked in the hallway and a tinny recording began to play.

"Welcome, sinners, to your first day on the path to redemption," a man said as upbeat vintage music played in the background. "Once you are purified, you will join God's mighty army and ready the souls of purgatory for final passage to Heaven."

"Bloody hell," Victoria said. "This sounds like a public service announcement from the fifties."

"*Perdition*, chapter one," the man said. "Though thou hast cast off thine mortal coil, thine path to redemption hast only begun," He hardly paused a beat before moving on. "For the path to salvation continues even in death. God demands his worthy servants purify the sinful masses."

"Oh my god, will you shut up?" I shouted. I tried to speak again but my voice went hoarse and I couldn't speak. Seeing as this was the second occurrence of losing my voice, I began to wonder if Mother or one of her minions might be doing it to me.

"*Perdition*, chapter two," the man said, and launched into the next verses.

I tried to talk again, but only hoarse whispers rasped from my throat. *This is torture!* I curled up on the bed and covered my head with the pillow. It did nothing to block the annoying reader.

I suffered in silence for nearly an hour. Sometime later I felt a slight pinch in my throat and was able to speak again. This time, I refrained from cursing out the recording.

"It's as if someone with a poor grasp of Middle English tried to make their own version of the Bible," Vallaena said in a low voice.

"Indeed." Jeremiah grunted. "Another charlatan building a cult."

Keeping my voice low, I asked, "Did any of you lose your voice?"

"Yes, right after I said it sounded like a public service announcement," Victoria said.

"It would seem these holy rollers have some abilities," Jeremiah said, "no doubt granted by the subconscious desires of their brainwashed masses."

"Wonderful," I groaned. "How are we going to escape this hellhole?"

"That is a very good question," Vallaena said. "There are hundreds of them between us and the border."

"And these cell doors don't even have locks," Victoria added.

I inspected the door and found only a smooth plate where a keyhole should be. I gripped the bars and pushed, but the door didn't budge. I tried shaking it, but I might as well have tried to move a boulder. Without demonic strength, I wasn't about to break down this door.

I couldn't help but chuckle. If these people had any idea I was demon spawn, they'd freak. But since I couldn't spawn or use any of those powers, was I even the same person anymore? I sat back down on the cot, stared at my hands, and sighed. *Who am I now?* I closed my eyes and tried to find Kalesh. Nada. Nothing. Just a void where he used to be.

I wondered if he was dead and gone, or maybe stuck in the body I'd vacated.

Meanwhile, the recording continued picking at my sanity. "Verily must thy soul be cleansed with fire, sayeth the Lord. The sinner shall not find peace until cleansed."

Victoria groaned. "He's literally saying the same thing over and over again."

I tried switching to demon vision by shifting focus like I normally did. I concentrated so hard I went cross-eyed and got a mild headache. Without my demon spirit, I couldn't even do the simplest of Daemos tricks.

"Vallaena, do you have any Daemos abilities?" I asked.

"No, nephew," she replied in a defeated voice.

I asked another question. "Can you sense your demon spirit?"

"That is a peculiar question," she said. "Technically, I was the demon spirit who merged with a human soul."

"Oh, yeah." As one of the original gangsta Daemos, she hadn't been born like that. "So your spirit and the human soul completely merged into one? And once that happened you never sensed a separate being again?"

Vallaena didn't answer right away. "At first, there was a distinct other being in the body with me. Sometimes we would fight for control."

"But you were dominant?" I said.

"Yes," she said. "But that was only the case for the original Daemos. The human soul is dominant in all Daemos born naturally."

My father had been the first demon to successfully merge with a human, much to the delight of Baal. Before then, demons had only possessed humans, and that rarely ended well. Dad had paved the way for Daemos to become a new supernatural species and created a new threat to Daelissa's original attempt to control the world. Daemos had been an ally of Baal, but for the good of the realms, had to become his enemy.

But for some reason, I couldn't reach my demon spirit and I couldn't access magic. What gave me the ability to use magic in the living world, but not here? My body was just a meat shell that housed my mind and soul. If the afterlife existed in the same dimension, then surely magic also existed here. If the primal fount was somewhere at the core of the afterlife, then this place had to be teeming with aether.

If true, then why couldn't I sense any magical power at all?

Since there was nothing else to do, it seemed a good time to attempt another lucid dream trip. I had to find out if Kalesh was on the other side of that window or if it had all been subconscious manifestations in the dream.

I closed my eyes, slowed my breathing, and drifted into the depths of my mind. The loft flickered into being around me. It once again hit me how strange it was that Kalesh created a place to live inside my subconscious. Did that make me his landlord?

Something was different. The television was back in place and fully repaired. And instead of the lone apartment building across a void, an entire city had sprung up outside. There were streets, buildings, trees, and the Atlanta skyline on the horizon.

As I walked toward the window, the television clicked on and static filled the screen. The sudden noise made me jump. "What the hell?" I twisted the power knob off.

Click. The television came back on, hissing white noise.

I groaned. "Dude, my mind must be really screwed up if I can't even keep the imaginary television off."

"...hope perhaps...not sure—"

The familiar voice got my attention. Black and white lines ran across the snow, interspersed with a fuzzy image. I stared at the outline of the person, straining to make out their features, but it was like trying to tune into a scrambled porn channel.

"...missions soon..." the person said. Though I couldn't see the face, it sounded just like Thomas.

"Thomas! Thomas, can you hear me?" I got up and banged on the top of the television. The image dissolved into snow and the television clicked off. I stared at the screen for several minutes, waiting for it to come back on, but it didn't.

I wondered if my mind was playing tricks on me. Maybe being dead had scrambled my senses more than I realized. On the other hand, what if my physical body had actually seen Thomas and this was how it relayed images to me?

I turned on the television and stared at the white noise for several minutes but nothing else appeared. I adjusted the antennae but failed to find another signal. I gave up and huffed. Messing with this dream television was a waste of time.

I headed toward the window again. Light glowed from the window in the building directly across from me. I saw something moving on the other side. The glass seemed less fogged this time and I could almost make out a face.

The world rocked violently. I stumbled away from the window and tripped backward onto the bed. Rain battered the window. The ceiling sagged and freezing cold water splashed on me.

"What the hell?" Strong hands gripped my arm. I blinked water from my eyes and realized I was face down in a puddle of water on the concrete floor in my cell. Something hard pressed into the small of my back.

"Lazy sinner," Gerald growled.

"Dude, I was sleeping!"

The pressure on my back increased and he pulled on my arm until I thought it was going to pop out of the socket. I screamed bloody murder. "Stop! Stop!"

Gerald flung my arms to the sides and got off me. He walked out of my cell and glared down at me. "On your feet, sinner."

Mother stood behind him, watching impassively.

Spitting water, I crawled to my feet, nursing the arm he'd nearly dislocated. Blood dripped from a cut in my lip where I'd hit the floor. "What the fuck is your problem, Gerald?" I had a lot more to say, but Mother held up two fingers and made a twisting flick motion with them. My voice dried up to a whisper again.

I pointed at her. "Witch!" Unfortunately, my whisper shout was barely audible even to me. Reluctantly, I closed my mouth and returned Gerald's glare.

Victoria, Jeremiah, and Vallaena stood just outside their cells, hands clasped in front of them. Vallaena stared at the floor, face impassive. Jeremiah looked at me with a curious expression.

Mother stepped up beside Gerald. "Sinners, you have heard the holy words from *The Book of Perdition*. You will memorize the book from beginning to end. Every day you will attend classes to learn the new word of God. If you have no faith, you will remain here until you find it. Once you find faith, it will be tested. Once you have proven yourself worthy, you will join the purified and be tasked with bringing sinners to God."

"Must we also learn the Bible?" Victoria asked.

Mother shook her head. "No. The Bible is for the living. *Perdition* is for the dead."

Victoria frowned, but said nothing else.

"Might I ask what your role is?" Jeremiah said.

"Is it not clear from my name?" Mother tsked. "Sinners are foolish children. I am the firm hand that teaches them to be wise. Gerald is the rod for those who do not listen."

"Is he the only one with a red suit?" Jeremiah said.

"He is my right hand," Mother said. "God grants him the strength of ten men so none can stand in his way."

Ten men? I tried to ask a question of my own, but my voice was still gone.

"And you have the ability to quiet us," Jeremiah said, apparently thinking the same thing.

"I have earned God's favor and he has given me talents," Mother said. She waved off Jeremiah before he asked anything else. "You will learn all about it in class, young sinner." She stepped behind her attack dog. "Now, follow me."

Mother turned and walked toward the stairs. Gerald gave us nasty stares while slapping his white cane against the palm of his hand. Then he trailed behind us. We followed Mother upstairs, down a hallway, and into a classroom with four desks neatly lined up.

"Are we the only students?" Jeremiah said.

Mother didn't answer.

I sat down in the last desk like a good little boy. Gerald placed a leather-bound tome on each of our desks. Gold font read: *The Book of Perdition.* I'd never been to church, so this was going to be a learning moment in more ways than one.

Bells chimed in the distance. Unlike the single bell I'd heard when we arrived, this was a whole chorus of the things. If the single bell celebrated our arrival, maybe these celebrated our initiation into their awful education system.

Shouts and screams from outside indicated the bells were for something else entirely. Gerald abruptly jumped up and rushed from the room. Mother followed behind him and shut the door behind her.

Victoria was up in a flash, testing the door. Like the cell doors, it had no lock and wouldn't budge. Vallaena walked to one of the large windows in the room and pounded on it. It rattled but didn't break. She clumsily hefted a chair and slammed it against the pane. It bounced back off and struck her in the chest.

Vallaena staggered back and somehow kept her feet. "It appears we are still trapped."

Jeremiah went to the window at the front of the room. "Come look at this."

A small army of men and women with swords charged from the forest and toward the church. Scores of bleeding men in white suits lay scattered in their wake.

Someone shouted, "Heretics!" over and over again.

Gerald rushed out to meet the charge. One of the attackers thrust a sword at him. It deflected off his suit. Gerald tore the sword from the grasp of the attacker and threw it to the side. Then he flicked his holy cane and it expanded to the size of a staff.

With a mighty swing, Gerald clubbed several attackers and sent them flying through the air.

"My god," Victoria breathed. "That man is a monster."

"No heretic shall withstand God's holy might!" Gerald roared.

If an army couldn't stop this dude, how in the hell were we supposed to escape him?

CHAPTER 13

Wearing long robes and leather sandals, the heretics looked like a bunch of hippies straight out of the sixties. But their swords and battle cries made it obvious they were anything but peaceniks.

Gerald parried sword attacks from three different heretics and beat them over the heads with his staff. He swept their legs out from beneath them and left them unconscious and bleeding on the grass. Within minutes, the conscious heretics fled for the forest, dragging some of their companions behind. The ushers took the rest into custody.

"The fanatical beliefs of these people give Gerald godlike strength and Mother magical powers." Jeremiah shook his head. "Subterfuge is our only way to freedom."

I watched as ushers retrieved their wounded comrades. A man in a beige suit walked up to each one, shouting something unintelligible and then slapping the wounded on their foreheads. Blood stains faded, leaving pristine suits, and the ushers got up looking just like new.

"What rubbish." Victoria grimaced. "The religious charlatans have certainly found the perfect flock of sheep."

"And through them have gained power," Jeremiah said.

I backed away from the window. "How do we play this?"

"We certainly can't fake our way out," Vallaena said. "Somehow, we must escape the church and slip through an army of ushers to make it to the border."

Jeremiah pressed his lips into a flat line. "Perhaps we could disguise ourselves and escape."

Victoria frowned. "You're wearing a white suit like the ushers, but they didn't mistake you for one of their own."

"The doors and windows don't even have locks." I blew out a sigh. "How are we supposed to open them?"

"A very good question." Jeremiah stared out the window. "How does one bend the will of rigid, dogmatic people?"

Outside, ushers knelt before Gerald, hands clasped. They looked upon him with naked adoration. Groups of men in brown suits and women in equally drab dresses were herded by women in white to view the captured heretics. Some of the people in brown looked just as happy to see Gerald as the ushers. Others looked uncertain and frightened.

"They must be in the early stages of conversion," Victoria said.

Jeremiah grunted. "We'll be in that group before long."

"Any delay is too long." Vallaena pressed a hand to the glass. "Justin may not have long to return to his body."

"I've dealt with people like Mother and Gerald before," Jeremiah said. "But in the real world, I had power even without magic. My followers would often take care of troublesome individuals."

"Aside from our wits and charm, I'm afraid we're completely powerless here," Victoria said dryly.

"No way." I shook my head. "Jeremiah and Vallaena, you two have been alive for thousands of years. You two should know all kinds of tricks by now."

"I'm afraid in this situation we're entirely powerless," Jeremiah said.

"I always had my demonic powers to rely on." Vallaena stared grimly out the window. "I hate it, but Jeremiah is right."

"Besides," Victoria said, "you can be sure the usual tricks won't work on people like these." "What we have here are the sort of people I used to work with in the Exorcists. They are bound by dogma—rigid, and unyielding. But what makes them strong, also makes them weak."

"Bend them even a little and they break," Jeremiah said. "But how do you bend them?"

"Challenging their beliefs won't help," I said. "Even if we had incontrovertible proof that Gerald is a child molester, the believers would simply find a way to justify and overlook it."

"They would consciously justify it," Jeremiah said, "but their subconscious belief would be shaken."

Victoria nodded. "Unlike Britannia where multiple subconscious beliefs create a varied environment, Heavenly seems to strictly adhere to one dogma. Shake it even a little, and the system crumbles. Unfortunately, we can't simply spread rumors."

"What about the heretics?" I said. "Wouldn't their beliefs undermine the collective?"

"To the contrary," Jeremiah said. "They strengthen it. A small outside force seen as the enemy will only fortify the resolve of those being attacked."

"Hmm." Victoria tapped a finger to her chin. "I noticed that the wounded heretics were hauled back into the forest rather than here into the prison. It would not surprise me if they're actually set free because the leaders here know it solidifies the support of the ignorant masses."

"That would make perfect sense," Vallaena said. "But how do we break such a system?"

"We would have to make someone important act out of character," Jeremiah said. "But I don't know how we'd accomplish such a thing."

"Man." I groaned. "If only we had a tiny bit of illusion magic. We could make it look like Gerald is masturbating in front of everyone."

Victoria smiled. "How lovely that would be."

"Lovely, but impossible." Vallaena frowned. "Perhaps there is another way."

I waited for her to elaborate, but she didn't. The door clicked open, and Mother and Gerald entered.

Mother raised an eyebrow. "Take your seats, sinners."

"As you wish." Vallaena sauntered toward a desk, her hips swaying suggestively. A man would have to be blind not to appreciate my aunt's beauty. She brushed past Gerald and smiled seductively at him.

Mother's eyes glinted with anger.

Gerald gripped Vallaena by the throat and slammed her against the wall. "Get thee away from me succubus," he hissed.

If only he knew how true that statement was.

Mother's lips spread into a pleased smile.

Vallaena moaned and gave Gerald a languid smile. "If it pleases you, master."

Gerald had his back to us so I couldn't see his expression, but he dropped Vallaena and roared, "To thy desk, temptress!"

Mother's chin rose and her smile broadened.

Victoria watched intently, a faint smile touching her lips. Jeremiah's face gave away nothing. I wasn't an expert on human emotions, but Mother's matronly façade had crumbled when Vallaena put the moves on Gerald. And she looked far too pleased by Gerald's harsh response. I wondered if there was something going on between them.

"Mother, may I ask a question?" I said.

Her gaze flicked from Gerald to me, as if jolted from a reverie. "What is it, sinner?"

"Are you married?"

Mother scowled. "There is no reason for marriage here."

I hadn't been expecting that answer. "So you can have sex without being married?"

Her eyes flashed. "Sex is for procreation, and we cannot bear children. Sex for pleasure is strictly forbidden." Her eyes flicked ever so slightly toward Gerald.

And that was when I knew for certain those two were banging each other. Someone once told me that the most religious people were the ones repressing the worst secrets. I kept my face neutral and nodded. "Thank you, Mother."

"You are welcome, sinner." She clasped her hands before us. "Now, let us pray and begin class."

Staying awake proved a huge challenge, even with Gerald or Mother rapping our knuckles when our attention waned. At noontime, we were brought bread and fish to eat. Mother and Gerald locked us in the room and went to eat elsewhere.

"Well, I think I've discovered a weakness," Vallaena said in a low voice.

"Indeed." Jeremiah sniffed the fish and took a small bite. "But will it be enough?"

"I suspect Mother is the brains around here," Victoria said. "Gerald is her enforcer—a brute who doesn't think too much."

"And they're screwing each other," I said, proud to let them know I hadn't missed the clues.

"Obviously," Victoria said.

"I assumed it the first time I saw them together," Vallaena said. "Even though I don't have my demon powers, I can still read people's faces."

I hadn't even thought about it until Vallaena's little stunt.

"So we do have some non-magic powers," Victoria said. "Now, how do we leverage them?"

"There are layers to the problem," Jeremiah said. "The masses actively and subconsciously believe Mother and Gerald have certain abilities. Because of this, Mother and Gerald manifest powers. Somehow we have to shake that subconscious belief."

Victoria scoffed. "How do you propose we shake the beliefs of an entire population while locked away?"

"What if we only need to shake the belief of one person?" I said. "Mother and Gerald are the ones who lock the doors. Maybe if we mess with Mother's mind it'd cause a few doors to spring open."

"Possibly." Victoria tapped a finger on her chin. "But I'd be very careful targeting Gerald with sexual advances. He's equally violent toward men and women."

"I have endured pain before," Vallaena said. "I am willing to risk it."

My forehead pinched. "By making Mother jealous?"

"Yes." Vallaena put a pinch of bread in her mouth. "Let us hope she is as quick to anger as Gerald."

Our favorite wardens returned right as the church bell chimed one o'clock. An usher followed them in, retrieved our plates, and left. Vallaena managed to brush Gerald's hand as he walked past her. His steps slowed noticeably as he passed her desk, but Mother was walking ahead of him and didn't see.

Class picked up where it left off with more reading and memorization of *Perdition*. Jeremiah and Vallaena were able to quote scripture from memory after hearing it only a couple of times with Victoria close behind. I was no slouch at memorization, thanks to my training at Arcane University, but I was definitely the slow kid in the class.

When the bells chimed six, we were a quarter of the way into the book.

"I must say I'm impressed by your progress." Mother looked down her nose at us. "Perhaps God already has plans for you."

Jeremiah clasped his hands and bowed. "As you say, Mother."

Gerald glared at him, obviously not impressed by our progress. Or maybe, just maybe, he was concerned we might shoot up the ladder faster than he did. Then I realized that Gerald wasn't actually looking at Jeremiah, but slightly to his right at Vallaena. He was interested, for sure.

Mother and Gerald escorted us back to our cells. Mother closed my door, but I noticed that Gerald seemed to make it a point to close Vallaena's himself.

"You will each find a copy of *Perdition* in your cells," Mother said. "Tonight, you will fast and pray upon God's word. Only those who hear his message will have sustenance in the morning."

"Wait, we don't get food unless god speaks to us?" I said.

"Precisely, sinner." Mother's chin lifted. "Do not seek to deceive me, for God always tells me the wisdom he's imparted to sinners." She gave Gerald a sideways look, then turned and left with him close at her heels.

"I certainly hope they don't make us wear hair shirts," Victoria said.

Jeremiah grunted. "I suggest we all pray if we're to pass her little test."

Victoria scoffed. "Are you bloody kidding me?"

"No, I'm quite serious," he said. "I believe we will literally hear something if we pray long enough, and I suspect the messages are unique to the individual."

"Yes, of course," Vallaena said. "Their beliefs include direct messages from God, so naturally they'll hear what they want to hear."

I threw up my hands even though the others couldn't see me. "Well, it's not like I have anything better to do."

"This is ridiculous," Victoria growled.

Jeremiah sighed. "Perhaps, but it's necessary if we wish to get in Mother's good graces."

I let out a long sigh of my own and sat on my cot. Then I started to pray in a low voice. "Dear God, please get me out of this mess. Please give Gerald eternal jock itch, and make Mother feel uncontrollable sexual urges." I prayed about returning to life, about my long-lost hellhound, Cutsauce, and even a few prayers about friends I hadn't seen in ages. It took a good hour of babbling before a loud voice spoke in my head.

YOU WILL FOLLOW MY FAITHFUL SERVANTS AND DO ALL THEY SAY! SO COMMANDETH YOUR GOD!

I shouted and jumped up, arms flailing wildly to keep from falling.

"You heard it too?" Jeremiah said.

I put a hand to my heart. Despite being dead, it was pounding away in my chest. "It yelled in my head!"

"I got my message about thirty minutes ago," Vallaena said. "It was quite predictable."

"Same," Victoria said.

I felt like a real slacker since it took me so long. "Was it along the lines of doing everything God's faithful servants command?" I said.

"Mine was that I should exalt and praise God's servants," Victoria said.

"I'm certain they're all similar," Jeremiah said. "Just remember the precise wording when Mother asks for it tomorrow."

"God shouted so loud, his words are literally embedded in my brain." I lay down on the bed, at least happy the ordeal was over. Unfortunately, I had only five minutes of respite before the loudspeaker came on with a shriek of feedback, and recorded scripture began to play.

My companions groaned.

So much for a peaceful rest. There was only one escape from the racket. I jammed the pillow over my head, slowed my breathing, and went into a meditative state.

There was a brief moment of darkness and then the loft faded in around me. The television blinked on, screen filled with static. Faint silhouettes moved within the static, but it was impossible to clearly see or hear them. I tried tuning with the remote, but it did nothing. I messed around with the antenna again, this time pointing it toward the window.

The picture improved, but only just barely. The cable connecting the antenna to the television had about twenty feet of slack, so I picked up the device and moved it closer to the window.

The picture became crystal clear and the static vanished.

"...and I hope you find peace," Thomas said. He seemed to be looking down at the camera. "You were like a son to me, and I'll miss you." Something glinted in the corner of his eye—a tear. He wiped it and walked out of view.

I choked back tears of my own. Thomas rarely showed emotion, and I didn't even remember him crying at the funeral of his own son.

"Justin!" The muffled shout startled me. I walked over to the window and peered outside.

My blue twin waved at me from the window across the street. I gaped at him for a moment, then tried to open my window. It slid open with no resistance.

"Kalesh!" I held out a hand even though our windows were at least a hundred feet apart. "I thought that was you, but the window was fogged up."

"Your window was covered in ice," he said. "I could see through mine but couldn't open it."

I waved a hand at the city. "None of this was here the first time, either. Where did it come from?"

"I thought by filling in the world, it would help us reach each other," he said. "It worked. You have finally opened the window in your soul."

At long last, we'd found each other.

CHAPTER 14

R elief warmed me like a hot apple pie on a winter morning. It was really damned good to see Kalesh again.

"This place is messed up," I said. "I don't remember it being so hard to open the window in my soul in the Gloom."

Kalesh shrugged. "The veil between Haedaemos and the afterlife is much harder to penetrate."

"That's for damned sure." I leaned on the windowsill. "Dude, I'm miserable. I don't have any powers, and we're prisoners of a freaking religious cult."

Kalesh frowned. "Are you in Hell?"

I scoffed. "I might as well be!"

"I'm barely able to hold onto our body," he said. "The preservation spell is helping, but our body is injured and cannot heal with the spell active."

"Yeah, but won't it die without the spell?" I said.

He nodded. "But if we are back together in the body, perhaps we can heal it."

"How do we accomplish that?" I leaned out of the window and looked down. We were about fifty stories above empty streets. "Aren't you usually over here?" I asked.

He nodded. "Even though we can see and talk to each other, something still keeps us apart."

I looked around the loft for an exit, but there were none. I imagined a white door in the far wall. It flickered into existence. I turned to the window. "I'm coming over."

He gave me a thumbs-up.

I opened the door and found a blank wall on the other side. I imagined an opening forming in the wall. A rectangular section vanished, but there was nothing but darkness on the other side. "What the hell?" I stepped through and stepped right back into the room.

I blinked. Looked around. My head spun as if I'd just gotten off an out of control merry-go-round. I went through the opening again and stepped right back into the loft. I had to brace myself against a wall to keep from falling over.

I stumbled back over to the window and leaned on the sill. "I can't leave the damned room."

Kalesh frowned. "Maybe there is no other way except across here."

I looked at the long fall. "Well, maybe I can fly. It is a dream state after all."

Kalesh shook his head. "This is not just a dream state. You are on the astral plane at the edge of our subconscious. It is only partially controlled by your thoughts."

"Astral plane?" I shook my head like a wet dog. "Like Nowhere?"

"Nowhere is a physical place," Kalesh said. "This is a place of pure consciousness. But our consciousness has split and we must somehow bridge the divide."

"That's not confusing at all." I pinched the bridge of my nose. "How did you create a loft in my subconscious?

"It is our subconscious," Kalesh said. "I wanted a comfortable place when I tired of watching the world through your eyes."

"God, that must be tortuous." I sagged. "I'm sorry it's like that for you."

"It's not bad. We are one, but also separate." Kalesh shrugged. "I can always go into Haedaemos if I wish to do my own thing."

"Wait, you can just waltz around Haedaemos?" I leaned out over the windowsill. "Isn't it really dangerous?"

"Not while I'm attached to you." He frowned. "But that is not important. We must reunite so we can heal our body."

I groaned. "Well, then we have to escape these religious nimrods and get to the primal fount."

His forehead pinched. "There is a primal fount in the afterlife?"

I nodded. "Jeremiah thinks that if he can get me to the birthing chamber near the fount, I can return to my body through the canal."

Kalesh blinked a few times. "Jeremiah Conroy is with you?"

I snapped my fingers. "Yeah, guess I didn't give you all the deets." I sighed. "You're usually with me all the time."

Kalesh nodded somberly. "If our body dies, will I be with you, or will I remain in Haedaemos?"

I paused a moment to think about it but came up with nothing. "Let's hope we don't have to find out." The floor rocked and the room seemed to tilt sideways.

Kalesh's eyes flared. "What happened?"

"Gerald is trying to wake me up." I groaned with frustration. "Look, see if you can find a way to bridge the gap between us, okay? Maybe we can—"

A white cane smacked me in the face. I jerked upright, shielding myself from another blow. Gerald glared at me. "Lazy fool."

I growled, deep and guttural. "I'll tear you to shreds, mortal."

Gerald's eyes flared and he leapt back with superhuman speed, cane raised in defense.

I blinked a few times, confused. For an instant, I'd felt demonic. But it was gone now. So I held up my hands in surrender and got up. "Apologies, master."

His lips peeled into a snarl and he yanked me out of my cell. "You'll apologize with flesh and blood, sinner."

"What the bloody hell?" Victoria gripped the bars to her door. "What happened?"

Jeremiah and the others were still in their cells as well. Mother was nowhere to be seen.

"Oh, master, please take me too." Vallaena slipped an arm through the bars and motioned Gerald over with a finger. "Dominate me."

Gerald's eyes lit with pleasure and lingered on her for a long moment. Then he reluctantly turned from her and dragged me down the hallway. We passed a dozen or so cells and reached a room on the right. Judging from the metal shackles and dried blood on the walls, it was definitely not a red room of pleasure.

"Are you fucking kidding me?" I planted my feet and tried to stop, but Gerald effortlessly shoved me toward two thick beams of wood that formed an X. He pinned my arms into the metal cuffs and secured me spread-eagled with my face through the crook of the crossed beams. I couldn't turn my head at all to look behind me.

"What kind of god condones torture?" I said. "God is love, not sadistic!"

Gerald grunted. "God is merciful."

A whip cracked and intense pain cut into my back.

"God is kind."

Another crack. A scream burst from my throat.

"God sees all."

I cried out as the whip sliced into my skin again. Gerald kept talking, his voice steadily filling with pleasure as he flogged me over and over again. I screamed until my throat went hoarse. And finally, I passed out.

When I came to, I was lying on something cold and hard. I pushed up wearily off the concrete floor and blinked my eyes into focus. Mother stood at the head of the classroom, reading from *The Book of Perdition*. Her gaze found me.

"Into your seat, sinner," she said.

I pushed up. My back was stiff, the skin raw. Every move felt as if someone was dragging a cheese grater across my skin. Gerald watched with grim satisfaction as I staggered to a desk. *This kind of suffering shouldn't be happening in the afterlife!*

Gritting my teeth, I leaned back against the desk chair and endured the pain. I stared straight ahead, fighting back the rage and indignation burning through me like a wildfire.

Vallaena continued to bat her eyelashes as Gerald, but I couldn't tell if it had any effect on him or not.

Gerald and Mother left us alone at lunch once again.

Jeremiah came over to me the moment they left. "Are you okay, son?" He lifted my shirt and winced. "The skin is already healing. At least injuries don't last long in the afterlife."

"Nor are they fatal." Vallaena's lips curled into a snarl. "If only I had my demon powers, I would teach that man a lesson."

"What did you do to anger him?" Victoria asked.

133

I pushed out of the chair like an old man. "I spoke with my demon spirit last night."

Vallaena's eyes flared. "How?"

I told them about the loft where my subconscious mind met the astral plane, and how I'd seen Thomas on the television. "Apparently, the window in my apartment is a projection of the window in my soul." I shrugged. "Kalesh was in a building across the street, but I couldn't leave the loft to cross the road."

"So Gerald was angry that you didn't wake up at once," Victoria said.

I shook my head. "No, he's angry because I almost made him piss his pants. Somehow, I spoke in my demon voice when I woke up."

Jeremiah picked at the creamed corn and pork that was our lunch. "Intriguing. For an instant, you were almost Daemos."

I turned to Vallaena. "Are you certain you and your demonic part are one and the same? What if your demon spirit is in Haedaemos like mine?"

She brushed aside a lock of golden hair, eyes lost in thought. "I once was only a demon spirit until I joined with a human to make myself Daemas. I cannot conceive of that part of me being separate." She blinked from her thoughts and looked at me. "Perhaps I should test your theory."

I squeezed her hand. "I think you should."

A wistful smile lifted the corners of her lips. "You have come such a long way from the hapless boy I first met."

I shrugged. "You and Dad were good teachers."

Vallaena's eyes saddened. "I hope Daevadius has found refuge in Haedaemos. If Baal finds your father's spirit, he will torture him."

I didn't want to think about what Baal would do if he caught Dad's spirit.

Our conversation was cut short by Gerald and Mother's return.

"The ushers have rescued more sinners," Mother announced proudly. "Soon, you will have more classmates."

Oh, joy, I thought. "Did they capture them in the seam between collectives?"

"No, they are prisoners of war," Mother said. "When you are purified and ready, you, too, will join our holy crusade."

I didn't like the sound of that at all.

By the end of class, we'd memorized most of *Perdition* and could recite it back to Mother. She and Gerald seemed confused by how such recalcitrant students could do so well. But we were apparently so well behaved, that they decided to give us a treat.

"You will see the glory that awaits you," Mother said as Gerald led us out of the classroom and the church. "Bask in the miracles of the Lord."

We walked across the church yards and through a trail in the forest. Cheers, shouts, and singing filtered through the trees from somewhere ahead. I already had an inkling of what we'd find, but none of us were ready for the vast valley that spread out below us when we emerged from the forest.

A giant statue of an angel towered over the simple buildings below. The statue rose as tall as a skyscraper and its feet were spread as wide as a football field. But that wasn't even the most shocking thing in the valley.

Countless people in their Sunday best crowded the streets below. Groups of men in white suits raised gleaming swords to the delight and cheers of the crowds. Crimson crosses were emblazoned on the backs of their white suits, leaving little doubt as to what they were.

"Behold our crusaders," Mother said proudly. "Not even the godless collectives can withstand our numbers. Our thoughts and prayers will tear down the heathen constructs and expand God's realm."

Jeremiah's mouth hung open. "How many souls are in your army?"

"Thousands," Mother said. "It has been too long since the last expansion. We are more than ready." She turned her smile on Jeremiah. "You have learned quickly, sinner. Soon, you will take your place in our holy crusade."

Jeremiah gulped.

Despite Mother's faith in us, Gerald put us back in our cells when we returned to the church. He gave me an extra-hard shove that sent me stumbling into the wall at the back of the cell.

"Such strength," Vallaena purred from her cell. "I dream of your hand clutching my throat."

Gerald still stood outside my cell. His gaze settled hungrily in Vallaena's direction, hands flexing. At this point, I had serious doubts Vallaena's plan to subvert his faith would work. There were just too many fanatics powering this collective to tear it down. After a moment of hesitation, he turned and left.

"He is more resistant than I thought," Vallaena said. She sounded a little hurt. "Without my demon powers, I must rely solely on my looks."

"You can't expect to undo a lifetime of indoctrination in a day," Jeremiah said. "You're obviously quite a temptation for him, but there's something holding him back."

An usher brought us our dinner some time later. I asked him a few questions, but he completely ignored me and left. Today's fare was an unidentifiable brown meat and potatoes. I wondered if they actually slaughtered imaginary animals for food, or if it just magically appeared somewhere.

Once I finished eating, I decided to meditate and tried to contact Kalesh again.

I lay down on the bed, closed my eyes, and concentrated on my breathing until everything faded away. Once again, I stood in the apartment. The television was off, so I went straight to the window and leaned out of it. Kalesh's window was closed, but I could see the blank wall on the other side.

"Kalesh!" I shouted. Seconds ticked past and no answer. "Kalesh!" Again, nothing.

Had he been waiting for me the last time, or did my presence here automatically draw him there? I went back into the room and looked for something to throw. Maybe hitting the window with something would get his attention. Unfortunately, the room didn't have anything I could throw clear across the road.

I focused on the bed and imagined a baseball. It flickered into existence a beat later. "Well, that was easy." I palmed it and went back to the window. I'd never been great at sports, at least not without my superpowers, so I cocked back my arm, aimed, and threw. The ball streaked across the space and bounced hard off the window, rattling the glass so hard I was surprised it didn't break.

I waited for a while, but still no Kalesh. That was when something else occurred to me. When I made the door to leave the apartment, it had just returned me here. Was that because I hadn't created the rest of the building like hallways and stairs? Maybe if I did that, I could wander down to the street and cross it.

If Kalesh had filled in the entire world outside, making the inside of a building should be easy, right? I sketched out the details in my mind, trying to figure out where the stairwell would be, how many flights it would take to reach the bottom and so forth. Or maybe it'd be easier to just make an elevator. I leaned out the window and tried to count how many stories it was to the bottom.

That was when I knew I was making this way too complicated. "Why don't I just make a ladder?" I muttered. "Or an elevator outside?" But then I'd have to make another way to climb up to Kalesh's window. "Why in the hell didn't he make these buildings one story tall?"

Then again, maybe he hadn't. Maybe this was how the astral plane interpreted our separation. I didn't need a ladder or an elevator—I needed to bridge the gap between us. And what more appropriate way than by simply creating a bridge?

I imagined a concrete walkway leading from my window to Kalesh's. As with the baseball, it flickered into existence and solidified.

I rubbed my hands together. "Holy crap, now I'm doing something!" I climbed out of the window, stood, and looked at the eerily empty city streets stretching into infinity both ways. Many of the buildings looked identical, mostly red-brick apartments in the same state of disrepair. There were skyscrapers on the skyline, but they looked flat and lacked detail, like badly rendered objects in a video game.

The sky was blue, but there were no clouds, and the sun was nothing but a small yellow ball hovering overhead.

"Okay, enough sightseeing," I muttered.

I began to walk. The first few steps were easy. But the air seemed to thicken, like wading first through water, and then through mud. When I reached the middle of the bridge, I hit an invisible wall. It flexed ever so slightly but refused to let me pass.

"Are you kidding me?" I pounded my fists against the barrier, but it didn't yield. The fifty feet between me and the opposite window might as well have been a mile.

I slid my hand along the barrier, confirming it ran even beyond the bridge. *What in the hell is blocking me?*

A faint howling reached my ears. I looked down the infinite street and saw a cloud of shadows swirling toward me. My skin prickled with fear. That storm certainly wasn't a part of my imagination. Whatever it was, I didn't want to be here when it reached the bridge. I turned back toward my window and tried to run.

But it was like jogging through waist-high mud. I pushed harder, flailing my arms as if they might help propel me through the thick air. Arctic wind howled, freezing my face and slowing my efforts even more. The shrieking cyclone grew closer and louder, until I could hardly think straight. It would reach me in seconds.

"No!" Gritting my teeth in determination, I surged against the thick air. Its grip lessened slightly as I put distance between me and the middle of the bridge, but by then, the shadows were less than two blocks away. I pushed harder.

One block away.

"Son of a bitch!" I strained as hard as I could. The invisible resistance dropped to almost nothing and I fell flat on my face just a foot from the window.

The cyclone was only yards away.

I gripped the windowsill and yanked myself through. I flopped on the floor like a fish, got to my knees and slammed the window shut.

The swirling malevolence paused outside the window. Ghoulish faces contorted with madness slapped against the glass. A human figure clung to the outside windowsill, desperately trying to hold on. The body was dark as a wraith, but the face was ghostly white, mouth twisted and slobbering. It moaned, banging its face against the window repeatedly.

More bodies crashed into him and tore him loose. The cyclone had nothing to do with weather. These souls were consumed—drained of life essence. There were so many of them, they literally formed a soul storm.

The storm passed. The howls and screams faded with distance.

My heart pounded. Cold sweat ran down my face and back. "Holy shit!"

The window across the way slid up and Kalesh poked out his head. He looked in the direction the storm had gone, eyes wide with fear.

I opened my window and dared look out. The shadows had already faded in the distance. "What in the actual fuck was that?"

Kalesh touched the bridge. "Did you make this?"

"Yes." I took a deep breath to calm myself. "I tried to cross but couldn't get past the center."

"It's the barrier between the afterlife and Haedaemos." He banged the windowsill. "I had hoped we could penetrate it."

I groaned. "Maybe there's no way to penetrate it."

"Then how can we see each other and communicate?" Kalesh said. "There must be a way through."

My hands still trembled from the close call. "I thought consumed souls were trapped in Haedaemos or Hell, not the afterlife."

Kalesh frowned. "I was told that when the souls of the living are drained, they are doomed to circle the infernal fount in Haedaemos." Kalesh said. "Perhaps what we saw is their remaining consciousness projected into the astral plane."

I scoffed. "Well whatever they were, they're fucking terrifying!"

"When you tried to breach the barrier, it must have drawn them to you." Kalesh patted the bridge. "At least they couldn't get through the window."

"Am I actually in danger here?" I said.

Kalesh nodded. "I think so. If you venture from your safe space, you are exposed fully to the astral plane."

"Well that's just freaking dandy." I leaned my forehead on the windowsill. "How are we supposed to figure this out if a tornado of consumed souls is waiting to devour me every time I step outside?"

Flames flickered in Kalesh's eyes. "Because we will keep trying no matter what."

I raised my fists at the imaginary heavens. "I hate being dead!" I glared at him. "Where were you, anyway?"

"I took a great risk," Kalesh said. "I think you will be happy."

I sighed. "I'm stuck in a freaking insane asylum for the dead. I don't think anything can make me happy."

Kalesh opened the door of his apartment, visible through the window. When I saw what was on the other side, I realized I was wrong—dead wrong.

CHAPTER 15

I whooped and nearly ran out onto the bridge again before common sense restrained me.

Another figure stepped up to the window and gave me his trademark smirk. "It's good to see you, kiddo."

"Dad!" I giggled like a kid.

It was, at least, the blue-skinned version of my dad, complete with little black horns on his forehead.

I reached out as if I could touch him across the distance. "You're alive!"

He shrugged. "What can I say? Baal was so happy with himself about kicking me out of my body that he didn't have anyone on the other side who could restrain me."

"So you've been hiding all this time?" I said.

He nodded. "Even though he ripped me from my body, I still have a link to it. That link makes me stronger than most demons, and I can even hide from the big man himself."

"How do you still have a link?" I said. "It doesn't make any sense."

"It makes plenty of sense." He patted Kalesh on the back. "Just like your demon spirit is still linked to your human soul and body even with you dead."

"Mostly dead," I said.

Dad nodded. "You know what I mean. Your demon spirit—"

"Kalesh," Kalesh said.

Dad raised an eyebrow. "Naming your demon spirit is kind of like naming your dick, isn't it?"

I snorted. "No. I mean, we're kind of separate entities."

"Weird. Most Daemos merge identities by the time they hit puberty." Dad waved off the tangent. "Anyway, *Kalesh* told me he's been looking for me for a while—like ever since Baal turned my body into Cain. It just so happened I was looking for him too, or he probably never would have found me."

"It's so damned good to see you, Dad." I started to tear up. "I almost captured Cain. We could have returned you to your body."

"Yeah, I know." He grinned. "My link lets me observe from time to time, so long as I'm careful. If Cain had any idea I was still linked, he could track me down or sever it." Dad's grin faded. "I saw your big fight on the beach."

"Yeah." I sagged. "That's how I ended up here."

"Well we're going to make sure you get back to life." Dad clapped Kalesh on the back.

My demon spirit nodded. "Yep."

"How?" I nodded at the invisible barrier. "I can throw imaginary stuff over there, but my soul can't pass through."

"We'll figure it out." Dad folded his arms across his chest. "I know a demon who crossed into the afterlife and back, but I haven't seen him for centuries. If I can track him down, maybe he can tell us what to do."

I wiped at my wet eyes and nodded. "Thanks, Dad."

He grinned again. "You got it, kiddo."

The world quaked. It was time to wake up again. I released my dream state and blinked my eyes open.

Gerald sneered down at me, cane raised. "Lazy wretch!" He whacked me in the face.

"I'm awake!" I shouted, doing my best not to anger him into another flogging session.

He gripped my shoulder and casually tossed me out of bed. "Into line, sinner!"

I bit back a smartass reply and staggered behind Jeremiah and the others. I ached to tell them about what had happened, but now was not the time.

Gerald marched us upstairs, but instead of the classroom, we went the opposite way. A chorus of singing voices reached our ears from a door ahead. Gerald opened it and organ music washed over us. He motioned us through and into a small area boxed in by low railings.

My butt cheeks clenched when I saw several hundred faces staring back at us from the chapel pews. A choir at least a hundred strong sang from a loft behind the pulpit, directed by a short woman I hadn't seen before.

Gerald remained on the other side of the door and shut it behind us.

The choir finished singing and a man in black robes rose from a chair, smiling broadly. "Blessings upon you, Sister."

The short woman beamed at him and bowed, then stepped down off the stage and took a seat in the pews.

"Salvation to all souls, sayeth the Lord," he boomed.

"Salvation!" the congregation thundered back.

I gulped and tried not to look at the crowd, but we were right out in front of them, sinners on display.

"Today, we are proud to show the progress Mother Karen has made with these sinners." The preacher held out a hand toward us. "Though they wallow in the filth of sin, they will soon be purified."

Of course her name is Karen. Karens were even more notorious than Susan and Bethany when it came to asking for the manager. But what happened when Karen *was* the freaking manager of souls?

Mother stepped up next to the pastor. "The sinners will recite *The Book of Perdition* today," she said proudly. She walked next to our box. "Sinners, you must do your best and prove your worthiness to proceed to the next phase of purification."

Since Gerald had flogged me for getting mad with him, I didn't want to imagine what he'd do if we messed this up.

Jeremiah cleared his throat, glanced at the rest of us, and began to recite from the beginning. "Though thou hast cast off thine mortal coil, the path to redemption hast only begun.

We joined him in a monotone chorus. "For the path to salvation continues in death. God demands his worthy servants purify the sinful masses."

And so it went for what felt like two hours until Mother stopped us, a pleased smile on her face.

"Verily hast thou done the work of God," the pastor said.

She clasped her hands and bowed. "God's grace shines, Father Mors."

Father Mors? What kind of name is that? He looked familiar and I soon realized why. The giant statue we'd seen yesterday wasn't an angel—it was this guy! He was obviously much more than just a preacher.

After Mother exchanged a few more pleasantries with him, Father Mors moved onto his sermon. He droned on and on for ages, until I could barely keep my eyes open or remain on my tired feet. Boos and hisses shook me from my drowsiness. I blinked and wiped my eyes.

Gerald dragged a man and woman dressed in sackcloth across the carpeted floor and forced them to their knees before the pulpit.

Father Mors looked down at the quaking couple. "Thou hast committed the sin of lust and sullied your souls. Had this been thine first offense, I would have found forgiveness. But thou hast proven your unworthiness. Verily must thou be cast from Purgatory."

"Geeze, can I be cast from this place too?" I muttered.

Jeremiah elbowed me.

"Please, no!" the woman screamed. "God is love! God is good! Why can we not be married under his grace?"

"Because it is a vestige of the mortals!" Mors roared. "Carnal lust has no place in God's kingdom."

"Mercy!" the man cried. "Have mercy!"

The pastor smiled. His eyes gleamed with wicked cruelty. Then he reached down and gripped the prisoners by the tops of their heads. He raised his gaze to the ceiling. "God, cast these sinners from Purgatory, for they will never earn your worth!"

The man's and woman's faces contorted, and their screams turned to horrific sucking noises. Black veins crept up their skin as their bodies trembled violently and withered. Their flesh turned black and their faces became ghostly pale. Within seconds, they were nothing more than shadows. The apparitions sank into the floor, arms flailing as if to grasp the ground and keep themselves from falling.

Holy shit balls! It took everything I had not to scream out loud. What kind of horrendous powers had the beliefs of this congregation given this man?

It was no wonder their army was so big. Once new recruits saw what this monster could do, they probably joined up, no questions asked.

Victoria trembled visibly, and Vallaena's lips curled up with horror. Jeremiah stared in blank disbelief. They probably realized the awful truth—we were never escaping this hell hole.

Gerald took us back to our cells after another long sermon. "It is a day of fasting," he declared before he left. "Pray, pray, and pray some more. For if you do not ascend to purification, you will share the fate of the sinners you saw today."

I didn't dare say a word until he left.

"We are well and bloody screwed," Victoria said.

Jeremiah grunted. "It doesn't look good."

"It is no wonder I could not tempt Gerald," Vallaena said. "Even he must fear true death."

I dropped onto my bed, body trembling with shock and anger. Mors hadn't given those people true death. He'd damned them to circle the infernal fount for eternity. How could this happen in the afterlife?

Where was a damned manager when you needed one?

"I'm sorry, everyone," Jeremiah said. "I thought I could navigate us safely to the primal fount."

Victoria scoffed. "Oh, it's not your bloody fault. After all our training and life experiences, we should have known to look before leaping."

"It's shameful," Vallaena said. "I was powerful in life. Here, I am weak and worthless."

Jeremiah sighed. "I know the feeling."

"We failed you, nephew," Vallaena said. "I am sorry."

Hearing the defeat in their voices really pissed me off. Oh, I wasn't mad at them. I was mad with this place and the people running it. Jeremiah,

Vallaena, and Victoria had been heroes. Victoria had died to protect Emily. Jeremiah had sacrificed himself to save me. Vallaena had died saving others. They deserved so much better than this god-awful fate.

It physically hurt to hear them tearing themselves down.

"Will you please stop?" I banged a fist on my wall. "You're all better than this and you know it!"

There was long moment of silence.

Jeremiah finally broke it. "Your boundless optimism won't help, I'm afraid."

"I'm not optimistic," I said. "I'm pissed and ready to do something about it!"

"And what would that be?" Victoria said. "Banging on the walls certainly won't help."

"I saw my dad," I said.

Vallaena gasped. "Where?"

"Through the window of my soul," I said. "He and Kalesh found each other."

"Your father was able to speak to you through Kalesh?" Vallaena said.

"Well, yeah," I said. "That's how Daemos talk to demons."

She huffed. "I'm aware of that. I have just never heard of talking to the spirit of another Daemos that way."

"Me neither, but that's how it happened." And it gave me an idea. "It's a long shot, but maybe Dad can help us."

"I certainly don't know how," Victoria said.

"If only I had more time." I dropped onto the bed. "Time doesn't work the same when I'm projecting to the astral plane. It seems like I've barely been there when Gerald comes and wakes me up."

"That's because they wake us at odd intervals," Jeremiah said. "The night and day cycle doesn't exist here."

"Oh." That made sense. "They just want to keep us off balance."

Jeremiah grunted. "It's a torture technique."

It had certainly kept me off balance. "I'm going to talk to him again," I said. "Vallaena, I'd like you to try to reach through the window of your soul as well. See if you can reach your demon spirit in Haedaemos."

"I've tried many times since I died," she said. "It hasn't worked."

"How did you usually contact her when you were alive?" I asked.

"I simply think about her and she is there," Vallaena said.

"Have you tried deep meditation?" I asked. "Like a lucid dream state?"

There was a pause. "No. It was never necessary for me. My demon powers were always at my beck and call."

"Can you give it a shot?" I wished I could see her instead of having to call out through the walls. "Things work differently here, so forget the normal way."

Another pause. "Yes, I will try."

"Great." I leaned back on the bed and made myself comfortable. "I'm going back in too." I closed my eyes and returned to the loft. I walked over to the window and saw Kalesh watching cartoons on an antique television.

He flinched and turned as if sensing my presence. "You're back at last."

"Yeah, and things are even worse than I thought."

Dad appeared at the window. "Can you ask your spirit to change the channel every once in a while? I'd love some HGTV instead of all these black and white cartoons."

I blinked. "You get cable in Haedaemos?"

149

Kalesh nodded. "Some aspects of Haedaemos mirror Eden."

"That's weird." I resisted exploring that further since Gerald could come wake me at any moment. "Unfortunately, we've got bigger problems than boring cartoons."

Dad raised an eyebrow. "I'm all ears."

"There's a priest named Father Mors who can drain souls."

Dad's other eyebrow arched in solidarity with the first. "You're shitting me."

"I shit you not," I said.

His brow pinched. "I thought powers didn't work in the afterlife."

"The beliefs of his followers give him powers," I said. "Just like Gerald has superhuman strength and can't be hurt by weapons."

"You told me about a fight between Gerald and heretics," Dad said. "He didn't drain any of them, did he?"

I shook my head. "No, he stabbed them a lot."

Dad nodded. "But no permanent damage, just like the flogging he gave you."

I shrugged. "They were all on their feet not long after the battle." I frowned. "Where are you going with this?"

"Truly draining a soul requires actual powers," Dad said. "I don't think even the most fanatical believers can grant someone that power."

My skin went cold. "You think Mors is a demon?"

"He's something," Dad said. "I mean, the name Mors should be a dead giveaway."

"Huh?"

He grinned. "It means death in Latin."

"So Father Death is running the show." I threw up my hands. "Perfect!"

"This is really good news, Justin." Dad's smile widened. "If Mors is working demon magic, that means you can too. It means, you're not powerless."

If I could figure out how that worked, it meant we might have a chance to get out of here.

CHAPTER 16

"I'm not powerless?" I let that sink in a moment before shaking my head. "How is he accessing his powers then and why can't I?" I held out my hands helplessly. "I can't reach Kalesh through the barrier between life and death."

Dad bit his lower lip and looked back at Kalesh. "I've got a plan that just might work."

I gulped in anticipation. "What is it?"

"You need to both reach into the barrier." He nodded as if suddenly making up his mind. "Yep, that's got to be it. Both of you go to the middle of the bridge and reach out to each other."

I stared at him for a moment. "Are you just making this up as you go?"

His grin faded. "Afraid so, son. Desperate times call for desperate measures."

"Well—" The building rocked violently. "Shit! Gerald's waking me up again." I jerked awake before Dad could respond. I opened my eyes to Gerald's glowering face just inches from my own.

It took a moment to realize he was holding me up by my shirt.

"He's awake," Mother said. "Bring him here."

Gerald dropped me on my feet and shoved me out of the cell. Mother stared at me with a disappointed look. But it was the person standing next to her who sent chills down my spine.

Father Mors smirked. "I hear you're quite the sound sleeper."

I glanced back at the other cells. Jeremiah and the others were gone. "Sorry, it's a disorder."

"Perhaps," Mors said. He walked around me, judging me like livestock. "Mother and Gerald, give us some privacy, please."

Mother's eyes danced between me and Mors, but she nodded and hastily walked away, Gerald close on her heels. When the door closed behind them, Mors smirked again. "It's been a long time since we had any recruits who memorized *Perdition* so quickly or passed class with such high marks."

I almost offered a lame excuse but decided to keep my mouth shut instead.

"To meet a group of four individuals with such excellent cognitive abilities is highly improbable." He walked behind me and stood there, sending chills up and down my back. "Did you know each other in life?"

Think quick, Justin! If this guy was a demon, he'd know about Arcanes and Daemos. He might see us as a threat and drain our souls on the spot. "Three of us went to college together," I said. "Victoria was our favorite professor." Jeremiah and Vallaena looked young, at least here in the afterlife. Victoria looked old enough to be our mentor.

Mors stepped around in front of me. He gripped my chin, eyes narrowed in concentration.

My knees went weak and I repressed a cry of alarm. "Are you going to kill me?"

He chuckled. "I'm simply using God's spirit to reveal who you really are."

Oh shit! It felt as if cold worms squirmed in my head. At first, I thought it was simply my revulsion from his touch, but then I realized it was some kind of psychic probe. Sweat broke out on my forehead.

He tsked. "No need to be frightened, boy. God only strikes down the unworthy."

Dad was right. There was something supernatural about this guy. I just prayed he wasn't a mind reader.

Mors released my chin a moment later. "Well, it seems you're just a normal human boy."

I feigned surprise. "What else would I be?"

His eyebrows pinched into a V. "God's enemies are numerous. One must always be vigilant."

I bowed. "Yes, Father."

"You and your friends have stronger minds than most." He put a finger under my chin and drew me upright. His pale irises stared into mine. "I will put your strength to good use, provided you become a loyal servant of God."

"It is our hope to make God proud," I said in a quavering voice. "Mother has helped us see the way."

He pursed his lips. "Perhaps. But God requires sacrifice." Mors turned away and began walking. "Follow me, boy."

I obeyed.

We left the church and walked around to the back. I did a double take when we rounded the corner. A wall at least fifty feet tall bordered the back of the church. I hadn't seen it before because the church building hid it. Mors walked to metal door and opened it without a key. I imagined he could open any locked door in this place. We walked through the gate and into a compound filled with single-story rectangular buildings.

"Are you the leader of Heavenly?" I asked.

"I am," he replied.

"Is there more to Heavenly than this church?" I asked.

Mors stopped and faced me. "This is one of many border facilities." He swung an arm to his right. "The capital city, Heavensgate lies in the middle. Only the purest of the pure are allowed to enjoy its splendors." He mussed my hair. "Perhaps you will one day earn that right, boy."

I barely repressed a shudder at his touch and managed to fake a pleased smile. "I hope so, Father."

"Good." He nodded. "Good." Then he turned and continued on.

We took a left and walked to the far end where a man in a pink suit stood outside a black building. The man bowed and stepped out of the way as Mors went to the door and opened it. Inside the building were two kneeling people, their heads concealed by black hoods.

"I'm going to test you, boy." Mors smiled amicably. "This is an important step in your purification, so do your best."

I looked apprehensively at the people and gulped. "What must I do, Father?"

"You must make a choice." Mors walked behind the pair of prisoners, touching each of them on the head. "You must decide which of these sinners is banished to Hell."

My jaw dropped open. "What?"

His smile turned to a smirk. "The pure of heart can make decisions quickly, because God guides them." Mors snatched the hood off the first person. A young woman looked up at me with terrified eyes. She wriggled, as if trying to move, but invisible bonds held her in place.

My insides clenched and I gasped, because I knew her and not in a good way. Judging from the look on her face, the feeling was mutual. Before I could recover from my shock, Mors tore off the hood of the other person.

The man beneath the hood regarded me with calm resignation.

I gasped again, because the man was Jeremiah.

Mors reared back his head and roared with laughter. "Perhaps there is divine justice in this universe after all." He smiled cruelly at me. "Because I have the man who killed me at my mercy."

I stared at him unable to identify him. "Who are you?"

Mors scowled and clenched his fists. "You do not even recognize me?"

I swallowed hard and backed up a step. "I died from brain injuries," I lied. "My memory hasn't been very good."

Some of the anger faded from his face. "Ah, yes. That would do it." His smirk returned. "You and I fought fiercely in the Battle of the Grand Nexus. Had it not been for the ceiling falling all around us, I would have bested you. But bad luck delivered me to my fate. Now a reverse of fortune has brought you to me."

I strained my brain and couldn't remember ever fighting this dude.

He continued speaking. "I am Astaeus, firstborn of Gaeus."

Neither name rang a bell, but I knew one thing for damned sure. "You're Seraphim—a Brightling."

His chest swelled with pride. "I am. And yet, I am consigned to the same fate as the kine."

This explained how he could drain souls. But it also made the female prisoner an even bigger mystery. Why in the hell was she a prisoner? Astaeus should be fawning at her feet like all the other Brightlings. In life, she had been his queen.

Because she was Daelissa.

CHAPTER 17

Neither Daelissa or Jeremiah seemed able to move in the slightest, nor could they speak. But the wild look in Daelissa's eyes spoke volumes about what she thought of me. I wondered if she knew who was kneeling right next to her.

I took a deep breath to keep myself calm, even though I was ready to run away screaming. Not that I could go far with the locked door behind me. "So you recognized me when you saw me?" I asked.

"Oh, yes." Mors shivered in pleasure. "I thought my prayers were answered when I found her." He nodded at Daelissa. "But it was nothing compared to finding you."

Jeremiah's eyes flicked to the side, but his expression didn't indicate he'd identified Daelissa in his peripheral vision.

"You have me at your mercy." I held up my hands in surrender. "What do you want?"

Mors pursed his lips and tapped a finger on his chin, mocking deep thought. "I shall eventually drain you, but not all at once. No, it will be a slow, torturous process. I will also drain your companions, but if you behave like a good boy, perhaps I'll let them live a little longer."

"I'll do whatever you want," I said.

"Of course you will." He sneered. "Your first task will be a decision." Mors put his hands on the heads of his prisoners. "Who shall I drain first?" He slapped Daelissa on the back of the head. "The fool who threw away all our lives?" He rubbed Jeremiah's head. "Or the one who died to save you?"

It seemed like a complete no-brainer. Daelissa deserved a fate worse than death. There was no way I'd ever choose Jeremiah for that. I paused a moment to give the illusion I had to think it over, but Mors knew as well as I did that it was a charade.

"I choose Daelissa," I said.

He nodded. "So be it." Mors put his hand on Jeremiah's head.

Jeremiah's eyes rolled into the back of his head and black veins crept up his skin.

"No!" I dove at Mors, but he batted me aside as if I was a fly.

I slammed into the wall and landed on the floor. I held out a hand imploringly. "Please, stop! Please!"

Mors laughed. Then he released Jeremiah and let him collapse to the floor. Mors touched Daelissa and she slumped to the floor as well.

He walked over and stared down at me. "Thus begins your true fate, Justin Slade. Never-ending torture by my hand." Mors reached down and touched my head. Cold, writhing worms seemed to burrow into my brain. I screamed and the world faded to black.

I woke up on the floor in my cell. But I was no longer alone. Mors had seen fit to give me a roommate.

I leapt to my feet. "What in the hell?"

Daelissa huddled in the back corner, staring at me. I couldn't tell if she was frightened or furious. Frankly, I was surprised she hadn't beat me to a pulp while I slept.

"You," she said miserably.

I waited for a follow up, but when none came, I nodded. "Yes, me." I kept my distance from her. Almost everything about her looked identical to Nightliss, except for her fair skin and blonde hair. But where Nightliss's voice was sweet, Daelissa's sounded haunted and slightly insane.

"Are you real?" she asked in a quavering voice.

I blinked a couple of times. "Yes, I'm real." I crouched, still keeping my distance. "Why do you ask?"

"He plays with my mind." She crawled toward me and stopped a foot away. Then she tentatively reached out and touched my arm. Daelissa recoiled, toppling backward onto her rear end. "You are real." She climbed unsteadily to her feet. "You are real!" she screamed.

And then she launched herself at me.

I jumped up and braced myself for impact, but instead of clawing me, she buried her face in my chest and cried.

"I cannot face myself." Daelissa shook with sobs. "You cursed me with the absolute truth, and it followed me even into death." She looked up at me with red eyes. "I beg of you, please let Mors kill me."

In the final battle against Daelissa, I'd hit her with Clarity. Unlike Brilliance, it didn't destroy. It wasn't a force of creation like Murk. And it didn't freeze objects like Stasis. Clarity burrowed right into the soul and revealed the unvarnished truth to the owner of that soul. Daelissa had been mostly insane for centuries, drunk on the essence of human souls.

The truth of her atrocities and instantly switching from insane to completely sane in the blink of an eye had killed her. Unfortunately for her, death had given her no relief. If anyone couldn't handle the truth, it was most definitely Daelissa.

It was also the strangest feeling in the world having someone who nearly took over the world and almost killed me and all my friends now soaking my shirt with tears.

I had no idea what to do, so I stroked her hair and said, "There, there, now." It was insanely surreal, even for the afterlife. Another part of me wanted to fling her away.

Daelissa continued to wail. After another minute, I'd had enough and pried her off me. Without her Seraphim powers, she couldn't offer much resistance. I sat her down on the bed and put some space between us.

"How long have you been a prisoner here?" I asked.

She shook her head. "I have no idea. It feels like a year or more has passed."

"Who was Astaeus to you?"

Daelissa's eyes lost focus. "He was husked when the Grand Nexus exploded. He was restored by our aether chambers. But I never knew him very well personally."

"So he's basically a little nobody with a big grudge," I said.

Her eyes met mine. "Yes."

"How does he have powers here?" I asked.

"I don't know." Her forehead pinched. "I cannot even feel aether. I am nothing." Her lips trembled.

I stared at my former nemesis. I couldn't stop thinking about how she, Qualan, and Qualas burned Jeremiah to ash with focused beams of Brilliance. About how her intense hatred and madness had led to the deaths of thousands. She alone was probably responsible for most of the consumed souls circling the infernal fount.

Now that she was powerless, I felt the urge to throttle her until she passed out. I wanted to scream at her about the countless souls she sent to the afterlife. Despite her suffering, she'd gotten off lightly compared to everyone she'd murdered or consumed during her long life.

The Overworld had been reduced to rubble trying to hold off Daelissa's army of Seraphim, Flarks, and other horrors. Everything she'd done had weakened the supernatural world and given Cephus, Victus, and Baal the perfect opportunities to unleash even more death and destruction.

In short, Daelissa was the queen of atrocities.

The only comfort I took was that enlightenment from Clarity continued to torment her even in the afterlife. I imagined Mors had probably tortured her relentlessly as he promised to do with me.

"Mors must think it's unbearable for us to share a cell," I said. "I'll bet he's having a really good laugh right now."

The door to the cell block opened and Gerald herded in Jeremiah, Victoria, and Vallaena. Their heads had been shaved bald. Cuts and bruises covered their faces and dried blood clung to their skin.

I gripped the bars to my door. "Did you beat them?"

Gerald bared his teeth in a grin. "God's punishment is just." He lined up the prisoners in front of my cell and watched Jeremiah closely, probably to gauge his reaction when he saw Daelissa.

Jeremiah looked calmly at his killer. "How ironic to be trapped in Hell with my murderer."

Daelissa stared at Jeremiah, her mouth hanging open in horror. "I killed him," she wailed. "As I killed so many. And for what? For nothing!"

Gerald grunted, obviously disappointed by the lack of fireworks, and shoved the prisoners out of sight and into their cells. He came back to my cell and opened it. "Come."

I glanced at Daelissa. "Me or her?"

His upper lip curled into a sneer. "You, sinner."

I stepped outside. Gerald closed the cell door and started walking. I followed him without comment outside the church, around it and into the compound. He ushered me into the same black building from earlier. Mors stood inside chatting with two women in brown dresses. He smiled at me. "Ah, Justin. I'd like you to meet Claudia and Margaret."

What in the hell is going on? I wondered. I stepped warily closer and nodded. "Nice to meet you."

"They are nearly through purification," Mors said.

I tried not to tremble with apprehension. "That's good to hear."

"Are you okay, young man?" Claudia asked. "You look pale as a ghost."

Margaret chuckled. "Well, we're all ghosts here, aren't we?"

Mors laughed. "Claudia, you're too much."

"Thank you, Father." Claudia smiled. "I do try my best."

"The path to purification is long and hard," Mors said. "And I have found that certain methods reap greater rewards." He put a hand on Claudia's shoulder. "Even though humans are weak, their souls are rich in energy." He smiled. "A super food, if you will."

Claudia and Margaret exchanged confused looks.

"Death has not changed that," Mors said. His eyes flashed and white wings blazed to life on his back.

Claudia screamed. "Heavens to Betsy, he's an angel!"

"Lord have mercy!" Margaret fell to her knees.

Mors gripped their heads. Black veins crawled up their skin and the women cried out. Their awful shrieks turned to awful sucking screams.

"Stop!" I shouted. But I was powerless to do anything but watch as the souls withered and turned black before sinking into the ground. I hadn't known the women more than a few seconds, but tears stung my eyes. This man was grade-A evil.

Mors's eyes and wings glowed brighter after his meal. He conjured a blazing orb of Brilliance in one hand and held it up to my cheek.

The heat caused me to flinch away. "How are you able to use magic?" I said. "I thought it was impossible."

Mors gripped my head with his free hand and forced it close to the burning orb. "I was more powerful than Daelissa, did you know that?"

I gasped as the heat began to burn my skin. "No."

"If Qualan and Qualas had not been resurrected before me, I would have been her right hand." He bared his teeth. "I would have overthrown Daelissa and shown her followers true power."

I tried to wriggle away from the terrible heat, but Mors held me in his iron grip. "What makes you stronger than Daelissa?"

Mors laughed. "I am third generation Seraphim. Those born after me are but shadows." He pressed the orb against my face.

I screamed. Flesh sizzled and smoked and the vision in my right eye went black.

"Now I am trapped here," Mors hissed. "But soon I will have enough souls to resurrect me. I will return to the living world and redeem myself." He traced the orb across my face.

I could barely hear him over the sounds of my own screams. I felt my flesh melting, my left eye searing shut until I was completely blind. And all I could do was scream in agony. Mors eventually let me collapse to the floor in a writhing heap. I wished more than anything I could pass out, but there was no merciful escape for me.

Mors chuckled. "I'm going to enjoy this, boy." He kicked me in the ribs. "Take him," Mors said to someone.

Someone grabbed me by the ankle, dragged me across the floor and outside. I weakly clawed at the ground, but there was no escaping the iron grip. There was only one person it could be.

"He's a monster, Gerald." My voice was hoarse. "He's the devil."

"He is God's angel of redemption," Gerald said. "He will purify you with flames, sinner."

The evil bastard dragged me all the way into the church and down the stairs into the prison, letting my head bounce off every step. Agonizing pain seared my burned flesh. Screams tore through my throat until it was raw. I prayed for sweet unconsciousness, but it never came.

Gerald dropped my foot and a metal door clanged. I barely had the presence of mind to realize I was back in my cell as his footsteps faded away.

"The true torture has begun," Daelissa said from nearby. "You are Mors's plaything now."

I wanted to cry, but my eyes and tear ducts were cauterized shut. The pain was constant, unending. I touched my face. The skin felt waxy. Seeping fluids dampened my fingers.

Vallaena called out from her cell. "Justin, what happened?"

"The bastard burned him," Jeremiah said. A fist pounded the wall.

"Burned him?" Victoria said.

"He will heal," Daelissa said. "The wounds are only manifestations. But the trauma will scar him mentally."

"I—I'll be able to see again?" I said in a quavering voice.

"Yes." Clothing rustled as she came closer. I felt her breath against my ear. "A part of me rejoices at your suffering," Daelissa whispered. "Mors has tormented me endlessly, but he could never scar me as you have." She whimpered. "I will never rid myself of the nightmares."

"You deserve it for what you did," I hissed. "You killed thousands and sentenced souls to eternal torment. Hate me all you want, but I'd do it again."

Her hand gripped my neck and squeezed. I gagged. Hot tears splashed on what was left of my face, drawing cries of pain from me.

"I am torn in twain, equal parts hate and regret," Daelissa hissed. "I do not know who I hate more, you or me." She released me and the bed springs squeaked.

"Get off my bed!" I flailed with a hand, trying to find it. The springs squeaked again, and I heard her walking around me. I expected a kick to the head, but it never came. My hand found a metal leg. I crawled to the bed and climbed onto it. It took everything not to groan and whimper from the excruciating pain in my face.

"Mors used Brilliance to burn me," I said loud enough for the others to hear me.

"Brilliance?" Jeremiah said. "Are you certain?"

"It looked and felt real," I said. "He can drain souls and channel magic. He has true power here."

"This is even worse than I thought," Victoria said.

"He drained two women right in front of me," I said. "It made him stronger."

"Now I understand," Vallaena said. "This collective is nothing but a soul farm. Mors has created a cult and feeds on them."

I told them everything Mors had said. "His endgame is to butcher his flock so he can resurrect himself."

"How?" Victoria said. "Draining souls won't give him life."

"I don't see how he could do such a thing," Jeremiah said. "But if he knows how to work magic in the afterlife, then perhaps he knows aspects of it we haven't considered."

"If he's using true magic," Vallaena said, "then he might as well be a god."

We were weak and helpless. Mors would crush us beneath his thumb until the day he decided to devour our souls.

CHAPTER 18

I'd been in all sorts of pain, but having my face seared like a well-done steak was something different. It was the kind of pain I couldn't just push aside. It was like having my face held against a hot griddle with no relief.

I was a ghost with no flesh, no nerve endings or anything else to generate pain. But the rules of this collective made me feel like I did. Try as I might, I couldn't slip into a meditative state or go to sleep. There was no way to achieve a peaceful state of mind when my skin felt like it was constantly on fire.

It made me wonder if the rules of Mors's world were even more twisted and sadistic than we realized. What if we felt pain more acutely here? What if you couldn't pass out from intense pain because the rules here didn't allow it?

"If Mors has powers, then maybe it's possible for all of us to have powers," Jeremiah said. "The trick is understanding how he accesses them."

"I sense nothing at all when I reach for my demon side," Vallaena said. "It is as if an appendage has been cut off."

"I never had any real powers," Victoria said. "Just an occasional flash of the future. I couldn't even control it."

"Have you experienced these flashes since death?" Jeremiah said.

Victoria didn't answer at first. "Yes, but only once."

I was in constant agony but concentrating on their conversation helped ignore some of the pain. I managed to complete a sentence. "You also contacted Emily, didn't you?"

"Yes," she replied. "I was in the outlands, though, not a collective."

"But you did it, nonetheless." Jeremiah grunted. "It must be possible, but perhaps the process is different."

It was so hard to think through the pain, but I managed to produce another thought. "The barrier between life and death prevents Daemos from reaching our demon spirits. "Maybe it doesn't affect magic users the same way."

"Perhaps," Jeremiah said in a soft voice. His footsteps paced back and forth. "The primal fount exists here. Magic is all around us, so what prevents us from touching it?" He continued to pace, muttering under his breath.

"It is hopeless!" Daelissa said. "Mors owns our souls."

"Nothing is ever hopeless," I said. "And you're living—er—dead proof of it!"

She whimpered and went silent. The pain had slowly faded over the last few minutes. It no longer felt as if flames were licking my face, but a gentle massage with a cheese grater. I'd take the cheese grater to the face any day over the red-hot griddle.

Ignoring the new level of pain was hard, but it was doable. It took me twice as long, but I finally slipped away into a meditative state. I breathed a sigh of relief when the loft appeared around me. The pain was still there, but distant and bearable. It was also nice having my face intact even if it was only in an induced dream state.

I went to the window and shouted, "I'm back. Are you here?"

Dad appeared at once. "Son, are you okay? Your face is beet red."

Even though I'd pushed away the pain, it seemed my subconscious was manifesting signs of distress on my dream body. "I'm not okay," I said. "Where's Kalesh?"

"He should be back soon," Dad said. "He ventured out to find help."

"Help?" I threw up my hands. "From whom?"

Dad shrugged. "Well, it might sound like a stupid idea, but it's all we've got."

I winced as pain lanced through my face.

He frowned. "What's going on, Justin?"

"We've got even bigger problems than I thought," I said. "Father Mors ain't no ordinary ghost."

Dad raised an eyebrow. "Anyone who can drain souls in the afterlife isn't ordinary."

"Yeah, but it's not because the collective gives him the ability to do it." I paused for dramatic effect. "It's because Mors actually has powers. He's a Seraphim."

"Well, shit." Dad blew out a breath. "And he's using Seraphim powers to drain souls?"

I nodded. "But wait, there's more."

"I can hardly wait to hear it," he said dryly.

"I have a new cellmate and her name is Daelissa."

Dad's mouth dropped open. "Damn, son. I guess the afterlife is more hellish than the real Hell."

"Oh, it sucks big time!" I blew out a breath. "I hate to say it, but I think we're totally screwed."

Dad shook his head. "We'll figure this out somehow."

"Man, I hope so." I filled in all the other details to bring him up to date.

"Hmm." Dad tapped a finger on his chin. "If Mors can use magic, then that means you can too."

"Yeah, but I can't sense aether at all." I shrugged. "So what's the missing link?"

Dad rubbed his cheek. Then he pinched it.

"Trying to see if you're asleep?" I said.

"No, just trying to put my finger on something." He pursed his lips. "You're not a meat machine anymore, you're a soul."

I scoffed. "I know. But I don't see how that changes anything."

"Maybe it changes a lot," Dad said. "Maybe you're so used to controlling things with a physical body that you don't know how to use just your mind and soul."

A smartass retort died on my lips. "Because the mind isn't physical. It's part of consciousness."

He nodded. "Your physical body just houses the mind and soul. But when you use magic, you're channeling it through those physical parts of you."

I paused a moment to think about it. "Willpower drives magic. But whether you're channeling or casting, you need a physical focus to push it through."

Dad grunted. "Or maybe, you're just so used to doing it physically, that you can't do it any other way."

I rubbed my cheek. It felt like real flesh even though in this dream state it was purely imaginary. In the afterlife, my soul felt like a physical body, but it was nothing of the sort. Perceiving myself as a physical being was nothing but a thoroughly ingrained subconscious routine. The question was, what exactly was a soul?

"Am I a being of pure energy now?" I said. "Or something else?"

"I don't think it matters," Dad said. "What's important is that you shift your perception. Maybe that will reveal what you are and how you can use magic again."

Kalesh appeared next to Dad. "I am back."

"Any luck?" Dad asked.

He nodded. "I found her."

"Found who?" I asked.

"Vallaena's demon spirit," Kalesh said. "She is alive and happy to learn after all these years that her human soul still exists."

"Whoa!" I slapped my forehead. "So her demon spirit is separate from her human soul."

Kalesh nodded. "Just like us and Dad."

I gave Kalesh a blank stare. It was weird hearing him be so familiar with Dad. But Dad didn't even seem to notice. I wondered just how much father-son stuff was going on over there and felt a twinge of jealously. Were they throwing a baseball in the front yard?

Dad grinned. "Now all we gotta do is figure out how to punch through the barrier between life and death."

I pshawed. "Gee, is that all?" I tried to look behind them, but their bodies blocked the window. "Where's Vallaena's spirit?"

"She remains in her safe place," Kalesh said. "Wandering Haedaemos without a link to a human soul is dangerous."

I blew out a breath. "She's cut off, just like us."

Kalesh nodded. "Perhaps it's impossible to penetrate the barrier."

"Let's not be negative," Dad said. "Where there's a will, there's a way."

I scratched my head. "I'm open to ideas."

"I don't really have any." Dad shrugged. "Maybe you should just try again."

The imaginary bridge I'd created earlier was gone, so I conjured a sturdy concrete walkway between my window and theirs. "I guess there's only one way to find out." I slapped a hand on the concrete. "Kalesh, meet me in the middle."

He bit his bottom lip and cast an apprehensive look at the bridge. Then he nodded and climbed out of the window. I followed his lead and crawled onto the bridge. We began walking toward each other, pacing each other step for step. Our movements slowed, caught in the invisible force that thickened like invisible mud all around us as we closed in on the center.

Shrieks echoed in the distance, growing closer with every passing second. Kalesh gritted his teeth and leaned forward, putting everything he had into reaching the middle. I grunted and groaned with effort until at last, my demon spirit and I stood face to face. We reached toward each other. Our fingertips hit the barrier, the distance between them barely as thick as a pane of glass. Blue electrical currents raced along the invisible surface where our fingers touched it.

Wind whipped my hair. The black tornado of consumed souls howled into view only a few blocks away.

"Push!" I shouted.

"I am!" Kalesh shouted back. His blue face reddened with the effort as we tried to punch through the divide.

It wasn't working—not even a little bit. And the soul storm was nearly upon us. "Get back inside!" I tried to pound a fist on the barrier, but it was like trying to punch through thick mud. "We'll try again later." I had to shout over the growing shrieks of the storm.

Kalesh turned in slow motion and headed back. I used the invisible barrier to push myself away and toward the window. The first few steps took a seeming eternity. The pressure abated so gradually it was hardly noticeable at first. The black cyclone of souls was less than a block away when I reached the halfway point.

"Run!" Dad shouted from behind me.

"I am running!" I growled. With less than four feet to go, I dove for the window. I almost made it, but my foot caught on the sill and I went down face-first onto the floor with my leg still protruding outside.

Blackness engulfed it. Arctic cold raced up my leg.

Father Mors reaches for me. I scream.

A hand reaches out. I shriek in terror and see the face of the priest.

I cower in a cell as the black-robed priest enters, a hungry look in his eyes. "Your soul will feed a god," Mors says.

Over and over again, I saw Mors coming for me. Over and over again, I felt myself drained. Heard my screams turn to howls. My head filled with the wails of countless souls. And then they went silent, replaced by the sounds of my screams.

I was fully inside the apartment, shivering violently. The soul storm seemed to hover outside a moment before howling off into the distance. "Holy shit." I hugged myself, desperate to feel warmth. I tugged off my tennis shoe and inspected my foot. It was ice cold but looked unharmed. I conjured a space heater, but it did nothing to thaw my flesh.

"Justin, are you okay?" Dad called.

I limped over the window on my numb foot. "It clipped me, but I'm okay."

Kalesh stood behind his own window, eyes wide. "You're unharmed?"

"My foot is ice cold and numb, but I feel okay." I pulled up my pants and looked at my leg but saw nothing wrong with it. "This is crazy. I never thought the astral plane was so dangerous."

Dad shook his head. "Son, that loft is the only safe place. Once you step out the window, you're projecting your consciousness into no-man's land."

I rubbed my foot. "Yeah, I get it. Loft good. Astral plane, bad."

Dad frowned. "What I don't understand is how the consumed souls from the infernal fount are able to reach you when Kalesh can't. Technically, they should be on this side of the barrier."

"Unless they're not." Those visions of Mors had come from the consumed—possibly their final moments of terror before he'd drained them. "I think the soul storm is actually here in the afterlife. I think these souls aren't the same as the ones trapped around the infernal fount."

"Really?" He quirked an eyebrow. "What makes you think that?"

I told him about the visions. "Mors has been trapped here for years. In that time, he's drained hundreds of souls."

"What a monster," Kalesh said.

Dad growled. "He's a complete psychopath if he's drained that many souls."

"Doomed to endless torment." Kalesh shook his head sadly. "He must be stopped."

"Yeah, but I need my damned powers back!" I slapped the windowsill. "There must be a way."

Kalesh seemed to be staring hard at the space between us. "It might be impossible."

Dad crossed his arms and leaned on the windowsill. "I've seen enough ghosts and heard enough stories to know that it's possible for the dead to reach out to the living. There's a way to punch through the barrier. We just need to find out how."

"In the meantime, Mors will torture me until I'm insane." I sighed and leaned on the windowsill. "If I don't escape, my body dies, and I'm stuck in the afterlife for good."

"We'll figure it out, son." Dad climbed out of the window and stood on the bridge.

"What are you doing?" I said.

"Testing a theory." He took a step forward and then another. A minute ticked past and nothing. Dad frowned. "Justin, step onto the bridge."

I climbed up and onto it. A moment later, the distant shrieks of the soul storm reached our ears. Within minutes the dark storm rumbled down the street.

Dad grunted. "It's drawn to you."

"Maybe not just me." I watched the encroaching tornado. "Maybe any consciousness that ventures into the astral plane unprotected."

"Yeah." Dad shooed me toward the window. "Maybe they sense your light essence and want to drain it for their own."

I hopped back inside the window. Within seconds, the sounds of the lost souls faded into the distance. It seemed Dad was right. "Just like the dark husks and shadow people drained by the Grand Nexus."

"Exactly like that." Dad shook his head. "If they get you, it's game over."

"Not if Mors gets me first," I said.

"We should ask other demons," Kalesh said. "Maybe they would know."

Dad nodded. "We'll have to be really careful, though." He looked back at me. "Hang in there, son. Try to figure out how Mors uses his powers while we work out this angle, okay?"

I nodded. "Good luck." Then I went and curled up on the small bed. I wanted to be optimistic but, considering what waited for me when I left this dream state, all I wanted to do was stay here and hide.

I had nothing to look forward to except torture.

CHAPTER 19

W hen I woke up, the first thing I noticed was that I could see again. My vision was blurry, but I could make out Daelissa huddled in the corner, eyes staring blankly. Mors had only been at me a day and I already understood how she felt.

Even though my face felt a lot better, my foot was still cold and slightly numb. The awful images of Mors reaching for me flickered through my mind. The final memories of those souls chilled me to the core.

If I was right, and if Mors was responsible for the soul storm in the afterlife, it meant he'd binged on souls the moment he figured out how to use his powers. I had no idea how many souls circled the infernal fount. I imagined Daelissa was directly responsible for hundreds if not thousands during her long life. That included all the human souls drained when the Grand Nexus exploded.

Only the Seraphim had come out of that more or less unscathed. Their bodies had survived being drained, and we'd figured out how to reverse the process. But the drained humans were lost. When we exposed their bodies to the process, they turned to dust.

Fresh outrage burned through me. If I could have my powers only for a moment, I'd drain Daelissa's soul and not lose a wink of sleep at night. There was nothing she could do to atone for her sins.

And then there was that soul-sucking son of a bitch named Mors. He was also here thanks to Daelissa. If she hadn't resurrected his husk he wouldn't be here. If she hadn't embarked on world domination not once, but twice, there would be thousands fewer consumed souls.

It seemed impossible two people were responsible for so many deaths and so many drained souls. And yet, I had the extreme displeasure of being trapped with one and imprisoned by the other.

Karma didn't seem to like me very much.

Daelissa watched me with wide eyes. "Today, he will be kind. And then at the last moment, he will do something horrible." She shivered and tears trickled down her cheeks. "He hungers for power as I once did."

I was sick to death of her pity party. "You just didn't care who you hurt to get what you wanted." My fists clenched. "Mors might be responsible for hundreds of consumed souls, but you and your wars doomed thousands!" I wanted to punch her in the face, but it'd be a slap on the wrist compared to what Mors had already done to her.

She shuddered. "Even my eternal suffering is not redemption enough."

"You got that right!" I pounded the flat of my fist on the bed. "You deserve a worse fate than death just like the souls of the people you consumed."

"I'm afraid justice is a rare commodity," Jeremiah said.

"Indeed," Victoria said. "And there's no great reward for doing good, either."

"Death is nothing but a miserable continuation of life," Vallaena added. "All our deeds were for naught."

Their chorus of doom only reiterated how I felt—hopeless. What was the point of fighting when there was always one more bad guy hiding in the shadows?

The outside door opened and Gerald marched in. Seeing him was the perfect capper to an already miserable day—and I'd only been awake for five minutes. He did a double take when he saw me and his brow furrowed.

I bit my tongue and held back any smartass remarks. "Is something wrong?" I asked.

He didn't answer.

Gerald opened the cell door, stepped inside, and yanked me off the bed.

"Jesus!" I shouted. "All you had to do was ask and I would've gotten up."

"Cease your profanities!" Still holding my arm, he slung me across the room. I cracked into the wall on the far side. Intense pain stabbed into my skull and the world blacked out for an instant. I climbed to my knees and went right back down in a puddle of blood. Gerald had zero shits to give. He dragged me upstairs by my ankle. I tried to resist but was too stunned from hitting the wall.

When he finally released my foot, I was back in the same room from earlier. I sat up and drunkenly looked around. I was alone for the moment. Like an infant trying to escape their crib, I crawled across the floor on hands and knees and tried to open the door.

No good. It was locked.

I groaned and leaned against the wall. "Fuck my afterlife."

As if on cue, Mors stepped inside. He blinked a few times when he saw me, as visibly confused as Gerald for some reason.

"What's wrong?" I asked. "Did Gerald bloody me up too much?"

Mors narrowed his eyes. "I must apologize for Gerald's handling of you." He motioned toward the door and two women bearing silver trays walked inside and set them on a table. They removed the lids and the delicious odor of bacon and eggs pleasured my nose. "In the meantime, please enjoy this breakfast."

The women knelt in front of me and began dabbing my face with damp cloths. Then they helped me to my feet and over to a chair. There was quite a spread on the table—orange juice, toast, bacon, eggs, and more.

Daelissa was right.

This was the nice treatment. At some point, he would spring his diabolical evil twist and screw me over hard. On one hand, there was nothing I could do about it. And on the other hand, there was bacon. I chose bacon and temporary happiness and chowed down. Mors took a seat at the end of the table and simply watched.

When I was full to bursting, I leaned back in my chair and patted my belly. "Stomach is full."

"I'm glad you enjoyed it," Mors said.

I watched him carefully. "So what's the catch?"

"I've been questioning your companions about events in the living world." He rested a hand on the table. "It seems Daelissa was not the last to seek power."

I hadn't realized he'd been interrogating the others. I nodded. "That's right. I assume you've heard of Baal?"

He nodded. "The demon overlord. The one who created the Daemos to fight us."

I realized I might have a chance to convince Mors to free us. "Are you familiar with the relics of Juranthemon?"

Another nod. "Yes. Moses told me of Baal's plot to combine them and recover his physical body." Mors leaned his elbows on the table. "He said undoing the Sundering could possibly wipe out the afterlife."

I nodded. "Exactly. But if you let us go, it's possible I can stop him."

Mors frowned. "How? Need I remind you that you're dead?"

It seemed the others hadn't told Mors I was only mostly dead. If I told him, would he be more likely to let me go or would his hate win out? It didn't seem like things could get much worse by taking my chances.

So I spilled the beans. "I'm not entirely dead. My body is in a preservation spell. If I can reach the birthing canal at the primal fount, it's possible I could return to my body."

Mors raised an eyebrow. "How do you know your body still lives?"

"I get glimpses of the living world sometimes." I leaned toward him. "If Baal isn't stopped, the afterlife will be wiped out before you have a chance to return to life."

Mors leaned back and steepled his fingers. "Those Seraphim alive during the Sundering knew little about what caused it. Your companions have enlightened me a great deal on the subject, but I would like to hear what you know."

I didn't see a reason to withhold anything at that point, so I gave him the full spiel. "Xanos lured the Apocryphan to Juranthemon with claims that one of the ancient gods, Elohim, planned to take over creation. Elohim was lured there with rumors of an impending battle between the Apocryphan."

Mors cracked a smile. "Very clever."

"I don't know exactly how it happened, but Saila, the daughter of Kathazal, tried to stop the battle. Elohim was watching from nearby when Xanos outed him." I shrugged. "The Apocryphan unleashed everything they had on him, and he fought back. The explosion sundered the world. Thousands of beings were killed, releasing so much spiritual energy that it created the realm Haedaemos."

Mors held up a hand. "Instead of the afterlife."

I nodded. "We think the afterlife was wiped out or reset in that instant, so the spirits had nowhere else to go."

"But spirits are different than souls," Mors said. "Spirits are alive and we are but ghosts."

It sounded a lot like what Baal told me during my short visit to Haedaemos. "Yes, they're alive as far as I know."

"This is very similar to what your companions told me." Mors pursed his lips. "You see, Daelissa would have seen no value to keeping you alive for information. Had I not, I wouldn't have seen the path back to the living."

I blinked. "What path is that?"

Mors raised a hand and one of the women brought him a glass of red wine. He took a sip. "Souls cannot be destroyed, boy. Even when I consume their essence, life remains."

I tried to keep the anger from my voice. "Life with almost no consciousness. Life in constant torment."

"But life, nonetheless." He smirked. "So the Sundering would not have wiped out the souls in the afterlife."

"Maybe they were consumed," I said. "They went somewhere."

"Oh, yes," he said. "Of that I'm sure. In fact, I believe they were transmuted into something more."

I frowned. "You've lost me."

"Isn't it obvious?" Mors took another sip of wine. "They were sent across the barrier between life and death, but without physical bodies, they had only one place to go—Haedaemos."

"It's possible," I said. "But it's a lot more likely they were drained."

"Why would an explosion of such magnitude drain souls?" Mors said. "They are not beings of flesh. The sundering breached the dimensional barriers in such a way that it literally created new dimensions we call realms. This means that in that instant, the barrier between the dead and living was also breached, releasing the souls into the spirit realm."

I hated to admit it, but his theory sounded as plausible as anything I'd heard. "Even if that's what happened, how does this..." The dots connected before I finished my question. "You think reversing the Sundering will open another breach?"

"I have little doubt it will," Mors said.

My mouth dropped open. "What if you're wrong? What if it wipes us all out?"

"I am not a fool, boy." Mors swirled the wine in his glass. "I am absolutely certain of my reasoning."

"But there's no proof you're right."

He smirked. "You've told me all I need to know. Now all I have to do is wait and pray Baal succeeds."

My stomach dropped like a rock. "Mors, you're wrong, dead wrong. If Baal succeeds, all the realms will come crashing back together and billions will die."

Mors set his wine glass down and stood. "I'm counting on it, boy. And in order to ensure my survival, I'll need as many souls as I can consume." He stepped toward me, hand outstretched. "Starting with you."

I leapt up and backed away, but the chair caught my feet and I fell on my backside. "Kill me and you kill yourself!"

"You're wrong." He leaned down and gripped me by the neck, lifted me off the floor until my feet dangled.

I gasped for air. My mind scrambled desperately for something, anything to say that might change his mind. Mors only cared for himself. If I couldn't convince him he was in danger, then there was only one other possibility. I forced myself to smile. "I'm glad I killed you. I hope you rot here forever."

Mors roared and slung me to the side. I crashed through platters of bacon and eggs, slid across the table, and hit the wall on the other side.

Throwing Justin against walls seemed to be the theme of the day. There was nowhere to run, so I climbed unsteadily to my feet and grinned. "That's right, Mors. Even if you suck me dry, you'll never forget that a teenage boy killed you." I spat out a glob of blood. "So much for your superiority."

Face livid with rage, Mors blurred toward me. He broke the table in half with a mighty blow from his fists. I squeaked and tried to run, but in this place, I was as helpless as a nom. The last thing I remembered was Mors's fist coming toward my face.

APPARENTLY, my ploy worked, because I woke up in agony. It felt as if every bone in my body was broken, including my skull. Daelissa appeared in my vision, her brow furrowed, mouth open in horror one moment, replaced by a smile of pleasure the next.

Tears formed in her eyes. "Your pain pleases me though I know it should not." She smiled through her tears. "Mors has crushed you to a bloody pulp."

I whimpered but couldn't move my jaw to speak. I couldn't even raise my head to look at the damage. Whatever was left of my body was wracked in pure pain. As with the burns, it was so intense, I couldn't push it aside and submerge myself in blissful unconsciousness.

Was it worse to be a terribly crushed and injured soul, or one of the mindless consumed? At that moment, I almost wished Mors had just drained me and gotten it over with.

"Turn his head toward me," Mors said from somewhere nearby.

Daelissa didn't even try to be gentle and pushed my face. A ragged scream tore from my throat and my vision blurred. When it resolved, I saw the cell door. Saw Mors standing outside with Jeremiah.

A smile slowly spread across his lips. "You were right to remind me why I'm here, boy. Dying by your hand has tormented me all this time, so why should I grant you respite?" Mors chuckled. "I will take great pleasure in torturing you, all while you wait helplessly for Baal to end the world you so love."

"Ungh." I tried to speak, but nothing worked.

"And what better start to that torture than to make Jeremiah die for you a second time?" Mors tilted back his head and roared with laughter as if he'd just heard the best joke in the world. When he finally recovered, he put a hand on Jeremiah's head. "Enjoy the show."

"I'd rather be a consumed soul than spend another moment in this hell," Jeremiah said. "Finish me quickly so I can be on my way."

"So brave," Mors said. "Let's see how brave you are when you feel your essence draining away." His grip tightened on Jeremiah's shaved head. "This will not be quick."

Jeremiah's eyes rolled up into his head. Black veins climbed up his skin and a ragged croak rasped in his throat. It only took a moment to see that Mors was taking it much slower with Jeremiah, savoring the man's pain instead of draining him as quickly as the others. But whether it took five minutes or an hour, the man who'd already died once for me would shrivel, blacken, and sink into the ground to join the swarm of wailing souls trapped in the afterlife.

I wondered if I'd see his tortured form the next time I tried to reach Kalesh. I wondered if his last memory would haunt me.

Goodbye again.

CHAPTER 20

I'd never felt so powerless in my entire death. Even if I hadn't been paralyzed, there was nothing I could do except watch helplessly. As it was, there was only part of my body I could use. So I took advantage of it and prayed it worked.

I closed my eyes.

A moment later, Jeremiah's croaking stopped. "Did he pass out?" Mors said. "Wake him."

A hand prodded my face. The pain was so intense, it was all I could do not to scream.

"I said wake him!" Mors shouted.

Daelissa slapped me.

I screamed in pain and tried to fake passing out again.

Mors was having none of it. "Hold open his eyes, you fool!"

Daelissa hissed but complied. Her fingers peeled open my eyelids and held them.

Mors smiled down at me. "There's no escaping this, boy." He turned back to Jeremiah.

Fury burned through my pain. *That son of a bitch!* But despite all my rage, I was still just a rat in a cage. Soon Jeremiah would be shriveled and black, forever trapped with this as his last memory.

An idea struck me out of nowhere. It was risky as hell but if I failed, it couldn't be any worse than this. The trick would be pulling it off with my eyes wide open. Despite the pain and my open eyes, I had to retreat into a lucid state. If this worked, I might be able to save Jeremiah. If it didn't, well, I wouldn't have any concerns anymore.

The pain had diminished somewhat, possibly due to my anger, or perhaps my soul had begun to heal. *Well, at least I've got that going for me.* I used the same trick I'd used countless times to shift into demon vision and let my eyes focus on nothing. Basically, it was like consciously zoning myself out. It wasn't quite as good as closing my eyes, but it did the trick.

The world faded away and darkness swallowed me. The loft flickered into existence around me. I went to the window and called across the street to Kalesh's side.

The window opened and Dad appeared. "Jesus, kiddo. What happened this time?"

"No time to explain. Is Kalesh there?"

He shook his head. "No, he got another bright idea and took off."

I climbed out of the window and onto the bridge. "Okay, well, if this doesn't work, tell him I hope he has a good life." I began to walk.

Dad held out his hand in the universal stop sign. "Justin, what in the hell are you doing?"

"Whatever it takes." I turned my gaze toward the growing sound of the soul storm and continued to press ahead.

"Don't get cryptic with me, son!" Dad climbed onto the bridge. "What are you doing?"

"I think the consumed souls might have answers." I waded through the invisible resistance toward the middle. "I'm positive they're trapped in the afterlife like me."

"How are you so certain?" Dad said.

"I just know it." I kept walking. "I feel it in my bones."

"You don't have any bones." Dad grimaced. "How are consumed souls supposed to give you answers to anything? They're going to drain you dry, son."

I stood next to the barrier between life and death and watched as the tornado churned through the void toward me. "I don't think they will." Or so I hoped. "They had the chance when my foot was stuck, but they didn't. I think they were trying to communicate with me."

"Just because you saw the last moments of the person before Mors drained them?" Dad said. "What's left of their minds is stuck in an endless loop, Justin. It doesn't mean anything!"

The howling swarm grew so loud I could barely hear Dad. They were less than a block away. "I've got no choice but to try. If I don't, Mors will drain Jeremiah, then Victoria, and then Vallaena."

Dad shouted over racket. "I love you, son!"

The swirling madness was nearly upon me. I spread my arms wide to welcome them. "I love you too, Dad!" And then darkness and cold swept over me.

Visions of Mors flooded my mind. There were too many to process, all jumbled into a chaotic mess. My entire body went numb with cold. I tried to scream. Tried to breathe. I couldn't do anything but feel my sanity slipping away.

It seemed this time I'd been wrong. My gamble was a bust and I was going to die here.

A seeming eternity passed, and the visions slowed and stopped. It was as if the consumed souls had sent me their memories all at once and had nothing more to say. Or else I was now a part of the swarm and didn't even realize it.

I still couldn't talk so I tried a little telepathy. *I need a memory. I need to see the first time Mors used his power here.*

The darkness remained.

Please, help me.

Still nothing.

I tried a different tact. *Show me the first memory.*

Apparently, telepathy wasn't working. Somehow, I had to speak.

We hear you. It was as if hundreds of terribly sad voices sounded inside my head, speaking in atonal unison.

Holy shit, you can talk?

Apart we are nothing. Together we combine what is left of ourselves.

So by combining what's left of your individual minds, you've created a group consciousness?

Yes, they replied.

It was fascinating, but I didn't have time for question and answers. So I skipped back to the point. *Do you have the first memory of Mors using his power?*

Who is the first among us? The voices whispered.

The visions began playing through my mind's eye. In the first one, I saw myself, a horrified expression on my face and realized it must have been from the perspective of the women he drained in my presence. The playback continued, going faster and faster until it was nothing but a blur. It abruptly slowed and stopped in darkness.

I stood in a room with white walls. The view rotated to take in a hunched figure in black robes.

An unseen man spoke. "You wished to see me, sir?"

The figure rose and turned, a feral grin on his face. It was Mors. "You were right. All I needed was a shift of perspective."

"God spoke to you?" the other man said.

Mors's eyes began to glow. "Oh, I am god now." He lifted his hand. The man whose eyes gave witness began to shudder violently. A cry rasped from his throat and the world began to fade.

That was the first memory?

Yes, the voices replied.

I hadn't seen a single clue that would help me. *Whose memory is it?*

Ours now, they replied.

What did Mors mean by a change of perspective? Can you show me what happened before that?

We have only the last moments, the voices said. *All else is lost.*

Show me the next memory, I said.

Mors appeared in front of me, dressed in his black robes.

"Father, I am here," a woman said.

"For now." A cruel smile spread his lips and he reached a hand out.

The woman gasped and her vision went dark.

The next one, I said.

And so it went, them playing back memory after memory of Mors and his smug little face as he drained his victims. But not once did he stop to give the bad guy speech and explain just how in the hell he was able to do it. I had only one clue from victim zero, and it certainly wasn't enough to go on.

I need to go, I said.

You are warm, the voices said. *You are our light.*

I didn't like the sound of that at all. *I'm sorry, I can't stay. Please let me go.* I tried to move, but my limbs were numb.

Stay and be our light.

I'm not a light, I'm a person! I summoned every ounce of strength in my being and tried to move, but I was locked in place, immobile in pitch black.

You are light. We have no light without you.

It was like trying to reason with a child. *I'm not a fucking light bulb!*

A tiny speck of light appeared in my vision. It grew larger and larger until it resolved into a humanoid shape floating in a void below me. The figure hung as if suspended by invisible strings. A soft white nimbus of light hung around it and tiny points of brighter light twinkled like stars beneath its skin. It looked like an alien.

I swooped down until I hovered right in front of it. I tried to gasp. The alien's mouth opened a fraction, mimicking my surprise. Because it was no alien at all. It was me.

Am I seeing this through your eyes? I asked.

Our eyes, the voices responded. *You are light.*

They weren't wrong. It was me, but my skin was translucent and glowed like starlight. My insides resembled a white nebula dusted with stars. It was like standing next to a fire on a cold night. The consumed souls were right—I was light. But how?

I stared at myself in awe for several heartbeats before shaking off the surreal feeling. *I don't look like this. Did you do something to me?* The glowing nimbus around my body flickered and faded slightly with every passing moment. The deathly cold of the consumed was leeching away my essence. If they held me much longer, I'd soon join the swarm.

We see you, they replied.

Obviously, but why do you see me this way?

I sensed confusion. *We see you.*

And then I understood.

The consumed souls had no individual consciousness. Their sight was no longer burdened by the preconceptions of the living. They saw only the naked truth. And it was the key to finally escaping hell.

You're holding me prisoner. If you keep me here, you will drain my light. The glow around my body faded perceptibly. *You will be no better than Mors.*

I sensed anger and sadness. My vision went black. Shrieks filled my ears and icy fingers ran down my back. Dim light grew brighter. And then I was free of the swarm. But my body was so cold I couldn't move.

"Justin!" Dad shouted.

I tried to respond, but my frozen lips wouldn't move. I toppled forward and fell off the bridge.

Dad cried out again. "Justin!"

The street rushed to meet me. But there was no impact. The ground swallowed me whole.

The cell floor flickered into view. I hadn't died. I was awake. Jeremiah knelt outside, streaks of darkness creeping up his skin as Mors slowly drained him.

"The boy's skin is like ice," Daelissa said. "I think you killed him."

"He can't die, you idiot." Mors leered at me. "Not unless I drain him."

The penetrating cold from the swarm made my broken body feel ten times worse than before. A ragged moan rattled from my throat.

Mors grinned even wider. "You see? He's alive and perfectly miserable."

Jeremiah looked really bad. I didn't have much time to figure things out if I wanted to save him. I'd hoped that my epiphany during my time in the swarm had carried over to the conscious world. Unfortunately, Mors and Jeremiah looked as physical as the last time I'd seen them. Somehow, I had to change my perspective.

I tried letting my gaze drift out of focus, but that did nothing but nearly put me into another trance. Jeremiah's skin began to shrivel like a rotting peach.

Damn it, how do I see like the consumed souls did? How was I supposed to shift my perspective when I had over twenty years of preconceived notions standing in the way? I couldn't just turn off my consciousness. I had to switch perspectives and see past what my eyes thought they saw.

There is no spoon.

I was going about this the wrong way. Shifting perspective didn't mean changing the way I saw things with my eyes. It meant shifting my beliefs to align with reality. It meant truly believing I was no longer made of meat and bones, but of something else.

Accept the truth.

It meant that all this pain, this agony didn't exist. I was allowing the collective to define my reality. I believed it had power over me and thus allowed it to control me. And by doing so, I'd given Mors complete control over my very existence.

Mors had beaten my soul to a pulp. He'd denigrated me and my friends and I'd just let him walk all over me.

No more!

I tried to move, but my body refused. *I don't have bones. I don't have muscles. I am stardust!* A ragged moan formed in my chest and crawled up my throat. *My jaw is not broken. I still have a voice!*

Mors's smirk widened. "Your misery is my joy, you little wretch. When I escape this Purgatory, I will revel in your eternal damnation."

"I'm not your toy," I rasped. Ignoring the agony of broken bones and torn ligaments, I lifted a hand to my face and finally saw it for what it was—a ghostly appendage, gently glowing and sparkling with inner light.

I had no bones, no skin, no meat. I was a being of pure life energy.

My soul snapped back into shape. It was damaged and in pain, but it was all mine to control.

I bared my teeth. "Let my friend go, you piece of fucking garbage."

Mors stumbled back from Jeremiah and the other man toppled over. Mors's eyes widened. "How did you—"

"I shifted perspective," I said. It was like plugging myself into an electrical grid. The aether I hadn't been able to sense earlier suddenly surrounded me. It felt so amazing to feel it again, I nearly cried. It wasn't the only thing I felt.

I am back! Kalesh shouted in my head. *How?*

No time to explain. I need to kick some ass. Then I reached back and kicked the cell door clean off its hinges.

Jeremiah lay unconscious on the floor. His skin was translucent and ghostly like mine, but his inner light had dimmed and didn't sparkle. Mors, on the other hand, pulsated and sparkled like a nineteen-seventies disco star.

He thrust his arms toward me. A narrow beam of Brilliance grazed my cheek. It burned like a hot branding iron. Even though Mors couldn't kill me, he could still hurt me and damage my soul. If he incapacitated me, he could drain me without breaking a sweat.

I dodged another blast from Mors and channeled a shield of Murk to block his next strike.

"Justin, what's happening?" Victoria shouted.

"Is he all right?" Vallaena said. "I cannot see anything!"

Mors snarled. "I have fed on the souls of hundreds. Do you really think you're a match for me?" He glowed bright as a star and lifted off the ground. "I will burn your soul to ash!" And then he unleashed a blinding blast. My shield evaporated. I flew backward through the air and slammed into something.

The last thing I saw was Daelissa's horrified face looking down at me.

CHAPTER 21

Daelissa's screams yanked me back to consciousness.

Mors gripped her by the hair and flung her out of the cell, then stormed toward me. I feigned unconsciousness until he reached down for me, then I unleashed my demon and manifested. It wasn't the same as morphing in the flesh. Instead, blue vapor flooded my ghostly form. I went from fun-sized to blue Hulk in an instant.

Before Mors had a chance to react, I let him get acquainted with my monstrous fist. The punch shot him straight up like a rocket. He plowed through the ceiling in a howl of rage and pain and vanished.

I was still woozy from the blast he'd given me, but for the first time in a long while, I could think clearly. He was too damned strong to fight. I raced to the cell next to Jeremiah's. Victoria leapt back from the door, mouth hanging open in astonishment.

"Justin?"

I nodded. "Yep." Then I ripped the door out of the frame.

"How?" Vallaena pressed her pale, tired face against her cell door. "I had lost all hope."

"No time to explain." I shooed her away from the door, then ripped it open. "We're leaving." I dashed over to Jeremiah and hoisted him over a shoulder. In demon form I was so tall my head kept hitting the low ceiling. I shrank back to normal size as easily as a deflating balloon.

I like this new morphing ability, Kalesh said.

Daelissa lay in a heap against the wall. The light in her soul was only marginally brighter than Jeremiah's. Inky fluid oozed from a wound in her head. I realized it was probably what I'd perceived as blood before my awakening. It only reinforced the realization that Mors could still beat the shit out of us.

I ran past the fallen angel, stopped, and looked back at her still form. She'd murdered thousands and drained the light from countless souls. If anyone deserved eternal torture from Mors, it was Daelissa.

Vallaena shook her head. "She is not worth saving, Justin."

But Victoria bent down and heaved the unconscious Seraphim over her shoulder. "I won't give Mors the pleasure of keeping her. If anyone gets to torture her, it will be us."

My aunt raised an eyebrow. "That is a valid point."

I heard a roar and a massive beam of Brilliance obliterated the ceiling of my former cell. We ran upstairs just as Mors pounced through the hole and landed.

Gerald was waiting on us in the hallway at the top of the stairs. He lunged at me and his fist connected with my temple. I stumbled sideways and Jeremiah tumbled off my shoulder and to the floor. Gerald blurred toward me. I dodged to the side and he smashed a hand through the drywall to my left.

Mors's shouts of anger echoed from the stairwell. He'd be on us in seconds. There was only one way to get out of this.

I turned to the others. "Vallaena, get Jeremiah and run. Get the hell out of this collective."

"You can't fight Mors," Vallaena said. "He's too powerful."

I shook my head. "I'm just buying you time. Now go!"

"He's right, " Victoria said. "We need to go."

Vallaena's jaw tightened. She nodded. "I am proud of you. We will see you soon."

Gerald came at me again, so I didn't have time to respond. I caught his fist inches from my face and easily held it at bay. His eyes flared in surprise.

I grinned back. "I'm going to enjoy this, you ball-licking son of a bitch." I cocked back a fist and punched him with everything I had.

Gerald screamed like a man falling off a tall building. His body left a nice big hole in the hallway wall and splintered four rows of pews in the chapel. Vallaena and Victoria were almost to the exit. All I had to do was hold of Mors until they got away.

I hadn't given it much thought until now, but I didn't perceive the actual building and physical surroundings any differently than before. They seemed to be every bit as real as those in the land of the living.

Mors burst out of the stairwell and glared at me. "How did you figure it out, boy? It took me years."

I shrugged. "I guess I'm just a lot smarter than a steaming pile of shit like you, Mors."

Brilliance coalesced in his hands. "I will burn your soul for eternity, boy."

I smirked. "Aw, shucks. I kind of made other plans. How about I kick your ass from one end of this church to the other, and then teabag your bleeding body while Gerald watches?"

His roar of rage was the only warning I had. A massive blast of Brilliance obliterated the wall where I'd been standing. Even though I blurred to the side, the blast threw me off my feet and sent me tumbling down the hall.

Mother rushed out of the door leading to the chapel, eyes wide with surprise when she saw the damage. "Father, what's happening?"

Mors still held crackling Brilliance in his hands. "God has granted me power to deal with an agent of hell."

I climbed to my feet and smiled innocently. "Who, me? I'm just a choir boy."

Mother stared at the destructive energy in Mors's hands. "God has truly chosen you, Father."

Vallaena and Victoria hadn't had a lot of time to get away, but it was probably a good head start. With Mother distracting Mors, now seemed the appropriate time to make a run for it myself. I turned and blurred away from them, heading in the opposite direction my companions had gone. I smashed through the door at the end and emerged outside between the church and the walled-in community where Gerald had taken me to meet Mors.

Judging from the roar of anger rapidly approaching my position, Mors was hot on my tail. Even with his supercharged angel powers, my demonic powers gave me more speed.

I went right, leapt over the wall and juked left. Then I jumped the wall on the far side and circled around the church. I took a moment to spot my companions. Victoria and Vallaena had made it as far as the edge of the forest. They wouldn't be going any further without my help because they were surrounded by ushers. Anger superheated my ghost blood.

"I fucking hate this place!" I unleashed Kalesh and swelled into Monster Smurf. I almost roared but didn't want to give away my position to Mors. I hoped he was hunting for me inside the walled-off section.

The ushers were so busy corralling my companions, they didn't even see me coming. I grabbed the first one I came to and used him like a base-ball bat on his fellows. Bodies flew like rag dolls.

"Satan!" one of the men screamed. I punted him like a soccer ball and sent him flying twenty feet through the air.

"Who's your daddy?" I said in my guttural voice. The others shrieked and ran for their lives.

I retrieved Daelissa and Jeremiah from the ground and cradled them like babies, one in each arm. "Run!"

Victoria and Vallaena took off and I paced behind them. They were so slow, I had to be careful not to run over them.

More shouts echoed from the church. A bell began to gong. And then I heard Mors's cries of rage behind us. The others couldn't catch us, but he could. I knelt down. "Get on my back, now."

Victoria looked taken aback, but Vallaena scrambled up my ten-foot frame and locked her legs on my torso.

"Get on," Vallaena said.

Victoria collected herself and climbed on, wedging herself against my side. Even encumbered as I was, my demon strength had little problem adjusting. I dashed through the forest at top speed. A moment later, we hit the void between collectives. I kept running straight and the next instant we were in the open desert.

At long last we'd escaped Heavenly, but now we were in Kalifa. I ran south along the border and up a tall dune so we'd have a hundred yards of buffer between us and the border.

"Maybe they won't follow us," I said.

"Bloody hell, it's hot." Victoria climbed off my back and wiped her brow.

Vallaena hopped down as well. "Yes, it is."

I felt the heat, but it didn't bother me nearly as much as it might in a real body. Knowing that we weren't actual flesh changed everything about perception. I crouched and watched the border for a moment. Just when I was about to declare us safe, a man in a white suit appeared out of thin air. A crowd of fellow ushers poured across the border behind him, followed shortly by Mors and Gerald.

"Son of a bitch!" I looked across the desert behind us and spotted a city in the distance. It was impossible to say how far it was, and it really didn't matter. I couldn't outrun Mors while carrying the others.

Gerald bared his teeth and began to run up the dune toward us. A look of surprise furrowed his brow when he moved no faster than the ushers running alongside him. In this collective, he had no powers. He was just another ordinary soul.

Mors, however, had no such limitations. Wings of white fire unfurled from his back and he rose into the air. The ushers cried out praises and dropped to their knees. Gerald must have known about Mors's Seraphim abilities because he didn't react.

"We should run," Victoria said.

"Where?" Vallaena waved a hand at the desert between us and the distant city. "The only city is miles away."

"South, back into Britannia," Victoria said. "Our chances are much better there."

Since the world looked as if it went on forever, I couldn't gauge how far it was to the border. But if memory served, it wasn't more than a few hundred yards away. "There's nowhere to hide here."

Mors was already gliding toward us and would reach us soon. I picked up Jeremiah and Daelissa. "Let's go for it."

Victoria and Vallaena hopped on my massive demon back and I sprinted south, hopefully toward the border. Mors shouted and his men began racing diagonally up the dune after us while he flew ahead. Thankfully, Mors didn't seem particularly adept at flying. If he'd been one of Daelissa's elite archangels he would've been on us in a hot minute.

I chugged along as fast as I could, but the sand wasn't helping anything. Even though my body was made of soul stuff and not flesh, fatigue spread slowly through my muscles. I didn't know if that was because of the rules of the collective, or if soul bodies also got tired.

On the upside, I had plenty of energy to run full out for a while, and Mors and gang were falling behind. Even burdened as I was, outpacing the pursuit wasn't going to be a problem. We'd make it to Britannia well before they did.

I should have knocked on wood.

The sand beneath my feet shifted and gave way. What had once been the angled top of a dune was suddenly a sheer drop. I cried out and flailed my arms, but there was nothing to grab onto. I dropped about ten feet and landed on a steep slope. Vallaena and Victoria let go and jumped away so I wouldn't land on them. Jeremiah and Daelissa flew from my arms and rolled down the slope.

I jammed my claws in the sand and managed to stop. The entire section of the dune had collapsed into a pit. And what waited at the bottom of the pit sent chills of terror up my spine—a gaping maw lined with teeth and tentacles.

"Jesus, it's a giant freaking sand worm!" And Daelissa and Jeremiah were rolling right toward it.

Victoria and Vallaena had dug in and slowed their descent. Since they were okay for the moment, I leapt down the slope toward Jeremiah. I landed on my butt, got my feet beneath me, and propelled myself down-hill again.

Unchecked, Jeremiah and Daelissa were rolling faster than I could leap after them.

It's good to be back, Kalesh said. *Life was boring without you.*

"Never a damned dull moment," I said, and launched myself again.

This will work better. Demon wings unfurled from my back and I glided at a steep angle toward the pit.

"Damn. Totally forgot about those." I angled them tight so I could glide faster. Jeremiah was nearly at the maw. I reached out a hand, but just before I reached him, a tentacle yanked him and Daelissa inside.

"No!" Victoria cried out behind me.

I gritted my teeth. "Not today, buddy."

Yes, never a dull moment, Kalesh said, almost to himself.

And then I dove right toward the mouth. A swarm of tentacles came at me. I sliced them to pieces with narrow beams of Brilliance. But when I angled to dive into the mouth, I miscalculated and glanced off the side. A sharp tooth sliced into my back. I crashed into another one jutting from the other side and roared in pain.

I used an old trick and channeled a shield of Murk from my body just in time to block the next tooth. I reached out and grabbed the next one, protected from the razor-sharp edges by the thin shield around my hands. I looked down and saw Jeremiah and Daelissa being pulled by the tentacles into the dark depths of the beast.

The space wasn't quite wide enough to spread my wings, and the teeth were likely to snag them if I tried, so I swung out from the tooth and let myself fall. I narrowly missed hitting Jeremiah and grasped a tooth just below him. A blast of Brilliance sheared off the tentacle holding him. I snagged him by the collar and used my feet to hold him so I could do the same for Daelissa.

You should let her suffer in the belly of the beast, Kalesh said.

I agreed with him, but my conscience put hands on hips and shook its head disapprovingly. I sighed and freed Daelissa. But with her tucked under an arm, climbing the hundred feet or so back to the mouth was going to take forever.

Keeping Jeremiah secure between my thighs, and Daelissa under an arm, I used my other arm to propel me up a few feet where I grabbed another tooth, then washed, rinsed, repeated. My arm began to ache after the tenth time.

"Come on, you can do this." I took a deep breath and launched myself up again.

The wall of teeth quivered, and daylight began to fade. It took a moment for me to realize the mouth was closing. At my current rate, there was no way I'd reach the top before it closed. If I dropped Daelissa, my chances were much improved. But what did that mean for her? Would she be trapped inside this monster for eternity?

She deserves it.

"Yeah, she does." I held her out over the void and let go.

CHAPTER 22

I sent the command to my fingers, but they refused to let go. I tried again, but my fingers held on. That was when I had to admit to myself that no matter how much I thought Daelissa deserved it, I couldn't bring myself to banish her to an eternity of torment. It was like killing someone in cold blood.

Daylight faded to a pinprick and then to black. I expected the neck to constrict and the teeth to start grinding us to a pulp, but nothing else happened. Jeremiah had said this collective was full of superstitious desert tribes. It seemed their superstitions weren't detailed enough to give the sand worms a fully functioning digestive tract.

I channeled a light sphere and sent it above me. Hopefully I could blast open the mouth when I got there, but I had other worries. Were Vallaena and Victoria up there somewhere, and would Mors reach them before I did?

"Think, man, think!" My aching arm told me I'd have to think fast, or it was going to give out soon. Thankfully, I didn't have to think long. I would have face palmed if I'd had a free hand, because the answer should have been obvious.

I channeled a sticky rope of Murk, coiled it around Daelissa, and hung it from a nearby tooth. I did the same for Jeremiah and hung him in place. With my legs and arms free, I vaulted up twenty feet at a time until I reached the top. The inside of the mouth resembled an anus coated in green slime. Like any sphincter, it constricted into a tight circle.

Instead of blasting it open, I channeled a wedge of ultraviolet Murk and rammed it up into the sphincter. It punched through. The walls of teeth quivered violently, but didn't constrict. I twisted the wedge back and forth. Green slime dripped on my face and arms. It didn't look like shit, but it sure smelled like it. With a violent twist, I pried open the mouth. Daylight streamed back inside.

The first thing I saw was Mors floating high above. White-suited ushers huddled at the edge of the crater far above. The next thing I saw were Victoria and Vallaena desperately trying to dig into the loose sand about five feet away. It seemed they were trying to dig a hole to hide in, but the sand kept sliding back in and spoiling their efforts.

There was no way in hell we were going to fight our way free of this crater. But if we stayed outside the worm, Mors would be able to blast us into submission from above. That meant there was only one way to go—down into the belly of the beast.

I pulled myself up over the lip of the mouth. "Victoria, Vallaena, let go."

They looked back at me with surprise.

"Are you serious?" Victoria said.

I nodded. "It won't be pleasant, but it's our only chance."

Vallaena rolled over on her bottom and slid the rest of the way. I caught her and eased her inside.

"Hold onto a tooth," I said, "but be careful. They're sharp."

Mors slashed a beam of energy toward Victoria. She let go and tumbled down the slope. I caught her arm as she slid over the edge. Mors slashed another sizzling beam at me. I fell back to avoid it and dropped into the mouth of the beast.

Victoria and I dropped like rocks through the gap between the sharp teeth. Aside from an initial cry of surprise, she didn't even scream. Emily's mom was definitely made of sterner stuff than most. I flung out a strand of Murk and snagged a tooth, but it snapped off due to our combined weight and momentum. I fired webs from all my fingers and snagged more teeth, but they shattered like porcelain.

We fell past Daelissa and Jeremiah, narrowly missing them.

"You've got to be kidding me!" I resorted to a different tact and stabbed a spear of Murk into the wall. It pierced through the flesh and held. The walls quivered and constricted violently. Shouts and cries from above drew my attention.

Jeremiah and Daelissa were awake, swinging back and forth on their tethers as the giant worm reacted to the stabbing pain on its insides.

"And I thought the stories about you were exaggerated," Victoria said dryly. She gripped a nearby tooth and pulled herself over to it. "Perhaps you should help the others."

Before I could respond, I saw a blonde bombshell falling toward us. Vallaena had apparently decided to jump after us. "Oh, shit!" I reflexively channeled a web of Murk below me, making it as thick as possible, then swung out of the way.

Vallaena flashed past. The web caught her and stretched for an instant before the teeth holding it up snapped off and plummeted into the darkness. A distant thud told me she'd found the bottom the hard way.

I grimaced. "That had to hurt." On the upside, she was already dead. "Are you okay?"

No response.

The sand worm began to tremble even more violently. Grains of sand rained down. At first, I thought Mors was firing inside the beast, but I soon realized he was doing something much worse. Drops of molten sand rained past me. One caught Daelissa on the cheek, drawing a scream of agony.

I channeled a Murk shield above them. There was no time for being gentle, so I willed Daelissa's tether to dissolve. Her scream turned to a shriek as she suddenly dropped. I almost let her freefall, but at the last minute, caught her on a tether and slowed her descent before letting it go. I freed Jeremiah next and did the same.

"Here I go," Victoria said, and jumped.

I gave her the same treatment and hoped I'd given them all enough tether to reach the bottom without breaking their legs. Then I jumped, channeling a tether from the end of my Murk spear. It turned out the bottom of the pit was still a good fifty feet down. I splashed down in pool of thick slime. It cushioned the fall a little, but my legs still ached from the twenty-foot fall.

I threw up a light sphere so I could see the situation.

Vallaena had somehow had the presence of mind to drag herself over to the side so the others wouldn't land on her. She was up to her neck in green goo, so I couldn't see the damage, but the grimace on her face said it all. The others looked shaken but staggered around on their feet.

I sent the light ball high into the worm until I could see the Murk shield. It was cracking under the weight of molten sand. We didn't have much time. I was tired and aching all the way down to my soul bones. I could channel another shield, but I wouldn't be able to hold it up under a ton of sand.

"My skin burns." Daelissa held up a hand. Her ghostly skin was red and swelling.

Victoria shook slime off her hand. "Bloody hell, It's stomach acid."

"Mors is dumping molten sand on us and we're trapped in a pit of slimy acid?" I threw up my hands. "Thank god we finally caught a break."

Jeremiah sagged against a nearby wall. "I suppose now is a bad time to ask where we are?"

"We escaped to Kalifa, but Mors followed us," Vallaena said. She pulled herself upright. "It's a wonder I didn't break my legs."

Victoria began to fill in the blanks about our escape, but I was too engrossed in figuring out what to do next. Being buried for all eternity in the belly of a sand worm wasn't what I'd planned on. Even with my super healing, the slime acid hurt like a bitch. And I was so damn tired I wanted to curl up in a ball and go to sleep.

Think, Justin, think! There were no teeth down here, just fleshy walls coated in slime.

"Why is the stomach at the bottom?" Vallaena said. "Does the worm have no digestive tract?"

I channeled a circle of Murk in the middle of the slime and widened it to clear away the center. There was nothing but purplish flesh beneath it. "It's just a poorly imagined monster," I said. There was no escaping through the worm's poop chute, so it seemed I'd have to improvise.

Drawing upon my reserves of energy, I channeled as much Brilliance as possible and unleashed it on the wall. It bored through the worm's flesh and melted through the sand on the other side. The giant worm trembled and shook as if in pain. I wasn't sure if I should feel bad or not.

Molten silica hissed as it flowed into the green slime. The others backed up to the far side of the stomach to get away from it. I kept firing until my energy fizzled out. I dropped to a knee, unable to stand upright. Vallaena and Victoria each grabbed me by an arm and dragged me away from the molten slag. A loud cracking from above told me our time had run out.

The slime and melted sand near my makeshift tunnel had congealed into a slab. Jeremiah touched it. "It's still very hot, but we'll have to endure it."

Victoria hoisted me out of the slime and onto the glassy slab. It was searing hot, but nothing compared to what Mors had done to me. The others followed, and Victoria dragged me along behind her. The glassy walls of the makeshift tunnel were still glowing orange, but we went inside. The half-dried slag cracked beneath our feet. The heat penetrated the soles of my shoes and began to melt them.

A massive slab of dirty glass crashed into the worm's belly behind us, followed by an avalanche of sand until it filled up past the opening of our tunnel. Miraculously only a small section of the wall in our cylindrical refuge cracked. Apparently, the heat from my magic had created a wall of glass thick enough to give it structural support.

On the downside, it was hot as an oven since the walls still glowed with heat. As they cooled, the light faded until we stood in sweltering darkness.

"Well, thank you for the rescue," Jeremiah said. "I suppose being buried down here is preferable to eternal torture."

Victoria barked a laugh. "I believe you're right."

I was too tired to summon a light sphere. The walls were uncomfortably warm, but they couldn't really hurt my soul body, so I lay down to rest. When my eyes blinked open, I was in the loft. Kalesh sat on the bed, a wide grin on his face.

"I didn't mean to come here," I said.

Kalesh nodded. "I have news, so I brought us here."

I blinked. "How in the world did you bring us here?"

"You're tired, so it was easy." His grin faded. "You're not mad, are you?"

I shook my head and walked over to the window. "I'm just glad you're on this side of the street now." I frowned. "There's no problem crossing back and forth?"

He shook his head. "Not anymore. Whatever you did opened the barrier."

My skin looked normal here, not translucent and ghostly. "What news do you have?"

"I found Kassallandra and told her you are alive." Kalesh flashed another grin. "She's going to tell the others about the plan to reach the birthing chamber."

"Dude, that's awesome!" I clapped him on the back. "I was worried they'd pull the plug on me."

"We still don't have much time." His grin faded. "I'm holding onto the body, but without a soul, it's getting weaker."

I grimaced. "Being buried a hundred feet underground doesn't help. I don't have a clue how to get out of this mess."

"Yes, that's a problem." He tapped a finger on his chin. "I don't know."

It was really odd how his speech patterns and gestures were becoming so much like mine. He'd been practically mindless at one time, stalking in the back of my mind like a mass murderer who only wanted to destroy. He'd evolved to speaking, though awkwardly, and now he looked just like a blue version of me with tiny little horns.

"Is Dad still over at your place?" I asked.

He shook his head. "Dad is trying to find out what Baal is up to. He said there are rumors that other overlords have gone missing."

I quirked an eyebrow. "Missing?"

Kalesh nodded. "Apparently, when Domathus failed to manifest in Eden all those years ago, it weakened him, and Baal devoured him. Dad thinks he might be killing off the competition in preparation for his grand finale."

"Oh, shit." I shuddered. "He must be really close to finishing the statue of Saila. We've got to get to the primal fount fast."

"I wish I knew how." Kalesh walked over to the window. "Since I can come over here, I wonder if you can go over there now."

My forehead scrunched. "Dude, that would be awesome." I climbed onto the bridge and began to walk. Kalesh stepped out behind me. This time, there was no resistance at all. I made it to the center in a few strides and stepped across. The distant wails of the soul storm reached my ears, but I didn't care. I reached the opposite window and stepped through.

A tremor ran through me, vibrating every molecule of my being. I shouted in alarm, but it was over nearly as quickly as it began. I touched myself to confirm I wasn't about to fly apart at the seams, but I seemed to be intact. "That was strange."

"You vibrated." Kalesh poked my shoulder. "Can you feel that?"

I nodded. "Yes."

"Then you're okay."

I took in my surroundings—an apartment similar to the loft across the street. I walked to the only door. "What's out there?"

"Haedaemos," Kalesh said.

"You think it's safe to look?"

He shrugged. "You're projecting your consciousness from your soul body over here, so the worst that can happen is you'll lose your mind."

I laughed. "Already lost it a long time ago." I bit my lower lip. Twisted the doorknob and opened the door. Outside I found a wide circular platform suspended in darkness. Stairs sprouted from all sides, some running straight up or down, some twisting back and forth, and others spiraling up or down in a corkscrew pattern. Just when my eyes adjusted to the confusing maze, the stairs undulated through random patterns and repositioned themselves.

Kalesh stood next to me. "Welcome to Bedlam."

"Bedlam?" I tried to trace the destination of a set of stairs and lost track of it. "I can't make sense of anything."

"Some parts of Haedaemos mirror Eden or other realms," Kalesh said. "Other areas are afterimages of cities destroyed in the Sundering."

"Like Juranthemon," I said.

He nodded. "But this area never stays the same. Only spirits with strong minds can travel the ever-changing maze. It's a good place to avoid lesser demons and hide yourself from greater dangers."

I looked back at the apartment door. "Why hasn't that changed?"

"There are pockets that remain the same." He shrugged. "It's a nice quiet place to live."

It wasn't exactly quiet with the stairs grinding around, but I certainly didn't see any neighbors. "How do we get to Haedaemos proper? I want to see it."

"Perhaps another time." Kalesh clapped my back. "We need to rest and figure out how to unbury ourselves."

I sighed. "Yeah, you're probably right." I took one last look around then went back through the door. "I kind of wish Dad was here right now."

Kalesh nodded. "He would be really happy to know that we reconnected."

I tried to release my lucid dream state, but my body bounced back as if I'd just hit a wall. I tried again and stumbled back from another invisible blow.

I was trapped on the astral plane.

CHAPTER 23

"I can't stop projecting!" I said.

Kalesh frowned. "Maybe you have to be back in the afterlife."

I blinked stupidly. "Oh. I think you're right."

As I climbed out of the window, my entire body vibrated as it had when I'd come through. Once the unpleasant sensation ended, everything felt normal again. "I vibrated again. Something about me seems to change when I cross to the other side."

Kalesh nodded. "The physics are different here. In the afterlife you're a soul. In Haedaemos, you're a ghost."

"At this point anything sounds reasonable." I walked across the bridge to my window and climbed inside.

Kalesh came in after me. "I wonder why I don't get the vibration when I cross over."

"No freaking telling." I scoffed. "I miss normal physics. Haedaemos and the afterlife are really screwing with my head."

He blew out a breath. "Am I a ghost here or still a spirit?"

I'd tried not to think about it too much because it didn't make sense. "Wish I knew."

"When we manifest, did you notice that our clothes don't tear, they just stretch?" he said. "But when you walked on the cooling sand, the soles began to melt."

"It's almost like cartoon logic," I said. "It's like some parts are really well thought out, and other parts are just movie props."

"That's a good analogy," Kalesh said. "The sandworm has tentacles and sharp teeth and is a hundred feet long, but there's nothing inside it except a pit of acid."

I shrugged. "What do you expect? The realities of collectives are literally projections of people's subconscious thoughts and fears. People aren't logical when it comes to things they fear."

"So how do we bypass their physics?" he said. "There must be a way."

"It'd require overcoming the subconscious fears of hundreds or thousands of people." I took in a deep breath. "I don't know if that's possible."

"If we sprouted angel wings and flew around, people would think we're a god." Kalesh grinned. "We could change hearts and minds."

I snorted. "Threaten to burn them if they don't bow down?"

"Exactly!"

"I'll keep that in mind." I clapped him on the back. "I'm going to actually sleep. I'll see you later."

He nodded. "Rest well."

I let go of the lucid dream and the world flicked away.

Sometime later, I woke up in stifling heat and darkness and wished I could go back to dreaming again. I channeled a tiny sphere of light and was happy to note that I didn't feel exhausted anymore. Despite the conditions in this literal hellhole, I'd managed to rest. I brightened the light to reveal the others and found Daelissa's ghostly blue eyes staring at me. The others were asleep.

Her soul body looked like a living body, except the skin was translucent, the colors were slightly washed out, and the insides sparkled. The gray dress she wore looked as normal as what I'd find in the living world.

"Why are you looking at me?" she said.

I blinked. "Why are you looking at me?"

"I did not realize I was," she said. "The light blinded me."

"I'm just trying to figure out why our clothes didn't vanish or change when we entered a different collective," I said.

Daelissa looked down at her dress. "I don't know. I try not to think about it, for being dead is even more confusing and miserable than being alive."

"On that we can agree." I sighed and tried not to think about why we hadn't run out of oxygen yet. For that matter, did I even need to breathe anymore? I stopped breathing. I no longer had lungs, a heart, or anything that required oxygen, so I didn't even feel the urge. I wondered if I could sigh dramatically without breathing, but that only took my mind back to the inconsistent physics of this place.

I sent the light ball drifting over to the mouth of the tunnel and examined the rubble blocking it. Unless Mors had completely packed the worm with sand, it might be the shallowest place to burrow our way free. Even so, it would be incredibly difficult. All that glass and sand had to go somewhere, and we didn't have much room in here.

Physically digging through the barrier might be our best bet. Digging through sand with my demon claws wouldn't be a problem, but I had to get through all the glassy chunks first. I really wished Adam was around to map out the physics, because I didn't want to end up trapped and buried. I was the only one with powers and the others couldn't help me if I messed up.

Which brought up another question—could I help the others reconnect with their powers?

I didn't understand how Vallaena and Jeremiah, both thousands of years old and wise, couldn't have figured it out by now. Then again, maybe they'd been alive for so long that maybe their minds weren't as flexible and accepting of such an alien reality.

Somehow, I had to help them bridge the gap. If they reconnected with their powers, escaping would be a hell of a lot easier. And having Vallaena's demon strength would take a load off of me. Heavenly and Kalifa wouldn't be the last dangerous collectives we had to traverse before reaching the core.

First of all, I needed to do something about the miserable temperature. I channeled a fine mist of Murk around the cave. The force of creation was naturally cold, so I used it to drain the heat until it was nice and comfortable.

Daelissa's lips peeled back in horror. She tried to back as far away from the mist as possible, but I made sure it covered her from head to toe.

"Why are you so afraid of Murk?" I said.

She shuddered. "The darkness is foul. The light is pure and sweet."

I scoffed. "Man, I thought Clarity would have made you see how stupid that is." I channeled an orb of Murk in my left hand, and Brilliance in my right. "Neither is inherently bad. One destroys, the other creates." I wove them into a gray sphere. "Together, they form balance and Stasis."

Daelissa squeezed her eyes shut. "The darkness is a taint on the soul."

I made a raspberry. "Maybe I should blast you with Clarity again so you can see just how wrong and stupid you are."

She tried to make herself even smaller. "Please, no!"

I shook my head. "Clarity might have shown you how awful you were, but it didn't make you a better person."

"I am beyond redemption." Tears trickled down her cheeks. "Because of you, I can never forget the evil I've done."

I smirked. "Well, my job here is done." During the war, I'd rarely had a chance to talk to Daelissa, primarily because she was too busy trying to kill me. Her motivations had been pretty simple—reclaiming Eden so she'd have a limitless supply of human souls to drain. So now that I could talk to her all I wanted, there was nothing I wanted to ask her. She'd been an awful person who wanted to do awful things for no compelling reason.

But threatening her had given me a great idea. I nudged Vallaena. It took a few tries before she finally woke up. Her legs were bruised and swollen from the long fall. Even the glittery stuff inside her soul body looked black and blue.

She blinked as if trying to focus on me. "Yes, nephew?"

"We need to get your powers back."

Wincing, she pushed herself into a sitting position. "How?"

"You need to see past your old perceptions and see the afterlife for what it truly is." I held out a hand. "This isn't flesh. It's a different body filled with glitter."

Vallaena's forehead pinched. "Glitter?"

"Well, sparkly energy." I shrugged. "You need to use meditation to see the truth. You lived a physical life for thousands of years, so overcoming perception might be harder for you than it was for me."

"How does this help me recover my powers?" she said.

"Because your false perceptions are blocking you."

She nodded. "I will try."

"Close your eyes and meditate on seeing the real afterlife," I said. "Don't let your mind fool you anymore."

Jeremiah sat up with a groan. "That's the trick?"

I nodded. "You have to see the Matrix."

He blinked.

"Sorry, bad reference." I held up my hand and wiggled my fingers. "Your mind thinks it's still in a physical body and that's why it can't connect to magic."

"I don't do magic," Victoria said. "I'm not like my daughter."

"Maybe you're more like her than you think," I said. "Eve might have culled your powers when you were a baby, but somehow you still have premonitions and Emily is practically a demi-goddess now."

Victoria nodded. "Emily thinks that when power auras are removed, they might eventually grow back. Perhaps after so many years, mine began to regrow."

If that was true, it presented a troubling problem. Xanos was still alive, and we definitely didn't want her powers growing back. I put that on my long checklist of things to consider when and if I made it back to the land of the living. "Regardless, you need to enlighten yourself too."

Daelissa watched us from the other side of the cave. She was too unstable mentally to enlighten herself, and that was exactly how I wanted it. Given time, she'd return to her old ways and terrorize the afterlife. Before I left this place, I needed to take care of her permanently. I just had to figure out how.

My three pupils began meditating. Victoria had been an Exorcist and a Templar and had excellent control over her mind. Emily hadn't told me a lot about her mother, but in the short time I'd known her, she'd impressed the hell out of me.

About an hour into the exercise, Victoria stared at me and gasped. "This is what souls look like?"

Jeremiah groaned. "I feel like quite the fool, because I'm not even close to enlightenment."

"I cannot do it either," Vallaena said. "I don't understand. I have so much experience, it should be no problem."

"You both spent thousands of years in physical bodies. That vast experience is holding you back." I grinned at Victoria. "I'm not surprised you figured it out first."

"I feel so light and airy." Victoria traced a finger along her arm. "What are we made of?"

"I have no idea," I said. "But it looks pretty cool."

She nodded. "It's beautiful."

I turned back to Jeremiah and Vallaena. "Keep trying. I need at least one of you to regain your powers if we're going to get out of this place."

Despite their ancient ages, they looked as ashamed as scolded children.

Time ticked on. At long last, Vallaena blinked her eyes open and stared at her hands.

I pumped a fist. "You did it!"

She buried her face in her hands and began to cry. "No, I am not even close! Death has reduced me to nothing but a pale shadow."

I grimaced and rubbed her back. "Hey, it's okay." I almost told her that she was starting to sound like Daelissa but decided that was probably the worst thing I could do.

Jeremiah shook his head. "I'm sorry, son. We've failed you."

It looked like I had no choice but to resort to the nuclear option and pray it actually worked. "I didn't want to have to do this, but I've got to try."

He raised an eyebrow. "Try what?"

"Clarity."

Jeremiah shook his head. "No, I don't think so. Son, the last thing I want is to see myself for what I truly am." He glanced at Daelissa. "I don't want to end up like her."

"It's not like you drained thousands of souls or anything." I shrugged. "You saved humanity back in your Moses days, then built Arcane University and the Overworld as Ezzek Moore. There's no way you'll end up like Daelissa."

"I don't know, son." He bit his lower lip. "There's no guarantee it'll help me see past my ingrained perceptions and no guarantee it won't make me regret ever existing."

Vallaena tried to rise, but her injured legs wouldn't respond. "I will do it. I have few regrets in life even if I haven't always made the right decisions."

I patted her shoulder. "Okay, then. Let's hope it works."

Weaving Clarity wasn't difficult, but it was draining. I'd used it to track portal scars in our search for Emily Glass. That adventure had taken us across several realms and nearly gotten us killed. Zapping Vallaena with a bit of Clarity hopefully wouldn't be too exhausting.

I channeled Brilliance and Murk through my opposing index fingers and wove them into a small orb of gray Stasis. Then I fired Murk and Brilliance from my eyes and into the Stasis. I heard a gasp from behind me—probably Daelissa. A clear beam rippled from the other side of Stasis and struck Vallaena in the chest.

Her head flew back, eyes wide, mouth frozen open in a silent scream. I cut off the flow immediately, but she remained locked in place, catatonic.

"Uh-oh." I snapped my fingers in front of her, but she didn't so much as blink. "Shit. I think I broke her."

"This is what I was afraid of," Jeremiah said. "To be exposed to every decision you've made over thousands of years is simply too much for the mind to handle."

I touched Vallaena's forehead. It felt cool. The sparkly stuff in her soul body swirled slowly, as if stirred by an invisible spoon. Otherwise, she seemed to be frozen like a statue.

Victoria held the other woman's hand. "You're okay, Vallaena. We're with you. Whatever you see can't harm you." She shivered. "Oh, that feels strange."

"What does?" I took Vallaena's other hand but felt nothing. "What's strange?"

"I saw something and smelled sulfur." She frowned. "It's like I saw something inside her."

"Just like how Emily sees auras?" I said.

Victoria nodded. She reached out and tentatively touched me. Flinched back. "That was bloody intense."

"What did you see?" I said.

"Too much to make sense of. I smelled sulfur and saw a great burning orb." She bit her lower lip. "But there was something else in the background, almost as if it was there, but not part of you."

I frowned. "I wonder if it's the Apocryphan aura." I hadn't given it much thought and hadn't sensed it since regaining my other powers.

"I wouldn't know," Victoria said. "I've never sensed such things before."

"Maybe you've always had more power than you thought," I said. "But whatever Eve did to you as a baby kept you from using it."

"Perhaps she muted my powers but didn't remove them." Victoria shook her head. "Whatever the case, it's rather unsettling."

"You smelled sulfur when you touched Vallaena?" I said. "Maybe she's reconnected to her powers again."

"Perhaps." Victoria put a hand on the other woman's cheek. "But I pray you haven't broken her mind."

We watched in silence for a moment, but nothing changed. My stomach clenched and roiled at the thought that I'd completely mind-fucked my aunt. Dad wasn't going to be happy to hear that. Or maybe he'd think it was the funniest thing ever.

Either way, it seemed we weren't getting out of this pit anytime soon.

CHAPTER 24

"Can you use magic like Emily does?" I asked Victoria.

"You mean blow up things?" She held out her hands and narrowed her eyes in concentration. A moment later she shook her head. "If I can, I don't know how to."

"Can you reactivate my Apocryphan powers?" I didn't know if using them could potentially damage my soul as it had my body, but I was willing to take the chance.

Victoria touched me and closed her eyes. She remained still for quite some time before shaking her head again. "I can almost reach out and touch it, but that's it."

I sighed. "Yeah, I can't expect you to learn everything in five minutes."

Jeremiah took Vallaena's hands and stared into her unblinking eyes. "I'm rather fond of your aunt. I hope you haven't destroyed her."

"Fond?" I grimaced. "Like in what way?" In his current form, he looked like a middle-aged man, but I still remembered him as a genteel old coot.

He sighed. "That's certainly none of your business, son."

I didn't know what to think about that, so I decided to think about more important things—like escape.

I paced back and forth. Daelissa shrank away from me anytime I came near, but I just ignored her. Daelissa had been thousands of years old when I hit her with Clarity and she'd responded instantly. Then again, she'd died pretty fast too. No one else had frozen like Vallaena, so what was the deal?

I wished I could read her mind, but that wasn't part of my skillset. So I tried the next best thing. I shifted into demon vision. Oddly, nothing changed. The only indication I'd done something was the pulsing power of nearby leylines and clouds of aether drifting nearby. The halo of light I'd seen around people in the living world was their soul shining through. We didn't have physical bodies anymore, so I was always looking at their soul.

I reached out with a tendril of soul essence and latched onto Vallaena. Most of the time, a mix of emotions hit me when I first connected, but in this case, it was something much different. There was no fear, no anger, or sadness. Just calm contentment.

What the hell?

There wasn't anything wrong with Vallaena. If anything, she'd found Nirvana. To feel that level of contentment was nearly impossible. I wondered if it might be best to just leave her there.

Jeremiah frowned. "What is it, Justin?"

"I think—" I blew out a breath and looked at him. "I think she's found peace."

"Oh?" He smoothed back her long blonde hair. "She's happy?"

"Happy and perfectly content." I shook my head. "I've never felt this emotion coming from someone I've connected with. Being content is probably the hardest emotion to achieve for a human."

"So she simply doesn't want to wake up?" Victoria asked.

I shrugged. "She might be stuck in a loop, or she just might not want to leave her happy place."

Daelissa crawled over to Vallaena on all fours. Tears sparkled down her cheeks. "I have never felt contentment, and I never will." She began to sob. "She is demon spawn, the lowest of the low!" Her sobs rose to a scream. "It's not right!" Before I could react, she slapped Vallaena hard across the cheek. Then she lunged and gripped Vallaena's throat.

My aunt toppled over to the side, eyes still wide, mouth open.

"You stupid bitch!" I reached for her, but Victoria beat me to the punch.

Victoria yanked Daelissa back by the dress and punched her square in the nose. The Seraphim tumbled backward and landed in a heap against the back wall. She curled into a ball and began sobbing like a child.

My mouth hung open. "Wow, you're packing some heat."

Victoria looked at her fist as if surprised. "I've never hit that hard in my life. Perhaps I do have a bit more power than I thought."

I regarded Vallaena for a moment, unsure what to do. As much as I hated to disrupt her peace, I needed her. I hoped she didn't hate me for what I was about to do. I reached out with a tendril of my essence and tapped into her aura. Then I let my emotions flow through the bond.

Vallaena gasped and jerked upright. She looked up at me with wide eyes, tears trickling down her cheeks. Her gaze settled on the tendril connecting us. "You brought me back."

"You have your demon powers?" I said.

Her face burned red and a shudder of anger ran through her body. "Perfection was in my grasp and you brought me back!"

I held up my hands defensively and backed up to the wall. "I'm sorry. I need you, Vallaena."

"All my life I did my duty." She wiped tears from her cheeks. "I lived for everyone else so I might be a good daughter for Baal. So the Daemos would become a viable race. So I might defeat evil and preserve Eden."

"You are the most honorable person I know, Aunt Vallaena." I was afraid to touch her. "I'm so sorry I brought you back. But we need you."

Her chin trembled, but this time it seemed with sadness rather than rage. "My moment of clarity was reward enough." Vallaena sagged. "But you are right. I can't think of myself now or ever. Even in death I must do everything I can to preserve what we fought and died for."

It was a bit melodramatic, but Vallaena didn't play games. She did her duty and expected the same of everyone else. I hadn't appreciated that about her when we first met, or even given it much thought during her life. If anyone deserved to rest in peace, it was her. And yet, she'd accepted her brief reward and was ready to keep on going even after sacrificing her life all those years ago.

I swallowed a lump in my throat and hugged her. She leaned her head on my shoulder and sagged.

"I'm proud of you, Aunt Vallaena." I squeezed her tight, then backed away. "I don't think I ever told you how much I looked up to you and how much you helped me. You're a rare soul and that's why I still need you."

Vallaena smiled and wiped her eyes. "Then I will see you through to the ends of the afterlife if I must, nephew."

I still felt horrible about it. "Thank you."

Daelissa's sobs nearly drowned out our precious moment. I resisted the urge to seal her mouth with magic.

Sharp black claws extended from Vallaena's fingers. She manifested into a slightly larger blue form, then shrank back to normal. A delighted smile flashed across her face. "I'm myself again." She shivered. "It's almost as good as being alive."

Jeremiah seemed entranced by her happiness. He blinked as if surprised and a little ashamed. "It seems Clarity does the trick."

I raised an eyebrow. "Your turn?"

He grimaced. "I am not the perfect being like your aunt, son. I fear facing the absolute truth about myself will end my sanity."

Vallaena scoffed. "I'm far from perfect, old man. If you wish for us to succeed, then you will do it."

Jeremiah swallowed hard. Took a deep breath and blew it out slowly. "Very well. Proceed." He took Vallaena's hand and squeezed it. "You are a remarkable woman." He let go and looked away uneasily. "I felt the need to say that in case I'm not right in the head afterward."

Vallaena kissed him on the cheek. "You were a good man when I met you during the first war against Daelissa, and just as good during the second. You'll be fine."

Jeremiah's forehead pinched in momentary confusion. "Yes, I suppose we have known each other a very long time."

It was amazing to think that their history went all the way back to the First Seraphim War. I imagined there'd been a lengthy gap between then and the second war, but it was still impressive.

I wove a ball of Stasis. "Ready?"

Jeremiah backed up. Nodded.

A narrow beam of Clarity rippled from the Stasis and struck Jeremiah in the chest. His gaze went distant. Then he blinked before I even stopped channeling Clarity. I released the weave and gave him a once-over. "Are you still sane?"

Jeremiah scoffed. "I'm a sane fool." He shook his head. "All those centuries wasted on pettiness. All that time I could have ended Daelissa before she regained her powers and threatened Eden. But I was too caught up in my own foolish ways."

"Well, if that's all it showed you, then you got off rather well," Victoria said. "Has the foolish man regained his powers?"

Jeremiah stared at his hands and grunted. "It was like having a façade peeled away to reveal the truth." Energy crackled from one finger to another. "I see us for what we are and can once again sense the primal fount."

"Then it's time to bust out of here." I held out a fist. "Wonder Twin powers, activate!"

Jeremiah's forehead pinched into a V, but he gingerly held out a fist and bumped mine. "Like so?"

Vallaena laughed. "Yes, like so, old man."

Victoria cleared her throat. "Levity aside, how do you propose we dig our way out without collapsing our little cave?"

"We tunnel diagonally up and into the sandworm," Vallaena said. "Then we climb out."

"And beat Mors to a bloody pulp." Victoria punched a fist into the palm of the other hand. "Retribution."

"Autobots, roll out!" I surged into demon form and flashed my claws.

Vallaena surged taller, her ghost form instantly shifting into a blue demon as I had. Long, red claws emerged from her fingertips.

I hadn't realized I could customize the color of my claws, but figured it wasn't really that important right now. I formed a shield of Murk around my fists and hers and we began pounding through the blocks of glass, turning them into rubble that would be easier to dig through. Then we dug up at an angle, while Jeremiah used his magic to shift sand and glass to the back of the cave.

As the cave began to fill, Daelissa had to abandon her pity party in the corner, scooting closer to us slowly but surely.

Victoria frowned. "I sense someone above us."

I raised an eyebrow. "You can sense people now?"

"It's the power I sense—the aura." She shook her head. "I think it's Mors."

"He is far more powerful than us," Jeremiah said. "We should avoid him at all costs."

I wanted nothing more than to punch that bastard's head off, but Jeremiah was right.

Vallaena slid out of the hole we'd dug. "I reached the top. The sand extends for about twenty feet up. We'll have to climb the teeth the rest of the way."

"Where Mors can blast us into submission," I said. "There's no way in hell I'm giving him free shots at us."

"He won't expect all of us to have powers," Jeremiah said. "Provided you can distract him long enough for us to get out."

I grimaced. "Yeah, that's the trick, isn't it?" If I could access the Apocryphan powers, then I could fly out. But I couldn't activate the aura and neither could Victoria. If Mors hadn't been sucking down souls for years, I could probably take him on solo, but the dude was seriously roided up and I didn't even think all of us could take him on.

I leaned against a wall and shrank down to normal size. "If Mors takes us down, he'll drain our souls. "

"What makes you think he can handle all of us?" Victoria said.

"You haven't seen him for what he is yet," I said. "Once you see his ghost form, you'll understand."

"He is brilliant with soul essence," Daelissa said in a tiny voice. "Drunk with power."

Jeremiah nodded soberly. "Mors deals in brute force. Perhaps we could turn that against him."

Vallaena looked at me. "Perhaps you should hit Mors with Clarity."

I tapped a finger on my chin. "Maybe you're right. Let's show him what a jackass he really is."

"But can you channel it before he strikes?" Jeremiah said.

That was a good question. "We need to climb eighty feet of sandworm teeth just to reach the mouth which is at the bottom of a steeply angled pit. Mors will have the high ground advantage. I know I don't have to remind you what happened to Anakin Skywalker when he attacked Ben Kenobi uphill."

They frowned and shook their heads.

"Who?" Victoria said.

I waved it off. "Bottom line is that we can't go back up the worm. We've got to find another way out."

Jeremiah looked around as if illustrating the obvious. "Unless I'm missing something, there is no other way out."

"We could wait him out," Victoria said. "Surely, he'll become bored and assume we're trapped for eternity."

I shook my head. "Mors has us cornered, but he's not leaving without my soul. With my powers, I'm too dangerous to him." There was no more room to pace since we'd filled the cave with sand and rubble, so I remained leaning against the wall. We couldn't very well dig in other directions. The sand was damp at these depths, but it still wasn't stable enough to tunnel through.

I imagined digging diagonally up for a hundred feet or more to reach the surface, using the worm to hold all the dislodged sand. It might work, but it'd take a long time.

But then it hit me. We had the perfect avenue to escape and it wasn't nearly as far away. I just had to remember how to find it.

CHAPTER 25

I couldn't hide my excitement. "When we entered Kalifa, we ran south along the border." I tried to get my bearings but tumbling into the worm pit had scrambled my sense of direction. "We're literally twenty feet away from the seam between collectives. I just don't know which direction it is."

"And we won't know until we cross the border," Jeremiah said. "The collectives appear to go on forever from the inside."

I closed my eyes and replayed the events in my mind. We'd entered Kalifa, turned south, and run up a dune. Once Mors and pals showed up, things had become a little chaotic. I'd turned back south again, but then the ridge of the dune had fallen away, and I'd tumbled into the worm pit.

The only way to figure it out for sure was to climb up the worm and look for the ridge I'd fallen down. But if Mors saw me poke my head out, he'd know for sure we were alive. If it was up to me, I'd like to escape and let him sit up there for the next hundred years waiting on me.

"Jeremiah, can you cloak me?" I said.

He nodded. "Of course, but I'll need to be fairly close to maintain the spell."

"I need to climb to the top of the worm and look around." I bit the inside of my lip. "You could ride on my back."

He snorted. "Son, I have magic again. I can climb on my own."

"Oh, yeah." I gave him a sheepish smile. "Guess you're right."

I looked down at Daelissa's huddled form and wondered if it was best to just leave her here to rot. She'd been nothing but a drag on the group and probably deserved it. And yet, I'd saved her from dropping into the pit in the first place. I still didn't understand my motivations for leaping to her rescue. I just hated the thought of anyone being eaten by a giant worm. In the end, it turned out that the worm wasn't much of a threat.

Victoria seemed to read my mind. "You want to leave her here?"

I sighed. Shook my head. "I'll leave that up to her." I nodded toward the tunnel. "Let's get out of here."

Vallaena went first, followed by Victoria and Jeremiah. I walked to the tunnel and looked back at Daelissa. She stared up at me with miserable eyes. I thought about sneering. About saying something nasty so she'd want to stay here. But when I looked at this miserable angel, all I could see was her sweet twin sister, Nightliss.

My mind flashed back to the last time I'd seen Daelissa alive. To that last moment at the end of the battle. So instead of being nasty, I gave her something to think about. "I'll never forget what you said to me in that final moment, Daelissa."

"Neither will I." Her lips trembled. "I was lost, but you found me."

I knelt next to her. "It looks to me as if you're still lost, Daelissa. And you'll stay lost if all you do is feel sorry for yourself."

Tears trickled down her ghostly cheeks. "In that moment, I felt the touch of salvation." She looked away. "But when I close my eyes, I see the faces of the dead staring back."

It was what she deserved, but I didn't rub it in. "Despite everything you did to her over the centuries, Nightliss was devastated when you died."

"She mourned me?" Daelissa said.

I nodded. "Even though you nearly killed her time and time again." I smiled at the thought of my sweet friend. "She's too good for any of us."

"I know." Daelissa's lips trembled. "I see that now. That is why I deserve this torment." She gripped my arms. "Why do you bother telling me such things, nemesis of mine? Let your hatred of me fill your heart with joy, for I am reduced to less than a shadow, filled with countless regrets. Let me suffer in peace and go."

I nodded and stood. Went to the tunnel and paused. "Maybe you can take solace that at least one person in this universe truly loves you no matter how awful you were."

"Naelissa," she said in a quiet voice.

That was Nightliss's given name—one she'd abandoned to separate herself from her mother, Kaelissa, and her crazy sister. "She despised what you did but loved her lost sister." I let that hang in the air a moment. "I'm sorry you're too filled with selfish pity to love anything."

Then I turned and climbed up the tunnel.

"Are we rid of her?" Vallaena said when I rejoined the others.

I nodded. "She's made her choice." I took a deep, albeit unnecessary breath, and rubbed my hands together. "Let's do this."

I manifested into demon form and began climbing the gauntlet of spiky teeth toward the distant light at the top. I looked back and saw Jeremiah floating up behind me. "Maybe I'm doing this wrong."

He shrugged. "Whatever suits you, young man."

I rolled my eyes and kept climbing. "Why do you avoid using my name, old man?"

Jeremiah remained silent a moment. "I suppose it's a character flaw." He shrugged. "I avoid familiarity."

I shot a grin over my shoulder. "You got pretty familiar with my aunt when I almost broke her."

His ascent faltered, and he reached out a hand to steady himself on a nearby tooth. "Ordinarily, I would deny this, but my brief dose of Clarity seems to have made me a bit more forthcoming than I'm usually comfortable with."

I waited for him to continue but had to prod him. "And?"

He cleared his throat. "I have grown close to your aunt during the last few years."

"Dude, you're dead, so just give it up." I shook my head. "You dig Vallaena."

Jeremiah cleared his throat again. "Now really isn't the time to talk about such things."

I wanted to disagree, but we were nearing the top and I didn't want to give away our position with unnecessary chatter. So I nodded. "Cloaking time?"

"Yes." Jeremiah flicked his fingers through a pattern and the air above me rippled. "No one will see you so long as they don't look too closely." He hovered in place. "I can maintain it from here."

I deftly climbed up the last few teeth and reached the rim of the mouth. The lips and most of the flesh were burned away at the top thanks to Mors's gentle ministrations. Even without poking my head out of the hole, I spotted a ring of white-suited ushers around the top of the pit. I remained a foot below the edge of the mouth and climbed around the inside so I could see in all directions.

Mors stood at the highest point above the pit. I stared at it until I was positive it was the ridge I'd been running along before falling into the pit. It didn't perfectly parallel the border of the collective, but it was close enough. I got my bearings and descended back into the worm.

"Figured it out?" Jeremiah said.

I nodded. "Let's get out of here."

The others looked at me expectantly when we reached the bottom. I jabbed a finger to my left. "This way out."

Vallaena smiled. "We'll escape and Mors will be none the wiser."

I studied the fleshy wall for a moment. "Might be best if I burn a hole instead of digging. The glass might provide some stability to the tunnel." I climbed a few feet up, turned, and traced a circle in the flesh on the opposite side with a narrow beam of Brilliance. The worm writhed and shuddered violently. Sand rained down from above and I nearly lost my footing.

"How in the hell is this thing still alive?" I said.

Jeremiah looked up past me. "I wonder if that got anyone's attention."

I peered at the distant mouth and waited to see if the commotion caused a reaction. A minute or so ticked past, but I didn't see anything. I increased the power of my beam and quickly sliced the flesh again. The worm shook again. Tracing a neat hole with that thing moving so much was like trying to put on lipstick while riding a rollercoaster.

Once the tremors died down, I yanked the severed slab of worm flesh with a thread of Murk and lowered it to the pile of debris below. Then I channeled a wide beam of destruction and began burrowing into the sand. Streams of red-hot glass flowed down the flesh and into the pit, drawing even more violent reactions from the worm.

The others stayed on the far side of the pit away from the superheated liquid, hanging onto whatever they could to remain on their feet as the worm continued its dance of pain. The sand seemed endless, but about thirty feet in, my burrowing beam stopped melting sand. It seemed to splash off of it without any effect whatsoever.

I sent jets of cold Murk into the tunnel and the sand cooled to an amorphous solid within seconds. "I think it's done." I climbed over from my perch and pulled myself into what I hoped was our escape route. I scrambled through the hole on all fours until I reached what looked like a dead end. When I reached out to touch it, my hand went through as if it were illusion. I hesitantly poked my head through and saw dark void on the other side.

"We're through!" I crawled back to the entrance. "Come on up!"

The others joined me, and we crawled to freedom. Vallaena came through last. I poked my hand back across the invisible barrier and expected to feel the inside of the tunnel. But all I felt was open air. I stepped back across and was surprised to find myself back on the surface of the desert. A dozen ushers stood twenty feet away from me, their backs to me. I leapt back into the seam.

"What's wrong?" Victoria asked.

"Apparently, stepping into the void resets your position." Making sense of this place was impossible, but I tried anyway. "So if you're underground in a collective and you leave it, you're back to zero on the Y axis." I frowned. "It's like leaving a holodeck."

That reference earned me more blank stares. I really missed Shelton and Adam.

"Which way now?" Victoria said. "Back to Britannia, or onward and upward?"

I wanted to press onward. My body could die at any time and I'd be stuck here for good. But my conscience locked my legs in place. Mors had an entire collective of souls under his control, and an army ready to claim even more at his disposal. With his powers, it seemed likely he could wreak havoc in the afterlife if no one stopped him.

Britannia and the death chamber would be his first conquest, and all incoming souls would be subject to his rule. How many souls would he enslave? How many more would be drained? No one deserved an eternity like that except Mors.

"I don't think we can go yet," I said.

Vallaena met my gaze and nodded. "Duty first."

"Oh, bloody hell." Victoria sighed. "We're going to fight Mors after you just said he's too powerful for us to fight?"

"We can't just leave him free to drain souls," I said.

"Justin is correct," Jeremiah said. "Leaving a maniac like Mors in control is unconscionable. We have the power to stop him once and for all."

I nodded. "Mors is powerful, but we can beat him. I just need to hit him with Clarity and see if it has the same effect it did on Daelissa."

"Easy enough," Victoria said. "We slip back into Kalifa and you hit him in the back."

"Well, when you put it like that, it sounds like it's super easy, barely an inconvenience." I paced north, counting off my steps until I figured I was close, and poked my head over the border. The desert appeared. The army of ushers were making their way down into the pit.

Mors hovered above the pit on blazing wings, his attention firmly fixed below. He was about fifty yards away. It wasn't ideal range, but with Clarity, it didn't need to be. Just a single dose seemed to be enough for most. I wove Stasis, channeled the other elements from my eyes, and fired a beam of Clarity at the target.

The transparent beam rippled through the air and struck Mors square in the back. He didn't even flinch. It was as if it hadn't even hit him at all. I nearly lost my concentration. *Is he out of range?* The ushers were too far down in the pit to spot me, so I walked toward my prey, nailing him with Clarity the entire time.

239

Mors continued to supervise his minions without a care in the world.

What in the hell is going on?

I released the weave and quickly backed out into the void again. "Bad new, folks. Clarity doesn't affect Mors."

That raised a few eyebrows.

"Not even a little bit?" Victoria said.

I shook my head. "He didn't even notice. Either he's got some kind of protection, or the dude has no conscience whatsoever."

"It's possible," Vallaena said. "Psychopaths have a very weak conscience."

"So you're saying Mors is an even worse person than Daelissa?" I blew out a breath. "Now that's saying something. We've got to end that bastard and there's only one way to do it."

"Drain him," Jeremiah said.

Victoria nodded in approval. "It's the only way."

"But how?" I pinched the bridge of my nose as if that would help me think better. "He's drained so many souls, it'd be like a nuclear-powered robot fighting a lawnmower."

"We need to drain him of excess power," Jeremiah said. "We'll have to goad him into fighting us and somehow survive."

"Illusions would work," Victoria said. "Emily used them when she had to fight Olivia."

"A solid idea, if I do say so myself." Jeremiah tapped a finger on his chin. "We'll lure him into a fake fight and exhaust him."

"The question is, where do we do it?" I said. "Kalifa is too dangerous and Heavenly is his home turf. There's too much potential for collateral damage in Britannia, but at least we'd be on even ground."

Vallaena nodded. "The outlands would be ideal. But how are we to lure him all the way there? It's much too far away."

"Yeah, you're right." I hated to do it, but Britannia seemed like the best place to pick a fight. But then something else occurred to me. Something that might kill two birds with one stone.

We might be able to end Heavenly once and for all.

CHAPTER 26

I told the others my idea.

"It's certainly worth a try," Victoria said. "And if it works, it might be the best thing to ever happen in this awful place."

"Amen to that," Jeremiah said.

As usual, my plan was simple and would either work or fail spectacularly. In which case, no harm done, we'd just have to go back to the drawing board. We stepped across the invisible border not to Kalifa, but to Heavenly.

Why Heavenly? After all, it was Mors's home turf and probably the worst place imaginable to take him on. Except he was across the road in Kalifa trying to extract his prey from the belly of a giant sandworm.

There was no one waiting for us in Heavenly. It seemed Mors had taken all his ushers with him. So we marched onward toward the white church. It took a lot of self-restraint not to blast the building to ashes. I summoned my power, holding it in the palms of my hands and kicked open the front doors.

Vallaena picked up a pew and hurled it toward the pulpit at the other side of the room. It made a tremendous crash, smashing both objects to splinters. This drew the response I wanted, but I was surprised by the first responder.

Gerald blurred into the room, eyes wide. They blazed with hatred when he saw it was us.

"What the hell are you doing here?" I said. "Shouldn't you have your nose up Mors's ass?"

"Feel the wrath of God, sinner." Gerald pounded a fist into his palm. "You will know nothing but pain."

I'd been hoping to find Mother first, but Gerald would do just fine. As much as I wanted to beat the shit out of him over and over again, we didn't have time to mess around. I unleashed my power and struck Gerald in the chest.

His back arched, eyes flared inhumanly wide, and then he collapsed. I stopped my attack but held onto the weave of power.

"What's happening?" Mother rushed through the door Gerald had come through and saw us. "You!" she shrieked.

"Yes, us." I struck her full in the face and she went down in a heap.

I released the weave and waited to see what happened. Mors might not have a conscience, but most of his brainwashed followers did. Hitting two of his most ardent followers with Clarity would be the litmus test to see if my plan sucked or shone.

Gerald rose to his knees and howled at the ceiling. Tears poured down his stricken face. Mother curled into a ball and sobbed uncontrollably.

"So far so good," Jeremiah said. "Let's make sure."

We walked over to the pair and gave them a moment to recover.

I stood in front of Gerald. "How do you feel?"

He looked up at me with miserable eyes. "I tried to be good but failed. I hated others for not adhering to what I saw as the truth." His shoulders sagged. "I tried to force my views on others. By hating others, I did not live my life by scripture."

I nodded. "Hating people is bad, mkay?"

He kept talking. "I have harmed many in the name of God but failed to live up to his standards. And now I happily follow a madman who is a demon in disguise."

"Everything has been for nothing." Mother looked at her hands in disbelief. "We are spirits and yet we pretend to be alive. We should seek the truth instead of remaining in the past."

Gerald slumped. "What have you done to us?"

"I showed you the absolute truth about yourselves." I gripped his arm and helped him rise to his feet. "It's the only way I could see to give you freedom from the prison you built for yourselves."

"What do we do now?" Mother asked.

I waved a hand toward the border. "Go help others realize the truth. Free them and seek enlightenment."

"I wasted my entire life being unhappy and judgmental," Gerald said softly. "I'm not worthy of anyone's trust."

"It'll take time." I patted him on the back even though I still wanted to punch him across the room. "Are there others in the church?"

He nodded. "Prisoners in the dungeon."

"I want you to ring the church bell," I said. "Get as many people here as fast as you can."

It was time to deliver a sermon no one would forget.

Gerald blurred away and the bell began to toll a moment later. Apparently, the collective still gave him superpowers even though he now knew the truth.

We stepped out of sight and waited.

It didn't take long for people to start filing inside. None of the damage from the earlier fight had been fixed, so most of the pews in the middle were nothing but splinters. This raised a lot of eyebrows, but the people were too scared to start asking questions now, especially when they saw Gerald standing up front. I stepped out next to Gerald when the influx slowed to a trickle.

"Is this everyone from the buildings in the walled off section?" I asked.

He nodded. "Those in the army worship at the feet of Mors's statue."

That figured. "This will do for now." I just hoped I had enough juice to hit the hundreds inside the chapel. I stepped up to the splintered pulpit and held up my arms. "Everyone, please close your eyes in prayer."

Many exchanged surprised looks as if wondering, *Who in the hell is this guy?* But with Gerald and Mother behind me, they didn't dare disobey. Once they bowed their heads and closed their eyes, I wove Clarity. This time, I willed it to split into multiple, crisscrossing beams and speared them through the entire congregation. Clarity passed right through the bodies in front and into those behind them.

Shouts of surprise and screams of anguish filled the church, as if a snake handler lost a basket full of rattlesnakes.

Gerald watched with tears in his eyes. "I don't know what to believe anymore."

"Well, that's a start." I covered my ears to mute the wailing voices of the newly initiated. "How many people are in Heavenly?"

"Another thousand plus are in the army," Gerald said. "Can you awaken them all?"

It was really amazing how a jolt of absolute reality could completely change a person as rotten as Gerald. "I have to."

"Then I will take you there." He paused. "If that's what you want."

"It is." I still wanted to punch the shit out of him. "Do you feel better now?"

He shook his head. "I put blinders over my own eyes and refused to take them off even though I knew deep down something was wrong. Seeing the truth made me realize I have a long way to go to atone for my real sins."

I nodded. "You just have to do your best and help others when you can." It sounded simple-minded but it was about as real as I could get with him. I turned to Mother. "Start talking with them and helping them deal with their new outlook on afterlife."

"But I can barely cope with it myself," she said.

I grunted. "Yeah, welcome to reality."

People in the crowd were already talking among themselves, many hugging and crying it out. I figured Mother wouldn't have to do much.

I motioned toward Gerald. "Lead the way."

It didn't take long to reach the field where Mors's giant statue towered over an army of crusaders. Gerald rang a bell at the base of its feet and a thousand plus souls began to gather. I was still feeling a bit washed out from channeling Clarity into everyone in the church. I hoped I had enough juice to finish the job here.

"Are you okay?" Vallaena touched my arm.

I nodded. "Yeah. Final stretch."

Jeremiah shook his head. "Perhaps you should rest first. You're looking a bit pale."

"Because I'm a ghost," I said.

He barely cracked a smile.

"I say we get it over with." Victoria put her hands on her hips. "What happens to this world when there are no more believers? Will it crumble and vanish?"

"That's a good question," I said.

A long line of confused faces in the front row looked from us to Gerald. Like those in the church, they didn't know what was going on but were too afraid to question authority. Their fear factor made my task a little easier.

A tall podium allowed me to look out at the masses of ghostly forms— Mors's brainwashed children—and I quickly realized that there was no way for me to hit so many people from one location. The back of the crowd was a good hundred yards distant, and that was too far to ensure I reached them.

I climbed back down the ladder from the podium and walked to Gerald. "Can you give them a speech to keep them occupied?"

He nodded and climbed up to the podium. "Brethren we are gathered here today to learn the truth about who we are and what we've become."

I wove Clarity, much to the shock of those on the first row, and channeled crisscrossing beams into those nearest to me. Using my demon speed, I ran around the edge of the crowd, nailing everyone with clarity as I went. People collapsed like mown grass, wailing and shouting, crying out in shock.

"Glory be!" I shouted out my best televangelist impressions. "Be healed, sinners! Send me all your money!"

When I was done, all but a few people in the center of the crowd were down on their knees or rolling piteously on the ground. The confusion on the faces of those untouched by Clarity was almost comical. But I was far too tired to laugh. Using up my last bits of endurance, I sprayed them like a pack of roaches and let them squirm in the light.

I'd extended myself past my limits. The exhaustion felt different than in a physical body. It wasn't bone-deep or aching, but more like a battery running out of juice. I just wanted to lie down and sleep.

Stone cracked and crumbled. People scattered as the giant statue of Mors collapsed in a heap of rubble. Some few brave souls stayed in place and let the dust wash over them.

I tried to walk, but my legs wouldn't cooperate. I dropped to my knees and tried not to lose consciousness.

Vallaena found me and cradled me like a baby. "You've overdone it, nephew."

"No more believers at least," I said in a whisper, unable to rally enough strength to be louder.

Victoria stepped up beside Vallaena. "Why did Mors's statue crumble, but the world didn't? If it's all a construct of thoughts and desires, it should fade to nothing."

I didn't know and was too tired to think about it.

"That's an excellent question," Jeremiah said. "Perhaps they let go of false idols, and that took care of Mors's statue, but there's something more basic about having ground beneath your feet."

"Or perhaps some constructs are more permanent than others," Vallaena said. She looked around at the mass hysteria—the wailing, screaming crowds of the newly enlightened. "I'm quite pleased how this turned out."

Jeremiah chuckled. "It is rather nice forcing people to see the truth even when they don't want to."

"I believe some people won't be able to cope with it." Victoria looked down at a sobbing man. "They'll end up eternally tormented like Daelissa even if they don't truly deserve it."

They continued talking but sight and sound faded to a dull blur. I strad-dled the line between wakefulness and sleep for some time, unable to fully cross to one side or the other. The dull roar of the crowd faded, replaced by the crunch of feet on leaves as Vallaena carried me through the forest. Shouts and screams echoed from ahead, but I couldn't muster the energy to open my eyes.

"No!" Gerald shouted loud enough to break through my muddled senses. "Mors has returned!"

I managed to crack open my eyes and saw a horrific sight. Screaming people ran in all directions, but none could escape the blurring form of Mors. He darted to the ground, splaying his fingers, and grabbing people left and right. Shrieking black shadows sank into the ground as he ripped the light from the souls of his former minions.

I tried to move—tried to shout—but I was too damned weak.

Vallaena tensed. "What now?"

"Run." Jeremiah pointed south. "Back to Britannia."

"And leave these poor souls here to be drained?" Victoria said. "We've got to stop this madman!"

"How?" Jeremiah said. "We don't even stand a chance with Justin fully awake and alert. We took away Mors's supporters. We should retreat and get Justin to the core."

I bounced in Vallaena's grasp as she ran away from the soul-thirsty madman. I must have lost consciousness because suddenly I stood in Kalesh's apartment room. I felt weary, even in my lucid dream.

Kalesh appeared in front of me. "We have doomed these people."

I blinked, unable to muster a coherent thought for a moment. "I wanted to free them."

He sighed. "It's not our fault, but I feel guilty."

"My god, that soul storm is going to swell by the hundreds today." It took everything I had to concentrate on talking. "How are we supposed to stop Mors?"

Kalesh bit his lower lip and stared out the window. "We have to drain him."

I managed a weak scoff. "How do you propose we do that? I'm too weak."

"Perhaps we and Vallaena combined could overpower him," he said.

I shook my head. "He'll drain us before we even latch onto him."

Kalesh frowned. "Then perhaps we should drain the souls of others so our powers are equal to his."

Mors had so much stolen soul essence that his powers bordered on godlike. If I drained souls, I'd be no better than him. But if I didn't use that advantage, then I had no hope of beating him. Dooming more souls to defeat him wasn't the answer. "I can't. If I drain them, they're tormented forever. I'd be just as bad as Vokan."

Kalesh nodded. "I suppose it's better to die good than bad. At least we saved some of the souls imprisoned by Vokan."

My eyes widened. "Holy farting fairies, dude. I think I know how we can win."

CHAPTER 27

K alesh frowned. Then he blinked. "That's a great idea."

"Huh?" It was my turn to blink. "When did you start reading my mind?"

"I'm part of you. Sometimes I hear what you're thinking."

The line between us was growing fuzzier, but I didn't have time to contemplate that. I leaned on my demon spirit. The bridge between life and death was still there. "Help me out here."

He touched me and strength flowed back into my legs. Then he stepped onto the bridge and started walking. I followed close behind. The wail of the soul storm grew in the near distance. We reached the middle of the bridge and waited for them to reach us.

The swarm had grown noticeably larger, swelling wider. The howl of hundreds of tortured voices threatened to overwhelm my senses. I started to have second thoughts about my idea an instant before they swallowed us.

You are back, the swarm said. *You are different.*

Yes. You helped me see the truth. Numbing cold penetrated my every pore. I clenched my teeth and continued. *I want to help you. Can you come to the place in the afterlife where my soul is now?*

A pause. *We cannot leave the void.*

Where are you? Kalesh asked. It was strange hearing his thoughts in my head.

We occupy the empty places. We cannot go into the light.

That made things a little more complicated, but we weren't down and out just yet. I pictured the place I wanted them to go. *Can you reach this place?*

Why? The tortured voices asked.

I have a gift for you. I sent them an image of the gift.

We come.

Kalesh beat me to the next question. *How long?*

The swarm left us without answering and vanished into the dark, leaving us alone on the bridge.

"Well, I hope they come soon." I blew out a breath. "Otherwise, Mors is going to eat us alive."

Kalesh nodded. "I have given us what strength I can. But our Seraphim powers are exhausted for now."

I clapped him on his back. "Thanks, dude."

He clapped me on my back. "You got it, dude."

And then I woke up to explosions and screaming. My body felt better even though my mind was still a bit dazed. I tried to talk, but Vallaena was running so hard, the bouncing made it almost impossible.

"Stop!" I shouted.

Vallaena skidded to a halt. Somehow, Victoria, and Jeremiah weren't far behind.

"What is it?" she said.

I looked around but couldn't get my bearings. "Which direction are we going?"

"We circled south back toward Britannia," Vallaena said.

"Southeast corner of Heavenly?" I said.

She nodded.

I patted her shoulder. "I can walk."

Vallaena quirked an eyebrow but set me on my feet. "You passed out."

I nodded. "Yeah, but I've got an idea." We'd stopped in the forest. I saw the burning ruins of the chapel barely visible through the trees to the north. It seemed Mors was tearing the entire place apart.

Jeremiah and Victoria sprinted up to us. Neither was out of breath which meant they'd realized souls didn't need to breathe anymore.

"I've got a plan, but we need to reach the seam between Heavenly, Kalifa, and Britannia." Using the chapel as a landmark I pointed in the general direction. "And we've got to bring Mors with us."

Wide eyes met my last statement.

"I'd love to hear this idea," Jeremiah said. "Because it certainly sounds like suicide."

I nodded. "Maybe it is." I told them my brilliant plan.

Victoria cocked an eyebrow. "It'll work for sure?"

"Maybe." I shrugged. "Or it might just piss him off."

Jeremiah barked a laugh. "Well, I say we piss off the son of a bitch one last time before we die."

"We won't die," I said. "We'll just be tormented wraiths for all eternity."

Blue energy flashed in his eyes. "Even better."

"Then let's do it." I took a deep breath and started walking toward the smoking chapel. Then I noticed someone was missing. "Where's Gerald?"

"He went to the chapel to see if he could save any souls." Victoria said.

"Oh, god." I grimaced. "He doesn't stand a chance."

When we cleared the forest, I looked around for any signs of a mad angel. It didn't take long to spot Mors on blazing wings a short distance to the northeast of the chapel. He hovered above a group of people, his lips curled up in a cruel smile.

Gerald stood in front of the frightened crowd, arms spread protectively, fear gripping his face. He shouted, but I couldn't hear what he said.

"Vallaena, come with me." I glanced at Victoria and Jeremiah. "You two are slower, so wait here, okay?"

They nodded.

My aunt and I blurred across the chapel grounds and stopped fifty yards from Gerald's group.

I waved my arms. "Hey Mors, you fuckwit. I'm over here."

Mors gave me a cool look. "There's nowhere to hide, boy. Why don't you take a seat and enjoy the show?"

"Please," Gerald said, "let them go. There's no need to drain them or anyone else."

Mors laughed. "My, how you've changed, little sheep. You were a mindless enforcer only hours ago, now you're a mindless protector of the weak."

"I saw the light," Gerald said. "I was wrong to follow you."

"And you still are." Mors swooped down and gripped Gerald by the head. He grinned and squeezed with both hands.

Gerald screamed in agony.

Even though a part of me thought Gerald deserved some punishment for all his jackassery, I didn't think Mors should be the one to enjoy it. "Stop!"

Mors only grinned harder, crushing Gerald's head. Even though it wasn't flesh and bone, it squished like a sponge. Gerald's screams went silent. Mors stared at me and drained Gerald down to a husk.

He continued staring at me and wiped his hands together. "Now it's your turn, boy." Mors blurred at us. He was so fast, I barely had time to react in my weakened state. His outstretched hand gripped my arm.

Vallaena punched him hard enough to splinter a tree, but the impact barely moved Mors an inch. His soul glow brightened to the intensity of a star where her fist struck him and then faded. He backhanded her and she sailed fifty feet through the air and landed on her back.

I tried to squirm free, but his hand was an immovable vice. I struggled and fought with all my remaining strength. Mors laughed. "How amusing. The little boy who defeated Daelissa is reduced to nothing." He smirked. "Soon to be less than nothing."

I waved at the others. "Run!"

Vallaena staggered to her feet, bracing herself to make another try for Mors. "We won't abandon you."

"Just do it!" I shouted.

Jeremiah shook his head and began walking our way. "No, son. We won't leave you."

Victoria squared her shoulders. "We all die together."

Mors guffawed. "You're making it too easy on me." He clenched a fist and a star of Brilliance nearly blinded me. "I am a god."

Jeremiah wove his hands in a pattern and fired a blast of azure energy at the Seraphim. Vallaena rushed in, fists blurring and pounding Mors. Victoria dashed forward and gripped the hand keeping me prisoner.

Mors grunted under the assault. He channeled a shield and held off Vallaena's and Jeremiah's attacks. Still holding me, he kicked Victoria away. She skidded across the grass and rolled to a stop.

Then she got back up and came again.

Tendrils of arctic cold snaked up my body. A horrible croak tore from my throat. *He's draining me!*

My struggles grew weaker. Victoria gripped his hand and tried to pry it off me, but Mors just looked at her and laughed.

I wanted them to run, to leave me, but my vocal chords were locked in a song of agony. There was nothing we could do to beat this monster. And because of him the living world and the afterlife would probably die.

A massive ball of ultraviolet force slammed into Mors's face so hard I felt the ground shake beneath me. His grip went slack and I slumped to the ground. A purple streak pounded into Mors again, sending him stumbling back another few feet. Inside the blaze of violet fire, I saw a petite figure I knew so well.

"Nightliss!" I shouted, in disbelief that my beloved friend was here.

She glared at me sideways and I suddenly realized it wasn't my friend.

"Daelissa?" Victoria said in disbelief.

The ultraviolet light surrounding her vanished. It had masked her blonde hair and blue eyes.

"She's channeling Murk?" I blinked. "Wait, how did you get your powers?"

Daelissa slashed a hand through the air. "Run!" She blurred into Mors, pounding him with Murk enhanced fists, pummeling him like the fastest boxer alive.

Mors threw up a fresh shield of Brilliance and roared in anger. "Zhuka! I will finally have your soul!" He slammed the shield into Daelissa, pounding her body so hard into the ground it sank a foot deep. He yanked her up by the neck. Glowing soul blood oozed from a gash in her head.

Daelissa stared him in the eyes and laughed. "Pathetic little worm. You were nothing in life and even less so in death." She spat in his face.

Mors gripped her neck tighter. "Says the squirming worm in my grasp."

She gagged and choked, but her body remained still, as if she refused to struggle. "Justin Slade didn't even know you existed, roach. Your life and death were meaningless."

"My life had meaning!" Mors screamed, his face a red mask of fury. "I should have taken power when I had the chance!"

Daelissa wheezed a laugh. "We used to laugh at you, Astaeus. You were pathetic."

A roar of pure rage tore from his throat and his hand squeezed Daelissa's neck harder. Mors drove Daelissa to her knees and put his hand on her head. Black veins crawled up her arms, neck and face.

She gritted her teeth, glared at me, and screamed, "Run, you fools!" With a final cry of agony, her soul withered into darkness and sank into the ground.

We ran.

I barely remembered the next few moments, feet pounding, weak legs pumping. Vallaena carried Jeremiah and Victoria beneath her arms so they wouldn't fall behind. I was still weak, but terror drove me like a whip. Mors's roars of rage were hot on our heels. I didn't dare glance back, not even for a second.

We dashed through the remaining trees and entered the void between the collectives. Something was waiting on us. Pitch black shadows swirled around us, visible even in the void. I skidded to a stop next to Vallaena. Mors burst into view just behind us, arms outstretched, eyes glowing with pure hatred.

And then darkness swept over us.

Icy numbness penetrated me to the core. I couldn't see. Couldn't move. Couldn't even scream. I didn't need to, because the soul storm screamed for me. Shrieks of despair, pain, and longing filled my ears. The bodies of the consumed buried me beneath the weight of eternal torment.

Encountering the swarm as an astral projection hadn't prepared me for this. The sensations were so intense I could hardly bear the weight of so many negative emotions.

Mors! The collective voice shrieked his name. *Mors!* I couldn't tell if the voices came from inside my head or out.

I felt weak as if the life force was being drained from me. I realized with horror that we were all caught in the storm and the consumed were so furious they didn't care who they attacked.

It took everything I had to send out a desperate plea. *It's me, Justin! Why are you attacking me?* I tried to struggle, but it was like sinking in tar. *My friends are innocent! Let them go!*

The swarm ignored me, screaming Mors's name over and over. They were blind in their rage. I tried to channel a shield, but my focus shattered. I caught glimpses of light to my left and right, quickly covered again by darkness.

I felt weaker and weaker. My trap, it seemed, had doomed us all. But maybe it was worth it. I would probably never know.

A strange sensation wormed its way up my body, like a python constricting around its prey. I felt the dark souls sliding off me and suddenly I fell into the open void just outside the writhing mass of oily darkness.

Jeremiah, Vallaena, and Victoria were a few feet away, feebly crawling from the swarm. I glanced back and saw a shadowy but familiar figure regarding me. Before I could say anything, it slid back into the swirling mass.

Brilliant light exploded and the swarm scattered. Mors glowed like a star, his face burning with rage. "You cannot harm a god!" he screamed.

A dark soul wrapped around his face. More latched onto him like black leeches. He screamed and tried to rip them away, but there were too many. They swarmed his soul, binding it until Mors was completely covered, a silhouette darker than even the void around us.

The consumed souls were paper-thin wisps, dark wraiths with barely more substance than tissue paper. But their collective despair was formidable. Mors flailed and jerked like a broken robot, vainly trying to free himself. But he'd created a monster even worse than himself—a collective of beings left with only a final memory of Mors ending their existence.

He'd created the darkness that now consumed him.

"My god, what are they doing to him?" Jeremiah said.

Victoria rubbed her arms. "Killing him, I hope."

Vallaena put her hand on my shoulder. "I can't believe it. Daelissa died for you."

I shook my head. "No. Death would be a blessing compared to what Mors did to her."

My aunt nodded. "Eternal damnation."

"She might have saved us," Jeremiah said, "but she still deserves damnation."

I couldn't disagree.

Mors looked like a mummy wrapped in black cloth. Arms flailing wildly, he fell and rolled around. His struggles gradually grew weaker until at last he went still. Something about the wraiths seemed different. Some of them had gone from pitch black to dark grey. At first, I thought it was my vision playing tricks on me. Then brilliant light speared through cracks between the souls. Mors began bucking uncontrollably. A faint humming grew louder and louder.

"Um, that can't be good, can it?" I pushed to my feet and backed away.

Victoria scrambled backward. "It sounds as if he's going explode!"

Everyone ran. But before we even made it a few feet, the void lit up like a super nova. For several heartbeats, the darkness turned white. I expected a blast to knock me to the ground and intense heat to fry my backside. But then the light vanished as quickly as it had come. Where there had been the howling storm, there was silence.

"Where am I?" a solitary voice called out.

I turned around and my eyes went wide as dinner plates.

The impossible had happened.

CHAPTER 28

The void was filled with souls—not the dark wraiths of the consumed, but actual living beings—hundreds of them. They were scattered across the ground, most of them seemingly unconscious.

"Where am I?" The source of the question was a man standing in the middle of the strewn bodies.

My mind couldn't make sense of what I was seeing. "Where did they come from?"

"It can't be." Jeremiah rubbed his eyes as if to clear them. "How?"

"I don't know, but let's not dither like fools." Victoria rushed to a dazed woman and helped her stand.

The rest of us came to our senses and began helping others regain their feet. As I turned to help another, I saw a familiar face watching me from a short distance. She looked weary and sad, but she offered the tiniest of smiles.

Daelissa was alive.

My mouth dropped open. "My god, they're not consumed anymore."

Jeremiah followed my gaze and nodded. "Well, I'll be a monkey's uncle."

Daelissa's eyes flared. She leaned over and yanked someone up by their hair. Mors's eyes flared with horror as he met her gaze.

"How?" he cried out in a ragged voice.

It was a damned good question. I strode over with the others and stood in front of him. His soul no longer glowed brighter than the others. If anything, it was slightly dimmer than normal.

"The consumed can be restored," Vallaena said.

I was still stunned by the revelation. "They weakened Mors and drained their soul essence back from him."

Jeremiah nodded. "I thought they were going to drain us in the process."

"We could not truly drain you," Daelissa said. "But I pushed you out."

"That was you who got us out?" I said. "How did you even have the mind to do it?"

"I have dealt with madness all my life," Daelissa said. "It seems being a wraith is only slightly worse."

"How does Mors still have his light?" Victoria said. "Why isn't he completely drained?"

"We could only reclaim that which was ours from him," Daelissa said. "It would have been impossible for one wraith to do it, but he could not resist all of us."

I looked down at Mors. "What now?"

Daelissa sighed. "We cannot leave him. With his powers, he would only repeat what he has done."

"There's no way to kill him," Jeremiah said. "And there's no good way to imprison him."

Victoria pursed her lips. "He has to be drained."

"No," Mors whimpered. "I won't allow it!" A sphere of Brilliance coalesced in his palm.

Daelissa punched him so hard in the temple that he slid sideways ten feet. She channeled beams of Murk from both hands and encased him from the neck down.

Mors screamed and jerked his head back and forth as if trying to break free.

I stared at Daelissa in disbelief. "Why are you channeling Murk? How did you get your powers back in the first place?"

Her bottom lip trembled. "Mors must be drained, but I can't bring myself to do it."

"No!" Mors began screaming over and over again. "No!"

"I've never drained a soul before," I said. "It's not right."

Vallaena patted my shoulder. "In this case, I think it's okay."

"It's justice," Jeremiah said.

Victoria bit her bottom lip. "It's the only way to keep others safe. Mors must be put in a powerless state and there's only one way to do it."

I stared at the helpless man. I let my hatred for him flow through me. If we'd been in the heat of battle, I probably could have done it. But not like this. It would be like killing someone in cold blood—an execution. "I can't."

Vallaena rubbed my shoulder. "You don't have to, nephew. I will consume him with my demonic abilities."

"Ah, yes." Jeremiah nodded. "I didn't consider that route."

Tendrils stretched out from Vallaena and latched onto Mors. His screams ceased and his face went slack. Gentle light pulsated across the tendrils and into my aunt. After a time, her brow furrowed and she shook her head. "Draining a Seraphim is extremely difficult even when subdued."

"Your people were never able to do it during the war," Daelissa said. "We have certain innate defenses."

"You can't do it?" I said.

Vallaena shook her head. "I'm afraid not. It's up to you."

I shook my head. "Hell to the no. This might be the most fucked up thing I've ever said, but I'm following Daelissa's lead on this one. I won't drain his soul."

"Bloody hell." Victoria clenched her fist. "Draining the bastard is the moral high ground under the circumstances. Unless you want to leave this monster free to do this all over again, I suggest you gird your loins and get on with it."

I looked around and realized a crowd of people had gathered around us. Most of them looked confused, probably because they didn't have a clue about the paranormal or what we were talking about.

"What won't you do?" a nearby man asked.

"He won't kill Mors," a woman answered.

"Because he's already dead." One man looked at his hands as if seeing them for the first time. "We're all just stardust."

Murmurs rose from the crowd. Others nodded in agreement.

"I didn't see the truth before," a man said. "But whatever happened to me made me see the light."

A little girl at the front of the crowd pointed up. "You mean that light up there?"

I followed her gaze and saw a single bright star in the sky. "Where did that come from?"

"Yes, I see it," someone else shouted. "I want to go to the light."

Others joined their assent. "Onward to the light."

A woman came from the crowd and hugged me. "Thank you, Brother." She hugged my companions, even Daelissa. "Thank you." Then she walked away, eyes locked on the star in the distance.

Others followed her, hugging us, giving thanks, and moving on. Before long, only Mors and our group remained.

Daelissa stared at the distant star. "Where does it lead?"

"You're all mad," Mors said. "There's nothing there but darkness!"

"I feel as if we should go there," Victoria said. "But not before taking care of Mors."

"We'll just have to bring him," I said. "Because I'm not draining him."

Vallaena sighed and nodded. "Then we will not ask you to compromise yourself, Justin." She kissed my cheek. "We'll find a way."

Victoria groaned. "I couldn't disagree more. If we don't make this animal powerless, he'll eventually drain more souls."

An idea twinkled to life in the back of my head. It was just a hunch, but maybe there was a way to have our cake and eat it too. I wove Clarity and speared Victoria in the chest. She stiffened, eyes going wide.

Jeremiah frowned. "What did you do, son?"

I shrugged. "I'm not sure if I did anything." I snapped my fingers in front of Victoria's face. She blinked as if from a trance. "How do you feel?"

A single tear trickled down her cheek, but a smile broke through the sadness. "That was very raw and beautiful." Victoria put a hand on my shoulder. "Though I have some regrets, I'm at peace with the path I chose through life." She laughed. "Oh, Patrick, I miss you so much, my love. I miss my children and wish Phillip knew more about the secrets we hid from him."

"Why did you use Clarity on her?" Vallaena asked me. "She shifted her perception already."

I nodded. "I was hoping it might knock loose something else."

Victoria wiped away her tears and sighed. "You mean like this?" Her hand reached into Mors and grasped the brightest star from the constellation of his soul. He gasped and convulsed violently. She plucked the star and regarded it in the palm of her hand. Then she shoved it inside Vallaena.

My aunt cried out in surprise.

"What are you doing to her?" Jeremiah shouted.

Victoria withdrew her hand and looked at Vallaena. "Playing with my powers."

Vallaena stared at a tiny orb of Brilliance in her hand. "What is this?"

"Congratulations," Victoria said dryly. "You're an angel now."

Jeremiah's mouth dropped open. "Well I do declare. Victoria has powers like her daughter's."

"And now Mors has no powers at all." Victoria stared down at the trembling man. "I daresay he's worse off now than if Justin drained him."

Mors sobbed uncontrollably. "You can't do this to me." He raised a fist at her. "I am a god!"

Daelissa reared back her foot and punted him. Mors flew through the void and vanished as he entered a collective. I was too disoriented from being inside the swarm to know which one it was. I decided it was better to know so I walked across the border and found myself back in the forest of Heavenly.

A group of people on the other side saw Mors slumped against a tree and ran screaming in the opposite direction.

"Wait!" I called out. "Stop!" A few of them slowed and turned. I dragged Mors by his ankle over to the crowd. "His powers are gone."

"Gone?" I woman asked. "I don't understand."

"What's happened to us?" a little girl said.

"Yes, please tell us." One of the men in the group knelt next to the girl and put a comforting hand on her shoulder. "Everything we knew before today was a lie, but now I feel even more lost than before."

I glanced up and saw the star in the sky, easily visible despite the bright sun. "Do you see that?"

They looked up.

"The sun?" someone asked.

I shook my head. "The star."

They looked confused.

"No," the man said.

"Oh, I see it." The girl pointed to it.

"I don't see it either," a woman said.

I still didn't know what the star meant but looking at it filled me with peace. I held my hand out to the little girl. "If you see it, then you should come with me."

She looked up at me with big, trusting eyes. "Okay." She walked over and took my hand.

The man's eyes widened. "You were the one who changed us. You were in the chapel."

I nodded. "I needed you to see that Mors had made you his slaves." I nudged Mors with my foot. "Now his powers are gone and he's as normal as anyone else here."

The man looked at his hands. "He's just a ghost like us."

I nodded. "And this world is what you make it." I walked back toward the border, paused and looked back at them. "So make it something good, okay?"

The man nodded. "I will do my best."

The others in the group nodded and murmured in agreement.

Then I walked back into the void to join the others.

Vallaena raised an eyebrow when she saw the girl. "Who's that?"

"She sees the light too," I said. "I left Mors with his former followers."

"What is it with that light?" Jeremiah scratched the top of his head. "Is it what I think it is?"

"Heaven?" Victoria pursed her lips. "Doubtful. But I don't think it's anything bad."

"I feel content when I look at it," Vallaena said. "Now that Mors is castrated, perhaps we should investigate."

Jeremiah stared harder at the light. "There's something so familiar about this, but I can't put my finger on it."

Vallaena took his hand. "Then let's find out together."

I swallowed a nervous lump in my throat because I wasn't feeling quite as content as the others. The little girl looked up at me and smiled. "Everything will be okay."

I managed a smile. "Thanks."

She rubbed my hand. "You're welcome."

"You're adorable." Victoria knelt next to the girl. "You remind me of my Emily when she was little."

"Oh, really?" the little girl let go of my hand and took Victoria's. "I really miss my mommy. Do you think we can find her?"

"Why don't we find out?" Victoria looked expectantly at the rest of us. "Well, let's stop dithering and go."

Jeremiah, still holding Vallaena's hand, nodded. "Lead the way."

Victoria set off with the girl and the others followed. I started to walk and realized something was off. I looked behind me.

Daelissa met my gaze, eyes uncertain.

"Are you coming?" I asked.

She shook her head, eyes watering. "I can't."

When I looked at her, I no longer saw the mad Seraphim who'd waged war on Eden. The same person who'd drained the souls of innocents to fuel her lust for power. She had done those things and worse. But when she came to our rescue in Heavenly, Daelissa had been someone else. It was like seeing the person who epitomized everything that was good—her sister, Nightliss.

She'd given up her very soul to save us.

I still harbored anger toward the Daelissa I'd known before, but this woman wasn't the same. She'd committed a selfless act and saved count-less souls.

I walked over to her and held out a hand. "Come with us."

Tears trickled down her cheeks. "I'm not worthy. I can never undo the horrible crimes I committed."

"Yeah, I know. But you went above and beyond when you sacrificed yourself for us." I stepped closer to her. "You were a hero, Daelissa. Nightliss would be so proud."

She bowed her face into her hands and sobbed. "I regret my entire life so much. I wish I could undo it all."

"You can't." I held out my hand again. "But you can move on with us and make the afterlife a better place." It sounded kind of corny, but I meant it. "Just drop the load and move on, Daelissa."

She raised her head and looked at my hand. Then she reached out and took it. "Thank you, Justin."

I smiled. "No. Thank you. Because of you, Mors is beaten, and hundreds of lost souls were brought back from damnation."

"Yes, I suppose I was a little bit of a hero," she said. Gone was the mad, overly proud voice. Also gone was the sobbing pity party. She sounded so much like Nightliss I could barely believe the difference.

Hand-in-hand with the woman who'd once been my mortal enemy, we followed my friends and walked toward the light. As we progressed, the star dropped lower and lower in the sky, growing larger as it neared the ground.

It touched down in the void just feet away from us, a serenely glowing portal. The others went through without hesitation. Daelissa and I looked at each other, then stepped through together.

A ten-foot tall man with crimson skin and hair of fire waited on the other side. "Now you're mine!" he boomed and raised giant fists above his head.

CHAPTER 29

"You've got to be kidding me!" I shouted.

"Watch out!" Daelissa channeled a shield around our entire party.

The man burst into laughter. The flames in his hair died out and he shrank to normal size. "Oh, you should've seen your faces." He roared with mirth. "Priceless!"

Daelissa blinked and released the shield. "What was the meaning of that?"

"Sometimes boredom gets the best of me." The man shrugged. "My duty has its rewards, but aside from the few who pass through, there is little to occupy my mind." He chuckled. "Though today has been really busy for some reason." He raised an eyebrow. "You wouldn't happen to know what's going on, would you?"

I'd been so focused on the man I hadn't noticed our surroundings. We stood on a slab of white marble in a round clearing bordered by tall hedges. Blue skies and yellow sunshine smiled down from above. A pair of bright orange birds flew past overhead, tweeting with excitement. A gravel path met the marble slab and led through a narrow opening in the hedges before vanishing around a curve.

"Where are we?" I said.

"That's what I'm here to tell you." He waved a hand toward the gravel path. "Beyond that point lies your final destination. Few souls ever make it this far, though today has been quite the exception." He chuckled. "Normally I see perhaps a dozen a year."

"We might have had something to do with that," I said.

He raised an eyebrow. "I thought I'd felt a great disturbance."

"In the force?" I said.

"I'm getting ahead of myself." The man put a hand to his chest. "I'm Yona, one of the keepers of the fount. Welcome to Paradise."

"Paradise?" Victoria frowned and pointed at the ground. "We're standing in Paradise right now?"

Yona nodded. "Well, the entrance anyway." He pointed to the path. "There's much more to see beyond."

"We came through the light," Jeremiah said. "Was it a portal like an Obsidian Arch? Does the path lead to the primal fount?"

Yona pursed his lips. "You're not ordinary folk like the others." He cocked his head and squinted at Jeremiah. "Oh, yes, you were the special case that came through here some time ago."

"What?" Jeremiah flinched. "I've been through here?"

Yona held up a hand. "I don't usually go into a lot of details with normal folks." He chuckled. "It just confuses them." His gaze lingered on Jeremiah. "The fount doesn't interfere in life very often, so I was astonished when it summoned someone who hadn't seen the light." He winked. "If you'll pardon the pun."

"I don't remember anything except being at the fount," Jeremiah said. "I saw Conrad there."

"When people die, they cling to the ways of life." Yona sat down and a marble bench appeared just in time to keep him from ass-planting on the ground. "They end up in stuck in Chaos, forever rooted to superstitions and their close-minded little worlds."

"You mean the collectives," I said.

"Chaos." He nodded as if indicating something beyond the dead-end in the hedge behind us. "Everything out there is subject to the infernal fount. The majority of souls trap themselves there, unable to conceive there could be anything more to life." Yona nodded his head the other way. "This way lies order and peace."

"So everything in this part of the afterlife is permanent?" I asked.

"That's correct." He waved an arm around as if indicating the unseen places beyond the hedge. "The fount created this place for enlightened souls. It senses those that are worthy and brings them through the light."

"Why did it find me worthy?" Daelissa asked in a quiet voice.

"That's not for me to say," Yona replied. "You can always visit the fount and perhaps it will give you the answers."

Vallaena flinched, as if remembering something. "We must visit the fount right away." She took my arm. "My nephew's body lives. We must get him to the birthing chamber so he can return to life."

A skeptical frown crossed Yona's face. "That's not how it works." He shook his head and stood. "That's not how any of this works."

"What do you mean?" I said.

Yona chuckled. "Let's move on with the tour so you'll understand."

Vallaena held out a hand "But—"

He shook his head again. "Follow and listen."

I gave her a *what can you do?* look and followed our tour guide but couldn't help the cold dread gripping the place where my heart used to be.

We followed Yona around the curve and up to a rusted iron gate. It squeaked and rattled when he pushed it open. Sound and sunlight washed over me the moment I stepped through. It was as if all my senses suddenly came alive. People laughed and played on the sandy shores of a vast crystal-clear lake. A great mountain rose on the other side, its ridges embracing the lake.

A forest of massive redwoods stretched in both directions. There were rows of craftsman cottages straight out of a fairy tale scattered among the trees, and dozens more suspended in the branches of the redwoods. Some of the redwoods had windows and doors as well.

It took a moment to realize I'd been standing still, mouth hanging open like a doofus. When I glanced at my companions, I realized I wasn't the only one. Jeremiah and Vallaena turned in circles, trying to take it all in. Daelissa fell to her knees and cried.

Victoria pursed her lips and nodded matter-of-factly. "This'll do just fine."

"The gate senses what place would make a person the happiest and takes them there." Yona closed it. "Since you're in a group, you all came to the same place together."

"How big is Paradise?" I asked.

Yona shrugged. "It's endless as far as I know." He motioned toward the lake. "If you choose not to stay here, you can go anywhere else in an instant. If you don't want to travel too fast, you can fly."

Victoria leapt into the air and hovered. Then she zipped around in a circle until her body was nothing but a blur. She landed, a grin on her face. "I love it!"

I gave it a try and found it as easy as thinking about it. I flitted back and forth across the lake, moving so fast it was like blinking from one location to the other. "This is insane!"

Daelissa wiped her wet cheeks and looked mournfully out at the water.

"Can you reach the fount the same way?" Vallaena asked.

"Of course." Yona held out a hand. "Everyone join hands, please."

We formed a circle, everyone but Daelissa grinning with delight. Before I could ask her what was wrong, the world flickered and changed. A carpet of perfect green grass spread out before us. Trees of every variety were scattered all around, some heavy with perfect apples, pears, and other exotic fruits I'd never seen.

A polar bear rolled lazily in the grass, moaning with pleasure. A golden leopard regarded us with emerald green eyes from the branch of a magnolia tree. Deer frolicked with a flock of geese around a pond of blue water.

An adorable little white rabbit hopped over to us and wiggled its nose. It didn't shy away when I reached down and picked it up. "You're so fluffy!"

"So I've been told," it said matter-of-factly.

I nearly dropped it. "Huh?"

"It talked!" Victoria looked delighted.

"All the animals here talk," Yona said. "People just love talking animals."

Daelissa stroked the white fur and managed a smile. "It's perfect."

The rabbit wiggled its nose and looked at her. "You're still in pain. You feel incomplete."

Fresh tears welled in her eyes. "Yes."

My eyes went wide. "Whoa, that's one smart rabbit."

JOHN CORWIN

"That's the primal fount talking now," Yona said. "The rabbits aren't that perceptive."

"Oh." I handed the rabbit to Daelissa.

Lower lip trembling, she waited in silence.

"You may come and go as you wish, child," the rabbit said. "There is only one balm for your self-inflicted wounds, and I believe your cause to be worthy."

Yona whistled. "That's a gift few receive."

"Come and go?" I said. "What does that mean?"

"Safe passage to and from Chaos," Yona said. "Granted, the primal fount can't protect her there, but she can summon the light whenever she's in the void."

I blinked. "Why would you want to go back to Chaos?"

Daelissa turned to me. "I am unworthy of Paradise until I can help the souls I harmed in life. I will spend eternity finding them and helping them find the light."

"That's an impossible task," Jeremiah said. He put a hand on Daelissa's shoulder. "But it is a worthy one. I would join you on such a venture if that's allowed." He looked at the rabbit. "May I?"

"I would also like to help," Vallaena said.

Victoria nodded. "As would I."

"I find you all worthy of such an endeavor," the rabbit said. "But there are many lost souls and great dangers in Chaos. There are those even more powerful than Astaeus who prey upon the weak-minded."

"What about the souls around the infernal fount?" Daelissa said. "Is that not where the souls I consumed would reside?"

"It is," the rabbit said. "Those reside in Haedaemos, the spirit realm. Travel there is possible, but even more dangerous for you. A soul without a body is stronger than a spirit, but some powerful demons can still consume you."

"And I would be gone," Daelissa said in a whisper.

The rabbit wiggled its ears. "Yes. Made a part of the spirit, absorbed into another whole."

I grimaced. "That's awful."

The rabbit turned its red eyes on me. "For most, but not for some."

"Why did you call me here the last time?" Jeremiah asked. "Why did I need to be present for Conrad?"

"It was better that way," the rabbit replied.

"Are you all-knowing?" Vallaena asked.

"I am not." The rabbit ran its little paws over its ears and face, cleaning itself. It was so adorable, it was hard to believe a vast power spoke through it. "My memory spans eons but it is not infallible."

"So you and the infernal fount are enemies?" I asked.

"No. We balance each other." The rabbit rose on its haunches. "I do not interfere often, because when I do, Chaos must react to keep the universe in balance."

I grunted. "So it's not good versus evil."

"Those qualities only resides in the hearts of the sentient," it said.

My eyebrows rose. "I noticed you didn't say humans."

It didn't reply.

"Can my nephew return to life?" Vallaena asked.

"Yes," the rabbit replied.

She breathed a sigh of relief. "If Baal succeeds, will he reset the afterlife?"

"All the souls in Chaos will form another spirit realm like Haedaemos," it said. "Those here will remain safe."

"Then Justin must return to his body." Vallaena leaned toward the little rabbit. "How can he do it?"

The rabbit looked at Yona. "You did not tell them?"

"I'm afraid they rushed the tour." Yona sighed. "Anyone who's made it here may return to life." Our surroundings flickered and we stood in a cavern lit by the azure waters of the primal fount. "You just jump into the water."

"That's it?" I said.

The rabbit gave me a serious look. "But you will not return to your body. You will be born anew, a baby."

CHAPTER 30

I grunted as if someone sucker-punched me in the stomach. "A baby?"

"With no memories of this place," the rabbit said.

"But my body is alive!" I began to shake. "Why can't I go back to it?"

"As I said, it cannot be done from here," the rabbit replied. "The birth chamber is for new life, not old."

I sank to the cave floor and buried my face in my hands. "I'll never see Elyssa again."

"Don't be so dramatic." Yona pulled me upright with ease. "You can't do it from here, but you could probably do it from the death chamber."

"The what?" I frowned. "The death chamber all the way back at the beginning?"

"Yes, where you enter the afterlife," the rabbit said. "The infernal fount is there."

I looked at the glowing pool. "Is this the same primal fount in the garden from a moment ago, or a different one?"

"Both founts exist across all space and time," Yona said.

"If the infernal fount grants you passage, you may return to your body," the rabbit said.

I groaned. "So all I had to do when I died was turn around and go to the death chamber instead of suffering all the abuse from Mors."

The rabbit's head twitched. "Just as you could not find me before, neither could you find the infernal fount. Your eyes were not yet opened."

I wasn't sure if I should feel relieved or not. "Well, it's been one hell of a journey." I bit my lower lip to hold back a question.

"I could not help you." The rabbit apparently read my mind. "But your journey has given us hope for the sentient beings on your planet in your universe."

"That is incredibly specific," I said.

"Who is us?" Vallaena said. "You and Yona?"

"Chaos and Order," it said. "We both want the universe filled with enlightened beings, for it opens the doors to endless possibilities."

"I don't know what gets more endless than this." I blew out a long breath. "Well, how do we get back to the death chamber?"

"Take a moment to appreciate what you have achieved," the rabbit said. "When you are ready, Yona can take you." The rabbit leapt from Daelissa's hands and into the fount. It vanished without a splash.

I turned to Yona. "I don't have time to spare. Baal might be destroying the world even as we speak."

"Perhaps," he said. "But I'd take at least a day to enjoy your reward." He patted me on the back. "After all, you earned it."

Jeremiah nodded. "Justin, one more day won't hurt."

"Can we be sure of that?" I said. "What if my body dies twelve hours from now?"

Our body is in stasis, Kalesh said in my mind. *I think we can spare one day.*

You sure? I asked.

I'm still connected to it, he replied. *It is safe to explore paradise for one day.*

I couldn't bear the thought of losing Elyssa and my friends forever. But it wasn't every day that you earned the right to enter paradise. *Let me know if you sense any changes,* I told Kalesh. *Because I will be in eternal anguish if this fucks us over.*

I will, he said.

I reached out and took Daelissa's hand. "If I'm doing this, then you are too."

She smiled. "Just one more day."

Yona clapped his hands together. "And I know just the place to go." The world flickered.

OUR DAY in paradise was almost too incredible for words. We walked the surface of Jupiter, chased each other across the rings of Saturn, swam the depths of an ocean full of wondrous alien creatures, and soared through the skies of a cloud city. Every single one of us let go of our worries and cares and enjoyed a single day of bliss.

But when it was over, I was more than ready to go. Paradise was amazing, but for me, heaven was a place on Earth. A place right next to Elyssa.

When I was ready to go, I thought of Yona and he appeared a moment later.

He looked at me expectantly. "You're ready?"

I tried to remain calm, but my insides were wracked with nerves. "Yes."

Jeremiah, Vallaena, Victoria, and Daelissa gathered around me.

"May we come?" Jeremiah asked.

Yona nodded. "I expected you'd want to see your friend off."

Jeremiah swallowed and nodded. "Yes. Yes, I would."

The world flickered and we stood in the place I'd arrived days ago. But this time there was a door I hadn't seen before. Yona waved a hand toward it. "The infernal fount is through there."

"Thank you." I walked toward the door. It had no knob but opened on my approach. A thin man with red skin and demon horns appeared on the other side.

"Not this joke again," I said.

The demon raised a fiery eyebrow. "Yona, have you been scaring the souls again?"

Yona smiled and shrugged. "Every chance I get."

The demon sighed and motioned us inside. "Welcome to Perdition."

I paused halfway through my step. "Say what?"

He shrugged. "Don't worry. I won't torture you."

"I've had enough of torture out here, thank you very much." I prayed he wasn't playing a terrible joke on us and stepped into a cave flickering with orange light with the others close on my heels.

The source of the light was a pool of bubbling lava. A terrible scream filled the room and a human form rose from the fires. The lava dried to a black crust and the form toppled over. The stone skin shattered with a loud crunch and the soul within floated through the door and out of sight.

"What in the fresh hell was that?" Before the question was fully out of my mouth another scream rose from the lava. Another soul took shape and floated from the room.

"The death chamber is a bit noisy," the demon said. "My name is Sakref, the keeper of Chaos."

A group of screaming souls rose from the lava.

"How do you deal with the sound?" I said.

He shrugged. "I rather enjoy the sound of humans screaming." He frowned. "Most don't make such a racket unless they died screaming. The majority are rather silent." Sakref clasped his hands. "But you're not here about that. The fount tells me that you wish to make a journey back to your body."

I gulped. "Yes. Is that possible?"

He nodded. "Absolutely. Many people die temporarily only to be pulled back to life by a doctor or healer. Almost none ever remain here for as long as you have." Sakref smiled and rubbed his hands together. "You'll have to jump into the fount while I give you a nice push. I guarantee it will be pure agony." His eyes lit with pleasure at the word.

I gulped again. "It's just that easy?"

Sakref smiled in a way that made me think it wasn't. "It sounds easier than it is. Both the primal and infernal founts have found your life fascinating. Thus it was easy for them to agree to let you return. But I think you'll find that returning to flesh and bone after living an enlightened life in paradise is unpleasant."

"I have to go," I said. "I can't just let Baal kill billions."

"Isn't Baal aligned with the infernal fount?" Jeremiah said. "And yet it allows Justin to return?"

Sakref shrugged. "Baal draws power from it yet. But he once drew power from the primal fount when he was flesh and blood. Neither fount expects or requires loyalty."

Jeremiah pressed him. "But Baal is an agent of Chaos."

"Just as he once was an agent of Order." The demon smiled. "Justin Slade is the counterbalance to Baal's ambitions. Chaos might win this time, but Order will prevail and return balance."

"And that's it?" I was a little disappointed. "There's no other rhyme or reason to things? Who gave me all those dreams about choosing between Murk and Brilliance when I was coming into my Seraphim powers? Who took me to the place where I saw all the rivers of power flowing in different directions from the primal fount to the infernal fount? Was it all just a dream?"

Sakref's eyes flared. "You've been to the Origin?"

"The what?" I was a little concerned by his shock.

"What you've described is the original universe," he said in a hushed voice. His eyes went distant as if listening to something I couldn't hear. He blinked. "The fount wants to know if you saw anything or anyone there."

It had been a while, but I remembered it like it was yesterday. "Just myself—a reflection."

Sakref went quiet again for a moment. "Well, it seems an even higher power is interested in you."

I refused to let my jaw drop open in shock again. "There's a higher power than the founts?"

"Of course." He rubbed his hands together. "This will be the most interesting thing to happen in a hundred thousand years if an architect has a hand in it."

"Architect?" I wasn't sure if I should be flattered or scared out of my mind. "What could possibly be more interesting than the all-out war in Eden over the past ten years? We've been fighting Apocryphan and the grand overlord of Haedaemos for the fate of the damned world!"

Sakref flicked his hand. "Yes, that's amusing, of course. But it's rather blasé compared to the human-dinosaur wars of the Plinthian Epoch."

Jeremiah looked aghast. "Humans warred against dinosaurs?"

"No, with them." Sakref scoffed. "The gods overstepped their boundaries by executing the wife of—" He shook his head. "Frankly, it doesn't matter. We could be here for years if I were to recite the history of Earth."

"I don't even understand how that lines up chronologically." I turned to Jeremiah. "Weren't you alive at the dawn of man?"

He shook his head. "Heavens no. I'm barely a few thousand years old."

"The age of gods was a much different time," Sakref said. "They vanished for a time and came back once man recovered from near-extinction." He shrugged. "They are as fickle as their subjects."

"So our accounting of history is wrong?" I said.

He waggled a hand. "Your historians have it partially right, but some mischievous gods made sure to hide real history."

"But dinosaurs and humans fighting gods would be the best history possible!" I said. "At least give me a history book on that."

Sakref tapped his head. "I'm afraid it's only in the memories of the founts."

I repressed a curse. "Then tell me about the architect."

"Architects," he replied. "And no." He dabbed a finger in the infernal fount and touched me with his other finger. "Your body lingers at the point of final separation. If you're going to go, you need to do it soon."

His warning sent a jolt of apprehension through me. I nodded. "One moment, please."

Sakref returned an understanding nod.

I held out a hand to Victoria. "I'll tell Emily everything."

She ignored my hand and squeezed me in a hug. "With my newfound powers, I can actually meet her in Nowhere. Please let her know that."

"I will."

She kissed my cheek. "Eden is in good hands with you, Justin." She backed away.

Vallaena took my hands, tears in her eyes. "It's been an honor fighting alongside you again, Justin. You've grown into a great man." She delivered a bone-crushing hug and kissed both my cheeks.

"Thank you, Aunt Vallaena." I blinked away tears of my own and squeezed her tight. "I couldn't have done it without you."

Jeremiah reached over and squeezed my shoulder. "Damn fine work as always, son. I'm glad I didn't kill you all those years ago."

I chuckled. "You gave me some serious scares."

"I underestimated you." He gave me a nod of respect. "You're most dangerous when others think you're down and out. Don't ever forget that."

"Can't be much more down and out than dead," I said.

Jeremiah chuckled. "True."

I turned to the last person I ever thought I'd bid a fond farewell to. The last person I thought I'd ever forgive. I took the hand of my former mortal enemy and pulled Daelissa in for a hug.

She squeezed me back and broke into sobs. "I will make amends for my crimes, Justin Slade. Tell my sister that she is the best of us, and I wished I loved her as much in life as I do in death."

I wiped my wet cheeks and backed away. "I never asked—how did you get your powers back?"

She smiled through her tears. "I'd never felt so low as I did when you left me in that hole, all alone and useless. I realized that for the first time in my miserable life I could do some good. I could be like you." Daelissa held out her hands and looked at them. "And in that moment, my perception shifted. I found my powers and went to find you."

"You found us," I said. "And you found yourself."

She nodded. "Now go find yourself, Justin." Daelissa backed away to stand with the others. "We will meet again."

It was a lot harder saying goodbye than I'd thought. So I took a deep breath and turned to Sakref. "I'm ready."

"Good." Without warning, he picked me up and plunged me into the infernal fount.

It was exactly like being dunked into lava. My screams of agony were drowned in the bubbling fires. My entire soul melted right down to the very core. Other screams rose from the orange depths. Souls of the newly dead slid past me, rising to the surface. I gripped Sakref's hand and tried desperately to free myself, but I had no strength left in me.

Oblivion claimed me.

Extreme cold replaced the heat. My skin felt as if it were coated ice. My bones ached and icepicks seemed to stab into my brain. I couldn't move. Couldn't breathe. Panic gripped me and I channeled Brilliance from every pore of my being. Ultraviolet crystal shattered and flew in all directions. I jerked upright and realized with a shock that I was on a table in the healing ward.

I was alive.

CHAPTER 31

I was back in the land of the living and I felt like shit. My bones creaked. My muscles ached. Every square inch of me itched, burned or hurt. Having been in a preservation spell, my wounds hadn't been able to heal. If anything, I felt like I was about to die all over again. My heart thudded wearily, a lump of lead barely able to pump blood through my body.

Unable to remain sitting, I flopped back down on the table, gasping for breath through lungs scarred by overuse of Apocryphan powers. I tried to speak, but barely a whisper emerged from my raw throat. I tried to drag myself off the table, but my arms refused to move. Simply sitting up had been a miracle.

So much for my triumphant return.

Keeping my eyes open became a chore, but I couldn't allow myself to go to sleep. If I lost consciousness, I might die again. I didn't think Sakref would be willing to plunge me back in a second time.

Kalesh, are you there?

Yes, he replied in a strained voice. *We hurt so much. I don't know if we can heal.*

I strained to draw another breath. What little air I drew in, my lungs struggled to process for oxygen. My heart feebly pumped what blood it could, and my brain starved. Staying conscious wasn't going to be possible for long.

Unless a healer gets here fast, I think we're about to make a return trip to the afterlife.

Kalesh growled. *We can't let that happen!*

I agreed, but there wasn't much I could do about it. If my supernatural healing didn't kick in soon, it was going to be lights out.

Someone tutted disapprovingly, but I couldn't look around to see who it was. "It would be embarrassing to have you return so soon after all those wonderful goodbyes." A drop of golden liquid pooled on the ceiling above and dropped straight toward my chest.

I didn't have the energy to cry out. It sizzled on my flesh, spreading out and searing right down to my core. My body convulsed. I drew in a ragged breath. Heaved it out. Sucked in longer breath and blew it out. The tempo of my heart increased, every beat throbbing stronger. My fuzzy vision clarified into sharp focus.

Fingers wiggled at my command, arms moved, and legs twitched. Within minutes, I was able to sit up again. My flesh looked red and itched like crazy. I scratched and skin began to peel like a healing sunburn. I tugged it off in sheets, shedding my skin like a snake. Within minutes, it lay in filmy sheets on the floor and my body was bald, bright pink, and completely healed.

"Sakref?" I looked all around the room, but the source of the voice wasn't there, and he didn't answer. He'd healed me. Or maybe the infernal fount had. I didn't know why except that I was supposed to make things interesting. It wouldn't be hard to live up to those expectations.

Then again, how in the hell could I top humans and dinosaur warring against ancient gods? "Those are some huge shoes to fill," I muttered.

There was only one thing I wanted to do right now. I dashed out of the healing ward, bare feet slapping on the stone, and ran down the corridor. I was somewhere inside the facility deep underground beneath the Ranch.

A startled Templar leapt out of my way as I rounded a curve, and a group of healers cried out in surprise when I dashed through their group.

"Who the hell was that?" someone shouted.

Someone else cursed. "Jesus Christ, is Jenkins streaking down the halls again?"

I jumped on the levitator at the end of the hall and rode it up to the command level. The war room there was empty, so I hopped back on the levitator and rode up to the underground parking garage. I blurred at top speed past the Templars on guard there and up the ramp to the surface. Whatever Sakref had done had healed me from head to toe. I felt amazing.

I dashed up to the house and inside without knocking. A lone figure sat in the kitchen, head bowed. Raven black hair hung over her face, but it didn't conceal the tears pooling on the table, or the trembling of her hands as she fought to contain the emotions tearing her apart.

My heart nearly broke seeing Elyssa like this. I went over to her and gently pushed her hair behind an ear. She gasped and flinched away from my touch. Then she saw my face and jumped back away from me. Her face went from sad to burning with rage in a heartbeat. "I'll kill you, you fucking Flark!"

Silver blades gleamed and blurred toward me. I cried out and leapt back. But my foot tangled in a chair behind me and I went down hard on my back. Elyssa pinned my arms with her knees and pressed a blade to my neck. Warm blood trickled across my skin.

"This brings back old memories," I gasped.

Her eyes flared. "What did you say?"

I smiled. "The first time you nearly killed me right after we won Kings and Castles."

Elyssa drew in a shuddering breath. The sai swords clinked to the tile floor. "Please kill me if I'm dreaming again."

I reached up a hand and caressed her cheek. "I came back to life just so I could kiss you one more time."

"Justin? It really is you, isn't it?" She laughed through her tears. "Only you could be so corny at a time like this!" Elyssa buried her face in my chest. She peppered my face with kisses and pressed her lips to mine until we both nearly passed out from oxygen deprivation. "How is this possible?" She sat on my crotch and looked me over. "And why are you naked and hairless?"

"Because I couldn't wait to find you." I pulled her back down to me. "You're my heaven on Earth, Elyssa. Not even Paradise can compare."

She pushed up slightly and regarded me seriously. "Why do I get the feeling you're being literal?"

"Because I died and have seen some shit." I rolled over so she was beneath me, then stood and pulled her up next to me. Without another word, I scooped her into my arms and carried her upstairs to her old bedroom. There was a lot to do, but right now, this was the most important thing in the world.

"I can't believe this is real," Elyssa said as I closed the door behind us.

I laid her down on the bed and sighed with bliss. "It's the realest thing I've felt in days."

I took my time and enjoyed every second of being reunited with my love again. We laughed, we cried, and we had sex—lots and lots of sex. And after that, cuddling—lots and lots of cuddling.

I relished the feel of her warm body wrapped against mine. Paradise had been indescribable, but it was nothing compared to this. Lying there half-asleep, memories of the battle on the beach replayed in my dreams. The searing pain and agony was still fresh in my mind, but I'd suffered far worse than that in Perdition.

So where to now? I was back, but there didn't seem to be any clear-cut paths to follow. Baal thought he'd killed me and was probably executing nefarious plans across a dozen realms. I had Apocryphan powers dormant in me. To reawaken them might give us the edge in the next battle, but they might also kill me again. But without them, I could barely hold my own against Cain, Olivia, and Baal's Hell demons.

Death sucked. But maybe, just maybe, it could be useful.

A plan formed in my mind. It was about as simple as it got, but it might just work. My *Aha!* moment jerked me awake. It was time to return to the real world—time to put on some pants, and return to duty.

The problem was, Elyssa didn't have any pants I could borrow. So I wrapped a towel around my waist and we walked all the way back to the underground complex laundry where we found some clothes that fit.

I got a lot of strange looks, but no one seemed to recognize the bald dude with a towel wrapped around his waist.

"I asked Dad to meet me in the war room," Elyssa said. "He'll be here in a few minutes. Would you mind sitting in a chair in plain sight of the door when he comes in? I want to get a picture of his face."

I chuckled. "I'll bet five tinsel he won't look surprised at all."

She tapped a finger on her chin. "Usually you'd be right. But your death hit him pretty hard." Elyssa looked down. "It hit everyone really hard."

"What was that comment about a Flark when you first saw me?" I said.

"Baal infiltrated the U.S. government not only with infernus, but with Flarks." Her jaw tightened. "He even had one that pretended to be you. It would actually come to the Ranch, stand on the lawn, and wave at us."

"Sick bastard." I rubbed my hands together. "Well, I dreamed up an idea to turn the tables on Baal. I want you and Thomas to tell me what you think."

Elyssa grinned. "Oh, I'm more than ready for payback." Her grin faded. "You should also let Shelton know you're alive ASAP. Poor guy has been so depressed he's just moping around instead of working on the infernus problem."

"Where is he?" I said. "And where's Nookli?"

"Shelton's in Washington and your phone is in our room in the barracks." Elyssa rubbed my bare arm and my head. "So I guess having no hair is your thing now?"

I'd lost all my hair to the infernal fount after jumping into it while in the Abyss. It'd only just started growing back and I'd lost it again after Sakref healed me with the infernal fount. I nodded. "It's sexy, right?"

"Not quite." She snorted. "I guess not having hairy balls is a plus."

I barked a laugh just in time to notice Thomas standing outside the door, mouth hanging open slightly, eyes locked onto me.

"Shit!" Elyssa tried to snap a picture with her phone, but it was too late.

Thomas walked toward me, face once again emotionless. "I assume since you're here with Elyssa that you're not a Flark."

I grinned. "It's really me. I'm back."

He sagged maybe a fraction of an inch. It was the equivalent of passing out for most people, but Thomas was a pro at hiding emotion. Then he surprised the hell out of both of us and gripped me in a firm hug. "It's damned good to have you back, son."

Tears wet my cheeks. "Thank you, sir."

Thomas backed off. "We've been battling Baal on multiple fronts, and it hasn't been going well. His dragon forces are massing in Seraphina for an attack on Atlantis, and he's subverted dozens of major nom governments, poising them all on the brink of nuclear war. Our agents are doing everything possible to turn back the tide, but we're spread too thin."

"Glad I didn't miss anything," I said with a scoff. "Do you really think he'd start a nuclear war?"

Elyssa nodded. "He's already willing to kill billions. We think he's setting up the endgame by making us chase our tails across the world so he can track down the final relics."

"We've managed to hold onto them, but he's already sent agents into the Glimmer." Thomas shook his head. "The rift guardians have held them off so far, but he's sure to find another way in."

It seemed things were even worse now than before I'd died. "We need to speak with Underborn about his relics."

"He's been hard to contact," Thomas said. "I'm sure he knows Baal wants his relics and has gone into even deeper hiding than usual."

I sighed. "Well, then we need to set up an endgame of our own. Being dead wasn't the most fun I've ever had, but it opens the door to an opportunity."

Thomas raised an eyebrow. "And what would that be?"

I'd fleshed out my plan a little bit during the walk here. On a scale of one to ten, its complexity was a zero. Compared to the battle plans Thomas and Elyssa designed, it was like something a kindergartener might come up with. But my death gave us the huge advantage we needed.

I told them my plan. "It's not much, and the payoff isn't huge, but it'd still be a major blow to Baal's overblown ego."

"I agree," Thomas said. "And the setup sounds perfect."

"Agreed," Elyssa said. "Let's recall the others."

I stood. "I'll save my story for when everyone else is here so I don't have to repeat myself."

"You should just wear a bodycam all the time," Elyssa said. "It'd save you so much time if you could just share the file."

I snorted and headed for the door. "That's for sure."

Elyssa stopped me. "Where are you going?"

"To the omniarch next to the underground mansion," I said. "I want to see Shelton."

"I'm coming with you." Elyssa turned to Thomas. "I'll be back soon."

He nodded. "I'll put out the recall so we can get everyone here ASAP."

Elyssa and I went to the underground garage and found a Templar guarding a square space boxed off by yellow paint. Once he got over his surprise at seeing me, he contacted a Templar at the omniarch, and a portal opened a moment later. We stepped through and into the omniarch room on the other side.

"My god!" The Templar who'd opened the portal for us nearly fell over backward. "You're back from the dead?"

Elyssa nodded. "Yes, he is. Let's keep it quiet for now."

The Templar pressed a hand to his chest and nodded. "Yes, sir."

She pulled up an image on her phone—a hotel suite with a stunning view of the Capital. The air between the arch columns split horizontally and flashed open into a portal to the same location. We stepped through to Washington D.C.

"Bella, that you?" Harry Shelton came out of the bathroom wearing nothing but his wide-brimmed hat and a pair of blue boxer shorts. His eyes flared and lips curled back with anger when he saw me. Shelton snatched his staff from a table and leveled it at me. "You mother fuckers don't quit, do you?"

He looked from me to Elyssa. "You think mimicking both of them is going to convince me?" Then he noticed the open portal and the Templar on the other side. The staff clattered to the marble floor. "Hang on…"

"It's really me, Shelton." I walked toward him. "I'm back."

"Back?" He stared at me slack-jawed for a beat, then dashed across the room. "No fucking way!" Shelton gripped me in a bear hug and spun me around like a man greeting his true love at the airport. "Holy farting fairies. You're alive!"

I giggled like a girl who'd just been swept off her feet.

"This bromance is killing me." Elyssa grinned. "Do I need to give you two some privacy?"

Shelton set me on my feet and stepped back, looking me up and down. He wiped tears from his eyes. "Son of a bitch. I knew if anyone could do it, you could." He dropped into a chair and took a deep breath. "Damn, I need a drink."

"I'm so glad to be back, I don't even care that you're only wearing underwear." I sat down in the chair across the small table from him. "I hate to cut the reunion short, but we need to hit Baal before he knows I'm back. I need you and the others to make it work."

"It's about god damned time for payback." Shelton got up and shuffled through piles of papers on a long table near the window. He found his phone and dialed.

"Don't tell Bella anything yet," Elyssa said. "We need Justin's comeback to be secret."

He nodded. "Hey, babe, I need you and the others to come back to the room. There's been a development." Shelton paused to listen and groaned. "No, I'm not moping around eating donuts and no, I didn't clog the toilet again. I really need you back here." Another pause. "Okay. Hurry." He hung up.

"Moping around eating donuts?" I raised an eyebrow.

"Clogging the toilet?" Elyssa made a gagging sound.

"Dude, I've been depressed as hell." Shelton picked up an empty donut box and tossed it in the garbage can. "This is what rock bottom looks like." He waved a hand at the piles of folders and papers on the table. "Hunting through all this mess for Baal's agents hasn't helped."

"Doesn't Adam have some way to detect infernus?" I said.

"We've identified almost a dozen infernus, but Baal's using Flarks too, and those are way harder to detect." He shook his head. "Either way, we can't go killing infernus and Flarks willy-nilly. The power vacuum would just make things worse."

Elyssa nodded. "It's a delicate situation."

"An impossible situation." Shelton scoffed. "Baal could start a nuclear war any time he wants, and there's nothing we can do about it."

CHAPTER 32

I didn't want to admit just how right Shelton probably was. "Let's hope it's not that easy for him."

Shelton shrugged. "Just saying. It's a hopeless task."

"Dude, I just came back from the dead," I said. "Nothing is hopeless."

He blinked a few times as if processing. "I'd probably rather die than dig through all this paperwork."

I thumbed through a thick dossier on a suspect and yawned. "Man, talk about torturous work." I looked up at him. "Do you think the original people are still alive or dead?"

"God only knows," Shelton said. "We think Baal's agents harvested soul fragments from the original host while they were asleep or drugged. Then they built the infernus and swapped them out overnight. What they did with the originals afterward is anyone's guess."

"Smooth operations." I blew out a breath. "And almost impossible to stop."

"That's what I said." Shelton got up and dug through a suitcase. "Baal doesn't care if we start killing off infernus. It'll create chaos either way."

"And there's no way to stop him." Elyssa flipped open another folder. "Support personnel like aides and secretaries are as important as members of Congress."

Shelton found a pair of jeans and slid them on. "Not gonna lie. It's been a real shit show. Even if we found every impostor it wouldn't really slow down Baal. We need to cut off the source of the infernus first."

"Baal's probably got a dozen foundries by now," Elyssa said.

An infernus foundry used complex patterns to summon powerful demons. During a summoning, demons took on a physical form controlled by the summoner. That meant someone skilled enough could manifest the demon as a copy of another human. To create the infernus, they fused a golem spark with a soul fragment, allowing the creation to also act like the person they replaced.

They were insidious creations—perfect agents of chaos that had overthrown governments on Seraphina and handed Baal the entire realm. Now it seemed Eden had an infestation we'd be hard pressed to exterminate without causing even more problems.

"Yeah, but if we don't cut off his production capabilities, we'll never get anywhere," Shelton said. "Besides, building one foundry takes months. I doubt Baal has more than one or two."

The pair continued to debate the issue while I sat back and just took it all in. I could hardly believe that only a few hours ago I'd been living it up in Paradise. It had been indescribably amazing, but there was no place in the world I'd rather be than with my friends even if faced with impossible odds.

It was so surreal and yet so normal.

Bella and Adam arrived about thirty minutes later. Their comical confusion upon seeing me was almost worth dying for in the first place.

Adam stared at me in slack-jawed disbelief. He looked from Elyssa to Shelton as if to confirm what his eyes were telling him.

"Yes, he's returned from the dead," Shelton said at last.

Adam slumped to the floor.

"Justin!" Bella ignored her unconscious sidekick and hugged me. She held on so long, I didn't think she'd ever let go.

I kissed the top of her head. "It's good to see you too, old Bella."

She laughed and stood on tiptoes to kiss my cheeks. "I knew you'd be back. I told everyone that the boy who led us through El Dorado and fought off hundreds of cherubs and three earth dragons would have no problem defeating death."

Shelton knelt next to Adam and gently slapped his friend on the cheek. "Hot damn, he really passed out hard."

Elyssa heaved Adam up off the floor, slung him over a shoulder, and relocated him on the bed. "Might need to splash some water on his face."

Adam moaned and sat up. His eyes locked onto me again. "I can't believe you're back." He staggered to his feet. "Oh my god, this is the best news ever!" Then he hugged me and burst into tears.

I patted him on the back. "It's okay. Just cry it out, man."

Shelton chuckled. "I think this calls for some tacos."

Bella patted his belly. "You need to lose weight first."

"Aw, come on, baby." Shelton sucked in his gut. "See? All better."

Once everyone was ready to go, Elyssa had the omniarch guards open a portal for us and we returned to the Ranch. Thomas was waiting on us in the war room, and he'd already assembled two people we'd need.

"Justin!" Emily greeted me with a long hug and a kiss on the cheek.

"Man, you put roaches to shame!" Tyler clapped me on the back and gave me a bro hug. "Thomas won't tell us how they healed you."

I was a little disappointed by their first reactions to seeing me. "Neither of you look very surprised to see me."

"I've been hanging around Em too long." Tyler grinned. "She can open portals to other realms and talk to the dead, so it takes a lot to surprise me these days."

I chuckled. "She's a tough act to follow."

Emily's gaze flicked to something behind me. I turned and saw Nightliss standing in the doorway, eyes wide in disbelief. "Justin?"

I walked over to her. "It's me." Seeing her made me want to tell her about Daelissa right then and there, but I forced myself to be patient.

Nightliss burst into tears and peppered my face with kisses. "Oh, how I missed you, dear friend." She held my face between her hands. "I thought I would never see this smile again."

"I'm so happy to be back." I kissed her forehead. "And I've got quite a story to tell you."

"I can hardly wait." Nightliss looked around the room. "How did you heal him?"

"We didn't," Elyssa said. "We were all just as surprised as you."

"I wasn't," Tyler said. "I totally called it."

Emily rolled her eyes.

Cinder stepped inside and stopped dead in his tracks. "Justin?"

"It's me." I held open my arms.

Cinder proceeded to give me the most awkward hug I'd had in a long time. He gave me three precise pats on the back. "This is quite unexpected." He stepped back and studied me. "But I am ecstatic to see you recovered."

I grinned. "I had a lot of help."

Elyssa frowned as if realizing something and turned to Emily. "Did you find Vitania in Aquilis?"

Tyler scoffed. "Oh, we found way more than we wanted."

I raised an eyebrow. "Aquilis?"

"Oh yes. We've had quite the adventure," Emily said. "We went to Aquilis to find Vitania since we haven't heard from her since she went there to ask for help. It seems Queen Dactia had her arrested on sight and caused a rift in the Siren hierarchy. Three of the seven Siren pods removed themselves from the council in protest and demanded that Vitania be released."

"That's putting it mildly," Tyler said. "The entire capital city was in an uproar. Vitania wasn't just a queen—she was a legend to the younger generations. Dactia even tried to have Vitania removed from the history books though she's literally the mother of the Sirens."

"We tried, and failed, to avert civil war." Emily sagged. "Dactia was overthrown, but Vitania refused to take the throne back."

"Dactia's brilliant plan was to have all the Sirens go to Atlantis to wait out the apocalypse so they'd emerge as the dominant race." He blew out a breath. "Talk about the queen bitch."

"If Vitania refused the throne, then what will the Sirens do?" Elyssa asked.

"Vitania called a vote. Either fight Baal with her or join Dactia in Atlantis." Emily looked glum. "I'm afraid the decision was split. Three pods voted for Dactia, and three for Vitania. The seventh was decimated during the civil war. Without a tiebreaker, three pods will return to Eden with Vitania. The others will likely follow Dactia's plan."

"Wait a minute." I shook my head like a wet dog. "I know I lost track of time when I was dead, but this sounds like a ridiculous amount of things to happen in a few days."

"You were mostly dead for ten days," Elyssa said.

"And unrest has been brewing for a long time among the Sirens," Emily said. "I'm afraid I might have been the catalyst that sparked bloodshed."

"Babe, it's not your fault." Tyler squeezed her hand. "Dactia is the dumbass who let it all happen because she wouldn't allow a fair vote."

"Sounds awful," I said. "How many Sirens are in a pod?"

"It varies," Emily said. "Anywhere from one to two thousand."

Tyler growled. "I'm still pissed Vitania let Dactia live after the shit she pulled."

"It wasn't entirely her fault," Emily said. "Her advisors took things way too far."

"Yeah, and destroyed Ganosha." Tyler threw up his hands. "Vitania should've chopped off Dactia's head and used it for a soccer ball."

Thomas gave him a grim look. "When can we expect Vitania to arrive?"

"They're already gathering in Iceland," Emily said. "Vitania said she'd be available for a formal planning session."

"Well, that's something." Elyssa sighed with relief. "I hope Lumia is having better success with the Fae."

"No word on that yet." Emily rolled her neck as if working out a kink. "I have a bad feeling we'll have to go intervene there too."

Someone slammed into me so hard, I stumbled forward into the table. Arms locked around me in a death grip. For an instant, I wondered if I was about to die all over again. "J-Justin!" My little sister sobbed. "You're alive!"

I managed to twist in her grip so I could hug her back. I stroked her hair. "I'm back, sis."

"My son!" Mom attacked me from the other side. "How are you alive?"

Max, Ambria, and Conrad piled through the door behind them.

"Justin!" Max wedged in next to Ivy, and Ambria forced her way into the group hug on the other side.

Conrad watched me with a puzzled expression. "I thought for sure you were dead."

Mom and Ivy were squeezing me so tight, it was hard to talk. "I was only mostly dead," I wheezed.

"Mostly." Max barked a laugh and backed away. "I thought your insides were all burned up."

"They were." I kissed Mom and Ivy on the tops of their heads and managed to disentangle myself.

"Knowing you could die isn't the same as seeing my little boy lying on a table." Mom stroked my cheek. "It was like a dagger through my heart."

"I know, Mom, I know." I kissed her forehead. "I felt the same way when Daelissa almost killed Elyssa."

"How are you back, bro?" Ivy gave me an imploring look. "How?"

I squeezed her again. "It's a long story."

"One which I look forward to hearing." Cora stepped into the room with Evadora close on her heels. "I'm astounded."

Conrad nodded. "Flabbergasted, even."

"Wow." Evadora leapt up on the table and grabbed the sides of my head so she could peer into my eyes. "You're still in there, but you feel different."

"I'd like to think dying changed me for the better," I said.

She nodded matter-of-factly, then leaned forward and whispered, "It's okay if you came back crazy. I like crazy people."

I managed an uneasy smile. "Um, thanks?"

She jumped off the table and began skipping around the room, singing a song in another language.

"Where's Thal?" I hadn't seen the dark Fae yet.

"I am here." The petite female fluttered into the room on gossamer wings. She regarded me curiously. "Evadora is right. Something is different about you."

I made a quick headcount to make sure all the players were here. The only people missing weren't here by design. I walked to the head of the table and took a seat. "It's damned good to be back in the land of the living." I gave myself a moment to let it sink in. The journey of the past ten days seemed so surreal and it was hard to believe I was actually standing here. I cleared my throat. "Without further ado, here's what happened."

And I started my bizarre story.

"Jesus H. on a pogo stick!" Shelton shouted when I got to the part about Daelissa.

Nightliss wiped tears from her eyes. "You saw my sister?"

I nodded. "Yeah."

Shelton grunted. "I hope you bitch slapped her a few times."

"She'd already been through far worse." I'd thought of giving Nightliss her sister's message in private, but we were all family here. I looked at her and smiled. "Before I left the afterlife, Daelissa told me to tell you that you are the best of us, and she wishes she had loved you as much in life as she does in death."

Fresh tears trickled down Nightliss's cheeks.

There were a lot of mixed emotions evident on the others' faces, but there weren't many dry eyes in the room. After I had a moment to recover my own breath, I continued the story, detailing the torture heaped on us by Gerald and Mors.

Nightliss wept. Mom and Ivy broke into silent tears when I told them about my conversations with Dad, but they seemed happy that he was relatively okay.

The next part of the story brought smiles to the room. I told them about our escape, enlightenment, and how Daelissa sacrificed herself to save us.

"Redemption." Nightliss smiled through her tears.

Everyone erupted in cheers when I got to the part where the soul storm absorbed the stolen essence from Mors and restored the consumed souls. Then I told them how we walked into the light and found paradise.

"Fascinating," Adam said. "The afterlife is your own personal hell if you don't rise above the life you left behind."

Shelton shuddered. "It sounds miserable."

"Chaos and Order." Thomas pursed his lips. "Two sides of the same coin."

"Man, I can't believe Daelissa came through for you." Shelton shook his head. "Your sister did you proud, Nightliss."

The petite angel smiled. "All she needed was a little push."

"Still doesn't make up for what she did, though." Shelton looked conflicted. "How do you redeem a someone who killed thousands?"

I pressed my lips into a flat line. "At least she's trying."

"I miss Dad so much," Ivy said. "Can you talk to him whenever you want now?"

I waggled a hand. "It depends on if he's in the house, so to speak. For now, he's sticking close to Kalesh so Baal can't find him."

"At least he's alive." A look of longing crossed Mom's face. "I want to see him so much."

"Well, that's why we're here." I leaned my hands on the table and tried on a fierce grin.

Shelton winced. "You look kinda crazy when you do that, especially since you're bald."

"It doesn't look wolfish and predatory?" I said.

Elyssa grimaced. "Justin, it looks like you're trying to poop but you're constipated."

The others burst into laughter.

"Oh, man." Adam slapped his knee. "Nailed it!"

I grinned. "Hey, wolves poop too, you know."

Shelton howled and clapped my back. "Good to have you back, man."

I leaned back in my chair and let the good feelings wash over me. "It's great to be back." When the laughter died down, I stood up. "Okay, once more without theatrics." I cleared my throat. "This mission is narrowly focused. We're not going to win the war, but we're going to collectively kick Baal square in the nuts."

"Oh, I like the sound of that," Shelton said.

Adam pounded the table. "Right in the scrote!"

Thal flinched and looked confused. "I did not realize Baal had testicles."

"It is a figure of speech," Cinder said. "But it is a notion I entirely agree with."

Mom's longing looked turned to hope. "Justin, is this a rescue mission?"

I nodded. "We're going to kidnap Cain and get Dad back."

CHAPTER 33

Operation Rescue Dad didn't have a lot of moving parts. It didn't require a lot of troops, and it was about as straightforward as plans get. I could've let Elyssa and Thomas construct a fifty-point battle plan complete with three backup plans and worst-case scenario analysis, but I hoped the element of surprise would be more than enough to win the battle.

Because we needed to execute it ASAP.

I'd refined the operation a few times in my head, so the plan I described to the group was more polished than the one I'd proposed to Thomas and Elyssa earlier. And the bait I suggested this time was even more irresistible than the last.

"Wow, that's almost Baal-worthy trickery," Shelton said.

Adam nodded. "I dig it."

"I also dig it heartily," Cinder said.

"We need to execute it tomorrow," Elyssa said. "I know it's short notice, but since it's a fairly simplistic plan, I don't think it'll be a problem." She projected a checklist above the table. "These are your assignments. Get on them right away."

I took Emily to the side. "I need the Apocryphan powers reactivated."

She studied me for a moment. "Your soul came back stronger, but it's still not strong enough. I think you proved beyond a shadow of a doubt that you'll kill yourself if I give you back the powers."

"If it means saving the people I love, I'd absolutely do it in a heartbeat all over again." I offered a half smile. "I promise."

She rolled her eyes. "Well, when you put it like that, how can I refuse?"

"I know, right?"

Emily sighed. "I didn't want to interrupt your story earlier, but I'd love to hear more about my mom when you have a chance."

"She was the strongest of us," I said. "When everyone else was ready to give up, she kept us going."

"Mom's willpower is legendary." Emily wiped a tear from her cheek. "I can't believe she had godlike powers hiding in her all this time too."

"With her guiding the others, I'm sure they'll clean up the afterlife in no time." I laughed. "They'll be like the Scooby gang of the dead."

Emily grinned. "Plenty of ghosts to find, that's for sure." She touched my arm. Deep inside my soul, the Apocryphan powers thrummed to life. "Please try not to sacrifice yourself this time, Justin. I don't know you very well, but it's easy to see that you're the heart and soul of this operation. You make the impossible sound possible, and that's a power even I can't steal."

I choked up a little. "Wow, thanks, Emily." I put a hand on her shoulder. "You might almost be a demi-god, but I saw where your real strength comes from. You're a lot like your mom."

It was her turn to tear up. "I used to hate her so much," Emily said. "She was unemotional and detached. When she finally found balance, it was just before she died." Emily took a deep breath. "I plan to visit her in Nowhere as soon as this mission is over. Now that she has powers, we can finally have that mother-daughter relationship I always wanted even though she's dead."

Tyler walked over. "So what's the dealio?"

Emily booped his nose. "Justin promised to kill himself again."

He blew out a breath. "Whew, what a relief."

AFTER THE MEETING WAS DONE, it was time to sit back and smell the roses. Elyssa snagged a Templar car and a sizeable group of us went out for tacos and margaritas.

Ivy stomped her foot after we refused to get her alcohol. "I'm totally old enough for a margarita!"

"You were in a preservation chamber for years," Mom said. "So your body isn't nearly old enough to start drinking."

Evadora didn't seem to care about permission. She camouflaged to near invisibility and stole someone's frozen drink. She took a sip and promptly spit it out, face screwed up in disgust. "It's too sour!"

Cora laughed.

"Man, this is something I never thought we'd do again." Shelton bit into a barbeque taco with gusto. "Thought I was doomed to just having Nosti as company."

Adam snorted. "Hey, you need someone around to wipe taco juice off your chin."

Bella dabbed Shelton's mouth with a napkin. "Oh, don't worry. I can take care of my baby."

Our table burst into laughter, drawing startled gazes from the noms around us.

Thal barely paid attention to the conversation, intent on finishing off the pile of tacos on her own plate. After trying them in London, they'd quickly become her favorite food. It was bizarre watching such a little body consume so much.

Several hours later, we left the taqueria and headed back to the Ranch. I had a pretty good buzz going, and it wasn't from margaritas.

"Is anyone up for a game of Scrabble?" Bella said after Elyssa parked the car.

Shelton scoffed. "Yeah, if I want to go to bed a loser."

Bella patted his arm. "Papi, you never go to bed a loser with me."

Adam pushed a finger up the bridge of his nose despite having not worn glasses in ages. "Frankly, Bella's the one who goes to bed a loser."

That brought on another round of laughter.

"Ha, ha." Shelton stuck out his tongue.

"What is Scrabble?" Thal asked.

Bella rubbed her hands together. "I'd be delighted to teach you."

"The woman doesn't lose," Shelton said. "Play at your own risk."

Elyssa clapped her hands together. "Look, it was great going out and having some fun to celebrate Justin's return, but don't forget we have a mission tomorrow." She turned her stern gaze on everyone, even Mom and Cora. "I suggest everyone get some rack time so we can be ready and refreshed in the morning."

Shelton saluted. "As you say, ultimate grand commander."

Adam mimicked Shelton. "Affirmative."

Bella took Shelton by the arm. "Let's see if I can't get something else to salute me in the bedroom."

I groaned. "Why do you have to torture me with that kind of imagery, Bella?"

She laughed. "Payback, of course."

"Yeah, you do kind of deserve it," Elyssa said.

She wasn't wrong.

"Has construction started on the new mansion yet?" I asked.

Elyssa nodded. "Construction golems demolished what was left of Galfandor's house a few days ago, so I imagine they've started building already."

"They're making it even bigger this time," Shelton said. "Hopefully it won't get blown up anytime soon."

"Oh, it won't," Max said with a knowing smile.

Ambria raised an eyebrow. "What makes you say that, Max?"

"Nothing much," he said. "But when the government decreed that my brother, mother, and sisters were outlaws, all their money and assets became mine."

"Say what?" Shelton stopped in his tracks. "I thought they were gonna freeze your family assets."

"Primus Takei thought this was a better idea." Max giggled. "So now they're poor as dirt!"

I remembered Max's glee when we'd discussed this before my almost death. "That's great, Max."

He nodded happily. "Tiberius Industries is doing construction on the new mansion, and I told them to use diamond fiber structural infusion, which should make the new house practically indestructible."

Shelton teared up. "Really, man?"

Max grinned at Shelton. "You taught me so much, I figured it was the least I could do."

Ambria tutted. "The boy worships you, Shelton, though I don't know why."

Conrad grinned. "Because Shelton shits gold and farts rainbows."

That brought on another round of laughter.

Shelton clapped Conrad on the back. "I knew this guy was smarter than he looks."

"Oh, man." Adam doubled over with laughter. "I'm commissioning that as a painting for the main foyer in the new mansion."

I guffawed. "Yeah, the first thing they need to see are rainbows shooting out of Shelton's bare ass."

When the laughter died down, Shelton gave Max a one-armed bro hug. "That's beautiful, man. Maybe we can finally have a home that'll last a few years."

Max beamed at him. "You're welcome."

I just hoped we'd all live to see it.

Elyssa and I went to our small room. The twin bed was tiny compared to what we'd had in the mansion, but I wouldn't mind being cooped up with her anywhere. Except maybe the bathroom.

I closed the door and took her hand. "We've got a few more items to get. Might as well do it now."

She stifled a yawn. "Fine, but let's make it quick."

Using my Apocryphan powers it would hopefully take no time at all to run our errands. Everything had to be perfect for tomorrow.

THE NEXT MORNING, I dug into my old bag of Arcane tricks and disguised myself with a mask of illusion. I really wanted to sit down and enjoy a big pancake breakfast, but Shelton didn't have time to cook, and we didn't have time to waste. So Elyssa and I grabbed a quick bite and then I used my Apocryphan powers to open a portal to a white sand beach overlooking crystal blue waters.

I kissed Elyssa. "Love you."

She kissed me back. "I love you too." Then she left me and went to join the crowd on the beach.

The location looked a lot like the beach for Emily's wedding, but this was a small island off the coast of South America. It had been a tourist resort thirty years ago, but the Colombian Templars had purchased it from the noms and ringed it with avoidance wards to keep them away. For a time, it had been used as a wilderness training facility until the war against Daelissa. It had lain dormant ever since Victus trapped the Eden army in Seraphina.

The island spanned fifteen miles, all thick jungles with an outer ring of sugary beaches. It really was the perfect place for the occasion. The crowd was already sizable. Cora, Evadora, and Thal stood on the right next to Cinder and a small group of Templars. Shelton, Adam, and Bella were opposite them. Mom and Ivy stood in front, heads bowed, faces stricken with grief. Even Stacey and Ryland had come to pay their respects.

Thomas stood at the front, facing the crowd with a grim expression.

Everyone I loved was here. The scenery was perfect, the weather was amazing, and I thought the silver Death Star urn was an amazing touch dreamed up by Adam and Shelton.

This was exactly how I wanted my real funeral to be.

There were several guests I didn't want at my real funeral, but they were necessary for the fake one. I spotted Vicky and her comrades mixed in with the Templars and hoped I was right about my hunch.

Thomas started the eulogy, his strong voice overpowering even the sounds of the ocean. "When I met Justin Slade, I despised him." His opening sentence caused a stir among the Templar side. "I harbored a deep hatred for Daemos that I refused to let go. I couldn't believe my daughter would abandon her duty and fall in love with a monster."

I smiled at the memory even though it'd been deadly serious at the time.

"But the demon boy I hated refused to let up and refused to give in," Thomas said. "Even though I nearly killed him, he continued to do what he thought was right. He showed me that it's not what you are or how you were born that defines you, but what you do with the life you're given."

Thomas paused a moment and took a deep breath. "I understood how he won my daughter's heart. Because Justin Slade, despite his faults, proved time and time again that he had the strength and tenacity to stand up to even her strong will."

That drew a round of laughs.

"Justin Slade was many things to many different people," Thomas continued. "One thing we can agree on is that he was the greatest hero of our time."

As much as I loved Thomas's words, I began to wonder if maybe my irresistible bait was resistible after all. Or maybe I'd been completely wrong about—

A portal ripped open to the left of the crowd. Cain and Olivia flew out, orange flames and black smoke trailing behind them.

"What is it with you people and beaches?" Cain shouted. "Try a little variety next time!"

Olivia cackled with delight. "What a little pity party you have here. Do you miss your wittle friend?"

Emily feigned surprise. "How in the hell did you find us?"

Olivia laughed again. "Wouldn't you love to know, sister?"

I couldn't see into the portal very well from this angle, but growls and thunderous roars told me a demon army waited on the other side. Which meant it was time for me to fly into action. I just hoped Olivia and Cain were so intent on mocking my friends that they didn't see me coming.

I fired up the Apocryphan powers and lifted into the air. "Please, dear magic man in the sky, make this work."

Then I jetted through the thick jungle, angling so I came out near the hell portal. A cluster of monkeys scattered across broad branches and trees, shrieking in surprise. I prayed their noise didn't give me away. Within seconds, I was just a scant thirty yards from the portal. I concentrated on what I needed to do and hoped I was up to the task.

I focused on the beach a few yards in front of the demon portal and cast Arcane magic. The sand shimmered slightly—the only indication my spell had worked. Then I used my Apocryphan powers to complete the second part of my magic trick. I tied off the weave and gave it enough juice to last several minutes.

Then I focused on the target.

Cain and Olivia stood about fifty yards out from the demon portal, backs to me. They didn't seem aware of my presence or my spellcasting. Another eighty yards from them, my friends were grouping to fight. It was going exactly as expected.

And then another voice joined the others.

"I've come to pay respects to my grandson." An infernus controlled by Baal stepped just outside the portal. "Perhaps we could have a mass burial today."

This was not part of the plan.

CHAPTER 34

"**I** like the sound of that." Cain cracked his knuckles. "One big funeral pyre."

"But who will we play with next time?" Olivia said. "Kitty needs her mice!"

Thomas stood in front of our people. "You're certainly welcome to try. Let's see whose funeral is next."

"No question about it." Baal cracked a grin and walked forward. "It'll be —" He abruptly vanished from sight.

And just like that, my plan was already going sideways.

But instead of realizing there was a trap, Cain thrust a hand forward and roared, "Demons attack!"

Olivia's forehead pinched as she scanned the area for Baal. It had been so unexpected, she apparently wasn't sure if Baal meant to just vanish or not.

Maybe my plan wasn't screwed after all.

"Oh, this is going to be fun." I poised myself, ready for the next part.

Screams and roars echoed from the demon portal and dozens of the tentacle demons rolled out, followed closely by giant hellfire demons. They were in such a rush to reach their prey, that none of them seemed aware their comrades vanished the moment they reached the enchanted patch of sand.

A hellfire demon stumbled forward and threw up clawed arms as it sank into the sand.

"What the fuck is going on?" Olivia shouted.

That was my cue. I prepared part two of my trick and flew at top speed out of the trees. The angle was right, and Olivia wasn't even looking at me

I struck Cain square in the back. He cried out in surprise. I slashed a hand in the air and ripped open another portal right in front of us. He twisted violently in my grasp as we jetted through, causing me to botch the landing. My foot caught on something and we tumbled across a rocky plateau beneath a blood red sky.

It was a place I'd never forget.

Cain was in my Dad's body, but I couldn't help myself. I punched him so hard in the jaw he spun in a circle and went down. Then I tossed him in the center of a diagram engraved in the stone. I hadn't created the diagram, but I was about to finish it.

I closed the portal with another slash of my hand, then knelt next to the pattern and sealed it with a drop of blood from Cain's nose. He groaned and staggered to his feet. "Where am I?"

I smirked at him. "Don't recognize the place?"

He lost his balance, still woozy from the sucker punch and looked at me with confusion. "Who the hell are you?"

I'd forgotten to remove my illusion disguise. "Aw, you don't recognize me? We went to grade school together."

Cain roared and leapt toward me. He slammed into an invisible barrier, trapped by the pattern. He looked down, flicked his eyes to another pattern right next to his, and then back at me. The pattern that trapped him was the very same that held my father when Baal captured him.

I smirked again. "Know where you are now, dear brother?" I wiped away the illusion and revealed myself.

"You, fucker." Cain pounded his fists against the barrier. "Wait until the others find us. The demon horde will tear you apart!"

"Most of that demon horde fell through a portal hidden in the sand," I said. "I sent them to this really nice vacation spot—a world where everything tries to eat you." The carnivorous world had nearly killed me and my friends during our multi-realm adventure to find Emily. "I kind of wish I was there to watch that battle."

"Impossible!" He rammed his body against the barrier to no avail.

Another portal opened and my friends spilled out. Only Vicky and her comrades were missing.

Emily closed the portal and burst into laughter. "Oh my god, that was so much fun. Olivia finally figured out there was a portal in the sand, but it closed before she saw where it went. So all the demons that fell through are trapped until they find them."

"God, I wish I could've videoed that," Shelton said. "That look on Baal's face the moment he dropped through the hidden portal was priceless."

Adam barked a laugh. "I hope the carnivorous world eats him alive."

Mom and Ivy made a beeline for me and Cain. Mom stared at my evil twin as if he were an exhibit at a zoo. She looked at me. "What now?"

I looked back at Emily. "That's where she comes in."

Elyssa squeezed between Adam and Shelton to join us. "The beach is evacuated. Emily sent the Templars back to the Ranch and brought us here before Olivia even knew what was going on."

"Well, looks like I was right." I flashed a grin. "Vicky, or one of her pals, is in contact with Olivia. They're the only common denominator between the wedding and the funeral."

Elyssa bared her teeth, fangs flashing. "I'll take care of her personally when we get back."

I shook my head. "Maybe we can use her again. Keep your enemies closer, right?"

"Maybe." Elyssa looked up at the blood red sky. "I'd feel better about getting this done and getting out of here."

I shuddered. "Yeah, Nowhere is a messed up place."

Emily approached, eyes on Cain. He snapped his teeth at her, a caged animal impotent in his rage. "You fucking bitch. Olivia could have killed you a dozen times over."

"My god, you've been—" Emily's eyes flashed wide and she broke off whatever she was going to say.

Cain's eyes flared with delight. He turned to Mom. "I've been fucking Olivia." He yanked down his pants and thrust his privates back and forth. "Your hubby's junk has been getting quite a workout."

Mom's face darkened. "Get him out of my husband's body."

Emily's eyes narrowed in concentration. A dark shadow took form and stepped forward. The shadows receded and suddenly Victoria was there.

"Hello again, Justin." She hugged Emily. "It's so good to see you dear. I'm delighted you thought to invite us." Victoria narrowed her eyes and three more shadows formed. They stepped into the light, revealing Vallaena, Jeremiah, and Daelissa.

A susurrus of gasps rose from the group. Nightliss cried out. "Sister?"

Daelissa looked around uncertainly and nodded. "Yes, sister. It's me."

Mom nodded at Jeremiah. "It's good to see you again, old man."

He smiled warmly. "It does my soul good to see you too, Alysea."

"Fuck all you!" Cain bared his teeth. "Think I'll go down easy like that weakling, David?" He slammed his faced against the invisible barrier hard enough to break his nose. Blood poured down his face. Grinning madly with crimson-stained teeth, Cain slammed his face into the barrier again and again.

"Stop him!" Mom shouted.

Emily slashed a golden beam across the pattern to break it, then snatched Cain by his throat and held him a foot off the ground. "Out foul demon!"

He squealed like a pig, feet and arms flailing. "Fuck you!"

Victoria reached into Cain's chest. "He's not an ordinary spirit. He's latched on like a parasite."

Emily nodded. "I feel it too."

Mom watched in open-mouthed horror as my doppelganger screeched while blood dripped and sprayed all over the two women.

"I've got it." Victoria pulled gently. "Unlatch him there, darling."

Emily nodded. "I'm untangling the roots."

I switched to demon vision and watched in fascination as a red-skinned version of Kalesh peeled loose from inside Cain's body. After several painstaking minutes, Victoria finally ripped it free and held the writhing mass aloft like a victory trophy. "I banish thee to Haedaemos, foul creature!"

A small portal winked open next to her hand. With a final shriek, Cain's spirit spun into a funnel of red smoke and vanished.

The body went limp. I reached out with my senses and latched onto the human soul, now freed of Cain. I closed my eyes and returned to the loft in my subconscious. I ran to the window and called out to Kalesh. "Is Dad there?"

"Yes." Kalesh moved aside and Dad came into view.

"Son, you made it back to your body?" he said.

"Yep."

Dad slapped the windowsill and laughed. "I knew you could do it!"

I walked onto the bridge. "Meet me halfway."

Dad walked out to the middle and gave me a hug. "I'm damned proud of you, Justin. Maybe you should take a break before risking your neck against Baal again. I think you deserve it."

"Yeah, maybe." I gripped his hand. "I've got a present for you, too." I let him feel the soul I touched back in the real world.

Dad gasped gently and a tear formed in one eye. "My god." He looked at Kalesh. "You knew, didn't you?"

Kalesh nodded. "It's time for you to get your own apartment, Dad."

I laughed. "Yeah. We're kicking you out."

Dad wiped another tear from his face. "Then I'd better get going." He turned and went back through the window, then vanished through the apartment door.

"How does this work?" I asked Kalesh.

"The moment he leaves our private space, he'll sense his soul and be able to go back to it." Kalesh sat down on the bridge and looked out at the cityscape. "In fact, he should be back any moment."

I clapped him on the back. "We're a good team, aren't we?"

Kalesh nodded. "Yes, we are."

I released the lucid dream state and blinked my eyes open. Emily held Dad under one arm and Mom held him up under the other. The body began to morph, its features shifting to a slightly older-looking version of me, but with a more chiseled jaw and wider nose.

"Oh, David," Mom said with such happiness, it hurt my heart.

"Holy shit," Dad moaned and blinked his eyes open. His head lolled to the side before he got control of it. He leaned heavily on Emily and looked over at her. "Alysea, you changed your hair color?" He stroked it. "I kind of like it, babe."

Mom huffed. "David, I swear to god—"

Dad laughed and turned to Mom, a mischievous grin on his face. "You're not even a little bit amused?"

Mom gripped him by the collar and yanked him close. Despite the blood caked on his mouth and nose, she kissed him hungrily.

Gasping for breath, Dad came up for air. "Maybe we should get a room."

Mom, face stained with his blood winked. "Damned right we should, and soon."

"A room?" Ivy said. "For what?"

"They wish to copulate," Cinder said helpfully. "Though for pleasure and not procreation."

Adam burst into laughter. "Cinder, did you really just say that?"

Shelton tried to talk but was laughing too hard to say anything.

Thal frowned. "Why are bodily functions such a source of amusement?"

Cora smiled. "It's just a human thing, I suppose."

Dad squeezed Ivy, then reached out a hand to me. "Thank you, son."

I joined the family group hug. "Anytime, Dad. Anytime."

The fam was finally back together. If not for the smiling ghosts of Jeremiah and Vallaena, I wouldn't even believe everything I'd been through. I wouldn't have been surprised to see Yoda and Anakin standing alongside them.

Dad saw Vallaena and blinked. "Whoa. Am I hallucinating?" He looked around. "Where are we?"

"Nowhere," I said. "I thought it would be kind of poetic if we brought Cain here before ripping him out of you."

"Brutal, savage, wrecked." Dad grinned. "I love it."

Ambria, Max, and Conrad talked among themselves while casting concerned glances at Daelissa. Nightliss and her sister spoke in hushed tones a distance from the rest of us.

"Dude, this is so surreal." Shelton grunted. "Man, I don't know if I should thank Daelissa for saving you or punch her for all the shit she did back in the day."

"You could probably do both," I said. "Hell, she murdered Jeremiah and I don't think he's hit her once."

"What a world," Adam said.

Nightliss and Daelissa embraced, tears running down their cheeks. I felt good for Nightliss, but no matter how hard I tried, still felt a little weird about Daelissa. I liked her and hated her for what she'd done. I figured it was one more contradiction in life I'd have to come to terms with.

Exhaustion weighed heavy on my bones, but I was grateful to have bones and flesh again. Deep inside, I felt the burn from using the Apocryphan powers. Opening portals was no mean feat, but I was surprised I felt so tired.

Emily and Victoria regarded me with narrowed eyes.

"You look a little sick," Emily said. "I don't think you had enough time to recover from death before using Apocryphan powers."

Victoria seemed to peer inside me. "His body certainly can't withstand the strain."

Emily reached out and I felt a little twinge inside. "For your own safety, I've turned them off again."

I sagged. "Damn, I was hoping maybe I'd come back from death a little stronger."

"It's not about growing stronger," Emily said, "it's about using powers that are incompatible with your body."

"You're a fifteen-amp fuse trying to channel sixty amps," Tyler said. "You can do it for a little while, but not for long."

"I guess it's time I just accept that and use the power sparingly," I said.

Emily exchanged a look with her mother. "We'll see."

Victoria smiled and put a hand on my arm. "For now, let's just enjoy each other's company, shall we?"

I smiled and looked at my family. Mocking her British accent, I said, "That's a bloody marvelous idea."

Somehow, we managed to turn this bizarre reunion of the living and the dead into a small soiree. Emily portaled in tacos and pizza, and those of us that could eat and drink, did so while the others watched with some small envy.

A loud voice cut through the hubbub of the crowd. "You saved my brother, but I'll never forgive you for what you did to me." Ivy stabbed a finger at Daelissa. "You manipulated me into being your little child soldier!" She stared daggers at Jeremiah. "And you helped her!" Ivy balled up her fists, tears streaming down her face. "I was just a little girl!"

Mom hugged her. "Ivy, it's okay. Things have changed."

"No!" Ivy struggled free. "I can never forget what they did."

"She's right." Daelissa sagged. "I used anything and anyone to get what I wanted. I even turned sister against brother." She looked up at me for a heartbeat before looking back down. "I am so sorry I wronged you, Ivy. I am sorry to all of you for the vile acts I committed. With Victoria's help, I will soon depart for Haedaemos and attempt to rescue the consumed souls around the infernal fount. We hope to find a way to restore them and save any I might have condemned."

No one responded, so I broke the awkward silence. "Daelissa did us all wrong. But it's only right that we help her any way we can. Her path to redemption might free souls that could otherwise be lost forever. She might help others reach Paradise."

"Agreed," Cora said.

"Today we've proven that nothing is impossible," Thomas said. "If Daelissa can save even one soul, then it's worth it."

"Hear, hear!" Shelton shouted.

Adam raised a fist. "Hear, hear."

Everyone joined the cry, raising drinks and fists high.

Ivy wiped tears from her face and turned away from Daelissa. She came over and hugged me around the waist. "I love you, bro, but I will always hate Daelissa."

I kissed the top of her head. "I love you too, sis." Time heals some wounds, but some scars ache forever. I just hoped Ivy could overcome the pain.

Nothing was perfect, but this was good enough for me.

We'd stolen Cain and saved Dad. It might be nothing more than a scratch on the mighty ego of Baal, but it was a damned good start. I felt like we'd walked up a step only to be confronted by a steep cliff. Overcoming Baal's massive advantage would take everything we had.

I still couldn't use Apocryphan powers to their fullest extent without hurting myself. Baal had an army of infernus agents controlling nom governments and a dragon army in Seraphina. A nuclear war among the noms might be on the horizon, and Atlantis might soon be overrun.

It was a lot to worry about.

But I decided that for now, it was okay to be happy. I'd returned from the dead, Dad was back, and Daelissa was no longer a psychotic bitch. All in all, things were looking up.

And it was good—damned good—to be alive.

EPILOGUE

Baal shouted in surprise when the ground swallowed him. One minute he'd been on a beach, and the next, falling thirty feet to land on an alien world. The ground jiggled like blubber when he slammed into it. He groaned in pain and rolled onto his back just in time to see dozens of octopods raining from a portal fifty feet up in the sky.

"Fuck!" Baal staggered upright and limped out of the way. The octopods smacked wetly into the rubbery ground. A deep roar drew Baal's attention back to the portal as a giant hellfire demon plummeted through.

"Where the fuck am I?" The infernus was just a host to a fragment of Baal's power, but they were specialized creations and he didn't like to lose them.

Purple and red clouds gathered in the sky. Strange birdlike creatures sprinted over a rise, squawking in unison. The portal vanished a moment later, leaving Baal, three hellfire demons, and dozens of octopods stranded.

The funeral had been a trap, which meant Thomas Borathen and his Templars suspected or knew about the moles in their organization. Baal smirked. "Well played." What they'd hoped to achieve, however, was a mystery. Surely they knew that this infernus body was disposable. The biggest loss would be the hellfire demons. Without a photo of this place, Olivia wouldn't be able to open a portal and recover them.

But even that obstacle could be overcome.

This amounted to nothing more than a taunt by the Overworlders. With Justin Slade dead, there was little else they could do to stop Baal's relentless march to victory.

He started walking toward the hellfire demons. And that was when the true horrors began. Hundreds of insects swarmed from the clouds, revealing bloated jellyfish creatures hidden beneath them. The insects stabbed into octopods with barbed legs, hauling the squirming demons up into the air toward the jellyfish.

Hellfire demons swatted the insects away with little problem, but weeds and vines crept across the blubbery ground and wrapped around their legs. Then the ground opened up beneath their feet, dragging them under.

A vine wrapped around Baal's leg, and then he realized the truth about this realm. The ground itself was alive. The vines were tentacles. "Shit!" Baal tore himself free from the tendril and leapt away as a hole began to open beneath him. Hellfire demons roared and struggled, ripping up great swaths of living ground. Viscous fluid seeped from the wounds in the blubbery flesh. Baal slipped in a puddle and skidded toward a small pond. A giant leech emerged from the muck, its tube-like mouth open in anticipation of a free meal. But the flock of flightless birds reached Baal first.

Their razor-sharp claws and beaks tore into his flesh, ripping chunks from his arms and face. Baal screamed. The demon flesh of the infernus would make a poor meal for the birds, but the pain and humiliation of being eaten alive incensed his rage. He wrapped his hands around the neck of the closest bird and squeezed with enhanced strength until the neck snapped.

Relentlessly, they tore into his flesh. Baal roared in pain and anger, fighting back and killing another bird until blood loss and shredded muscles drained his strength.

"Fuck you!" Baal screamed. "I will burn this realm to ash!" And then his vision went dark.

The fragment of Baal's spirit controlling the infernus returned to him. Though he could control more than one infernus at a time, this outrage had drawn his full attention. He roared in impotent rage and stomped across the complex patterns etched into the floor. Reaching out through the patterns, he searched for another infernus near the hell portal Olivia had opened.

He found it and slipped it on like a glove. It was one of the older infernus, but it would do. He raced across the cavern floor and reached the staging area deep in Hell. The portal to the beach was gone. Olivia stood among the octopods and remaining hellfire demons, eyes filled with fear.

"What happened?" Baal stormed over to her and gripped her shirt. He yanked her toward him, though without the enhanced strength of the new infernus, it wasn't quite as satisfying.

"I don't know." Her eyes seemed lost. "They knew we were coming. They took Cain. He's gone!"

Baal's hands slackened their grip on her shirt. "Did they try to take you?"

She shook her head. "No. Someone flew out of the jungle and took Cain through a portal before I could react. Then the rest of them vanished through another portal."

"Who took Cain?" Baal softened his voice to make her feel safe.

Olivia looked even more frightened because she knew better. "I barely saw the face, but it wasn't anyone I recognized."

Baal tried to make sense of it. "Did your sister open the portal?"

She shook her head. "Emily was too far away. Whoever took Cain made the portal."

"Then it was the Edison boy. He's the only one potentially strong enough to do it."

"No, I saw him near Emily." Olivia shook her head. "It wasn't him."

Baal paced around an octopod. "Then who? Some new ally?" It didn't make sense. And then he sensed something back in Haedaemos. He flicked back into the spirit realm and extended his senses. Someone was crying out for him. Baal blurred from the control room and out into the palace.

"Baal!" the voice cried out from the hallway.

"I'm here, Cain." Baal extended a tendril of essence and drew him in.

Cain ran to him, face burning with rage and pain. "They took my body!"

It took everything to hold Baal's fury in check. "Tell me what happened."

"The funeral was a trap." Cain started blubbering like a child. "Justin Slade took me to Nowhere and they trapped me in the same pattern you used to trap his father. Then Emily and Victoria ripped me out and banished me here."

"Justin Slade?" Baal's question emerged as a razor-sharp whisper.

Cain nodded. "Jeremiah Conroy and Daelissa were there too."

For once, Baal was speechless. "Justin Slade came back from the dead with ghosts in tow?"

"I need my body again, Father. I want my revenge!"

Baal needed more information. "Of course, child. Come to me."

"Thank you, Father." Cain walked over and held out his arms for a hug.

Baal smiled and reached out. Cain was literally made from a seed of his essence, so welcoming him back was easy. Baal gripped Cain by the head.

Cain screamed in terror. "No, Father!"

"Shh, child. Go to sleep." Baal opened his mouth inhumanly wide. Light poured from Cain and into him. Cain's feet folded in on themselves, followed by his legs and torso. Then the head sucked inward like a deflating balloon and the remaining essence of Cain rejoined the might of Baal.

Cain's memories were there, clear and crisp. Baal watched everything from the abduction over and over again. It was true. Justin Slade had returned from the dead and he'd claimed his father back as a prize.

For the first time in eons, Baal was concerned. He could no longer afford to watch the dominoes he'd carefully placed fall out of turn and disrupt his intricate plans. Justin Slade had to die, as did all the Over-worlders. The time for subterfuge was over.

"Fight all you want, boy. You'll still lose in the end." Baal clenched his fist. "Elohim will rise again."

And the one true god would reclaim his throne.

BOOKS BY JOHN CORWIN

THE OVERWORLD CHRONICLES

OVERWORLD UNDERGROUND

Infernal Blade

OVERWORLD ARCANUM

Conrad Edison and the Living Curse

Conrad Edison and the Anchored World

Conrad Edison and the Broken Relic

Conrad Edison and the Infernal Design

Conrad Edison and the First Power

STAND ALONE NOVELS

Mars Rising

No Darker Fate

The Next Thing I Knew

Outsourced

For the latest on new releases, free ebooks, and more, join John Corwin's Newsletter at www.johncorwin.net!

ABOUT THE AUTHOR

John Corwin is the bestselling author of the Overworld Chronicles. He enjoys long walks on the beach and is a firm believer in puppies and kittens.

After years of getting into trouble thanks to his overactive imagination, John abandoned his male modeling career to write books.

He resides in Atlanta.

Connect with John Corwin online:
Facebook: http://www.facebook.com/johnhcorwinauthor
Website: http://www.johncorwin.net
Twitter: http://twitter.com/#!/John_Corwin

www.ingramcontent.com/pod-product-compliance
Lightning Source LLC
Chambersburg PA
CBHW030922260626
47169CB00002B/358